HYMN OF ASHES

By: Andrea Andersen

Developmental Edits by Yara Gharios

Copy Edits & Proofreading by Kelly Andersen

Cover Art by McKenzie Green

GLOSSARY

HYVENMERE *(high-ven-meer)*
SAMMARA *(sahm-ah-rah)*
ENHARRA *(en-hahr-uh)*
ENHAVENN *(en-ha-venn)*
VANYARA *(vahn-yah-rah)*
VANHIRRA *(vahn-heer-uh)*
LYNDORUUN *(lynn-door-uhn)*
LYDHAVN *(leed-hawn)*
MELLHAWN *(mell-hawn)*
GRAVHUNE *(grahv-hoon)*
TYNARA *(tin-nah-rah)*
WHISMERRA *(whis-meer-uh)*
LYSKIFT *(lee-shift)*
SINNDRA *(sin-drah)*
BANDTHRAL *(band-thrawl)*
FJELLENHEIM *(fyehl-en-hyme)*
SOLVYRN *(sol-vern)*

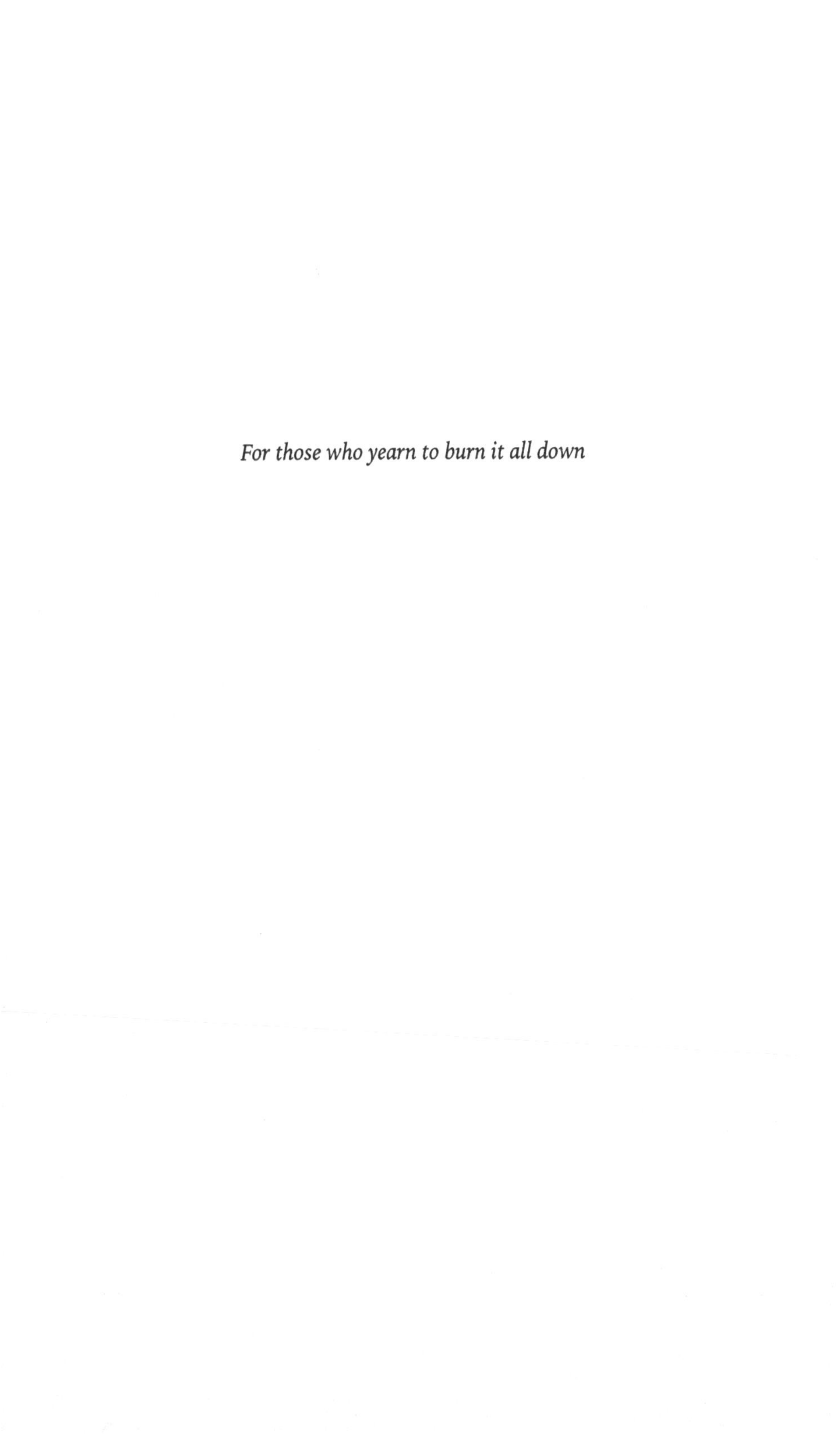

For those who yearn to burn it all down

PROLOGUE
AUDREY'S LETTER

Dear Vanessa,

I'm sorry. I wish I could be honest with you. I wish I could tell you where I run off to or what I've been doing every spare minute I have. I see the way you look at me when I blow you off. I've seen how you have become more guarded over the years.

This letter is selfish of me to write, because you'll probably never read it. Either I'll chicken out and never give it to you, or by the time I do try to give it to you, I'll have pushed you away so much that you won't consider reading a letter from me.

But please understand, I'm so sorry for everything.

I have lit a match to our fifteen years of friendship, because my entire world has been turned completely upside down.

A couple of years ago, I was sleeping at my desk at the library on a late shift. I woke up to the feeling of something tightening around my neck, arms, and legs. I was being strangled, but when I tried to get my bearings, I couldn't see anyone. The only thing nearby was the pothos plant, growing at an impossible rate, attacking me, choking me. I screamed, but no one was around to hear. I was terrified. I thought I was going to die.

Suddenly, Liam was there.

It was the first time he and I met, and after he cut the vines and dragged me outside the library for fresh air, he waited for me to calm down from my panic attack before he introduced himself to me. That was when I got my first good look at him. Liam is beautiful. He's very large, but with kind eyes. He immediately offered me help and guidance.

Nothing was the same after that night, because then Liam took me to Hyvenmere.

That's the name of his realm. Hyvenmere is filled with magical creatures and a rare beauty in the landscape that does not exist in ours. I've seen things I can't explain without someone telling me I'm hallucinating. I've learned about cultures that I thought only existed in fairy tales.

I've learned that I'm not entirely human.

Liam suspects that I am half-fae. It's why I suddenly developed my magical green thumb. It was the first gift of mine to manifest, the second being my healing touch. I guess he and our friend Fergus had been using some type of spell to track down human halflings like me, searching for someone to fulfill a prophecy of theirs. Obviously, that person isn't me, even though some Hyvenmerians are convinced otherwise.

As I type this out, I can vividly picture you thinking about me fulfilling a prophecy and scoffing. Or holding back a laugh. Or holding in an inappropriate joke. It's moments like this that I wish I could safely bring you into this world that I often escape to.

The goddess's blessings are abundant in Hyvenmere right now. No, I'm not religious. But nature and the goddess that's referenced in Hyvenmere is a...unique belief. Nature is both a science and a deity in Hyvenmere. It's pretty legit. What is the goddess of nature and balance blessing Hyvenmere with, you might ask? Mating bonds. They are snapping into place left and right. Hyvenmerian's have desired to have families, but have struggled with infertility for thousands of years, until about three decades ago.

No one knows why fertility has risen, or why the goddess of Hyvenmere is even allowing more mating bonds to develop. But everyone seems to be going with it, paying respects and taking care of their environment more intentionally to ensure the blessings continue.

I think that's partly why I love it here so much. Humans just haven't learned to love our land as much.

But unfortunately, I don't feel comfortable bringing you to Hyvenmere yet. You're human. It's dangerous over here for full-blooded humans. Some political leaders don't even like that other halflings and I set foot in Hyvenmere. Liam has spent hundreds of hours training me in hand-to-hand combat just in case I'm jumped, which has happened a handful of times already, by extremists who are very anti-human anything.

I've also learned how to wield nerdy-ass weapons like swords and daggers. You'd think that dealing with political leaders calling for my expulsion and being attacked by extremists who agree would keep me from going back to Hyvenmere so often. But I can't stay away.

I still haven't found my fae family. That was why I originally agreed to explore Hyvenmere with Liam and strengthen my gifts. But it's been years, and I don't feel any closer to finding them.

The Mellhawn Gates, linking our realms together, have been open for quite some time. Oddly enough, the majority of Hyvenmerians weren't aware that they were open until halflings like me started to appear— around the same time that more bonds started to snap into place.

The fae and the nereid governments seem fine with the Mellhawn Gates being opened because of the number of mating bonds that have been produced, many including human halflings like me. The fae and nereids think it's worth the risk of giving humans access to their realm if it means their people will continue to prosper.

Then there are the sirens. Well, the siren government, specifically.

The King of the Sirens was originally the one thought to be the fulfiller of the prophecy. But someone started a rumor that it wasn't him at all, and was probably me instead, and it's lowkey ruined my life. I guess the Siren King defeated the only solvyrn seen in thousands of years back in the day, or as the prophecy says, an "ancient beast."

But me? I haven't slain anything. You know me, I cry if I accidentally kill a spider instead of capturing it safely to return it outside.

Liam suspects that the "ancient beast" hasn't been slain yet, but even he doesn't know what kind of beast that would be, if not a solvyrn.

It would be convenient for me if the Siren King continued to be the prophesied one, because that would mean less responsibility on my part. I could focus more of my attention on finding my family, instead of bringing peace to the realm.

What else could I fill you in on?

Well, Liam is my best friend in Hyvenmere, and because of his royalty status, I've become a weird celebrity figure. Hyvenmere's Halfling Sweetheart, if you will. It's weird. I don't know how to deal with the constant attention. I wish I could talk to you about it.

But I can't. Because, unfortunately, the Siren King, who doesn't like humans that much, is dangerous. I think he hates me and all human halflings. I haven't spoken with him personally, but I've seen enough interviews of him spewing resentment and fear about my presence to get the message loud and clear.

Maybe if he and I hung out once, he'd come around.

I can see you shaking your head at me, saying not to waste my time on getting a man's attention. Don't worry, the Siren King is over two hundred years old and dangerously powerful. Trust me, I'm not trying to get his attention.

Unfortunately, the last time Hyvenmere was widely open to humans was during the seventeenth century. During that period, Hyvenmere's political leaders all unanimously agreed to close the gates to protect the realm from humans and their destructive habits. Barring them from sailing Hyvenmerian seas.

So the Siren King kind of has a point, because as you and I know, humans generally suck. But the thought of the one single door leading me to my family, my history, being closed forever, makes me sick to my stomach.

Thankfully, I'm not the only one who feels that. The other human halflings want to be able to walk both realms freely, and a lot of Hyvenmerians want an opportunity to see if their mates are in the human realm, too.

What would you do, Van?

I feel like you'd give the Siren King the finger while holding the gate open yourself—assuming you believe everything I'm telling you in this letter.

That, again, you may or may not ever read.

I could also see you stepping foot in this realm, seeing all the danger and uncertainty, and shaking your head with a dramatic frown, before you moonwalk out of it.

And I wouldn't blame you one bit, because you and I have been through enough.

I've opened up to Liam about a lot, including what you and I experienced in the foster system. He was filled with rage. It was also the first time a man had held me in years, and I cried through the whole thing.

God, I wish I could talk to you more about Liam. About my very inappropriate feelings toward him, which sadly seem to be unreciprocated. I swear every man in this realm only has "mate-eyes." It's all or nothing with them.

But I love you. And I prioritize your safety. Maybe I can win the Siren King over so that he's less aggressive toward humans and halflings like me.

Maybe then, I can let you into this world if you'd like.

Unfortunately, I don't think that will happen.

For now, all I can do is write this letter. Maybe one day you'll find it. Maybe you'll get a chance to read it. But, if our friendship is destroyed because I've kept too many secrets from you to trust me again, I wouldn't blame you.

I'm so sorry, Vanessa.

I'm so, so sorry.

-Audrey

CHAPTER I

I had finally ditched the guy who was following me.

Maybe he wasn't actually following me. Maybe I was just being paranoid.

But I was *pretty* confident he was following me.

I sensed that I was being watched as soon as I stepped out of my home earlier this morning. I glanced around, expecting to make eye contact with someone, but there was no one around. No one on my street looked suspicious, either. My neighbors were approaching, and they waved politely as they entered our apartment building behind me, but they weren't the reason I felt watched. As I did another scan of my street, tourists who were shouldering heavy, brightly colored beach totes, smiled at me as they passed.

I decided to walk a different route to my coffee shop, playing it safe.

I kept checking over my shoulder as I made my way through the narrow streets of Marina Vista, a touristy beach town in southern California. The place I had called home for most of my thirty years.

The marine layer was thick and humid this early in the

morning, just as I liked it. I passed the public library, as well as my favorite pizzeria. I made a mental note to go there for lunch, since the painted letters on their glass windows announced a special on their veggie-lovers pizza.

All the while, the uneasy feeling that I was being watched never truly left. Not when I opened my coffee shop for the day, not when I spent hours brewing drinks and wiping surfaces. Not when my employees and I prepped for Jam Night, and not when I closed down the shop and decided to make my way to the harbor to pout.

The sun had set hours ago. The moon's reflection danced along the salty waves. Following the habit I had maintained all day, I checked over my shoulder again before I turned a corner.

A few yards away, a man was walking on the same sidewalk, casually headed right toward me. He was tall and wearing a nondescript dark outfit with the hood of his sweatshirt up, concealing any noticeable features.

A spike of adrenaline made me speed up as I made my way through the quiet town. I made another turn, checking over my shoulder again. But he was gone.

He disappeared into the night.

Well then.

I shrugged my shoulders and smiled at the security guy when I approached the docks. He was drinking a beer and hanging out in security's little room near the main gate to the harbor. The harbor was closed. No one was supposed to be out here this late at night.

But, like I had many times before, I slipped him a fifty, and he let me in.

That's what happens when the city chooses to hire young twenty-somethings for minimum wage to work security.

After quietly walking the dock, I boarded my boat and entered the main cabin. I pulled out a bottle of scotch and got myself settled in a chair on the second level of my sizeable vessel.

I took a moment to admit to myself that I looked like the biggest asshole.

Sipping my scotch, sitting on a cushioned bench on my mini yacht, getting emotional over the fact that I was all alone. Not even the guy who —I was ninety-seven percent positive— was following me, even bothered to see through whatever he'd had in mind.

I was just…alone.

The harbor was protected from most of the ocean's larger waves by the jetty, but a gentle sway still comforted me as I stared at the full moon's reflection over the Pacific.

In the back of my mind, I wondered if this was how the ultra-wealthy felt. Surrounded by material things others yearned for, while feeling more alone in the world than ever.

The only reason I had this stupid three-level mini yacht—lovingly named the *Knotty Boy*—was because of my roommate, Audrey. A long-lost aunt bestowed her hoarder house in the Bay Area on me a couple of years ago when she passed. I wanted to light a match to the mess, but Audrey convinced me to clean up the estate and sell it. Which, she was right to do. Because now I had a decent amount of savings and a boat. A feat not a lot of thirty-year-old women could say in this economy.

I used the money to buy the building that I had been renting for my coffee shop, the Sun Bean. Thankfully, when I approached the property owner with a cash offer, he was ready to retire and get the property out of his hands.

He also liked the idea of selling it to a "spitfire woman" like me, whatever the hell that meant.

So here I was, financially stable. A business owner. Wallowing in self-pity on my own boat because I was, yet again, stood up by my best friend, Audrey. Because ever since she met some fuck stick named Liam two years ago, Audrey had been flaky as hell.

We shared a condo a five-minute walk from the Sun Bean.

Audrey and I were literal *roommates*, and yet, I hardly saw her anymore.

Oftentimes, I'd track her location to find her off the coast of Catalina Island. Which was weird, because if you grew up in Southern California, you didn't go to Catalina Island all that often. It's a special occasion place. A touristy spot you take friends who haven't visited Southern California before. Once you've gone to Catalina Island once or twice, you don't usually go again. Not until you've seen and done everything else in the state.

But Audrey was at Catalina Island at least once a month.

Because her good-buddy-who-she-claimed-wasn't-her-boyfriend-but-was-definitely-her-boyfriend, Liam, lived there.

Which made me side-eye him even more.

Did she ever think to invite me to his (what I assumed) fancy-ass house on Catalina Island?

No.

Had she introduced me to this mystery man of hers after two whole years?

Also, no.

Part of me worried she had joined a cult. Catalina Island has some isolated areas on it. People could easily set up a cult compound there if they had the money.

The number of times Audrey would randomly come home, after several nights of being out with Liam, covered in scrapes and bruises, pissed me the hell off.

I wasn't upset with Audrey.

No, I was pissed at whoever this *Liam* guy is. I couldn't find information about him online *anywhere*.

Shady. As. Hell.

I have promised myself that if I ever met him, I'd punch him in the throat.

Audrey probably blew me off tonight to see Liam again. She was probably out at Catalina Island right now. As I took another sip of scotch and savored the smooth burn it provided in my core, I stared in the direction of the island.

Wondering what changed in Audrey.

Wondering how some *guy* could cause this much distance to appear between us. We had been best friends for fifteen years. We grew up in the foster care system together. Graduated together. Went to college together.

Yet, I wasn't sure if we were still each other's best friend after the last two years. Because she was gone more often than not.

Glaring in the direction of Catalina Island, I pulled out my cell to send off a text—not surprised I didn't have one from her.

> Me: If you need me, I'll be drinking on my boat. Alone.

Then I rested my cell on my thigh. Waiting for three dots to show up. Waiting. After five whole minutes, I received nothing.

Nothing. But she'd *read* the message four minutes ago. So, in a moment of pure pettiness, I sent another text.

> Me: I think I'm going to move out.

She never bothered to read that one. Thus, I continued my pity party on my mini yacht.

God, that sentence *really* made me feel like an ass.

I could sleep here until I found my own place, I thought. I also considered converting the attic of the Sun Bean into a small studio apartment. I wasn't sure if either of those options were perfectly legal, but I couldn't find it within me to care.

I didn't want to move out, though.

If Audrey was a victim of domestic abuse, the logical explanation for the scrapes and bruises I'd seen on her, the best thing I could do is be there for her when she is *hopefully* ready to address it. But what if she wasn't? What if I was overreacting to the scrapes and bruises that I'd seen her with? What if she felt like our friendship was a burden to her? What if she was simply embracing a male-centered life? I had no way of knowing *what* exactly was going on with her, because she wouldn't fucking talk to me about anything.

A gust of wind hit me, making my dark hair brush away from my shoulders. I shivered, even though I was wearing a hoodie to protect me from the chill of the ocean.

A throat cleared behind me, and I yelped and jumped out of my seat to whirl on whoever it was.

I assumed it would be Audrey—for some stupid reason.

But it wasn't.

It was a man.

No, wait, *two* men.

"What the—" I backed away from them at the same time my heart rate kicked up. One of them was definitely the man who followed me earlier tonight. But I couldn't recognize which one specifically followed me, because they looked so similar.

The two men stood between me and the cabin. Behind me was the railing of my boat, and the muddy ocean water of the harbor.

I immediately tried recalling the dozens of self-defense courses I'd taken throughout my twenties. The movements that felt natural after hours and hours of training, designed to disarm and incapacitate a large man long enough for me to escape.

The one on the right stepped forward, raising his hands as if to show he wasn't a threat.

He had dark, shoulder-length hair and a very light color to his eyes.

I wondered if it was the night sky and the moonlight that

made them look so light, so *bright*. But I didn't focus on his eye color for too long because the next detail I noticed was how tall he was.

How tall they *both* were.

I was five feet, eleven inches tall. I rarely looked up to a man. Most often, I was eye-level or looked down at them.

But I was eye level with their chests.

Were they truly close to seven feet tall, or did I have too much scotch?

"Calm, female," the man said in an accent I couldn't place, but in a soothing voice that made me want to relax.

Did he deadass refer to me as female? I narrowed my eyes at them, flicking my gaze over to study the second man. He had blond shoulder-length hair and a very light eye color.

And pointy ears.

They both did.

What the fu—

"You have three seconds to get off my property," I told them in a stern tone. Adrenaline surged through my body, and the sound of sand rushing in my ears made me realize how much danger I was in.

I was completely alone.

At the docks.

"You need to come with us," the blond man said in a bored tone. He looked me up and down with a look of dismissiveness. As if he were inconvenienced by being on my boat, he demanded that I go with them.

I snorted at them, "Absolutely not."

Then I noted their pointy ears again. Their clothing. It was dark, so I couldn't catch all the details, but they wore leather chest pieces and thigh coverings. Their long-sleeved shirts and pants looked...odd.

A European style, maybe?

Perhaps that's why they had accents, but I couldn't place

where in Europe they were from. I was determined to figure it out. If anything went down, I would need to remember as many details as I could about them when I filed a police report.

With their fake-pointy ears, I wondered if they were actors of some kind? There was a Renaissance fair thing forty minutes north up in Buena Park. Perhaps they came from there? But I couldn't recall for sure, because I wasn't tapped into Live-Action-Role-Play culture.

They had black, thin scarves around their neck. It almost looked like a headpiece I'd seen snowboarders wear under their masks, which didn't bode well for me. If they had those facial coverings, but were showing me their faces now, it probably meant that they didn't plan on me being around to identify them after this.

Shit.

"Please," the brunet said, lifting his hands up higher to prove a point. "We don't want trouble, just come with us."

I frowned, glancing at my bag a foot away.

"Why?" I asked, stalling.

The blond man rolled his eyes. "Because we have orders."

The brunet threw the blond an annoyed look, before focusing back on me. "I'm afraid we have to bring you with us—but please trust that we don't want to hurt you." Was I more valuable to them without bruises or cuts, or scrapes? My stomach twisted at the thought.

"You expect me to just go with you?"

"You are coming with us whether you want to or not, human," the blond responded with a downturn of his lips. With his words, ice-cold, paralyzing fear started to drip down my spine, coating my bones, stiffening my muscles.

Terror consumed me. My heart was beating too fast; it couldn't have been healthy.

Usually, I was excellent at regulating my emotions. But I couldn't grab hold of this sudden panic. The adrenaline from the surge of my anxiety was paralyzing. It gripped me like a vise, making me feel like a ghost watching my own body react.

I'd never experienced dread like this, and I had no idea why this was my body's reaction to these men. To the blond's voice.

It made it difficult for me to keep a level head, but something in my chest wanted to just get this over with and go with them. The fear of the unknown was scrambling my nervous system, making it almost impossible to properly formulate a plan to get myself out of this.

Almost impossible.

"Okay." My voice shook, exposing my fear as I stepped toward my backpack.

The brunet threw an annoyed look at the blond, "You did not have to use your sinndra on her, you impatient prick."

Slowly, stiffly, I reached down to grab my backpack.

"She was being unreasonable," the blond replied, unrepentant.

As if in response to his words, my fear was starting to fade, but the men looked disarmed by my fear, so I leaned into it while I opened my bag and started slowly going through it, "L-let me just make sure I-I have everything."

Jesus, was it because they were tall? Larger than any man I had ever seen? Perhaps that's why my fight, flight, or (in this case) freeze instincts were at the wheel right now.

"Hurry up," the blond muttered, standing taller as he glanced around the docks. "It reeks here."

"Do not be rude," the brunet grumbled, studying me. "But we do need to hurry."

I nodded, stepping toward them. "Okay."

I waited until the blond reached his hand toward me, because I determined him to be the bigger threat at the moment. His obvious disdain and annoyance gave me less of a chance to make it out of this, whereas I suspected the brunet man had some compassion. He was trying a gentler approach with me.

Perhaps it was their weird version of the good cop, bad cop act.

When the blond reached for me, stupidly expecting me to take his hand, I wrapped my fingers around the police stick that I carried around in my purse my entire adult life. Ever since I stole it from one of my foster fathers the night that he—*no*. I shook my head, pushing the horrid memories away.

Instead, I snapped the police stick open.

And *thwacked* it across the blond's head.

This was the very first time I actually had to use it, but I couldn't feel excited about it.

Because even though there was a satisfying sound when it connected with his skull, he didn't drop to the ground as I expected. He stumbled, bracing himself, shouting in a language I didn't understand. Then he kicked his leg out and swiped my feet, and I fell to the ground.

"Our orders were *unharmed*," the dark-haired man growled, reaching down for me.

I grunted and tried to hit him with my police stick instead, but he snatched the weapon and yanked it out of my hand. I watched in horror as the brunet gripped both ends of the police stick with his large hands, bent it in half, and tossed it overboard.

Through my shock, I still managed to punch the brunet in the face.

Hard. Right across his cheek and nose. Blood should have started spouting from his nostrils at this point. But he barely flinched from the hit, even though my knuckles were throbbing now.

What the fuck, what the fuck.

My dread spiked again as the blond reached down to wrap

his fingers around my biceps and yank me up, but I was panicking. Flailing. Screaming.

"You escalated this," the brunet scolded his companion. Then he started shushing me as he grabbed both of my wrists, turning me to face him as he said, "We don't want to hurt you." The only proof I had that I had just successfully punched him in the face was a quick sniff and twitch of his nose.

"But *I'm* going to hurt you," I promised, lifting my knee up to impact him in the groin. His clear, bright eyes widened in pain before he grunted, tightening his hold on my wrists to a painful grip. His accomplice groaned behind me, and when I turned around to see where he was, he released one of my biceps to snap his fist back and punch me in the face. The base of my neck made an audible cracking sound, and as stars danced across my vision, fear that I was now paralyzed flittered through my mind.

The brunet shouted something at his companion from somewhere nearby. I was so disoriented that I couldn't stand. As soon as the two men let go of me, I collapsed to the deck of my boat.

Desperately blinking, I rolled to the side to see the men bickering with each other in another language. The blond was glaring down at me with disgust, and the brunet was shoving him hard. Scolding him.

Even while seeing double, I rolled onto my stomach and started slowly army crawling to the main cabin.

"Stop." The blond's voice was the only warning I had before something heavy pressed itself down on my ankle.

I heard, rather than felt, the snap of the joint. White hot pain scorched my leg.

I shouted in anger, looking over my shoulder to glare at the blond, who smiled mischievously down at me. The brunet shoved him off of me, kneeling to grab my arms and pull me up.

I spat in his face.

He blatantly ignored it as he spoke in a soft voice, "We don't want to hurt you, but we must hurry."

"Say that—" I clenched my teeth through a groan of sharp pain as the brunet failed to get me to my knees, "to my *broken fucking ankle.*" Then I wrenched my grip out of his and clawed at his eyes as aggressively as I could. He shouted, and the cry of his pain made my mind go dizzy again. He dropped his hold on me, covering his eyes, which were finally starting to bleed.

As the brunet struggled to collect himself, though, the blond grabbed a handful of my hair and yanked me up to him. My feet were dangling, unable to find purchase, and I thought my scalp might be on fire due to the burn of his grip on my hair. I desperately clutched his fist as he held me close to his face, desperate to bring relief.

"You're difficult." He leered at me with a gross smirk, ignoring me when I spat in his face, too. "That just means you'll be that much more fun to break."

I screamed, kicking him once with my non-injured foot, before he roughly threw me into the main cabin of the boat. The door was open; my head made impact with the doorframe as the rest of my body flew through the threshold.

Warm wetness started to soak my head as I collected myself enough to realize that I was on my back on the main level, where the lounge area and a small kitchen were. My head was throbbing; my ankle was on fire. My neck was in the worst pain I'd ever felt. I may not be paralyzed, but I definitely had a spine injury of some sort.

Heavy footfalls entered the cabin, and the blond's face towered over me.

Then he kicked me in the head again.

Everything went black.

A thick, heavy fog surrounded my existence.

"Don't!" I didn't recognize that masculine voice at all. "Don't accidentally kill them, Aud."

"I—I—" That was Audrey, and she sounded distraught.

Everything was weighted down on me. I couldn't move my body. It took every ounce of concentration and determination to open my eyes. But I did. And through the threshold of the cabin entrance, I saw Audrey standing on the deck.

"Who sent you?" That was the man's voice I didn't recognize. He was new and had long curly hair. He towered over Audrey but stood at her side, facing the men. I blinked, and Audrey quickly flicked her wrist, throwing the two men who attacked me right off the boat and into the harbor.

Then everything went black again.

CHAPTER 2

Before I opened my eyes, I was distinctly aware of bedsheets around me, and I almost whimpered in relief from the sensation. Sometimes, my gummies that I took to help me get a full night's sleep, hit me harder than usual. It really depended on what brands the dispensary was stocking whenever I walked in.

It really was just a fuck ass dream.

My bed sheets had never felt this good. I'd never felt this warm and cozy and safe as I slowly rose to the surface of consciousness. This was the most comfortable my bed had ever felt. There wasn't a single joint in my body that ached. I rolled over, desperate to squish my face into the comforting smell of my pillowcases.

Except when I did, I didn't recognize the smell.

My pillows smelled good, fresh, and clean, but they weren't mine.

"Van?" Audrey asked.

Audrey was here. Maybe I fell asleep in her bed? Had her bed always been better than mine? When did she get a new bed?

Somewhere in the room, the sound of a TV was going, but the people weren't speaking English.

"Van?" Audrey asked again.

"What?" I replied, my mouth muffled in the pillows.

Audrey snorted before pressing her hand on my shoulder and asking, "How are you feeling?" in a gentle voice. She spoke to me like she was trying not to scare me off. As if I were a little fawn, seconds from bolting.

"Confused," I replied into the pillows, then turned my head to face her. I pried one eye open to address her, "When the hell did you get a new mattress?"

Audrey's brows pinched in confusion briefly before her lips pulled back in the corners, smiling at me, "This isn't my bed."

"You sure about that?" a familiar male voice asked.

No.

I widened my eyes and sat up in a panic, utterly disappointed to see a man standing at the foot of my bed.

His curly blond hair was draped over his shoulders. Oddly enough, he also had stupid pointy ears poking out of his curls. He was wearing linen pants with a...tunic? Is that what those were called? It looked like a pirate shirt, with billowy long sleeves and a deep V that had loose laces around the cut, showing off male cleavage.

His large arms were crossed over his chest, and while I caught him smirking at Audrey, he gave me a shyer smile when I sat up.

"Who are you?" I practically growled at him before throwing a confused look at Audrey.

"Van," Audrey lifted her palms as she addressed me. "This is Liam."

I was already pulling my covers back before she finished speaking his name. I barely acknowledged that I was not, in fact, in Audrey's room.

Liam's eyes widened when I swung my legs over the end of

the bed and stood, my hands in fists as I marched toward him. He threw a concerned look toward Audrey before looking down at me and my sudden approach.

"Wait—" but Liam was cut off as soon as my fist collided with his throat. Shock colored his expression as he choked, stumbling away from me. Before I could lay into him again, Audrey was there, wrapping her arms around me and holding me back.

"Oh my god! Why did you do that?" Audrey asked as she threw me back on the bed. The move startled me. I'd never been so thoroughly handled by her. She was always so gentle. So soft. And yet, her strength was undeniable. I landed on my butt on the edge of the mattress with a confused *oomph*.

But she asked me a question, and it deserved an answer.

"He took you from me." I pointed an accusing finger at Liam, and surprisingly, he looked guilty at my claim. Which probably meant that I was right.

"No, no." Audrey shook her head and stood in my line of sight, blocking Liam with her body. "Liam hasn't done anything wrong, Van."

"Really?" I challenged. "Because as soon as *he* came into your life, things haven't been the same for us."

Audrey flinched from my words and argued, "You're right, but that's not his fault."

"It *clearly* is, everything was fine until you started running off with—" I cut myself off with a dramatic wave of my hand toward Liam, too upset to address him by name. I glared at his pointy ears, so annoyed that the man who encouraged Audrey to lead a male-centered life also seemed to wear fake elf ears unironically.

Staring at his ears suddenly triggered the memories of my dream.

The two men who also had pointy ears who tried to kidnap me.

The sound my ankle made when the blond man stepped on it.

"Van?" Audrey asked as she sat down beside me. The channel changed on the TV, and when I glanced up at it, it looked like a news station. A blonde woman with a microphone was talking into the camera while standing on a busy street filled with pedestrians.

Drapes and signage in a language that reminded me a lot of ancient Nordic runes were scattered on various buildings around her. People walked in the background of the shot, shopping, going about their day.

I stood from my seat on the bed, walking toward the flatscreen playing the news station. Because, as the woman was speaking, she tucked a blonde strand behind her pointed ear. I stepped closer to the TV, noticing how the pedestrians walking behind her also had pointy ears. Every single one of them. Even the kids.

At the bottom of the screen were English subtitles.

"...sources say that two unidentified sirens found their way through the Mellhawn Gates and into the human realm, before the fae prince and Hyvenmere's favorite halfling were able to..."

I ignored the subtitles because none of that meant anything to me.

"Aud?" I asked without looking at her. The soft sound of fabric moving was the only indication I had that she stood from the bed.

"Yeah?"

"Where are we?" I asked as I walked toward the floor-to-ceiling window of the room. I studied the delicate and intricate details of the drapes that framed the window before looking outside.

We were high up, maybe six stories or so, in a marble building that overlooked a charming city. It reminded me of a

European cottage town—not that I had the chance to visit Europe yet—but with thousands and thousands of buildings.

Trees were everywhere.

Flowers were everywhere.

Whatever building we were in had a courtyard, and below were dozens of people milling around, doing landscaping and gardening, some just sitting on blankets and enjoying the sunlight. I cupped my hands and pressed my face against the glass, focusing on the people in the courtyard.

They had pointed ears, too.

"Well…" Audrey approached my side, staring at the window, seeing everything I was, with a confidence I couldn't comprehend quite yet. "We're in Liam's home—well, his family's home."

I nodded, but based on what I was seeing, this wasn't Catalina Island.

"And where is Liam's family home?" I pressed.

Audrey turned to look at me, waiting for me to meet her eyes before she calmly replied, "In a magical realm." I pressed my lips together at her words, wondering how far gone my friend was. "Vanessa…welcome to Hyvenmere."

CHAPTER 3

"I don't understand," I muttered. "Is this like a theme park?" I glanced around the room, looking at the exposed stone on the accent wall of the large suite we were in. The bed I woke up in pressed against it. A bed made with soft silks and a wool throw.

The TV was still going in the corner, at a low enough volume not to disturb our conversation.

"No." Audrey sighed. "You're just in Hyvenmere. A real place where real people live."

"You keep saying that word, *Hyvenmere*." I walked around the room, ignoring the cautious stare of Liam and the worried lip biting of Audrey, as I studied the art on the walls. The landscape was unrecognizable. I mean, it was mountains and trees and flowers, but not of a land I had seen before. "What is Hyvenmere?"

"A magical realm," Liam answered. "As Audrey said."

"But what does that even *mean*?" I asked him, walking back to the window, just to make sure the city I saw before was still there.

"Be patient with her," Audrey told Liam before turning to me. "It's a lot to explain, but this—" Audrey spread her arms wide and glanced around the room. "—this is why I've been so busy."

"You haven't been *busy*." I shook my head at her, giving a fleeting glance toward the TV. "You've been *gone*."

"She's been here—" Liam tried to add, but he stopped himself when I whirled on him and gave him my harshest death glare, complete with my index finger pointed at him in warning.

"You're on thin ice, my guy," I spoke low, threatening, and I grinned when I saw Liam silently swallow around nothing. "As far as I'm concerned, you're still the reason Audrey's left me."

"I didn't *want* to leave you, Van," Audrey interjected, making both of us turn our attention toward her. She was playing with the sleeves of her sweater, her wide hazel eyes pleading with me. "I wanted to *protect* you. Hyvenmere is amazing, and I've come to learn and love so much about it—but it's also very dangerous for humans—because of what you dealt with two nights ago."

I felt the pinch in my forehead from her words, and the sudden, crystal-clear memory of bright eyes and a leering sneer. The sound of the crack in my spine.

I instinctively reached a hand up to press against my neck.

I should be in more pain.

If what I experienced *wasn't* a dream, and only happened two nights ago, then how the hell was I walking around and not in any pain?

"...How am I okay?" I asked, rubbing the back of my neck, counting the vertebrae. How many vertebrae were people supposed to have in their necks? Four? Five? However many I had, they were all fine. No pain accompanied my touch.

"That's actually why we had to bring you here, to save you," Liam spoke up again, ignoring my dramatic frown toward him. "Audrey was too distraught to trust herself to heal you properly after seeing you broken and bleeding from a head injury, unconscious. We brought you back here to take you to our best healers."

"What do you mean by, heal me herself?" I asked.

"I can heal people with my touch." Audrey's lips played around with a smile as she wiggled her fingers at me. "Among other things. It's why I've spent so much time here in Hyvenmere. I'm learning about who I am, and what all I can do..." her voice trailed off, and her gaze grew distant. "...but now things are way more complicated." She lifted her hands to wrap her palms around the back of her neck, tugging as she met my gaze.

"I still don't understand..." but my voice trailed off. I was pretty sure I was following everything she was saying, but it was a lot to take in. I turned away from her in thought, toward the TV. On it, a new reporter with dark hair and—again—pointy ears, copper-toned skin, and blue eyes spoke into the microphone as he approached someone from behind. Someone with shoulder-length red hair.

English subtitles trailed along the bottom of the screen, but my entire focus was on the face of the red-haired man as he turned to give a withering glare toward the reporter speaking to him.

They were at a bar, and the red-haired man held a glass of some dark-colored alcoholic beverage as the reporter rattled off something.

"I don't know why they keep interviewing him." Audrey frowned as she studied the TV with me. "He never provides a substantial take beyond 'fuck off.'"

"I don't know why they don't send him back to the Gravhune," Liam grumbled. He strode across the room where a drink cart was set up and started pouring himself a glass.

The red-haired man had gold, shimmering irises that made me step toward the TV to get a better look. His pink lips pulled into a clearly condescending smirk as the reporter asked his question and tilted the microphone toward him. Instead of giving the reporter a response, the red-haired man engaged in direct eye contact while tipping his glass up to take another silent drink.

Watching him swallow his drink made my cheeks heat, and I lifted a hand to rub against my chest, attempting to brush the heat away. He was attractive, undoubtedly so, but something about him felt very...off.

My eyes fell to the bottom of the screen, where the English subtitles were, when the reporter tried again.

"...affect your father's claim that he's the one destined to unite the realm?"

The red-haired man lifted an eyebrow, taking another quick sip of his drink before resting his now-empty glass on the bar top and standing. He was several inches taller than the reporter, and the visual of him leaning in with clear intimidation toward the poor man made my heart start to drum in my chest. His lips started moving, and I focused on the English subtitles.

"...If the halfling wants to prove herself truly worthy of our realm, making an adversary of my father, guardian of the Fjellenheim Mountains, is an unintelligent way to do so..." Listening to his voice made my skin erupt in goosebumps.

The red-haired man had a very nice voice. Even though he was clearly being rude and condescending toward whoever he was talking about.

"He sounds like a prick. Who is 'the halfling?'" I asked, pointing at the TV screen.

Audrey slowly raised her hand. "That would be me."

I raised my eyebrows at her. "Oh shit."

"Yeah..." Audrey rubbed the back of her neck again. "I have a lot to catch you up on. But first, I need the healer to come and clear you."

I frowned, scanning my body. "I feel fine."

"That's great," Liam interjected after tossing back his drink. He then pulled out what looked like a cellphone from his pocket, tapped on it, and gave the TV another glare as it showed a montage of footage of the attractive red-haired man, before it powered off. "But you're an undocumented human in Hyvenmere, and we need to ensure the territories don't get upset with Audrey for healing you and bringing you here."

I frowned at her. "Why did you bring me here, then?"

Audrey stomped toward me, resting her hands on my shoulders so I would face her. "I don't think you understand the severity of your head injury. I did not spend the last two years keeping secrets from you, letting you hate me, allowing our friendship to grow apart, just for you to die as soon as you're exposed to this part of my life for the very first time." Audrey's lip quivered. "I love you, Van. You're my only family."

A piece of my heart that had hardened over the years, watching Audrey become shadier and shadier, keeping me at arm's length, thawed at her words.

Perhaps our friendship wasn't completely ruined.

Maybe there was a way for us to get back to who we used to be, as Audrey and Vanessa.

If this meant Audrey wasn't keeping secrets from me—even if I still couldn't comprehend what all her secrets were—I wanted to find a way to nourish the bond between us.

I wrapped her up in a hug, almost letting an emotional tear escape my eye when her arms immediately wrapped around me, too.

"I don't hate you," I muttered, squeezing her tighter, encouraging her to do the same to me. "I don't understand what's happening, but I love you, too. Don't worry." I pulled back, looking her in the eye, noticing the red lining her lids as well. "We're still good."

Liam set his glass down on the drink cart, reminding me that he was here, as he gave the two of us a soft smile.

"You can still fuck off, though."

Audrey snorted and laughed, whereas Liam sighed dramatically with an unimpressed frown at me.

"I don't want to be enemies, Van."

"Tough shit, Liam."

CHAPTER 4

A few minutes later, an older woman known as a healer, entered my suite. She came complete with pointed ears and white robes that looked very doctorly. Her demeanor was calm as she came in and took my vitals. It was weird, because all she did was stick little square stickers on the back of my neck, wrist, and front of my chest, and told me to chill for a bit while her tablet—one that looked very similar to what I see at home, just a little more oval—logged my heart rate and oxygen levels.

"So...what are you?" I asked Liam, trying to hold still while the stickers did their thing.

"You can move," the doctor—or rather—*healer* told me with a gentle smile.

"I'm fae," Liam answered. He was reclining in a leather chair and flipping through channels. "You're in the fae territory of Enharra."

"En-hahr-uh," I slowly spoke, and Audrey nodded confirmation at my pronunciation. "At your family home."

"The Dahl Family Palace," the healer interjected with an excited smile. The way she stared at me was unsettling. Like she was fascinated with me. I gave her what I hoped was a friendly smile before turning away.

"Palace? Like royalty?" My clarification was directed toward Liam, but my gaze shifted to Audrey, who lifted a shoulder in a casual, *believe-it-or-not* way.

The healer's eyes widened at me with curiosity as she asked, "Do humans not have royalty in your realm?"

"Humans?" I asked her.

"Some territories do," Audrey answered the healer. "Not the one we're from—well, we're not supposed to, anyway. Celebrities often get idolized to the level of royalty, though."

"Interesting," the healer responded.

"Okay, wait. Back up." I shook my head, trying to keep a steady head during this mindfuck of an experience. "What the hell is a fae?"

Audrey giggled while Liam and the healer both waited for her to answer. "Think of fae as like...faeries?"

I blinked at her. "...Like Tinkerbell?"

Audrey jutted a thumb toward Liam's massive frame lying back in the chair. "Does he look like a Tinkerbell to you?"

"Okay, well, where are your wings?" I asked both the healer and Liam.

"They don't have any," a feminine voice answered, making all three of us turn toward the double doors. A tall woman gently strode into the room. She wore a pale green gown that exposed her waist, covering her bust all the way up to her neck. The gown shimmered with her steps as she entered and closed the doors behind her, but it wasn't sparkly. I couldn't place what the material was.

When her back was toward the room, though, I saw wings.

Clear, insect-like wings. Almost transparent if it weren't for the tendons that flexed them. They were folded against her back but flittered as she turned and smoothed some wrinkles out of her gown.

She smiled at me in a warm, friendly greeting. Her blonde hair was knotted with a crown of braids, keeping it all out of her face and encouraging the curls to flow down her back, over her wings.

As she stepped toward me on the bed, the healer stood and clasped her hands in front of her, dipping her chin lightly. The woman smiled at the healer, at the same moment as she ruffled Liam's hair in passing, dodging his hand as he swatted at her in retaliation.

"Are you two siblings?" I asked the woman, noting how similar their features were. Blonde hair, blue eyes, sharp features.

"I'm Liam's twin sister, yes." The woman nodded as she made it over to my bed.

"Vanessa." Audrey gestured toward the blonde-winged woman. "This is Ada Dahl, Liam's sister, and Queen of the Fae." I raised my eyes and nodded, smiling, panicking, because how the hell do you address royalty in a magical realm?

"Shit—sorry—hi—" I made my way to stand so I could properly bow.

"Please." Ada raised her hand to stop me. "We don't need to be so formal in the privacy of my home."

Oh, thank god.

"When you greet her in public, though," Audrey interjected, "It's best that you dip your chin to show respect, at least."

"Got it." I gave Ada a thumbs up, and she pressed her lips together with her smile at me.

"What did the council say?" Liam asked Ada. I looked toward Audrey for any sort of context, but she was busy focusing on Ada and Liam.

Ada blew out a tired breath and crossed her arms, "They're annoyed, but not upset. Additionally, King Ilia denies any involvement."

"Well, he's lying. His men were there. But the fact that

everyone is only *annoyed* is good." Audrey placed a hand over her heart in relief. "So what do they want us to do?"

"The good news is they approved her grant, which she should have in the next day or so. You'll be able to return to your realm soon."

"Hold up," I interjected. "I'm stuck here until I get a grant?" Like a money grant?

"A grant is documentation," Audrey explained. "Think of it like a tourist visa to visit Hyvenmere."

"Oh." I nodded. "I won't get arrested for being here?"

Ada frowned at me and asked, "Did you commit a crime?"

"Not that I'm aware of, but did I accidentally enter this—er —realm 'illegally?'"

Audrey muttered, "That's a loaded question."

Understanding dawned on Ada's face, and she flicked a glance over to Audrey before explaining to me, "It is not 'illegal,'" she emphasized the word with air quotes, "to enter Hyvenmere if you are not an official citizen of Hyvenmere. We are not cruel like the human realm seems to be." I was filled with relief from her words. "Your realm does not know about our realm, as has been the design for hundreds of years. However, because several discussions are going on about *officially* opening the Mellhawn Gates to the human realm again, the council has decided that the humans who *are* aware of Hyvenmere and its territories must have proper documentation, so governments can be aware of who is exploring our lands."

"I—" I shook my head once. "I don't see myself paying this place a ton of visits." I didn't understand how a person traveled between realms. How did we even get here? Was there a bus? A train? A boat? Who the hell knew?

At my words, Audrey's face fell a little bit, and I immediately wanted to take it back.

But I was still trying to fight off memories of the men who attacked me on my boat, and if those were normal occurrences here, then whatever the hell was going on in Hyvenmere was none of my business.

"That's fine, but this way, when you carry your grant on you, my court will be notified of your arrival in the realm."

"Ada is basically vouching for you," Audrey summarized. "So if you do decide to visit, you're her responsibility."

I quirked my lips to the side and slid my gaze over to the Queen of the Fae. "Thank you. That's nice to do for someone you've never met."

"It's not without a request of my own." Ada settled herself on the edge of my bed, folding her hands in her lap as she tilted her head at me. "Would you be willing to tell me what happened? In your own words?"

I inhaled a deep breath before saying, "I don't know if I even understand what happened, yet."

"Maybe just start from the beginning." Audrey kneeled next to me on the bed, resting a hand on my shoulder. I reached up to squeeze her fingers with mine before addressing Queen Ada directly.

"It was nighttime, and I had a drink." I blew out a breath at the feel of my heart picking up speed, my body remembering the anxiety of the moment all too well. "At first, I thought I was too intoxicated. That's why the men seemed very tall and very... odd."

Ada's blonde brows pinched at my words before she turned to Audrey. "You said it was Leon and Sergei trying to take her?"

Audrey nodded. "Yes. Without a doubt."

"You don't happen to have any evidence that it was them?" Ada pressed.

I frowned at her question. "I don't have security cameras on my boat. Never thought I needed them."

Ada hummed in understanding. "What happened after they showed up?"

"They were very...I don't know. Annoyed. The blond specifically acted inconvenienced."

"Leon." Audrey chimed in.

"Sure, whatever." I waved my hand. "They were bickering. Leon sounded like he just wanted to grab me and go. I jutted a thumb over my shoulder. "But the brunet mentioned something about me needing to be...unharmed. He just kept telling me to come with them."

I still ended up being, what I considered, very much harmed.

I rubbed at my chest, attempting to soothe the burning anger I felt from the memory. The fact that my well-being was being debated between two seven-foot-tall men was disgusting.

"Interesting." Ada frowned, her gaze shifting to the side. "Did you consider listening to them?"

"Absolutely not," I snorted with my reply. "I can usually keep a level head when men try to push me around," (or attack me, tomayto-tomahto). "But then Leon said something, and I suddenly felt stuck."

"Stuck?" Ada pressed.

"Yeah." I curled in on myself. "What he said wasn't even that much more threatening, but for some reason, my fear just..." I paused, not sure how to describe the reaction I had, "...took over. I think I may have considered going with them for half a second, because I was so terrified." I glanced up, making brief eye contact with all four people in the room, finding comfort in Audrey's empathetic gaze and Ada's respectful one. "I don't usually let my fear of men control me like that. It caught me off guard."

Liam released a deep, heavy sigh from his spot on the recliner. "Sounds like he used his sinndra on her."

I perked up at that and pointed at Liam. "Yeah, I think they said that word."

"They *said* they were using their sinndra on you?" Audrey asked, scooting closer so that her thigh was against mine.

"No." I shook my head, dropping my gaze to my lap to try to remember. "...the brunet, uh..." I looked to Audrey.

"Sergei," she filled in for me.

"Yeah, Sergei," I nodded and continued. "He scolded Leon. Called him a prick for, what was it...*using* his sinndra on me."

"Huh." Ada frowned in thought. "What an odd interaction. He was allegedly willing to steal a human but had a moral code when it came to the unlawful use of sinndra."

"You're telling me." I sighed, then lifted a finger. "Also. What is sinndra?"

Ada was about to speak up before Audrey beat her to the punch.

"All sirens have sinndra to some extent," Audrey explained. "In the simplest of terms, it's their ability to sense your emotions and amplify them to their liking. Some sirens have a stronger sinndra than others. Leon's must have been strong, but not strong enough to fully manipulate you, since you were still willing to fight back anyway."

"Good job." Ada gave me a smile and a thumbs-up, which didn't feel *queenly* at all, but I appreciated the praise.

"Thank you." I gave her a thumbs-up back, and she grinned wider.

Then I thought about Audrey's explanation and asked, "Sirens?" I glanced around the room, "I thought you were all fae?"

"We are," Liam muttered. "Leon and Sergei are sirens, though. Known to do the Siren King, Ilia's, bidding."

"And this Siren King, he's claiming he had nothing to do with my attack?" I pointed to Ada, who nodded as I tried to piece all of this together. "So how are sirens different from fae?"

"We're not pricks, for one," Liam grunted.

Audrey and Ada both turned to Liam to scold him.

"Enough," Ada snapped.

"Liam," Audrey groaned, before turning to me. "Biologically, they're very similar. But sirens are shapeshifters, whereas fae are not."

I stared at Audrey before shrugging my shoulders and shaking my head in defeat.

"Yeah. Sure. Of course they are." This was all so insane. What else was I to do, besides go along with all of the crazy shit flowing out of everyone's mouths?

Ada gave me a bright smile, as if sensing my overwhelm at her world, before pulling a more oval cellphone out of the pockets of her gown and frowning at it.

"I need to take this." She nodded to the room, and the healer at my side dipped her chin again, so I followed suit. "I'm glad you're doing well, Vanessa."

"Me too," I replied. "Thank you."

"Of course." With that, Ada pinched Liam's arm in passing, avoiding his swatting hand yet again, and let herself out.

When the doors closed, the healer quietly removed my vitals stickers and cleared me.

"Your ribs have healed," she read off her tablet. "No more internal bleeding. Your concussion and fractured skull left no scarring. Your ankle is healed, and your oxygen and heart rate are steady for human standards."

I decided to let "for human standards" lie.

"Goddamn." My heart rate picked up as she listed off all my injuries, and how I definitely would have been in one of those refrigerator cubbies at a morgue in the human realm if this one didn't exist. "And you healed all of that with just your hands?"

"The halfl—Audrey—kept you stable until they brought you to me. But I've also been doing this for a very long time," the healer smiled as she asked me one last question. "Are you in need of any pain management? Would you like a tea?"

Audrey giggled. "It's strong stuff. Only take it if you're in genuine pain, or you'll be stoned."

I shook my head in the negative at the healer. "I'm not in any pain at all—" Then I held up a finger in thought. "Do you have anything if I'm sensing a panic attack coming on, though?"

Audrey frowned at me, but the healer gave me a rueful smile and replied, "Unfortunately, nothing that we have has been tested enough on humans. I can't guarantee it's safe for you to take."

"Oh, for sure." I waved her off. "I probably won't need that, anyway." Audrey's shoulders dropped in relief.

The healer started packing up her things as she said, "It was a pleasure to meet you. I haven't met a full-blooded human until today."

"Um, I'm honored to be your first." If that was true, what the hell was Audrey? The healer just chuckled at me and let herself out of the suite.

I didn't even hesitate as soon as the click of the latch echoed in the room.

"Why do people call you 'the halfling'?"

Audrey bit her lip with a shy smile because she always hated having attention on herself.

"I'm half fae." She lifted a shoulder and shoved her hands in the pockets of her linen pants. They were tighter on her legs, but when her fists went into them, I realized the linen stretched. I wondered how that worked with linen. Was this another detail of being in something called a "magical realm"?

Liam grumbled, and the two of us turned to see what caused his mood to drop.

The red-haired man was on the TV again, this time wearing a black leather outfit that looked a lot like some type of spy or military wear. It was very similar to the outfit that the men—I'm sorry, *sirens*—who attacked me wore, and I found myself frowning at the screen.

He was walking down a cobbled-stone street, with other tall men walking behind him, wearing face masks. He didn't wear his, though. The hood that seemed to come with his military uniform was down. Instead, he strutted down the street with a relaxed, casual air of indifference.

The red-haired man nodded politely at pedestrians he passed, even though his lips stayed in a firm line; a couple of teenage-looking girls with gold eyes and more pointed ears giggled at his attention. Apparently, even the teenagers in this realm were capable of fangirling.

"Everyone in that shot has gold eyes," I murmured, mostly to myself, but loud enough for them to hear.

"All sirens have gold eyes," Audrey quickly explained before she sighed to Liam. "Just turn it off."

"I hate that the sirens are still pretending that it's okay for *him* to be on their streets like this," Liam muttered.

Liam and this guy clearly had beef, and while I was curious what it was, I was more concerned with Audrey and how the fucking hell she discovered a whole ass magical realm in the first place.

As if she read my mind, Audrey strolled over to the desk in the corner of the room, near the large window, and unplugged a laptop from it before walking back to me.

"I was writing you a letter the night of, well—" She vaguely waved her arm toward me, and I took that to mean, *The night you were attacked by seven foot tall men you mistook for LARPers but were actually evil sirens*, before she continued. "And I didn't expect you to read it so soon, but it might provide some answers to questions you're having right now."

I gently grabbed the laptop from her, setting it on my lap. I was healed, I didn't need to stay in bed, but I also didn't know what else to do while I waited for my grant from Queen Ada.

Plus, this bed was cozy as hell.

"Do you want me to read it out loud?" I asked her.

Audrey's hazel eyes widened in horror. "Oh dear god, no." She laughed to herself, and settled in next to me on the bed. She pulled her cellphone out—an oval one from the realm we were in—and started checking through various apps.

I opened the laptop, and sure enough, a document that was clearly a letter from Audrey was left open. I scrolled back to the top and started to read.

Not knowing what to expect.

Not really caring what was in this letter from her.

Just grateful that I was here, sitting next to my best friend, who was finally willing to answer questions I've had for years.

After I read her letter, Audrey gave me time to sit with my newfound knowledge of Hyvenmere and what she's been up to, by leaving to get food. She asked Liam to stay with me while she was gone.

I made an "ew, what the fuck?" face at her request, which she blatantly ignored.

Liam obliged, also ignoring my expression, and we have been sitting here in unbearable silence since. He sat in the recliner again, flipping through channels on the TV, while I stared daggers at him.

Sure, Audrey liked him. Had a friendship with him.

But I still hated him.

"Are you going to say anything, or just continue to sit there, picturing my death?" Liam sighed without looking at me.

I narrowed my eyes at him. "I was just glaring at you, but I can picture your death too, if you'd like."

"What is your issue with me, specifically?" Liam turned to look at me then. "You got along with my sister. The healer, too. It can't be a general grudge against fae."

Obviously not, considering I learned about fae five minutes ago, and I had been building up this resentment toward Liam for just under two years.

"They didn't pull Audrey away from our friendship for two years straight." I crossed my arms over my chest and my ankles over each other on the bed, legs stretched out. "According to her letter, you Kool-Aid-Manned your way into her life and stole her away."

His facial expression made me realize he probably had no idea what I meant by "Kool-Aid-Manned," but with a shake of his head, it was clear he decided not to ask about the slang.

I wasn't sure if Audrey remembered that she wrote about her unrequited crush on Liam in her letter, but that detail was in there, and I wouldn't forget it.

They may not be dating, but she definitely wasn't opposed to the idea.

"I did not encourage her to keep so many secrets from you, Vanessa." Liam stood from his recliner, stepping toward the bed to lean against one of the large bedposts at the foot of it. "Audrey always wanted to keep you safe. You are precious to her." Liam's blue eyes locked onto mine. "Who was I to tell her otherwise?"

I frowned at him. "I still don't like it when men come between Audrey and me, even if you're claiming that it was unintentional."

Liam's eyes narrowed at my words, and his chest rose with something like irritation; his nostrils flared as he composed himself enough to ask me, "Are you and Audrey lovers?"

I opened my mouth to say no, but I hesitated.

Because what if Liam was homophobic? That made me want to say yes, just to spite him. But I had no idea if lying about this was dangerous. The more I studied Liam's body language, though, the more I realized his heated reaction to his question wasn't one of bigotry.

No. He had tense shoulders, tight fists, uneven breathing through his nose. Liam's reaction looked…jealous.

Well, I'll be damned.

Audrey's little crush might not be so unreciprocated after all.

"What's it to you?" I asked, leaning forward to bend my knees enough to rest my elbows on them. "Would you back off? Would you let us live our happily ever after in my realm without putting weird pressure on her to hang out here?"

Liam closed his eyes, attempting to compose himself. His shoulders inched higher; his irritation with my non-answer made me grin. Without looking at me, he returned to the drink cart. He poured his second drink of the day.

This *thrilled* me. I loved irritating men.

Suddenly, Audrey threw the suite door open, holding a brown bag of what smelled like food in each hand.

I immediately jumped off my bed, walking toward the table in the corner where Audrey dumped the bags of food and started unpacking them.

"I got these skewers I think you'll love, Van." Audrey grinned at me, and she held one up.

I moaned, sexually. "Babe, I could kiss you on the mouth."

Audrey just snickered, rolled her eyes, and continued to unpack the food. I glanced over my shoulder to see Liam taking a deep pull of his drink as he kept his eyes on us.

I turned back to Audrey, "Can I?"

Audrey grinned, pulling out little cardboard cups of what I assumed were side-dishes. "Yeah, sure." She clearly didn't think I was being serious. "But let me show you what else I got—" Audrey was cut off because I had cupped both of her cheeks with my hands and slammed my lips on hers, dramatically.

Audrey immediately tried to retreat, startled and confused, and I followed after her, bending my body over hers, like lovers.

I released her lips with a loud smack, and Audrey laughed out loud.

"What the hell was—" Audrey was cut off once again by the sound of glass shattering, making both of us turn to see Liam *fuming*. The glass in his hand was shattered into pieces on the floor at his feet, his hand bleeding. He had gripped the glass so hard that it shattered in his massive mitts.

"Oh, Liam!" Audrey slapped my hands off her face and ran toward him, wrapping her hands around his injured and bloody hand. Light started to glow from their touch, and Liam's shoulders immediately relaxed at her proximity. When Audrey removed her hand from his, the cuts were completely gone. As if he had never hurt himself in the first place.

When he lifted his gaze, his expression was no longer furious, but smug. He had the look of a man who felt like he had just won a challenge, but when he saw me, his smug look faltered. Because I was standing there, my weight shifted on one hip, arms crossed, with a shit eating grin.

Liam just showed me all his cards.

"So, tell me, Liam." I pulled a chair out while Audrey grabbed a rag from the drink cart and dabbed away the blood from Liam's freshly healed palm. "How long have you—"

"Let's eat!" Liam clasped his fingers in Audrey's and pulled her to the table, practically throwing her down in a chair he pulled out for her with one hand. "Vanessa must be famished."

"She is," I replied and decided to let this go, because I really was starving. According to them, I hadn't eaten in a couple of days while I was healing. I reached over to open one of the cardboard cups Audrey had set out before I attacked her face and moaned at the familiar look of mashed potatoes.

"Oh, and Vanessa?" Audrey said as she helped distribute the food.

"Yeah?" I replied before shoveling a heaping spoonful of mashed potatoes into my mouth.

"You know you're not my type." Audrey raised an eyebrow at me with a smirk. "Right?"

"I was thanking you for saving my life and bringing us food." I scooped another heap of mashed potatoes, because damn, these were delicious. "Can't a woman express gratitude with a passionate kiss on the mouth?"

Audrey rolled her eyes and shook her head at Liam. "You should know that Vanessa is a bit of a wild card at times."

"I'm starting to see that." Liam smiled at Audrey, but when she looked down at her Hyvenmerian cellphone that was resting face up on the table, he turned and glared at me.

In response, I stuck my tongue out at him.

His face twisted up in annoyance, and I dramatically dragged my thumb across my neck in a clear threat.

Audrey glanced up when my thumb was halfway across my throat, and watched Liam shake his head at me.

"You two are going to get along beautifully, I see." Audrey sighed to herself before she returned her focus to her phone and scooped green beans into her mouth.

CHAPTER 5

The next morning, I woke up to Audrey spooning me in bed.

I turned my head over my shoulder and blasted her with my morning breath with a very dramatic yawn.

"Dude." Audrey wrinkled her nose and shoved herself away from me.

"Oh, I'm sorry." I rolled over onto my back to look at her. "Did I disturb you?"

"My nose hairs are burning off from how foul your morning breath is, which isn't my preferred way to start the day." Audrey stretched her arms above her head with her words, before throwing the blankets off and rushing out of bed. "Your grant should be here soon, if it isn't already." She pulled out a duffel bag from under the bed and plopped it on the space where she had been sleeping before, pulling out clothing I recognized.

Her *human* clothes.

I groaned and tugged the covers around my body more as I watched her get dressed, "Did I interrupt a dream about a certain Temu-Thor?"

Audrey's cheeks immediately flamed bright red, almost as red as her hair, as she playfully glared at me. "I know you don't like him, yet."

"That is correct." I stretched under the covers as I spoke. "He has a bit of groveling to do."

"He's a nice guy." Audrey paused her sentence to lift a palm toward me. "And not like in an incel way. He just genuinely is a good guy. I...I don't know. I like him."

"You've always had a thing for blond partners, I'm not too surprised," I replied. Whereas I always preferred dark-haired partners.

Audrey hummed while she pulled a comb out of her bag and started tugging through the knots in her hair. I finally pulled the covers back and stood from the bed, stretching my back out as I added, "His massive body and muscles really don't suck, either."

Audrey cackled, blushing again.

"The men and women in this realm, I'm telling you..." Audrey tugged the collar of her shirt and panted dramatically, "It's like there's something in the water that makes everyone ridiculously beautiful."

"Based on the beautiful people I saw on TV, I think I believe you." I smirked, thinking about how the reporters were also undeniably gorgeous. But then the image of the red-haired man smirking as he sipped his drink filled my mind. I shook it away, before I asked, "Why there are English subtitles, if everyone seems to speak in another language?" Liam, Queen Ada, and the healer had similar accents to Liam and the men who attacked me. The reporters also had an accent that, I suddenly realized, wasn't European at all. It was an accent that didn't exist in our realm.

Audrey smiled, "That depends on the news station. The one we were flipping through yesterday just happened to be pro-human-inclusive mating bonds."

I was making the bed when I froze at her words, looking up at her suspiciously. "I beg your pardon?"

Audrey rolled her eyes. "I assume you know what I mean by mating bonds, then." Yes, because she mentioned them in her letter. Context clues helped me figure out what exactly that meant.

"Are you telling me that there are English subtitles on news networks, because the owners of those networks want to..." I inserted my index finger into a hole my other hand made, in a dirty gesture. "...with humans like us?"

Audrey sat on the edge of the bed, lacing her sneakers up as she casually lifted a shoulder. "Yeah, I guess that's the simplest way to put it."

Get me the hell out of here.

The fact that I woke up this morning, still in a magical realm named Hyvenmere, in a fae Prince's family castle, and *didn't* have a nervous breakdown was a win. Audrey had me read enough of her paranormal romance novels for me to know exactly what "mating" and "bond" implied.

While I was generally monogamous in my sexual relationships, I wasn't sure I was ready to settle down, yet. I had my coffee shop to run, and I liked having all my free time to myself. I liked being able to hole up in our condo for days at a time to start a new composition whenever I pleased.

Plus, I still had to wrap my head around the fact that my best friend had magical powers and spent half of her time in a place called Hyvenmere.

Audrey and I finished getting dressed in our human clothes, which the castle servants had washed and pressed for us. Then Liam knocked on our door. He held in his hand a thick paper that was the size of a business card, but I couldn't read the language that was on it. Again, it reminded me of runes of some kind. But apparently that was what I needed to have on me should I choose to enter this realm again. I pulled out my wallet from my bag, thankful that all my personal belongings were still in there after the clusterfuck I've experienced. I tucked my grant into my wallet, then stowed it away in my bag.

Leaving the castle was a surreal experience. It was difficult to imagine that I spent the last twenty-four hours of my (awake) time in a legitimate, occupied, functioning castle. When we walked out the front doors, escorted by Liam, I turned around with my hands on my backpack straps. The marble was a cream color, with flowers and vines circling up each side. Every window and doorway had a decorative, but natural foliage haloing them. Seeing all the blooming flowers and greenery made my nose itch, and I sneezed once as I turned around to follow my friend through the courtyard.

Other fae were there, watching us with curious eyes.

A younger boy, I would guess around the age of ten, was with his mother, who was picking flowers. He stared more blatantly than the rest of the pointy-ear creatures, and as I stayed in step behind Audrey and Liam, I gave him a tentative wave.

He smiled brightly and waved enthusiastically back.

I turned forward right when we were about to walk through an iron gate that led to the rest of the city, only to meet Audrey's eye. She was smiling at me, happy with that exchange I just had with the little boy.

Queen Ada had mentioned that humans hadn't had access to this realm for hundreds of years, but if Audrey was half-fae, would that imply that this realm at least had access to ours? How did that work?

I was wondering this as I got distracted by the smell of a delicious pastry from a shop that we passed. I bumped into someone, and as I apologized to them in passing, I realized something odd about Hyvenmerians.

Compared to them, I was considered average, or even small,

in height. This was unnerving to wrap my head around, considering I usually towered over everyone I met. I had been tall since my middle-school growth spurt. I was used to being tall.

What I wasn't used to, I quickly realized, was feeling small.

Especially in a sea of people.

A person I bumped into never broke their stride, and soon they were lost in the crowd while I jogged to keep up with Audrey and Liam, who led us through the stone streets. They weren't exactly cobblestone, because they were smoother. There was just enough texture to keep people from sliding on the stone if it were wet but not displaced enough to easily trip over.

I also expected the trees to thin out to make room for such a busy, massive city. However, that wasn't the case. The tall, skyscraper-height trees stood next to modern-looking buildings. It was obvious that the forest had been here way before these people were, and instead of cutting everything down, everything was woven together with it. Streets, bicycles, buildings, and shops.

Every establishment looked small, but a short walk to a slightly higher elevation showed how far the city development had expanded. We also passed a small creek with canoes that reminded me of the ones I've seen on Italian tourist sites. It cut through the center of the city, but the water wasn't polluted, like it would be back home.

Suddenly, something started to tickle my ears.

At first, I wasn't sure what I was experiencing. It wasn't until I could identify individual notes that I realized I was *hearing* something. A song. Perhaps someone was playing music in the distance, since this seemed like a lively city.

"That sounds beautiful," I said.

"What does?" Audrey asked.

"The music," I replied.

Liam and Audrey gave me curious looks before Audrey asked, "What music?"

"The music." I turned around, trying to locate where it was coming from, but I couldn't pick out a certain direction. It was still so faint, but when I faced her again, she just gave me a confused look.

She didn't hear it.

Oh my god, maybe I was having a breakdown after all.

"Never mind." I waved my hand dismissively. "I thought I heard music. I think it was just someone talking."

Audrey nodded. "The languages do sound beautiful, don't they?"

I agreed and moved on. I still heard the tune but kept it to myself.

I couldn't track where the melody was coming from, but it brought me comfort to hear music, an art that brought me relief in my darkest and lowest times. I sent a silent prayer up to the universe, thanking it for letting me experience a tranquil melody in this realm as I adjusted to my new reality.

I was lost in my thoughts as we walked throughout Liam's flowery home city, Enhavenn. Which apparently was in the fae territory (country) of Enharra. There were little to no cars or vehicles at all. Everyone rode bikes or walked, which made the city feel cozy, even though it was large.

Audrey led us to an EV train station, which I would have thought would clash with the classic stone structure of the city, but it didn't. It didn't look like a metal rusty tube like the main train system California had. It looked like a tube of polished wood, stained with a light oak, with green and yellow paint to make it feel like it belonged with the city's architecture.

"First, we need to take the train out of Enharra and to Sammara," Audrey explained as we took our seats. They were comfy, with embroidered cushions. A quick look around the full space made me realize that this was a very common form of transportation. Families, businesspeople, the elderly, and teens all took their seats around us.

"Is Sammara another fae city?" I asked as I made eye contact with a young child again. I smiled and waved, and she blushed and turned away from me in her seat, toward her parent.

"Sammara is the capital of Hyvenmere," Liam explained as he settled next to Audrey, facing me. There was a stone table in between us, with an electronic tablet built into the surface, with the Hyvenmerian language dancing across the screen. It looked like a map showing us the route we were about to take. "It's a city where all the people of Hyvenmere gather to celebrate each other. Sammara is where you go when you want to experience every territory's cuisine, art, and culture. It's also where the Mellhawn Gates are, which is how we'll get you back home."

The train started to take off, and when I glanced out the window, I was shocked.

We were traveling *so* fast.

Enharra was very green, with a thick forest that reminded me a lot of Northern California, covered in the largest redwood trees I'd ever seen. Watching the massive trees zoom past us as the train practically flew under ancient canopies, until the landscape opened up wide enough for us to see for miles, was surreal. By my estimate, we were easily traveling over one hundred miles per hour, if not one hundred and fifty.

I could feel Audrey's eyes on me as I watched the landscape zoom past us.

After the vast landscape was exposed, and my jaw audibly dropped, Liam excused himself, saying he was going to find us coffee.

Thank fuck they had coffee in Hyvenmere.

In the far distance, a city made of bricks and stones, surrounded by large evergreens and redwoods—at least, trees that *looked* like evergreens and redwoods, started to come into view.

Audrey studied me, and I focused on her reflection in the glass. The tall and short buildings of what I assumed to be

Sammara slowly crawled closer to us as the train left the old-growth forest and traveled over a large body of water. Far away in the distance, on another green landmass separated by a large river, were mountains capped with a dusting of snow.

"Those are the Fjellenheim Mountains of Lyndoruun," Audrey nodded her head toward them as she spoke. "Legend has it that the goddess Tynara used to reside there. Watching over the continent of Hyvenmere. Keeping everything balanced and fruitful."

I grinned. "I'm glad it's a goddess."

Audrey smiled at me and replied, "I am, too."

"Have you snowboarded down them or anything?" I asked, wondering how far away they truly were.

Audrey shook her head and responded, "No. They're protected, so there are no resorts or anything there. Think of them as a national park that's also kind of a universal temple, not many Hyvenmerians have visited, out of respect." She tilted her head as we studied the mountains, until the path of the train pivoted, and they were out of our sight. "They're also *huge*. Imagine being able to see a mountain range in San Francisco while standing in LA."

"Whoa, they're that far away?" I widened my eyes. "They don't look *that* far away."

Audrey lifted a shoulder, "That's how large the landscape is here. I think the earth is just...bigger. Making the curve of the planet not as drastic as it is in our realm."

I stared at her wide-eyed and focused back on the city we were entering. The train was going fast, and suddenly the landscape started to make a subtle shift. There were several land masses in the distance over the body of water we were crossing, one where the Fjellenheim mountains resided, and another that was very tropical. Reminding me of home.

"It's all so beautiful," I breathed.

The air was cleaner here.

I could taste it on my tongue, even on the train.

"It is," Audrey sighed. "I'm glad I can finally show you."

I nodded in agreement, then asked my next question, "Why don't you just…stay here?"

Audrey's reflection turned to look at me. "…It's not my home?" She said it like a question, with an insecure little chuckle. "I mean, sure, half of me belongs here. But the other half? The half that was raised near the beach. With my favorite people…" She reached across the table to poke my arm with her finger. "I can't imagine leaving you behind."

I bit the inside of my cheek at that. "Don't get me wrong, I'm glad you didn't disappear completely." I inhaled through my nose, admiring the gorgeous deep greens and earth tones of the landscape. "But I've only been here for hours, and I can already see that you practically shine here."

I thought about her interacting with Liam and Ada, and the friendly and familiar waves she gave Hyvenmerians as we made our way to the train station. She was open. The last couple of years, she had only looked guarded in front of me. Sure, she was keeping several secrets that I now had the context for. But seeing her here, not hiding any part of herself, and cautiously studying my reactions to things as they were revealed to me, made me see the Audrey I once knew. The Audrey I wanted to find again.

I doubted anyone would be the same after discovering that they had magical powers and descended from a magical realm, but all things considered, Audrey was handling it well as far as I could see.

Audrey faced the window again, staring at the passing foliage in silence.

"…You could shine here, too," she murmured.

I snorted, "I don't know about that." I lifted an eyebrow at her. "If those two men have any interest in putting their paws on me again, I don't know if I feel safe wandering around here."

Audrey nodded in understanding, "The good news is that you're protected by the fae government now. Hyvenmere knows of your existence. You're not an unknown, easy target. As long as you have your grant on you, Queen Ada will be able to find you."

I frowned. "I...I guess I don't understand why anyone felt the need to attack me in the first place."

Audrey blew out a heavy breath. "We can discuss theories once we're back home and you feel safer."

I smiled at her with relief. "Thanks."

Then Liam returned with a drink holder with coffee, and the conversation turned more casual after that. Like the weather. Apparently, seasons operated similarly in Hyvenmere as they did in the human realm. They had winter, spring, summer, and fall. Liam started telling me more about his fae territory, specifically, and the holidays they celebrated there. I was only half listening, surrounded by new smells and fragrances as soon as we stepped off the train and into the city of Sammara.

According to Audrey, Sammara was both a city and a small country. It was similar in size to Texas.

"This is...wow..." I struggled to take everything in.

People were laughing and chatting and shouting in a myriad of different languages, shuffling past, going about their day.

Including English.

"Why do Hyvenmerians even speak English in this realm? I mean, you explained why news stations have English subtitles —" I immediately ignored the *mating bond* part of that conversation. "But why do so many people seem to speak English amongst themselves?" I asked Audrey while eavesdropping on a young couple chatting about new fabric they wanted to buy. One of them gave me a double-take. Perhaps they felt me staring at their pointed ears, or they didn't recognize me as one of the humans who apparently frequented this realm.

They eventually hurried along the street with their partner.

Audrey smiled and replied, "Learning languages is significantly easier over here. When the other halflings and I first started visiting a couple of years ago, it became trendy to learn English and Spanish—and Mandarin. Sirens have it easy because they can learn any language that they hear themselves, even if it's just a few words. But technology is advanced enough that nereids and fae can essentially download languages in their brain."

I gave her a horrified look and asked, "What the fuck? Like a computer chip?"

Audrey shook her head and replied, "No, no one is microchipped. It's a type of technology-magic fusion. I guess more like a spell to become fluent in a language...anyway, language barriers aren't really a thing here. Anyone can learn any language at any time they want."

I gave her a blank stare, absorbing. Processing.

"Sure. Why not?" I replied. Liam chuckled at my reaction, nodding politely at people who stared wide-eyed at our little group as we walked through this, much busier, city.

Eventually, we made our way to some docks, and I smiled at the familiar sight that reminded me of home. Home. I was almost home.

I did a double-take at seeing my mini yacht, though.

"How?" I asked Audrey with a finger pointing toward it.

"Liam brought it over while you were recovering." Audrey patted my shoulder in reassurance. "We're leaving the old-fashioned way, as opposed to how you arrived here."

"Dare I ask, how did I arrive here, if not on my own boat?" I followed Liam and Audrey onto my boat, side-eyeing how familiar Liam seemed to be as he held an arm toward us to enter the cabin, settling himself into the captain's seat. How many times had they driven this thing without my knowledge?

"Lyskifting," Audrey said.

"Bless you," I replied.

She snorted as she dropped our bags on the interior couch before walking out to the main deck. Since Liam took it upon himself to steer, and he actually knew the way out, I followed her.

"Think of it as moving really fast. Faster than the human eye can see. Faster than light, even," Audrey explained with a sigh as she settled herself on one of the lounge chairs.

I sat down and stared at her, waiting for her to turn her head and look at me.

"Are you seriously trying to tell me that I teleported here?"

Audrey tipped her head back and laughed. "It's not teleporting—but whatever helps you understand it, I guess."

I shook my head and settled into my own lounge chair, scanning everything. The water was large enough to remind me of the Bay Area, with four different land masses being visible. The land mass with the distant mountains, the one with more tropical foliage, the land mass that was Sammara, and the land mass that was Liam's territory.

As we traveled, I pointed toward the mountains. "What is that place called again?"

"Lyndoruun," Audrey replied.

"And you said it's the siren territory?" I lifted a brow. "Where the two men who attacked me are from?"

Audrey nodded, confirming that I would not be visiting that territory anytime soon. Then I identified Sammara and Enharra correctly, feeding off of Audrey's excitement when I did so. I was getting ready to ask about the tropical land mass next, as we followed the curve of Sammara's land, exposing two massive, ancient-looking black pillars the size of skyscrapers. They were made of stone and jutted out of the water that I was starting to suspect was more ocean than river. The pillars stood perfectly between Sammara, Lyndoruun, and the tropical land mass.

"These are the gates to our home?" I asked Audrey. She

nodded, pointing toward a couple of structures at the base of them.

"Historically, sirens have been the guardians of the Mellhawn Gates back when they were open. But no one has formally stood guard for hundreds of years due to them being closed—well, due to everyone *believing* that they were closed," Audrey said. "But now nereids have partnered with the siren government to guard them since they are open."

I quirked my lips to the side as we approached. "Why are they open?"

Audrey tipped her head side to side as we approached one of the stone structures at the base of the left pillar. "No one knows. No one knows how to actually close them, either. Past spells and locks don't seem to be working, no matter what the governments try."

I frowned. "That's unsettling."

"Beyond destroying them, which no one really wants to do." Audrey shrugged. "The Hyvenmerian governments are at a loss." Liam cut the engine to my boat as soon as we pulled up to a small dock that led to the small housing unit. It reminded me of the fancy gates to neighborhoods that the ultra-rich lived in, in Southern California. Where the gatekeepers had a small apartment to hang out in, as they allowed or denied passage.

A couple of men stepped up to the boat, boarding my vessel. I tensed, hating the sight of people just sauntering onto my boat. They held clipboards as they nodded politely at us, one of them doing a curious double-take at me, as the two men spread out and casually searched my boat. They didn't break anything, at least.

"Grant?" one of them asked as they stepped toward Audrey and me. Audrey casually slipped hers out of her wallet, reminding me that I also needed to do that.

The man stepped forward and sat down on Audrey's lounge

chair, making me give her a confused look. She smirked, remaining relaxed.

"How are the kids, Emil?" Audrey asked. Ah, she knew him. I slowly became less tense.

He lifted a massive shoulder as he eyeballed both our grants and returned them to us. His blond hair was cropped short, and as he scratched his neck in response, I noticed a flash of pink.

Three pink lines flexed with his words as he told Audrey about school and extracurriculars his children were involved in, much like any human parent would. But I couldn't focus on anything coming out of his mouth, because this man literally had gills on his neck.

"Finished," the second man who boarded the boat called, exiting immediately.

Before he did, though, he gave me a harsh glare with his gold eyes.

I didn't notice any gills, though.

Audrey waved goodbye to the gatekeeper as he stood and exited the boat, allowing us passage through the gates.

As soon as Liam pulled the boat away from the dock and toward the two pillars, a shimmer started to dance over the waves.

Keeping my eyes locked on the water, I asked Audrey, "Do you and Liam have gills, too?"

"Nope." Audrey lifted a shoulder, not bothered at all by my questions. "Nereids have gills, fae do not."

"Nereids are mermaids?" I asked. Audrey snorted and tipped her head side to side.

"Not exactly—but, again, whatever helps you understand them better," Audrey replied.

"Do sirens have gills?" I asked, picturing an evil-looking mermaid. Even though the men who attacked me didn't look mermaid-ish at all.

"If their shapeshifting is powerful enough to produce gills, then sure," Audrey replied. I rubbed my eyes but could see the shimmer on the water get thicker and thicker. As we traveled through the pillars, the land around us was blurry. Changing. Like a vintage TV screen changing channels, but instead of the grey static of a transitioning image, more shimmering sparkles coated everything around us. I lifted my hand, shocked to see my fingers creating small waves throughout the sparkling, shimmering air.

"It's magic, in its most visible form," Audrey murmured. I assumed as much at this point, but I nodded anyway to let her know I heard her just fine. The scenery finished transitioning, and I was shocked to recognize the ocean around me, with our tiny beach town far in the distance. When I sat up and looked behind us, a large island I had only ever admired from the comfort of my docks was directly behind us.

The unpopulated side of Catalina Island, that is.

It was as if we emerged from the large earthy edge, even though that was impossible. But a few random shimmers fading into the light of day let me know that we did, in fact, just casually emerge out of the flat edge of the earth.

As Liam steered the boat around the curve of the island for a few silent minutes, the popular tourist stop of Avalon came into view.

"Oh my god," I breathed.

Audrey giggled as she said, "Welcome home, Van."

I shared a shocked laugh with her as we sailed away from Catalina and toward Marina Vista, our home. One thing I immediately noticed as we made it through the Mellhawn Gates was something that I didn't think would bother me so much.

The subtle, melodical tune that seemed to travel in the air of Hyvenmere was suddenly gone. I tried my best to recall the details of it; how soothing it was to me. But I couldn't. I rubbed my chest as a weird sense of longing for the melody filled it. I immediately pushed the feeling away, focusing on the utter relief of going home soon. Liam's fancy castle bed was great and all, but it wasn't *mine*.

The first thing I was going to do when we got back to our condo was take a long, overdue nap. Then, if I had time, perhaps try to recall the melody I heard in Hyvenmere. If I could recreate that peaceful sound on my own, surely, I wouldn't feel any longing nonsense for the magical realm again.

CHAPTER 6

If anyone were to ask me how you're supposed to go on with life after discovering magical people exist, as well as entire realms, I'm not sure I'd have an answer for them. Every day after that adventure with Audrey and Liam felt weird. Every time I walked to work, or went grocery shopping, or ran errands, I felt like I was in a simulation. I would find myself staring at everyone walking by. People were casually going about their day, most likely completely unaware of people like Liam and Audrey. Of the magical realm.

Just like I used to be.

It was unsettling to exist in this world now.

I was constantly glancing over my shoulder while desperately trying to cling to any sense of normalcy I had. Having the unstable childhood I did, I didn't like a lot of sudden changes. It triggered my fight or flight.

But I was coping. I found peace in getting back into my routines. Opening and closing the coffee house. Chatting with my employees. Cleaning the custom live-edge wood countertop I special-ordered from a carpenter I used to date. Watering the dozens of indoor plants that hung sporadically throughout the open concept space, soaking up all the natural light from the front wall of windows. Ordering baked goods from the bakery a couple of blocks away.

Audrey was spending more time at the condo, and Liam would only show up half the time. I wanted to ask Audrey more about her uncomfortably platonic relationship with him, but I refrained because she was so touchy about it. I did, however, ask him yesterday if he had a job, when he showed up unannounced, and he just rolled his eyes and raided our pantry.

Audrey had started throwing together a casserole for all of us, which meant that she made one for us and one for him.

I was playing music more often and relied on the grounding that instruments brought me. I couldn't correctly remember the melody I heard in Hyvenmere, though, and it was irritating me more and more. No instrument I played compared to the song in the air. Everything felt off. I wasn't even sure I was remembering the cadence correctly.

About a week later, I was gently tapping away on the drums set up in the far corner of Sun Bean and part of me considered asking Audrey to go back there, just to walk around. I was confident I wouldn't even have to leave my boat, as soon as we traveled through the Mellhawn Gates, I would surely hear the melody again.

Yesterday, when I asked Audrey if she had heard the gentle song in the air whenever she visited Hyvenmere, she gave me a funny look and shook her head. I haven't brought it up with her again.

I wanted to feel more connected to Audrey, but I didn't want to concern her with the possibility that learning about Hyvenmere may or may not be driving me insane.

However, I knew her secret now. I couldn't forget that night I was attacked on my boat. I couldn't forget the gifts Audrey had. Or the giant fae prince who often lounged on our couch and ate all our food.

No, I couldn't pretend I didn't know any of this, but part of me wondered what this meant. I wanted to support Audrey and this new adventure of hers, but was that just because I wanted to be close to my friend? Did I want these gates to be open between our realms? Those men who attacked me were dangerous, and even though I was lucky enough to hold them off until Audrey showed up, who knows how other creatures would react to being here?

The front door opened on the far side of Sun Bean, and I glanced up to smile at the new customer. The man tilted his head forward just enough to fit through the doorway, and part of me remembered how Liam's large frame barely made it through.

I narrowed my eyes, studying the man.

When he turned his head, and his ears appeared rounded, I relaxed, starting another rhythm on the drums. He turned toward me; the sound of the instrument having caught his attention.

I gave him a half smirk as I continued to play, my thoughts still buzzing with my new reality. This man returned my half smirk as he slowly stepped toward the counter, glancing up at the menu before studying me again.

I studied him back, completely unashamed and refusing to hide it.

He was attractive.

He had dark, thick hair, a sharp jawline coated with a light layer of stubble. He wore a long coat that covered most of his frame, but when he reached into his pocket to pull out bills for his drink, I could see how fit his form was. He wore sunglasses, as most visitors in this beach town did.

Once I finished my set on the drums, I stood, stretching my shoulders. The man watched me with polite curiosity while glancing around the warm, naturally lit space. There were only a handful of other patrons in the shop, used to music randomly playing.

"Hi there," I waved, waltzing toward the counter.

His dark eyebrows twitched, and I thought I noticed him swallow once before giving me what looked like a shy smile. Frankly, this man was too attractive to be shy about anything.

"Did you want whipped cream on this?" Emma asked the customer.

He didn't respond to her question. I wasn't positive he even heard her question. He just stared at me, even when I approached the counter and leaned a hip against it, crossing my arms. I raised my eyebrows as my smile widened.

"Sir?" Emma asked again after giving me a conspiratorial look.

His head jerked toward her then, and the angle revealed dark brown irises behind his sunglasses.

"Huh?"

"Do you want whipped cream on this?" Emma repeated.

"Yes, thank you," he replied, stepping toward the other end of the counter where she was finishing his order.

The man was polite, too, which was another plus. A quick check on his hand indicated his ring finger was empty, so I squared my shoulders and walked toward him.

Being tall wasn't a requirement for me to date someone. I learned how to date men who were shorter than me early on, considering my almost six feet of height. He had a couple of inches on me, though, which was nice.

I hadn't been with a taller man in a long time, now that I thought about it.

"Have you been here before?" I asked the customer. I leaned forward and made my way around him, letting my eyes rake over him in a blatant pass. When I flirted, I was obvious. I didn't want any miscommunication. Any second-guessing. I liked getting straight to the point, so that if the person I was flirting with wasn't interested, they could tell me or hint at it as soon as possible.

"Hmm?" he asked as his head turned to follow my path. I bit my lip to hide my smile as I made my way to the entrance hidden in the counter.

"It's just…" I rested my hand on his bicep, a light touch, to silently ask him to move out of my way. His hip was blocking the hinge that lifted the countertop. "I don't think I've seen you here before."

He didn't startle from my touch, which was good. It wasn't until he stepped to the side and allowed me to get behind the counter that he cleared his throat and gave me another shy grin.

"Only once before," he replied.

"Oh, yeah?" I smiled at him as I tied an apron around my waist. Emma handed me his drink, sans whipped cream, while she stepped through the door that led to the kitchen. "I'm glad we were worth visiting again."

He hummed as I grabbed the can of whipped cream and sprayed the top of his drink. He ordered a very sugary one, so I added the sprinkle of cinnamon on top that the recipe called for. I glanced at him out of the side of my eye as I grabbed the cardboard sleeve.

"You were playing then, too," he said the words in a rush, as if he wasn't sure how to continue the conversation. "When I came before, I mean."

"Yeah?" I raised my eyebrow before sliding his cup across the counter to him. "And I didn't scare you away?" I wanted him to keep talking.

If I played my cards right, I could get him to ask for my number. Going on a date and exchanging orgasms would be a good way for me to feel stable again after the several bombs Audrey dropped on me recently.

"Not at all." He shook his head as he retrieved his cup. He

held it cautiously in his hand, as if he were studying the beverage, before slowly bringing the drink to his lips.

As he took a sip, he seemed surprised. Dark eyebrows rose behind his sunglasses.

"This is delicious," he said.

"Thank you," I said, giving him a bright smile as I studied him again. My eyes blatantly dragged over him, before I met his gaze—well, sunglasses. "Maybe you'll want to come back again, then."

He was taking another sip when I replied, and when he lowered the cup, he cleared his throat once before giving me a handsome smile of his own.

"Yeah, or maybe I—" He cut himself off when I stiffened and looked over his shoulder.

Another customer had just walked through the door, ringing the bell hung above it. Harmonizing with the bell, however, was the melody. The one I heard in Hyvenmere. As soon as the door shut, though, the melody was gone.

"I'm sorry, I—" It was my turn to cut myself off, because another customer left, opening the door, revealing the melody again. It was a little louder. I held a finger up to the man and hopped over the counter, startling him as he backed away enough to let me land on my feet. I scrambled through the tables and chairs, running toward the door before it slammed shut.

But as soon as I stepped outside onto the sidewalk, the melody faded into the distance. I grumbled, rubbing my head, wondering if I should find a psychiatrist to talk to about this. I shook my head and turned back toward the Sun Bean, just in time to see the handsome stranger nod politely with a nervous smile as he left with his drink in hand.

Damn. I totally blew that.

Emma stepped out of the kitchen slowly, her brows raised as she whispered to me, "What happened?"

"I—" How did I explain that I was chasing a song that may or may not exist? "I thought I saw a celebrity." Those were fairly common to see in our tourist town.

"Who?" Emma asked.

"Um," I scratched my head, trying to recall a random celebrity off the cuff. "The lead singer of Carbon Cut."

Emma gave me a blank look before throwing on a grin and nodding, reminding me that she was a couple of years younger than me, and not into rock music. She wouldn't know who Joshua Madey was.

A moment later, the back door chime sounded, letting me know someone had entered the shop from the hallway.

"Hey, Emma!" Audrey greeted my employee after stepping into the open space. She pulled a stool over and sat at the counter in front of us.

"Did you see the man who just left the shop?" Emma asked her immediately.

Audrey widened her eyes a little. "No. Why?"

"God, he was so attractive." Emma sighed as she started to restock the syrups. "I thought for sure he was going to ask Van out."

"I was *hoping* he would ask me out." Then I leaned on my elbows, leveling Audrey with a look. "How about you, Aud? Is there anyone out there that you're hoping will ask you out?"

Audrey lifted a shoulder. "Um. No."

"Really?" I gave her a disbelieving look.

She narrowed her eyes at me in response. "No."

"Van's tone implies otherwise." Emma smirked as she pulled her phone out of her back pocket and widened her eyes at the screen. "Shit! I lost track of time!" She threw her apron off and tossed it at me before hopping over the counter, "Bye!"

"Bye!" I laughed as I folded her apron and set it on the counter in front of us. The shop would be closing in an hour or so, and that meant it was going to be slow beyond the handful of customers who had already ordered something and were set up at random tables with their computers.

"I have a question for you." I steepled my fingertips together as Audrey dropped her elbows onto the counter.

Audrey copied my pose and grinned. "Hit me."

"Want to go out on the boat tonight?" I grinned. She and I had only hung out on the boat by ourselves a couple of times since I got it during her "I need to keep Van at arm's length" phase.

"Sure." She grinned. "Can Liam come?"

I immediately frowned. She immediately frowned back.

"Sorry, it's just that he already planned—you know what? I'll just tell him to go home when he shows up." She waved it off, clearly disappointed in my reaction, but humoring me anyway. I crossed my arms and cocked a hip out.

"Just text him." I nodded toward where I assumed her phone was in her pocket.

"I can't, well, not on this phone. I can only text on my other phone." Her Hyvenmerian one, I assumed. "But only when he is also, um, here. The signal can't travel through *realms* yet." She lowered her voice to a whisper when she said realms, so I nodded and didn't push it.

"If he's going to show up anyway, might as well let him drive," I grumbled. He was lowkey better at it than I was, based on what I saw about a week ago when he steered us out of Hyvenmere.

Audrey gave me a nervous look. "I'm sorry that he's so... present."

"It's fine." I was still bitter about it, but beyond being in our space and taking up some of Audrey's attention, I didn't see any major red flags in him. I just couldn't get over my harsh feelings toward him, yet.

"It's just—" Audrey bit her lip and lowered her voice so only I could hear again, "He wants to make sure we're safe. That whoever wanted to take you that night doesn't try again." I quirked my lips to the side at that. I mean, if his intentions were pure, I couldn't fault him for volunteering to be our personal bodyguard until things cooled down.

"That's nice of him," I forced myself to say. I was good at holding grudges. I was decent at identifying when I was being unfair. Unfortunately, I was a petty and prideful woman and didn't always want to admit when I was being unfair toward someone.

I never said I was perfect.

"He'll just drive," Audrey promised with a nod.

"Shirtless," I muttered. Audrey gave me a quizzical scowl.

"Excuse me?" Her tone immediately lowered to aggravated, which caught me off guard. I blinked at her, startled by her immediate hostile reaction.

"I mean, if Temu-Thor is determined to crash the party, the least he could do is show off his rippling abs and look pretty for us—" Audrey's nostrils flared, so I raised my eyebrows and changed course. "—or more accurately, *you*, since blond men aren't my type." Audrey deflated at that, her shoulders lowering, and her scowl loosening into one of embarrassment.

"I'm so sorry—I have no idea what that was." She placed a hand over her heart as her light hazel eyes studied the grain in the countertop, genuinely looking concerned. I waved her off before starting the lock-up routine during the last hour of business. The sun started to set when she and I finally left the Sun Bean, and I locked the doors behind us. We walked toward the harbor where my boat was docked, admiring the pinks and oranges of the sky, when her *other* phone vibrated in her pocket.

She pulled it out and let Liam know where we would be for the evening, then looped her arm in mine as we made our way toward the docks for an overdue girls-night.

The sun was below the shoreline, painting the sky in a deep purple with a bright strip of orange, as Audrey and I shared one more drink. We weren't huge drinkers, but we were tipsy and giggly and having a lot of fun. Even Liam's presence didn't sour my mood, and when I boldly suggested he take off his shirt after our first drink, I wasn't too surprised to see him dart a look toward Audrey and blush.

They just needed to bang it out already.

I wasn't too far gone to say those words out loud, though. But Liam obliged and even made a show of flexing his arms and abs, which made me laugh, and made Audrey's eyes widen in admiration. The way the sun reflected off the ocean lit up the subtle streaks of gold in her irises as she ogled Liam.

Then I threw an ice cube at her face, and we've been joking around and sharing stories ever since.

"Okay, okay." I fanned my face, calming my heart after telling Liam a hilarious story of Audrey and I getting lost in Big Bear during college. "Not to change the subject, but I think I'm ready to talk about all of this—" I waved my arms vaguely toward Liam and the direction of Catalina Island. "—more."

Audrey lit up. "Really? Because I'm *dying* to talk to you about this more."

I snickered and replied, "I guess I just have some questions." I cleared my throat and tucked my legs underneath myself. We should probably find our way back to the docks soon, but we were anchored in the water, and I could still see the harbor in the distance, so it wasn't like we could get lost.

"Ask away," Audrey encouraged, patting the seat next to her for Liam to take.

"First." I held up one finger. "What the hell do you do in Hyvenmere when you go there?" My question made Liam smirk, and Audrey groan. "Do you just hang out in Liam's castle all day? Do you play tourist? I mean, a lot of people seemed to recognize you."

"That's another loaded question," Liam muttered with an elbow against Audrey's arm.

"Why?" I pressed.

"It's just—ugh." Audrey scraped a hand down her face as she settled in. "Back when Liam first found me outside the library, originally, I went there so often because I wanted to learn more about my culture. I'm half-fae, after all." I nodded, because that made sense to me. "Plus, I was able to meet a handful of other halflings who have been secretly traveling there for years. Some halflings have known about their Hyvenmerian lineage their whole lives, but others just stumbled upon it when I did, when powers manifested, or when Liam and Fergus found them. But then rumors about me being Hyvenmerian's Chosen One started spreading this last year or so, and I'm not sure who started it or why, but it's caused a lot of contention between Hyvenmerians and halflings like myself. So now when I'm over there, it feels like a lot of shaking hands and political peacekeeping—which Liam and Ada have been able to help me with."

"We also train over there," Liam added, as he stretched his legs out to cross his ankles.

"What makes people think you're the Chosen One?"

"No idea," Audrey sighed, gently swirling her glass as she watched the liquid slosh around. "I don't fit the requirements of the prophecy—the details we know of it, anyway. But the Siren King, Ilia, *does*. So, naturally, I'm not exactly the siren government's favorite person right now. Thus..." Audrey wiggled her fingers in a flourish. "...weird contention with halflings."

I considered her words for a moment before saying, "If this Ilia man is actually confident that *he's* the Chosen One the prophecy talks about, then he shouldn't be so threatened by you."

Audrey released a humorless laugh. "Unfortunately, that's not—"

Our conversation was interrupted by a loud, guttural, haunting roar.

All three of us froze to turn toward the water. It was one of those noises that felt huge. My ears just knew that whatever was making that sound was massive. It almost sounded like the cry of a whale, if the whale was pissed off and able to amplify the sound by twenty units or so.

"Here?" Audrey whispered in horror. I turned over my shoulder to look at her, and even though Audrey was already incredibly pale, even I could notice the blood drain from her face in the dim light of night.

Liam stood tall and reached behind himself.

When he pulled his hand forward, he was grasping a large sword.

A real one, based on how the steel of the blade reflected the moonlight above.

"Did you just pull a sword out of your ass?" I asked him.

My question was ignored, and instead of replying, Audrey stood to shove me behind her as she stepped toward Liam.

"What do we do?" Her question was followed by another deafening roar, and far out in the water, a large creature emerged, tilting its head back as it released another haunting bellow.

I almost fainted from the sight of it.

It was as if a dragon was crawling out of the ocean. One clawed hand broke the surface of the water, flexing its massive claws. Pale scales glistened against the night sky, and the creature turned its huge reptilian snout toward us, parting its mouth and hissing.

It took every muscle in my body not to soil myself in devastating fear.

"We need to keep it away from civilians," Liam muttered before he disappeared into thin air.

He was standing there, then he wasn't. Perhaps he did the not-teleporting thing Audrey mentioned earlier.

"Hide!" Audrey shouted at me, pointing inside the cabin of my mini yacht, before she took off in a sprint, jumping off the boat into the ocean.

I was standing there on my deck, paralyzed with fear, unable to believe what I was seeing.

A masculine shout danced across the water, and the sword Liam held glinted against the moon's glow when I realized he was jumping onto the long spine of the monster.

A flash of red hair followed him out of the water.

"No!" I shouted to myself. I had no idea what was happening, but I was not about to let some fuck ass guy lead Audrey to her death. Perhaps I was hallucinating, and I wasn't actually seeing a sea-dragon-like thing emerging from the Pacific Ocean. I was convinced, however, that what was really happening was still dangerous.

Audrey was risking her life to get involved.

I would *not* let that happen.

Not after she saved me from those two men who tried to kidnap me only a week ago.

I sprinted to unanchor my boat, revving the engine as I slammed myself down in the captain's chair. I scanned the water out of the windshield to find my friend. But the monster was gone; the normal, gentle waves of the ocean crashed against the harbor barrier behind me.

Oh no.

The sound of a sudden splash made me turn to follow the noise, because breaking through the surface was the scaly, yellow-eyed head of the beast that I had seen before.

It was just *a lot* closer now. My boat almost tipped over from the size and speed of the creature breaking through the surface.

"Jesus fucking Christ," I gasped, as I steered the boat away,

deciding to stay out of its line of sight. However, on the snout of the dragon-or-lizard-or-whatever-the-hell, was Audrey.

"Aud!" Liam shouted, as he emerged from the ocean, clinging to the monster's long, serpent-like neck. He emphasized his shout by stabbing his sword into the neck of the beast, eliciting a sharp cry, showing narrow and razor-sharp teeth that looked to be the length of my legs.

"Audrey!" I shouted over the piercing noise that came from the monster's mouth—that Audrey seemed to be trying to tie shut.

Once the beast was restrained with more seaweed that Audrey was conducting with her hands, she shouted back to Liam.

"We don't need to kill it!" Audrey cried as the beast swung its head, successfully knocking her off and into the ocean a few yards from my boat. The beast dove back under the waves, and I grabbed my comm while flipping on the external speakers.

"Audrey!" I shouted, catching her attention as her head resurfaced from the ocean, gasping for air. "Get on!"

She swung her head toward me, her eyes widening in horror as she started swimming toward the boat.

Swimming *really* fucking fast.

"Van! Get out of here!" Audrey gasped while spitting ocean water out of her mouth at the same time. Obviously, I ignored her as I ditched my captain's seat to run to the edge of the boat and pull her up.

Right when Audrey clasped my hands, the beast broke through the surface of the water again, and a loud, wet *thunk* crashed onto the outer deck.

Audrey scrambled onto my boat, screaming at whatever landed behind us.

I followed her gaze to see the unmoving body of Liam, who had a large gash in his core that was bleeding rapidly.

"Shit—*fuck*—" I muttered as Audrey ran toward Liam, her

hands glowing hot again. She knelt and slapped her palms onto his unmoving body, and within seconds, the blood started to stop.

"What do we do?" I asked, running over to grab the first-aid kit I kept under one of the exterior seats. I always kept several on board, always wanting to be prepared.

Even though no one on planet Earth could have prepared me for something like this.

"...Aud," Liam groaned, before clasping her wrists with his hands. "You have to stop it. Before it gets to shore."

"I can't," Audrey shook her head. "It won't stop—"

A sharp bellow erupted from the beast, and while it was facing the docks of our town moments before, it quickly turned its sharp head toward my vessel, before tipping its head back and crying out a pained screech again.

"His sword is in its nose," I gasped. Liam's large blade was pierced through the top of the dragon-like snout, keeping it from closing its mouth completely, because the blade had already pierced its tongue.

"Stop it, Aud," Liam groaned, inhaling a deep breath. His bleeding was completely stopped now, and when Aud lifted his shirt to check the wound, all that was left was a light pink scar. "Go."

"I—" a large, scaly tail broke the surface of the water, and heavy dread sank in my stomach at the sight of it closing in on us.

"Do it!" Liam shouted.

"Shit!" Audrey cried in feral anger before standing up and screaming at the beast. It snarled back at her, hissing its foul breath down at us as it rose higher and higher. I was frozen, completely useless, as I stayed in a kneeling position at Liam's side, watching Audrey flex her hands.

More seaweed and oceanic foliage erupted out of the Pacific, aggressively wrapping itself around the beast. With a flick of her wrist, more and more sprouted from the sea, successfully detaining and holding the monster back as it cried and bellowed.

"You need to stop!" Audrey screeched at the monster, who obviously didn't listen at all. It became more hostile and aggressive the more her seaweed wrapped around it. It thrashed and thrashed, dislodging the sword in its snout, sending it clattering on the deck.

Audrey picked it up, anger pinching her fingers as she pointed Liam's massive blade toward the beast. It screeched and groaned as a clutch of her fist brought the beast's head down toward her level.

"Enough!" Audrey even stomped her foot with her command, which made the creature more upset. Even though seaweed was securely tightened around its jaw, with a threatening growl, it snapped its mouth open, tearing the seaweed off its face as it lunged toward Audrey.

Right as I reached my hand out—with no idea how I would actually help in this situation—Audrey cried and leaped in the air, aiming the sword right between the beast's eyes.

As soon as Liam's sword was buried to the hilt, the head of the monster immediately fell onto the deck of my boat, mere feet away from me and Liam, who was recovering well enough to grab the collar of my shirt so I wouldn't slide off the boat and into the ocean. The beast had no life left in its eyes, and when Audrey removed Liam's sword with a grunt and jumped back on the deck, the massive head the size of a car, unceremoniously slid off my boat, back into the dark depths of the ocean.

The boat rocked back and forth dramatically, and the only reason I was able to stay on board was due to Liam's hold on me until it stabilized.

The only sound was the Pacific waves crashing against the boat, the heavy breaths the three of us were desperately inhaling, and the ringing in my ears. I couldn't tell how long we all sat on the deck, reveling in the silence after that disaster. Maybe it was five minutes. Maybe it was an hour.

Liam seemed to be fine now, thanks to Audrey's healing touch, and Audrey was soaking wet, but not injured or shivering. I also had no injuries I could identify in the moment, so I shook my head and got to my feet before marching toward the cabin.

"What are you doing?" Audrey asked me.

"I'm getting another fucking drink."

CHAPTER 7

Liam automatically took the captain's chair again. When I asked him if he was good to drive, he waved me off. Apparently, getting his entire chest cavity ripped open and healed within minutes wasn't that traumatizing. He steered us back to the harbor, perfectly docking the boat. We walked back to our little condo in silence, noting that Audrey was starting to shiver. Perhaps the adrenaline of what just went down was finally starting to recede.

Liam automatically wrapped her in one of his massive arms, and her shivering started to die down as we finally made it into the condo.

"Are you okay?" I asked her as we set our things down. "Do you need to warm up in the shower?" Audrey nodded at my question as she wordlessly sauntered down the hall. Liam sighed and scraped both hands down his face.

"You're staying, right?" I asked him as the door shut to Audrey's suite.

He lifted his head at me with a curious look. "You want me to?"

I gave him a look of disbelief. "I think she would feel better if you did."

Liam raised a blond eyebrow at me as he pressed, "Would *you?*"

I rolled my eyes. "Don't push it."

Liam chuckled as I stomped down the hall to my room.

Audrey and Liam were still asleep when I left the next morning. I wasn't too surprised to see them in bed together. It wasn't like our thrifted couch was large enough for him, and our carpet was worn down enough that it probably needed to be replaced soon, so Liam sleeping in bed with Audrey made the most sense. But even though she slept on a California King-sized mattress, his feet still hung off the edge from under her covers. They weren't cuddling or anything, which surprised me. Audrey was a cuddler.

When I arrived at work, I found myself stuck at the front door. Was I really about to just casually go to work after getting attacked by a monster the night before? Was that really how I was choosing to cope with that?

I started to mentally go down a rabbit hole on how Capitalism affected the American psyche when my employee waved his hand in front of my face.

"You good, Van?" Shane asked. He looked like he had just rolled out of bed, too. He hadn't shaved in a couple of days, and his dark hair looked a bit shaggier than normal. His cocoa-colored eyes also had dark circles under them.

"So good, Shane." I grinned brightly at him, meeting him at eye level, and unlocked the door to let us in.

A couple of hours later, I noticed surfers strolling along the sidewalk outside the shop, their hair damp from the ocean. I was suddenly petrified. *They had no idea how close they were to—*

"Van," Shane called, making me snap my head up and grin at him. His ever-present frown was on his face. "Did we get that shipment in?"

"Oh." I lifted the divider in the countertop to let me out. "Yes. It's in my office. I'll go grab it." I strode past him to walk down the hallway that led to both the restrooms and my office, a smaller room that barely fit a desk, storage shelves, and a thrifted loveseat. I pulled my keys out to unlock it, only to find that the door was already unlocked.

I figured Shane must have used his keys already to go in there for something else, but when I opened the door and saw a woman standing in the far corner, gazing at all the random trinkets I had collected over the years, I froze.

"Um," was all I managed to get out before she turned her head, revealing that the majority of her face was covered up. She wore a scarf covering the bottom half of her head, exposing only the gold shimmer of her eyes. The rest of her outfit had dark leather chest and leg pieces—much like the ones on the men who attacked me that horrifying night.

Like what the attractive but rude red-haired man on TV wore.

I immediately stepped back before her melodic voice chimed, "I'm a friend."

My brain was scrambling; she was barely taller than me. She wore a large cloak with a hood over her wrapped head, shielding most of the shape of her body, and the dark clothing she had on underneath. She lifted a hand, her pale fingers the only thing poking out of her gloves, "You're safe."

"Sure." I narrowed my eyes at her.

"Don't make a scene, they don't know I'm here." Her golden eyes flicked over in the direction of the front of the shop, where Shane was. I glared at her, slowly stepping into my office and shutting the door behind me.

"Who the hell are you?" I asked.

"Your friends call me Hush," she replied. Then she crossed her arms and turned back toward my shelf to admire a picture of Audrey and me. We were on the beach, sunbathing. Except the flash from the camera practically made Audrey invisible on the sand, "I'm a friend. At least, I'm trying to be."

"Why?" I asked. I grabbed the box that Shane needed and cautiously made my way to the door again.

"We want the same things," Hush replied.

"Ah." I nodded, not yet convinced.

Hush turned to watch me open the door to set the box Shane needed just outside of it, before closing the door and locking it.

"Our previous meeting spot in my realm has been compromised," Hush explained. "I was told to meet here instead."

"Who told you to meet here?"

Hush flitted her gaze to the door seconds before the doorknob jiggled and knuckles wrapped on the door, "Van, let us in." Audrey said.

I glanced around my small space. Four people, one of them being the size of Liam, would be a tight fit. But there would still be enough seating for everyone, thanks to the loveseat I squished against the far wall. I flicked the lock open and let my two friends inside, giving Audrey a very obvious, pointed glare.

"I know, I know." Audrey winced under my expression. "But we need to talk to Hush about what happened last night."

"And we're just gonna do that here?" I countered, relocking the door behind them. The box was still there, so Shane hadn't come looking for it, yet. I looked up at Liam, surprised to see him slouching so much. He wore a beanie on his head, concealing his pointed ears. His swim trunks were back, and I recognized it as his human disguise.

"We must be quick," Hush replied, finally turning away from my memorabilia shelf to watch Audrey and Liam plop themselves on the loveseat. "I can't linger here." I leaned back against my desk, mirroring our new friend by crossing my arms.

Well, a new friend to me.

I guess Liam and Audrey had known her beforehand.

"Well, spit it out." I waved for them to get a move on. "I have employees here. I can't have secret Hyvenmere stuff going on in my place of work."

"I am no threat to your employees," Hush said again, before turning that eerie golden gaze to my friends. "What was so urgent that you needed me to come so quickly?"

"Audrey killed a solvyrn last night," Liam said, point-blank. He sat forward and clasped his fingers together. Even hunched, his massive frame still took up space.

"What?" Hush stiffened, her golden eyes widening. "Where? How?"

"Here, out in the ocean." Audrey tipped her head in the direction of the ocean as she crossed her arms over her chest. "I had no choice—it was too wild and was a danger—"

"Of course, you had no choice—there was a *solvyrn* in your territory," Hush whispered as she started pacing the small room. Her blonde brows pinched together as she processed this, "How did a solvyrn get through the gates?"

"That's what we want to know." Liam sighed, leaning back on the loveseat.

"This sucks." Audrey groaned, dropping her face into her hands. "This fucking sucks."

"Where is it?" Hush asked, ignoring Audrey's agony.

"The bottom of the ocean," Liam replied. Hush nodded, rubbing her brow with her fingertips.

"You'll need to tell the Fae Queen about this; that way, the governments can coordinate to clean it up before humans discover it."

"I informed my sister first thing this morning," Liam nodded. "She was in the process of reaching out to the other governments when I came back."

"How the hell did you travel there and back so fast?" I asked.

Liam lifted a massive shoulder. "I lyskifted."

Teleported. He teleported there and back. Because of course he did. Jesus Christ.

Hush stopped her pacing and stared at Audrey intensely, a stare that Audrey immediately felt and addressed with a glare. Hush raised a blonde eyebrow in a clear, silent challenge. A challenge that Audrey groaned at, throwing her hands up in exasperation, before declaring, "I'm not—"

"You *are*," Hush interrupted her. "You can't possibly still be in denial of it."

I picked up on what they were arguing about and inserted my own two cents, "Doesn't the Siren King think *he's* the Chosen One? Why would it be Audrey?"

"King Ilia was deemed the prophesied one fifty years ago, when he single-handedly defeated the first solvyrn to emerge from the oceans and touch Hyvenmere soil in hundreds of years," Hush interrupted me with a withering glare in my direction.

I slid my gaze over to Audrey as I asked, "How many, uh, solvyrn's have shown up since?"

"One." The three of them replied.

Well, shit.

"Does the prophecy talk about killing solvyrn, specifically?"

"The language of the prophecy has been translated and rewritten dozens of times over thousands of years," Liam explained. "The original language and meaning are probably lost, leaving a lot of Hyvenmere to guess the interpretation. Two pieces of it have remained consistent, though. One piece is that the person will have several powerful gifts, whereas Hyvenmerians generally only have one, if any. Audrey has *two*. The second is the prediction that the prophesied hero will 'slay an ancient beast'."

I scrunched my nose. "Okay, but, like—" I pinched the bridge of my nose. "Why does it matter?"

Hush tilted her head at me, her eyes the only part of her face that allowed me to interpret her quizzical expression. "What do you mean?"

"Why does it matter if Audrey or Ilia is the prophesied Chosen One?" Perhaps if I understood the significance of this role more, I would be more helpful.

Hush sighed as she crossed the room to lean against my shelf of trinkets.

"Things are already tense in Lyndoruun," Hush explained. She flicked her eyes over to Liam and Audrey, who nodded in agreement. "Ilia is a dangerous ruler who has become more aggressive with age and the loss of his queen. He takes pride in his role as King of the Sirens, protector of the Fjellenheim Mountains, and as the Chosen One the prophecy foretold. Hyvenmerian governments have been able to keep peaceful trades under his and Queen Astrid's rule—before she passed, that is."

"Before his bastard son—" Liam started, before Audrey interrupted him.

"Being the Chosen One gave Ilia all his success," Audrey explained, looking to Hush for her nod of confirmation. "He killed the solvyrn that directly endangered Astrid, the former Siren Queen. That accomplishment is what allowed Astrid's parents to bless their union, so he could take the throne next to her. Who better to guard the Fjellenheim Mountains than the Chosen One from a prophecy designed to unite all the lands?"

"So basically, if he's not actually the Chosen One..." I pointed toward Audrey. "And *you* are, his seat on the throne will have been because of a misunderstanding."

"Imagine the distrust his people will have toward him," Hush added with a nod. "Especially when he's already losing his grip on them."

I glanced around the room, waiting for an explanation.

Everyone just stared silently in thought, so I rolled my eyes and groaned before saying, "I'm new to literally all of this; stop speaking in vague cliffhangers."

"It's just so much." Audrey sighed with a pinch on the bridge of her nose. "Where do I start with this?"

Hush rolled her golden eyes. "If you must know, human, Lyndoruun has its own mess to deal with, on top of our king possibly *not* being the prophesied peacekeeper we were all raised to believe he was." Hush crossed her arms over her chest and danced her fingertips on her bicep. "We also have a very significant problem where siren mothers and children are continuing to go missing."

My heart ached. "Oh."

"Yes, *oh*." Hush shook her head as she stared at something on the wall behind me, a divot formed between her brows. "It's gotten worse over the last couple of years. Even more so this year. Every week, a new siren female and her child are reported missing. Every time Ilia's guard is close to finding answers, the trail goes dry." Hush shook her head once. "My people are scared. We don't know who is hunting us or why. If they're even alive or not. Sometimes we manage to find a blood trail, but then...nothing. All we know is that it's getting increasingly unsafe for siren females to wander the realm alone."

I huffed and dropped my eyes, understanding all too well how dangerous it was for women to travel alone. But Hush was speaking as if this were a *new* phenomenon. Was that not a common threat in Hyvenmere? Were Hyvenmerian women not raised to hold their car keys in between their knuckles when walking in a parking lot at night?

"And your people are upset with the Siren King for not being able to find them," I concluded.

"Which he is responding to by alluding that the halflings, like Audrey, must be the reason for the missing sirens. The uptick in missing reports escalated right when halflings started coming and going into our realm as they pleased."

I raised my brows at that. "What? No way." I turned to Audrey, who nodded her head. "The Siren King thinks you're just wandering in and kidnapping his people?"

"Yes, which is another reason why he probably doesn't want to entertain the idea that *I'm* the Chosen One—not that I'm entirely convinced that I am."

"Which is also why the Siren King has been strongly advocating with the fae and nereids for the Mellhawn Gates to permanently close," Hush added.

I shook my head and tried to summarize, "Instead of entertaining the idea that the Siren King might not be as grand as he thought he was." Liam smirked at my simplified explanation. "He's blaming Audrey and the other halflings for his large number of missing persons, and advocating for the gates to close, cutting off Audrey and the other halflings from half of their lineage forever."

"That's about it," Audrey replied in a bored tone.

"Audrey is powerful," Hush added, staring at my friend thoughtfully. "She has the common fae gift of manipulating horticulture, and a common siren gift of healing. If she happens to develop a third commonly nereid gift, that identifies the three main territories of Hyvenmere. I, personally, wouldn't need any more convincing that it's Audrey who was meant to unite our realm."

Damn. Uniting an entire realm could not have been an easy feat, which explained Audrey's reluctance to accept the role. The responsibility was heavy, and when I glanced at her, I could practically see her shoulders sag with the weight of it.

"I never kill anything..." Audrey murmured. "I've never been put in a position where I needed—" She cut herself off, flicking her hazel gaze up at me. I shook my head at her, knowing why she did. *I* had been put in that position at too young an age. But now was not the time to talk about it. It was the past.

"But the gates haven't been closed yet..." I changed the

subject, looking back at Hush and Liam. They both shook their heads.

"Ilia has yet to convince the fae and nereids," Hush replied.

"Why do they want them open? Beyond just being decent people." I asked. Audrey smirked, and something flared in her eyes as she looked at me. I narrowed mine back at her, wondering what sparked the mischievousness.

"The fae and nereids have seen success with human—or halfling—inclusive mating bonds," Audrey replied. It was my turn to roll my eyes.

"Okay, gross." I shook my head and ignored Hush's confused look. "So basically the only reason Liam's sister and the people with gills want to keep the gates open is just that they want the opportunity to fuck humans."

"Why does that disturb you?" Hush asked.

"It's not just about sex, Van," Liam chimed in. "It's about compatibility. The opportunity to start families with fewer obstacles. Hyvenmerian mating bonds had been forming less and less over the last several hundred years—until about thirty years ago. There was a subtle rise in mating bonds snapping into place." The way he talked about mating bonds made it seem like they were this tangible, physical tie between people, not just hormones. "Then, when halflings started to wander back into Hyvenmere, several of them formed mating bonds with fae and nereids. It's a joyous time now, after a very dark one, and if we can keep the gates open and allow more Hyvenmerians to find their partners, why wouldn't we do that?"

I nodded. It sounded like creating a mating bond was the equivalent of getting married. Something to be respected. I tipped my head back and forth as I thought about it.

"The Siren King just doesn't give a shit about that? He doesn't care if his people find their—um—" I stuttered over the wording, but Hush filled it in.

"Mates. There has been no siren on record who has formed a

mating bond with anyone with human DNA. So, to Ilia, and a large amount of his people, there is not much to lose by shutting the gates to the human realm."

"I guess that means we just gotta match a siren up to a willing halfling." I held two thumbs up, mostly joking at the simplicity of my suggestion. "And help Audrey with her new role as Hyvenmere's Hero." I wiggled my eyebrows at her with jest, but Audrey smiled at me back, looking like she was about to be sick. I immediately walked over and sat on the arm of the loveseat next to her.

"Easier said than done," Audrey sighed. "I still don't know if I'm totally convinced...but I did just *defeat*, you know..." She let her sentence go unfinished as she leaned back against the loveseat. "This is basically going to be a nightmare once word gets out of what I did."

"The good news is, my sweet little halfling..." I wrapped my arm around her neck and pulled her close, wrapping her up completely in my arms while she struggled to free herself. "Is that you have *me* now."

Hush tipped her head to the side as Audrey finally freed herself and asked, "What do you do?"

I shrugged and replied, "I'll be the Robin to her Batman." Hush just looked more confused. "But even less cool because I wasn't raised in the circus." I looked down at Audrey, nudging her arm with mine. "You can tell me about all of this now. I can be a listening ear and be waiting with a warm cup of coffee when the stress of being the Chosen One becomes too much. Hell, I can even go with you if—"

"You will?" Audrey sat up, eyebrows raised. I hesitated before lifting a shoulder to act like my suggestion was no big deal.

"I'm not going to lie. I was really freaked out when I woke up in Hyvenmere the other day," I said, ignoring Hush's curious glances between us. "But I've had time to absorb...all this. Hell, because of *you*, we survived getting attacked by a dragon last night, and I was able to come into work as if everything was normal today."

"You were attacked by a solvyrn," Liam corrected.

"Oh my god, who the hell cares?" I shook my head at him and addressed Audrey, "All that to say, I want to help. Even though I don't have cool powers or anything, I still want to support you." I was also dying to see if I heard that distant melody as soon as I set foot in Hyvenmere again, but Audrey didn't need to know that or be concerned that her friend was on the verge of having a mental breakdown.

That just seemed so unimportant in comparison to being a Chosen One destined to unite a whole ass secret magical realm.

Audrey's eyes watered at the rims seconds before she wrapped me in a hug.

"Thank you." Audrey sniffed as she pulled back to release me. "I really don't deserve you as a friend."

"Touching," Hush muttered. She didn't sound touched at all, actually. "However, I must leave soon. Before I can, we need to form a plan to address the headache your latest adventure is surely going to cause me."

"My sister is already starting to believe the rumors that it's Audrey, and not Ilia," Liam spoke up. "As soon as Audrey developed her second gift, Ada didn't need much convincing either. She's mostly been waiting for Audrey to continue fulfilling the prophecy."

Audrey frowned at that.

"What about the people with gills?" I asked.

Hush gave me a disturbed look and clarified, "You mean the nereids?"

"Yes," I nodded. "The mermaids."

"Nereids," all three of them corrected in unison.

"Whatever." I flicked my hands in a gesture that looked like shooing the terminology away. "Where are they leaning with all of this?"

"Entirely neutral at the moment." Liam scrubbed his chin with his words. "However, if we can talk to Fergus, he might be able to sway his parents in our favor. Which would help us keep the gates open regardless of Ilia's temper tantrums."

"Fergus is…?" I asked, sliding my gaze over to Audrey.

"The First Prince of the Nereids, next in line for the throne," she replied. "And also one of my favorite people in Hyvenmere."

This was good. Liam being the exception to the rule, if Audrey liked this Fergus fellow, I probably would, too. Later, though, I wanted to chat with Audrey about how she casually befriended several princes in Hyvenmere as if she were collecting them like baseball cards.

"Let's go talk to Fergie." I sat up from my desk, rolling my shoulders back. "Just give me a couple of days to enjoy the mundane routine of running a coffee shop, and I can tag along."

"He does have his birthday celebration this weekend." Liam lifted a brow at Audrey, who grinned with excitement.

"Oh, that's perfect. It'll be a more casual setting," Audrey said.

Hush nodded and added, "I'll let you know how Ilia's mood is after learning about Audrey's solvyrn…disposal." She shook her head and stared at the ground. "He's getting more unsettled each day that passes; just this morning, he announced that he's considering banning siren females from leaving Lyndoruun without a member of the king's guard to escort them."

I still couldn't get over how Hyvenmerian's referred to people as males and females. Did they not have nonbinary Hyvenmerians? Did gender and sexuality really stay so strictly within the bounds of a person's genitalia? But instead of voicing these questions, I stayed silent while the conversation, thankfully, started to wrap up in my office.

"Once we can guarantee that Audrey and the other halflings

are safe to travel to and from Hyvenmere," Liam said to Hush. "We will do everything we can to help you find them. And stop whoever is hunting them."

Hush nodded at him before turning to me. "Thank you for hosting." She bowed with a flourish, and even though I was still learning about Hyvenmerian customs, it felt a little mocking. As if Hush was bowing sarcastically.

I smirked and bowed back to her. I thought I caught her eyes crinkle in amusement, but it was hard to tell with half her face covered up. Then, without saying another word, she froze a second before I heard Shane's voice on the other side of the door.

"Is this all, Van?"

My heart started racing as I replied in a panic, "Yup! Just that box!"

Hush was unnaturally still, her eyes on the door that separated her and my employee. The sound of Shane's heavy footfalls echoed down the hallway, and she only waited one more second until we all heard the thud of him dropping the box on the countertop, before she vanished into thin air.

I gave Audrey and Liam a wide-eyed look and said, "She just teleported out of my office."

Liam rolled his eyes and said, "She *lyskifted* out of your office."

I immediately mocked him in a ridiculous voice, "*She lee-shifted out of your office.*"

"Enjoy your mundane routine the next couple of days," Audrey interrupted our bickering. "Because this weekend, I'm taking you back to Hyvenmere."

CHAPTER 8

"I'm obsessed with Hyvenmerian fashion," I announced as I twirled in front of the standing mirror, watching the many layers of my sheer skirts twirl. They were thin enough to see my fingers through, but because of how many layers there were, no one could see my ass through them. They were made of the lightest, most breathable fabric. I was covered but felt naked.

We departed on *The Knotty Boy* early this morning so that Liam could sail us to Catalina Island through the Mellhawn Gates, where I got to show off my fancy Hyvenmerian Grant and be allowed entry. As soon as the shimmering magic revealed Hyvenmere to us, the faint melody in the air that I was desperately trying to hear again was there. It sounded more distant than the first time I heard it, but it was there, nevertheless. I immediately pulled out my notebook and wrote down a few notes I could identify before we approached the gatehouses where the guards were stationed. Sirens with golden eyes were the ones guarding the gates today, and they both gave me a stink eye that made my skin crawl, but allowed us passage into Sammara, where Audrey and Liam took us to get fitted for the party tonight.

"This is more Vanyara fashion, actually," the nereid seamstress named Áma corrected me with a smile. Her copper-toned hair was pulled back in intricate braids that showcased all the jewelry hanging from her pointed ears, and her lip rings sparkled with her grin.

"This is Fergus." Audrey lifted her phone, displaying an incoming call as she stepped out of her dressing room. "I'm going to take it really quick."

"Okay." I swished my skirts back and forth as she stepped out of the little boutique.

There was a small flatscreen TV up in the corner, and as the copper-haired nereid seamstress came over to adjust the band holding my skirts on my waist, another nereid seamstress with purple hair named Frida flipped through the channels. She stopped at a station that felt a lot like old-school MTV, or some kind of news station that was only focused on gossip. There were no English subtitles on this one, though.

What made me do a double-take as my skirts were being adjusted and pinned by the seamstress, though, was the image of the red-haired, golden-eyed man I saw on TV my first day in Hyvenmere.

I tipped my head to the side and asked the woman, "Who is that?"

Áma glanced up at the TV and replied, "Drustan Shaw."

"And what is so significant about Drustan Shaw?" Saying his name out loud did things to me. A shiver of awareness danced down my spine with my words, as if saying his name or acknowledging my fascination with the blood-haired, golden-eyed Greek god was putting dangerous energy into the air.

"He's the Mad Siren Prince of Lyndoruun," Frida replied with her eyes glued to the TV. Ah, so he's a *siren* prince. Because princes are a dime a dozen in Hyvenmere, I guess. That simple answer revealed so much; it implied that the Siren King, Ilia, who hated Audrey and believed that *he* was the Chosen One, was Drustan's father.

"What are they saying about him?" I asked, while noticing how deep in conversation Audrey seemed to be with another prince on the phone through the glass windows of the shop.

"The anniversary of his leaving the Gravhune is approaching," the nereid who was helping me replied in a reverent tone. "And they're discussing if he's still fit to command his father's guard." I had no idea what the hell the Gravhune was, but I also didn't want to pry too much. I watched the broadcast with Frida while Áma finished sticking pins in my skirts.

An older stream of Drustan, shackled, thrashing violently against other golden-eyed siren guards, made my heart jump in my chest. The stream immediately cut to him crawling out of what looked like a crazy large pit, with siren guards pointing swords at him. He was thin, dirty, shirtless, and covered with various injuries as he addressed the terrified guards. Then the stream cut to the same one I saw before, where he marched on the street in that dark leather uniform, looking much more filled out while refusing to look at the camera.

"Anyone would be unwell if they survived the Gravhune," Frida said absentmindedly, entranced by the TV.

"She forgets that one must be unwell to be *sent* to the Gravhune," Áma countered with an exhausted scowl in Frida's direction before whispering to me. "Frida is easily distracted by a pretty siren face." Frida didn't argue; she just winked at me. On the TV, a woman making a recording on what I assumed to be her cell phone, took over, speaking in a hushed tone to the camera as she stood outside of a busy establishment. When she panned the phone over to view inside, it looked like a bar. Apparently, that's where anyone could find the Mad Siren Prince. The woman zoomed in on the camera, just in time to see another golden-eyed woman dance over to Drustan and delicately plop herself on his lap. He took her invitation without question and offered her some of his drink. She nodded and opened her mouth, and he gave her a heated look as he poured the liquid in.

A sour, burning sensation churned in my stomach watching the exchange, and I forced myself to look away from the screen as Audrey re-entered the boutique. I still had no idea what the Gravhune was, but based on the vibes of our brief discussion, it sounded like a bad place where bad people go. An odd thing for the son of Hyvenmere's supposed "Chosen One" to experience.

"How much time will you need to make the final adjustments?" Audrey asked Áma as she pocketed her phone. Frida changed the channel, shooting a weary glance toward Audrey as she did so.

"A couple of hours and your attire will be ready for you," Áma replied, standing tall and gesturing for me to go change in the fitting room. Áma and Audrey continued to chat while I quickly disrobed and returned to my human clothes, shrugging on my favorite leather jacket before I stepped out into the boutique again.

"Let's eat lunch, then we can come back and grab our outfits before we board the train," Audrey encouraged as she looped her arm through mine. I squeezed her against me, feeling comfort that I was with her now. Joining her in this secret part of her life.

When we stepped out of the boutique, the soothing sound of that distant, airy melody that only seemed to exist in Hyvenmere, blessed my ears.

We rode the train from Sammara to the nereid capital of Vanhirra, the capital of the nereid territory of Vanyara. We stepped off the train and walked through a coastal forest before approaching a tropical beach. On the beach, a cream-colored stone castle overlooked the ocean, half of it submerged into the gentle waves. Vanhirra was a smaller settlement based on what we saw cruising in, but still beautiful. The white sandy beaches, the green grass leading into a coastal forest just beyond. It reminded me of our little town if it had ancient structures, like castles.

The sun was setting, and it was a warm summer night. The air was comfortable on my exposed shoulders and arms. I didn't shiver from the coastal breeze that brushed past us as we were escorted to the gates of the castle by more armored nereid guards. They flexed their neck gills as they greeted us with warm smiles. Their breastplates had waves marked on them, which I assumed was some indicator that they were nereid guards, as opposed to sirens or fae.

"Are you ready?" Audrey grinned, looping her arm through mine as we entered the large building. "I'm so excited. Fergus throws the *best* parties."

"I am." I could hear the music playing down the large corridor we walked in, and nerves seemed to hum on my skin. Our sandals were soft on the floor. They were strappy, useless things that would fall apart if I had to run or walk a longer distance, tied in intricate knots on my calves.

These sandals were meant for fashion and nothing else.

Liam wore closed-toed shoes, but they looked more like slippers than sandals.

We approached large wooden doors, where nereid guards lifted a hand for us to wait while they reached forward to open them for us. It was all so formal, but I only felt out of place for a moment until the live sound from the ballroom filled the space, and music soothed the anxiety inside of me.

"You look hot," Audrey whispered from over her shoulder. She and Liam were standing one pace ahead of me, leading us through the ballroom doors.

"You do too." I winked at her, making her grin as Liam lifted his arm for her to take. I was very much a third wheel tonight, but it was worth it to be included.

The nereids' styles were a little more risqué. Formalwear included a sleeveless corset, showing off my midriff and lifting my cleavage. The flowy skirt from the boutique brushed against my skin with every step I took, and when I caught my reflection, I smiled at my choice of maroon and grey fabrics tied around me with a shimmery gold band. Audrey's skirts were green and yellow, held with a brown leather belt that matched the leather of her corset, which emphasized her voluptuous chest.

We both wore our hair half up, half down. Braids holding back the loose strands from our faces, adorned with gold jewelry that made me want to formally do my hair more often.

Liam wore dress pants and a dress shirt, which was a little disappointing.

The two of us were showing off plenty of skin and cleavage, and Liam's clothing did nothing to show off what he was packing underneath. His shirt wasn't even that tight. It was a real bummer, and when I told Audrey this in a hushed whisper on the train ride here, she just rolled her eyes at me.

The guards held open the doors to the ballroom, and a gorgeous Black man with dark blue eyes stepped into view. "Liam," he greeted as he shoved past the guards and embraced the fae. "Glad you finally made it."

"Wouldn't want to personally insult the prince and his people." Liam and the nereid pounded each other on the back in greeting again. Ah, so this was Fergus.

I tilted my head back to study the two of them when I realized that Fergus might even be an inch or two taller than Liam. His dark blue eyes slid over Audrey, whom he embraced with just as much enthusiasm, as she patted his back during their hug.

"How is my favorite halfling?" Fergus asked after leaning

back and snagging Audrey's hand to twirl her once. His gaze studied the flow of her skirt as she did so.

"Starving," Audrey replied after completing her twirl. "Point me toward the food."

I was watching this interaction quietly, realizing how close these three must be, when our host's head turned toward me, and a devastating grin spread across his face.

Good lord, Fergus was *handsome*.

He wore a long-sleeved tunic with a deep enough V at the collar. He was able to show off his toned pecks and abs. His dark brown hair fell into neat dreadlocks at his mid-back, with caramel-colored highlights braided throughout.

"As long as your human friend promises me a dance." Fergus's eyes scanned my attire too, eliciting a flutter in my heart at his attention. Because apparently, I was *that* attention starved. I wasn't normally one to preen under a man's approving gaze, but something about Fergus made me feel safe. He wasn't leering at me; he was appreciating what he was seeing and nothing else.

My gut immediately trusted him.

"If you're patient with me." I stepped forward and held my hand out, and to my surprise, Fergus took my hand as he bowed, pressing a warm kiss against my knuckles.

I pressed my lips together, trying not to laugh at the formality of it all.

Fergus was the only man who had ever, in my thirty years, kissed my knuckles.

Fergus stood tall but kept his fingers wrapped around my hand.

"I can be patient." He winked at me as he leaned down closer, something he probably wasn't used to doing. "Anything to be close to a gorgeous female's beauty."

I internally cringed at his terminology before deciding to move past it. "You know what? I like you," I told him with a smile, stepping closer to his space. He released his hold on my hand and provided his arm for me to loop mine through. "Feel free to give me more compliments while showing us to the food."

"It would be my honor." Fergus chuckled as he did just that. Then Liam and Audrey were following behind the two of us, moving us through a crowd of creatures who gave us curious glances.

I could get lost in this ballroom, because it wasn't a typical square or rectangular shape. The walls didn't have sharp corners; they had smooth curves. I had no idea what shape it was in, but the architecture did a good job of creating an open concept look while providing little pockets of privacy as well. It was difficult for me to appreciate all the gold and marble artwork and décor because I couldn't see well over all the taller bodies. The ceiling was a couple of stories high, and murals of beautiful landscapes were painted above. The style was so unique, I couldn't find anything to compare to the artwork in my world.

There was a moment where, as we were moving past a louder group of people who were starting a dance in the center of the main space, Fergus released his hold on my arm to place his palm on the small of my back, where my skin was exposed. I shot Audrey a wide-eyed look of appreciation over my shoulder, who was already smirking at me with an eyebrow wiggle of her own.

Excellent, she was cool with me sleeping with Fergus at some point.

If he wanted to, at least.

Finally, we made it to the food, and Fergus released his hold on my lower back to face us, "I'm not quite sure what compares to human food." He made the cutest pinch in his brow, as if concerned that I couldn't eat the salad or exotic fruit that adorned the table. "But perhaps I can ask—"

"This is perfect." I picked up a strawberry and took a bite, savoring its flavor and licking my lips before glancing at our host. "Thank you." For a prince, he seemed super chill and laid back. Now that I thought about it, so did Liam. Neither carried themselves with this weird, holier-than-thou air that I assumed a prince would.

After contemplating that little thought, I realized that my dramatic bite of a strawberry didn't catch Fergus's attention in a way that let him know I was available. He just smiled politely at us before his eyes started scanning the room.

"Are you ready to dance, Van?" he asked.

I nodded enthusiastically. "If you lead, I can learn—oh!" I didn't get to finish my sentence because Fergus had tugged my hand and led us to the dance floor. I barely had time for Audrey to take the rest of my strawberry, laughing, before we were off.

Fergus was an excellent dance partner, but I had I feeling I was going to strike out with him. No matter how sensual and dramatic I made my dance moves, his eyes never stayed on me longer than a few moments at a time. Sometimes we would stay close to Audrey and Liam, chatting about upcoming events.

Other times, I caught him staring at a couple far off to the side of the room. It wasn't until I purposefully studied them to see what drew Fergus's attention over there that I realized the woman's ears were rounded, like mine and Audrey's.

Human.

She must have been a halfling, like Audrey, if she were here.

The man, however, had pointed ears like everyone else in this realm.

The couple looked completely enthralled with each other. In their own world, while standing in a ballroom filled with people.

"Do you know them?" I asked Fergus after we joined another group dance.

He blinked before turning back to face me, "Yes." He smiled good-naturedly. His movements were loose, and his dancing fun, but something about him felt guarded now. "They became mated this year."

I grinned at the couple, watching the man kiss the knuckles of the woman just like Fergus had done with me. "That's exciting."

"It is." Fergus nodded with a sigh, and I caught a longing look on his expression before he glanced over my shoulder. "It's an exciting time for us. For our people."

"Sounds like," I replied, turning away from the nereid and halfling couple once they started kissing.

"Can I ask you something?" Fergus asked.

"Sure."

"You made a face earlier, when I attempted to give you a compliment." Fergus pressed his lips together. "I'm worried I offended you."

"Oh." I shook my head before I attempted to reassure him, "It wasn't—It's just—" How did I explain this?

"What specifically caused your reaction?" Fergus pressed. "I —if there is some human offense I mentioned, I want to be aware. I don't want to offend other humans I speak to." He seemed so earnest and genuine, too. Like he wanted to get his human interactions *just* right.

And then it clicked for me when he gave another fleeting— but clearly *longing*—look toward the couple in the corner. Fergus wanted a mate. He wanted a mate *really* badly.

I squeezed his hand in mine and gave him an appreciative look.

"You're the sweetest," I told him. Fergus gave me a nervous smirk in response, so I did my best to ease his concerns. "It's just..." I inhaled a breath, desperate to make this as clear and simple as possible. "In my realm, I am more than what is just between my legs." A divot formed between Fergus's dark eyebrows as he looked down at me, so I elaborated, "While *female* is technically accurate for *me*, I am more than that. I'm a woman."

The divot in his brow smoothed. "It wasn't me admiring your beauty. You took offense to me referring to you as a female, specifically?"

"But that's the thing," I rushed to explain. "I know that *man* and *woman* aren't really words your people say here."

Fergus shook his head, straightening. "*Man* and *woman* haven't been terms here in thousands of years, but that does not mean they never will be. Additionally, I agree with your state-ment. We are all more than what is between our legs, are we not?"

Fergus glanced up and turned us so we could both face the couple in the corner again. They weren't making out anymore; instead, they were sipping drinks, deep in conversation.

"That nereid over there, while presenting outwardly as a male, has made it known that they prefer identifiers that do not shove them so tightly into a specific expectation."

That made me smile.

"That's encouraging to hear," I smiled up at Fergus, who was still staring eagerly at the couple.

His smile was still on his lips, but softer. He was lost in thought as he stared at them. I concluded that Fergus was a romantic. Which made me think that he probably wouldn't be one to quickly jump into bed with someone, but rather longed for a deeper connection, as the couple in the corner had. A mate.

I decided that I wouldn't try to sleep with him tonight, because I wasn't convinced all that soulmate talk was for me quite yet.

"I guess—" I stopped myself when a gasp sounded nearby, and I glanced around to see what spooked someone. Fergus's hand tightened around mine as his head turned toward the large ballroom doors.

"Shit," Audrey cursed from nearby. She and Liam were a few feet away, slowing the steps of their dance.

"This is ridiculous," Fergus sighed, only sounding a little inconvenienced.

"We shouldn't have expected anything less," Liam grumbled.

"What is happening?" I reached up on tiptoes to see, but Fergus released his hold on me and straightened his shoulders before I could see anything.

"Stay with us." Audrey wrapped her fingers around my bicep. Fergus gave us a conspiratorial look before he sauntered toward whoever had just entered his party. Low whispers of partygoers started to erupt around us, and among them I recognized words like "siren" and "prince."

Oh. *Interesting*.

I leaned around a particularly tall woman to see Fergus spread his arms out in a welcoming gesture.

"To what do I owe the pleasure?" Fergus sounded jolly, friendly, which was the complete opposite energy that everyone else in the room was giving off. Another shift in attendees revealed the newcomers, because everyone was giving them a wide berth.

Standing there, with his hands in his pockets, was the red-haired man I had seen on TV my first day in this realm. Drustan Shaw. The Mad Siren Prince of Lyndoruun. The son of the man who had a personal vendetta against Audrey.

And he was…utterly dashing.

His thick, dark red hair was half pulled back out of his face. He wore a plain cream tunic and dark pants, not nearly as dressed up as everyone else. The only gold jewelry he wore was a few hoops in his pointed ears. Fergus stepped forward to shake his hand, which he returned absentmindedly as the siren prince's gold eyes scanned the party around him.

"His eyes are…Wow," I whispered to Audrey. Drustan's gaze continued to glance around, even checking over his shoulder, as Audrey whispered back.

"The gold irises of a siren. It's the one feature sirens can't shapeshift out of."

Fergus reached over and shook the hand of the blonde woman on the siren prince's arm.

Something pinched in my chest at the sight of them. I rubbed at it, above my exposed cleavage. A familiar melody filled my mind at the same time Drustan turned to mutter something low to Fergus.

I knew better than to ask if Audrey heard the music again. I knew she didn't. Part of me wondered if this mental melody was a defense mechanism. If it was my brain trying to protect my mind from the stress of being in the magical realm, interacting with friendly but dangerous creatures.

Or if it was just the result of being in a land where sirens, fae, and nereids exist.

"I was feeling a bit left out, Fergus." Drustan turned and gave the nereid a condescending smile, adjusting his arm, which his blonde date gripped tighter. She wore a similar outfit to the rest of the women. Cream corset with cream skirts. Her nails were painted gold to match the several necklaces that hung low over her exposed navel.

"Did he truly expect an invitation?" Liam whispered to us in annoyance.

"I apologize." Fergus placed a hand over his heart. "Had I known the siren prince's feelings were so delicate, I would have delivered an invite to you myself."

I pressed my lips together, loving Fergus a little bit more after that line.

Drustan's lips tipped up in the corners, not as offended as I'd assume a Mad Siren Prince to be, before he scanned the crowd again. His gaze was about to land where we stood, but someone

in the crowd shifted, concealing us while he searched for...
something.

I rubbed my chest again.

Drustan said something to Fergus in return, but I didn't
catch what it was because Audrey tightened her grip on my
bicep. Then released it. Her voice distracted me from the tune
playing in the background of my consciousness.

"This might get weird," Audrey whispered low, her lips near
my hair. "We might need to bail quickly." She threw a glance
toward Liam at her other side, who stood tall with his arms
crossed. A fuming expression pinched his face.

I nodded. "Got it."

Clapping made us turn our heads toward Fergus and
Drustan, now released from the beautiful siren woman's hold
on his arm. Fergus looped an arm around Drustan's shoulders
while waving a server over to deliver a drink.

Once the cup was in Drustan's hands, Fergus smiled at the
audience they held, while murmuring something in Drustan's
ear. Drustan didn't react at all; he kept his eyes on the attendees
while taking a small sip of whatever drink Fergus gave him.

"Come, enjoy!" Fergus bellowed, nodding toward the band
to continue the music they had paused playing for the spectacle.

I turned around and walked toward the food table. Audrey
and Liam followed, both looking over their shoulders toward
Fergus, guiding Drustan and his date through the party.

"Hungry?" Audrey asked me with a smile as she focused
back on me while I loaded up my plate.

"The fruits here are *so* much sweeter, if we need to, you
know—" I jerked my head behind me in a general "skedaddle"
gesture. "I want to enjoy this as much as I can first."

"Good idea," Audrey said, snagging a few grapes off my plate
and biting into them.

A moment later, Fergus came back to us, smiling and
greeting his guests as he did so. He clapped his hands on the

backs of Audrey and Liam, positioning himself between the two as he lowered his head and murmured for only us to hear.

"This just got a lot more interesting."

"You can't get rid of him?" Liam asked, full volume. Clearly not giving a shit if Drustan heard him.

"Now, Liam…" Fergus lifted a dark brow with his words. "You know as well as I do that it would be in poor taste to publicly refuse the siren prince's presence at a peaceful celebration of my birth."

"We just won't talk to him." Audrey lifted a shoulder and plopped another grape in her mouth. "I doubt he really wants to talk to us, anyway. We do, however, need to speak with you in private, Ferg."

Fergus looked intrigued at her words. Then a tap on my shoulder made me jump. My friends halted their conversation as we all turned to see who was tapping me.

A young nereid man smiled down at me. Nerves coated his features as he cleared his throat; pink blossomed on his cheeks from all our direct attention to him. Standing tall, he placed both of his hands behind his back and addressed me.

"Would you be interested in a dance—when you're finished, that is?" He nodded toward the fruits on my plate.

I grinned as I replied, "Sure," and finished my bites. The young nereid man beamed as he patiently waited for me to clean my fingers off with a napkin before holding his hand out for me to take.

Fergus winked at me as the nereid man pulled me into the crowd of couples dancing.

It only took about three seconds for me to realize, based on the hungry gaze the young nereid man kept giving me as he led us through the steps, that this may have been a bad idea. My gut was reminding me that nothing about his demeanor felt predatory, but the way his eyes kept dropping to my lips made me picture hearts in his eyes.

I didn't want to lead anyone on. I wasn't looking for a life partner or mate in this realm. I was just here to dance, eat delicious food, and become musically inspired by a melody that kept humming in the back of my mind. I went out of my way to keep a couple inches of space between our bodies at all times.

After dancing with the nereid, a fae man approached, tapping me on the shoulder, asking if he could have a dance, too.

I hesitantly obliged, feeling more eyes on me as I realized the men at this party seemed to be taking a direct interest in me. Perhaps it was because I was the only full human in attendance. Perhaps it was because they genuinely found me attractive. But I knew I wasn't mistaking the attention itself. Everywhere I looked, eager eyes watched.

A third man approached, tapping me on the shoulder, politely asking for a dance, and I accepted.

This would be the last time I accepted an invitation to dance, though. My feet were getting tired, and it was becoming increasingly difficult to keep track of where Audrey, Liam, and Fergus were in the large ballroom. Last I saw, they were standing close together in between some drapes near an open window, haloed by the sunset. Their conversation seemed hushed and intense, but then the man I was dancing with pulled me out for a spin, and when I looked back, they weren't there anymore.

I knew Audrey wouldn't abandon me, but Fergus's party was a full one. For the first time in my adult life, I was experiencing just how difficult it was to find people when everyone else was either the same height or a head taller than me.

Instead of another tap on my shoulder, a throat cleared behind us. I held back a sigh of annoyance.

The nereid I was dancing with, who was in the middle of asking me about my interests, almost stumbled when he saw who approached. Thankfully, he caught himself, but I didn't miss the way he gripped my hand and waist a little tighter.

Our steps slowed so that I could turn to see who startled him.

There he was.

Drustan stood about a foot taller than me. I had to crane my neck to look up and meet his golden gaze. He stood so closely that I was able to inhale a deep breath of his spicy, masculine scent through my nose. His musk was delicious, but I couldn't tell if it was a cologne or just what he naturally smelled like.

His tunic was opened low, low enough for me to admire his defined pectorals and abdomen. Lower than it was when he first entered the party. My mind immediately went to a cheese-grater joke, but I kept the thought to myself. When he lifted his arm to hold his palm face-up for me to take, I noted how snug the fabric bunched on his biceps.

This man was the definition of big and tall.

Drustan dipped his chin once at us, his lips in a line. No smile. No grin. Just a straight face as he lifted his eyes to address the nereid holding me tight.

"May I cut in?"

CHAPTER 9

G od, his voice was good. Hearing him speak this closely filled my chest with warmth. His voice was unbelievably smooth. The four simple words that slipped past his lips felt like a physical caress on my ears. Muscles I didn't know existed in my ears and head relaxed at the sound. If sound had a feeling, his voice would be slowly stepping into a warm pool of sweet honey, savoring the sensation of being coated with it, inch by inch.

Instead of ice-cold fear racing down my arms and spine, a heat ignited in my core that I hadn't experienced in a very long time. Maybe ever. It was enticing. His voice was calling to me; it made me want to lean toward him.

Absolutely not.

I studied the nereid I was dancing with, whose complexion had gone pale. Perhaps his grip on me wasn't a protective one, but a fearful reaction.

While it was obvious that Drustan was asking to dance with me, I was serious about not accepting another offer, so without thinking too much about the consequences, I turned back to the siren prince and gave him a bright smile.

"Oh, of course." I squeezed the nereid's hand to get him to let go of me, but when he did, I quickly guided his hand into Drustan's palm. "He's all yours."

And then I turned on my heel and made my way toward a dessert table, all too aware of the siren prince's piercing gaze on my retreating form.

Off to the side, a woman laughed. Following the sound, I caught sight of Drustan's date smiling into her beverage before taking a sip. She had just witnessed her prince casually getting rejected by me. When I looked around, several guests had their phones out, and a human woman rejecting a dance with the siren prince was now probably recorded at several different angles.

Whoops.

I helped myself to a cookie, biting into it. This cookie had a fruity flavor, and I hummed in appreciation as I turned around to see if I could find my friends.

I stood up on my tiptoes, looking, listening. But I couldn't find them. All these tall Hyvenmerians were blocking my view of wherever they were.

I did, however, lock eyes with the siren prince.

Like a good sport, Drustan was now dancing with the terrified nereid man. But his eyes weren't on his dance partner; they were on me. Their hands clasped together for a few steps, and the visual of his large hands grasping the nereid's made my blood simmer. Perhaps it was the way the siren prince kept his eyes on me, no matter how they turned and danced together. Perhaps it was watching the way he moved, sensual and confident, as he shared a dance with someone that he originally had no intention of dancing with.

It was easy to picture myself in the nereid's place. Studying Drustan's hands, his body, how careful and assured the siren was with his steps, made warmth pool in my belly. I knew deep in my soul that the feel of Drustan's touch on me would be rousing. That I could easily be seduced by an attractive, large, dangerous man like him after sharing one dance. I pictured him pulling me flush against his hard, chiseled body. Even though he kept a couple of inches of space between him and the nereid that I practically pushed into his arms.

Every time he turned and was able to meet my eyes again, my pulse spiked with a surge of awareness. My cheeks were getting more heated the longer he and I held eye contact. The cookie in my hand was forgotten.

Murmurs from male voices caught my attention, pulling me out of Drustan's spell. There was a group of men discussing something amongst themselves on the opposite side of the food table, looking back and forth between the siren prince and me.

One of them specifically appeared like he was working himself up to approach me, while his friends were holding his arm and encouraging him not to.

Oh, for fuck's sake.

Acknowledging my lack of strength and power compared to all these creatures, whose general interest in me only seemed to be growing, I set the cookie down on the dessert table. As I did, I spotted a clean, unused knife that was intended for cutting slices of cake. As slyly as I could, I slid it off the table and into my hand, gripping the handle close to my many layers of sheer skirts, attempting to conceal the weapon. Feeling better about having a way to defend myself from unsolicited advances, I sped away from the table and curious male eyes.

I kept scanning the party.

Still no Audrey or Liam. No Fergus.

Where the hell are they?

Walking the perimeter of the room allowed me to brush past the luxurious linens and silks that lined the walls, framing portraits and works of art I admired as quickly as I could in passing. Once I arrived at a side door with no guards stationed at it, I took it as an opportunity to slip out and get some fresh air.

The noise of the party quieted as I gently shut the door behind me. I grabbed my knife and slipped the blade into the waistband of my skirts, with the handle sticking out against my hip, in case I needed to grab it.

I was probably being dramatic.

But I still stood by my impulsive decision to bring it with me.

I padded down a smaller hallway, toward where I suspected the ocean to be, quietly admiring the pottery that occasionally stood proud against the walls. I reminded myself that Audrey, Liam, and even Fergus all had super-Hyvenmerian hearing. I figured that they knew how to find me whenever they decided it was time to leave.

The farther I got from the ballroom and the musicians playing in it, the more I focused on the melody humming in my mind. Why did I only hear it here? Why didn't I hear it back home? But here at Fergus's ball, it seemed much clearer now. The specific notes were easy for me to identify. I quietly hummed along with the mental melody as I traced my finger over the texture of a vase that stood almost as tall as me, admiring all the beautiful carvings and colors the artist used on it.

I moved on, approaching a stained-glass window that over-looked the ocean. *Ha, I was right*. The colors of the sunset shining through the warm reds and oranges of the glass were breathtaking, but what caught my eye was the creamy material of the drapes that framed it. I pinched the fabric between my fingers, holding it closer to my eyes as I noticed how it shimmered against the sunlight.

Every detail in this world was breathtaking.

Suddenly, a large presence appeared behind me, and I stiffened in alarm. A throat cleared, and I gasped at the same time I straightened, clutching the handle of my cake knife.

Without hesitating, I whirled around and struck.

Plunging the blade right into the side of the Mad Siren Prince.

Drustan grunted from the impact, his gold eyes widening in shock.

My eyes were also wide with shock, realizing what I had done.

I just stabbed someone.

Oh my god.

His hand was lifted as if he was about to tap me on the shoulder, but instead, he tightened his hand into a fist as he breathed through the pain.

He and I stood there, frozen in the moment. Paralyzed with the knowledge that I currently had a hand on a knife that was buried in his side, to the hilt. My jaw dropped, my lips parted in horror as I watched his nostrils flare with pain. He squeezed his eyes closed, clenching his jaw, as if attempting to compose himself.

We were so close I could smell him again, and the seduction of his scent made my head spin. But I couldn't enjoy it, because again, I just *stabbed* him.

The longest seconds of my life passed before he released a pained sound in his chest and took a step toward me. I released my hold on the knife and backed away. The silk of the drapes brushed against my skin right when he slapped a palm on the wall, bracing himself. His forearm almost brushed against my shoulder.

Drustan's eyes opened, and they were darker.

No, that wasn't quite right.

His pupils had expanded. A lot. Color touched his cheeks as he huffed out short, pained breaths through his nose. The muscles in his cheeks popped as he continued to work his jaw behind the firm press of his lips. My heart was racing out of my chest, both from proximity to this handsome creature and from only being able to think one single thought.

I just stabbed him.

His other arm moved, drawing my attention to his grip on the knife I had left in his side.

While holding eye contact with me, mere inches away from my face, the siren prince slowly started to pull the knife out. His eyes winced, but that was the only thing indicating that what he was doing did, in fact, cause him pain.

I couldn't look away from him, not even when he lifted the knife, releasing me from his gaze to study the way his own blood coated the blade.

I had just stabbed him, and in response, he had simply pulled the knife back out.

His tunic was stained with some blood, but he wasn't bleeding nearly as much as someone who had just been stabbed in the kidney should. Audrey had mentioned a couple of days ago that Hyvenmerian's healed a lot quicker in this realm, but I had no idea stabbing a man would be *this* uneventful. That he could act this nonchalantly about it.

It didn't subdue him like it would a human man.

He hummed low in his chest as he turned the blade this way and that between us, and that's when a familiar burn of arousal filled my lower stomach.

The temperature in this hallway was too warm. A bead of sweat dripped between my shoulder blades, pooling in my lower back. His scent, mixed with the low timbre of his hum, and his exposed torso that allowed me to count how many abs he had, disarmed me. Every moment that passed between us, the more my muscles started to relax.

It's not real, I reminded myself. *What did sirens have? Sin... sinndra. He could weaponize my emotions, and I just happened to be horny right now.*

Locking his eyes on mine again, Drustan adjusted his grip on the knife to angle the tip of the blade toward me. My breathing staggered, and heat bloomed from my chest to my vagina as he gently started to drag the blade across my collarbones. Not enough to break the skin, but enough to make a flurry of goosebumps erupt. The hairs on the back of my neck stood up straight, recognizing the danger I was in. But instead of fear, all I felt was wetness start to gather between my thighs.

He made one pass across my collarbones, keeping his other hand braced against the wall near my head, as he towered over me in the secluded hallway. I was pinned between his arm and the decorative vase I was admiring earlier.

Nowhere to escape to.

And yet, when he parted his lips, I wondered what they would taste like against mine.

"Is this how humans show their interest?"

With his words, he started to gently drag the knife in the opposite direction against my collar bones, and another hot flush coated my entire body. All the way down to my toes. I clenched my thighs together, suddenly craving friction as I struggled to understand his words.

"Huh?" I asked, gripping my skirts in my hands, desperate to hold on to something.

"If you wanted my attention," he hummed, his eyes dropping to my mouth as he stepped even closer, "You did not need to resort to such extreme measures." The knife slowly dragged down, down, toward my lifted and proudly on display cleavage.

Right when he began to tease the top of my breasts with the knife, my nipples hardened. The knife was still coated in his own blood, and when I noticed some of it leaving a trail on my skin, that's when I fully registered what he was saying.

"Excuse me?" I asked with a pant. I swallowed around nothing, my throat dry.

The corner of his mouth lifted, and his eyes locked on mine

again. I watched in real time as his pupils kept expanding and contracting, almost filling the entirety of his golden irises as he leaned even closer, dragging the knife back up my chest, teasing the side of my neck.

"Stunning," he whispered, ignoring my question. "...*mine.*" His tone changed to a low growl with the claim, and my knees almost buckled from the dominance he manifested with it. The one word from him melted parts of me I didn't realize needed to thaw. My shoulders instinctively dropped. My jaw unclenched, and my lips parted.

Towering over me with his massive body, he studied me with an intensity that made me shiver. I had never, ever, felt so small. I was vulnerable, dressed in flimsy skirts and a corset that was feeling too tight. My nipples were probably poking holes through the leather, and I fought the urge to check.

But then I realized what he said.

Mine.

"Oh..." I breathed as I watched him lean down, his eyes on my lips. His intention was clear. I waited until his breath was able to fan my face. I considered letting it happen for half a second. Stealing at least one taste of him before I put a stop to this madness. My sudden, surging hormones were begging me to lean into him in return. He got so close that his face was blurry, before I finally forced myself to speak, "No."

He froze; his lips close enough to ghost over mine. He stared at me, and I wondered if I was blurry in his vision, too, or if Hyvenmerians didn't deal with blurry vision when in proximity as humans did.

But then his lips pulled back into a smile, and my confusion surged with my libido.

"No?" he asked with his devilish grin, softly dragging the knife along my jaw.

He still had the knife. The one I stabbed him with. This man was holding me against a wall at knifepoint. And yet my clit was throbbing.

Your arousal isn't real. It's just his sinndra. His sinndra.

I needed to get out of here.

"No." I repeated and swallowed around a dry lump in my throat. "Actually, I should leave."

Surprisingly, he nodded his agreement, but then he said, "With me."

I snorted, surprised that *that* was my reaction as he used the tip of the bloody blade to admire my dangly hoop earrings, creating a new wave of fire under my skin. His grin twitched, as if he found his own amusement in my reaction.

"No thanks." I slowly shook my head, dislodging the blade from my earring with the movement. "I—"

"Should leave with me," he interrupted, taking the final step that closed the distance between us. Our chests were now completely flush together. His feet bracketed both of mine, drowning me in his body heat as he removed the blade from my skin, twirled it in his grip, and tucked his arm behind his lower back.

"No."

"Why not?" he asked, leaning in to brush his lips against my jaw. I tilted my head back, hating myself just a little bit as I gave him more room to explore my skin.

"That's—" I bit back a whimper as his lips gently nipped at my earlobe, before trailing up the shell of my ear. "That's not how this works."

His chest rumbled against mine, sending a new wave of shivers down my body as I clenched my thighs together even tighter, my underwear completely ruined.

"Then, tell me," he whispered, his hot breath fanning my neck. "How will this work between us, Vanessa?"

Oh *god*.

It was unfair how seductive he made my name sound. I

didn't remember my eyes falling closed, but I fluttered them open at the sound of him deeply inhaling my hair, as if breathing me in affected him as much as breathing in his scent affected me. It took every muscle in my body to hold perfectly still; to not start grinding against him like an animal in heat.

Then I realized something. I'd never once introduced myself to him. Alarm bells started going off in my head right when Audrey's voice broke through our intimate moment.

"Vanessa?"

That was Audrey's voice, and it made me jump.

Oh my god, Audrey. Liam. Fergus. The party. It was as if a bucket of cold water had been splashed over me, snuffing out any flame of arousal from the moment.

Well, not *any* flame. I could still count my pulse based on the throbbing between my legs. But it was snuffed out enough for me to get a clearer head again.

The growl in Drustan's chest turned threatening, and his massive body tensed over me as he turned toward my best friend.

Her hazel eyes were wide, her expression horrified, as Drustan lifted the bloody blade toward her, no longer hidden behind his back.

Liam and Fergus stood on either side of Audrey. Liam, wearing his constant hostile expression toward the siren prince. In contrast, Fergus only looked disappointed while standing tall with crossed arms. Like a chaperone who caught teenagers canoodling at a high school prom.

"Aud," I gasped. As Drustan turned his body toward my friends, with his mouth pulled back in a threatening grimace, complete with the bloody cake knife raised in a defensive hold, I shoved him away from me.

He barely budged, but I still managed to bolt toward Audrey, who opened her arms for me as I ran into her.

"Are you okay?" she asked me in a whisper.

"I'm okay," I assured her as I turned back toward the siren prince.

His eyes were on me, back to their gold color. He pushed himself off the wall and sighed, flipping the knife in his hands casually.

"Hello, old friends," Drustan muttered.

Something sank in my gut at his words. Like a veil of manipulation was being pulled off of me.

"Explain to me," Fergus sighed in annoyance. "How and why the Prince of Lyndoruun ended up hidden in the drapes with a human at my ball?"

As Drustan's eyes locked on mine. A mocking tone coated his voice as he replied, "Have you seen the female, Fergus? How could I possibly resist such a creature?"

I scowled, anger boiling my blood as I stepped forward and spat, "Call me a female one more time. See what happens."

Confusion marred Drustan's features for a moment before a cool, uninterested expression smoothed over them. I was manipulated so *easily* by him. I understood Liam's constant hostile energy toward Drustan. I was completely powerless against a siren like him. Had Drustan kept me tucked away for a few more seconds, I probably would have caved and gone anywhere he asked me to.

Drustan's lips twitched before he gave his attention to Liam, who took a threatening step toward him.

"Why are you holding a bloody knife, Shaw?" Liam asked accusingly. Audrey immediately started to coat her hands over my body in a panic, before I shooed her off.

"Why don't you ask the human, *Dahl*?" Drustan replied, sounding more bored than anything as he danced the blade between his fingers without cutting himself once.

Fergus turned to give me a proud smirk, then he faced Drustan again as he said, "It's getting late, and it's a bit of a journey back to Lydhavn."

"That it is," Drustan replied. "Though I am intrigued. Where have the three of you been, while you left your human companion unprotected?" I glared at him, but he didn't react. "It almost looked as if the fae and nereid princes were conspiring with the halfling." The threat was clear in his voice, and I balled my hands into fists as everyone stayed quiet. Drustan's eyes fell on each one of my friends before he released a heavy sigh of exhaustion, "Hopefully, the peace our territories have been able to maintain over the decades will remain intact."

I'm going to strangle him, I thought, picturing my hands wrapping around his neck.

Drustan's eyes landed on me as his lips tipped up in a grin.

We'll work our way up to that, my song. His hypnotic, warm voice rang in my mind.

I immediately gasped and took a step back, "What the fu—"

"Don't be delusional," Fergus said calmly. "Why are you suddenly interested in our affairs now, instead of finding the bottom of every bottle within your reach?"

Drustan's gaze flitted around the room behind us, as if searching for an answer.

"Time will tell." He lifted a shoulder before stepping forward with the knife. The three of them immediately blocked Drustan from approaching me, and his red eyebrows jumped at the threatening positions all my friends took. He chuckled to himself, amused at the obvious hostility, before he twirled the knife one last time.

Drustan slowly lowered to a kneel on the ground, gently placing the weapon on the ground, before smirking at me and standing tall again.

"Until next time, Vanessa." Drustan winked and lyskifted into thin air.

I released the breath I had been holding as soon as his voice echoed in my mind.

Liam grumbled but relaxed with the siren prince's absence, turning toward Audrey and me, "I'm sorry that he—"

"He spoke in my mind," I muttered. All three of them froze, and it was the first time I had seen Fergus look genuinely concerned about anything all night.

"What?" Audrey asked, resting her hand on my shoulder.

"Drustan, he—" I shook my head, barely comprehending my own words. "He spoke in my mind. He talked to me."

Liam's nostrils flared, Fergus's eyes widened, and Audrey stood stock still.

A beat of silence filled the hallway before Liam finally grunted out, "How is that fucker still *alive?*"

CHAPTER 10

"It doesn't make any sense," Audrey muttered the next morning after Fergus's birthday. She had bags under her eyes, and her hair was a mess, similar to mine. We stayed out late, taking the train back to Sammara and sailing my *Knotty Boy* through the gates again. As soon as I got home, I popped two gummies and knocked myself out. I had a nice little, slightly groggy, afterglow from the marijuana.

"It doesn't, and yet Drustan is—hold on," Liam stepped up behind Audrey when she reached for a new bag of coffee. He rested his hand on the small of her back and only released it when he handed it to her. "And yet, Drustan is not only gifted with whismerra, but he's also not afraid to use it."

When he stepped away, he glanced down to stare at her exposed ass cheeks, because her tiny sleep shorts rode up with her stretch. I cleared my throat, and his gaze snapped up to mine. An embarrassed blush coated his cheeks as he sauntered back to our small folding kitchen table.

"Telepathy is a no-no?" I asked, rubbing the last sleep out of my eyes.

"Whismerric sirens haven't existed in thousands of years,"

Audrey yawned as she waited for the coffee to brew. "Long ago, it was decided that any siren who developed whismerra at the age of maturity was to be executed immediately. The governments of Hyvenmere considered whismerric sirens to be too powerful to allow. They claimed that they disrupted the balance of nature and needed to be eliminated. They created a narrative that painted whismerric sirens as threats to the peace of Hyvenmere. So, after the fae, nereid, and siren governments agreed on this barbaric and, what I consider to be purely evil law, the gene ended up completely wiped from the pool."

"What's the age of maturity?" I asked with an uneasy churn of my stomach.

"Twenty-six," Liam replied to Audrey's ass. I propped my chin on my fist, staring at him, waiting until he felt my attention. I sat on our couch, facing the tiny kitchen in our condo. Eventually, Liam glanced at me again and looked down at the table, sufficiently caught.

"So, sirens didn't develop this gift until they were fully grown adults?" I asked. They both confirmed my statement with nods.

"If Drustan has this whismerra thing, and he felt comfy-cozy talking to me with it, does that mean that the law is no longer in effect?" I asked. Audrey walked over to me to give me a cup of coffee first, and when she turned around to give Liam his, I made sure to stick my tongue out at him.

He stuck his tongue out at me as soon as she looked away to take a seat next to him at the tiny folding table.

"I doubt Ilia is eager to execute his only heir," Audrey hypothesized. "But he's also historically traditional about things. A hundred years ago, Ilia tried to push males and females to take on specific roles and identities in a typical lifestyle that ancient Hyvenmerian society used to have, but it did not go well for him." Thank god. I privately wished that my realm would shut that shit down immediately, too.

Then I widened my eyes when I realized what Audrey said. "I'm sorry, *how* old is the Siren King?"

Liam smirked. "Oh, that's right, I forgot human lifespans aren't as long as ours." He chuckled to himself and then answered, "He's two hundred and fifty-one years old." I released a low whistle because *damn*.

"How old are you?" I asked Liam.

"Thirty-five," he replied. I sighed with relief, because thank *fuck* Audrey wasn't crushing on a man old enough to be her great-great-great-great-grandparent.

"I think we should assume Ilia knows about Drustan's whismerra." Audrey scrubbed her cheek with her hand as she sipped her coffee, both elbows on the table. "Because Drustan wouldn't keep something like that from his own father, then share it with Van the second they met. This also means we need to assume Drustan knows *exactly* what we discussed with Fergus, and that Ilia now knows that I'm officially a threat to his role as the prophesied one, too."

"We should also assume that Drustan has, again, confirmed to his father that Vanessa is a weakness of yours," Liam added with annoyance laced in his voice. "Which would have already been confirmed the night Ilia sent Sergei and Leon to take her. Unfortunately, Drustan now knows how easy it is to manipulate Vanessa." I frowned at my coffee mug. I already put that together myself, but the fact that Liam and Audrey seemed to understand just how out of control I was during those heated moments with Drustan in the hallway made me feel embarrassed. I didn't want to be a liability to them, but rather someone helpful. I immediately panicked, worrying that Audrey wouldn't want me to go with her to Hyvenmere anymore or would start keeping secrets from me again to protect me.

We hadn't had the formal conversation yet, because Audrey didn't want to overwhelm me with everything all at once. But based on everything everyone had told me about Hyvenmerian politics and Audrey's specific role, I started to put together a narrative on my own. If Ilia didn't want Audrey around and wanted to close the gates between realms for good, it would make sense for him to send his men after me. Holding me hostage and forcing Audrey's hand was something that human dictators did all the time. This was also me hoping that Ilia didn't have any desire to kill me once he got a hold of me. But Liam had a point. Ilia now had irrefutable evidence that I was important to Audrey. A powerless human. A pawn to weaponize to get his way. The concept made my nerves flip in my stomach, and a bit of anger simmered in my chest at the situation.

Then I had an idea.

Liam grumbled as he sipped his coffee, before nudging Audrey's leg with his under the table in solidarity. After letting everyone enjoy their morning brew for a few moments, I raised my hand. The two of them turned to me, Audrey with a slightly more amused expression as she asked me, "Yes, Van?"

"Can I make a request, as the powerless human who wants to be more help than hindrance?"

I told Audrey that I wanted to train with her and Liam. Liam had mentioned that he trained Audrey the day the solvyrn attacked our boat and, based on how skilled Audrey was when confronting the beast, I figured I should familiarize myself with her skillset.

I got lucky being able to stab Drustan; the element of surprise was on my side. I wanted to be better prepared should I ever find myself in the presence of another fucking siren with obvious ulterior, dangerous motives. I had always been big on strength training. I had taken many self-defense courses throughout my twenties, especially after the horror Audrey and I experienced as teens. I considered myself stronger than most women my age. However, I didn't think it was enough to defend myself from anything Hyvenmerian. I needed to do more.

"I can hardly lift this." I used both hands to try to hold a large sword. I hadn't seen one since we were attacked by the solvyrn, and Liam used his fae magic to summon his. Other than that, I'd only seen swords on TV or in random museums. After grunting and letting the blade hit the ground, Liam's large hand wrapped around both of mine to take hold of the weapon.

I understood the muscles in his arms better now. He handled the large sword with ease and familiarity. He stepped away from me before showing off and doing a couple of flippy sword trick things that illustrated how familiar he was with wielding one.

"Yeah, that's not for me." I wandered over toward the knives Audrey set out.

We were in a warehouse, about half an hour south of Orange County. There wasn't a lot between Orange County and Oceanside, but there were scattered abandoned buildings in the hills against the coastline. We were in one of those, with the open, exposed ceilings allowing just enough sunlight in for our training session.

I was pretty sure I'd attended a pop-up rave here back in college.

"I prefer knives, too." Audrey tossed one, catching the tip of the blade between a pinch in her fingers, before flicking her wrist and grasping the handle.

"You're such a badass now." I smiled at her.

According to Audrey, Hyvenmere didn't have guns. Like, at all. They were outlawed, but most civilians didn't even know that they existed in the human realm. The magical governments, however, seemed to agree on that one specific issue. Guns were out. Bringing one into Hyvenmere would result in destroying the weapon and a one-way ticket to the Gravhune for the person who dared sneak it in under the radar.

Blades and swords seemed so much more...brutal. Intimate.

You couldn't distance yourself from the life you took with a sword or knife.

Off to the side, Liam was going through a series of movements with his huge ass sword.

"What exactly *is* the Gravhune?" I asked. "The nereids at the boutique mentioned it."

"It's a prison," Audrey explained, balancing a knife on her index finger. "Hidden miles underground, on a secluded island between Vanyara and Lyndoruun—the nereid and siren territories." I nodded my thanks at her reminder. "It's cursed with ancient, dark magic. Once you go in, you don't come out. No one ever has."

"Unless you're fucking Drustan." Liam grunted, slicing the air aggressively.

Liam's words made the TV segment about him walking out of the Gravhune, looking tortured, that much more newsworthy. That implied that Drustan was the only Hyvenmerian to survive the prison.

Audrey inhaled and blew out a long breath before handing me a blade she plucked from the assortment on the table.

"This one feels like you."

I had no idea what that meant, but while there was weight to the knife, it felt comfortable in my hand. "Okay." I pointed at her with the knife, making her grin. "Now fill me in. Why is Liam moodier and more annoying than normal?"

"I can hear you, Van," Liam replied while continuing his exercises.

"I know, Liam." I rolled my eyes before leveling Audrey with a look. "I'm going to keep asking about it. The more secretive you are, the more my curiosity is piqued."

She tucked her bottom lip between her teeth.

She nodded and leaned against the old, folding table on which all the blades were displayed.

"Drustan, Fergus, and Liam used to all be friends." Audrey

looked sadly over at the fae, who was now stretching his arms as he sauntered toward us.

"What happened?" I asked. I refused to step aside as Liam reached forward to drop his sword on the table. My form of dominance—never stepping aside for a man.

"He killed my parents," Liam grunted before taking one of the spare seventy-two-ounce water bottles we brought from our condo and chugging half of it in one go. "That's why he was sent to the Gravhune."

"Oh my god," I whispered. I had been assuming Drustan slept with Liam's high school girlfriend or something. I didn't realize—*oh my god*. Liam's parents were the former Fae King and Queen. Drustan murdered the leaders of an entire country.

"Yeah," Audrey sighed, resting a hand on Liam's forearm as he settled in to elaborate.

"Why did he do that?" I asked.

"Because Drustan is a monster," Liam replied.

"Okay—but—like—" I shook my head, suddenly feeling restless. I decided to pull my ponytail out and start braiding my hair to keep my hands busy. "Why?"

"No one knows," Liam sighed. I could see so many emotions pass over his expression as he paused in thought. Anger. Hurt. Pain. Rage. Sadness, "...He just...snapped. No one saw it coming."

A psychotic break, maybe? That would explain why everyone referred to Drustan as mad, even though he didn't seem so during our brief interaction together. Beyond barely reacting to getting stabbed, that is.

I frowned, but Liam continued speaking, staring at his water bottle as he did, "Our families were close. Being children of political leaders, we were pretty much raised together. Me, Fergus, and...Drustan." Liam's lips grimaced just from uttering his name. "This was a little over a decade ago. Right as the three of us were becoming adults. Everyone was at my parents' estate.

The nereid royals with Fergus and his siblings. The siren royals, who were just Ilia, Drustan, and Drustan's cousin; the female he brought to Fergus's ball." A weird, very inappropriate relief filled my core at the knowledge that the woman was Drustan's cousin, and I forced myself not to dwell on that piece of information as Liam continued, "Everyone was celebrating my sister's future on the throne. After we had gone to bed, I suddenly woke to the sound of my parents screaming." Rocks formed in my gut, watching Liam inhale a breath of what looked like determination as he lifted his gaze to continue the story. "After finding their guards disemboweled in the hallway, I stormed into their chambers with Fergus. We found Drustan standing over my parents' bed with—with—" Liam's lips twisted in disgust as he scraped a hand down his face. "...their hearts in his claws."

I blinked at him, throwing a shocked look toward Audrey. She gave me the barest nod of confirmation as she squeezed Liam's forearm in a small attempt to comfort him.

"...In his...claws?" I asked. Drustan didn't have claws. He had normal, slender, human-like fingers with veins that circled up his wrists, down his forearm—

"Sirens have a specific...form." Audrey sighed as she dropped her hold on Liam's arm. In response, he scooted closer to her, as if missing her touch.

"And it involves claws?" I pressed.

"Yeah, black claws. Almost as long as their fingers themselves. Their eyes turn jet black, too. Sometimes black veins appear under their skin; it's very...unsettling to see."

"You've seen it?" I asked her. Drustan's eyes had gone all black a couple of times during those fleeting moments in the hallway of Fergus's palace. I suppressed a shiver from the memory of those dark eyes.

"I've seen other sirens show it to me, like, as a party trick. But it's still nerve-wracking to witness."

I hummed at that, letting a few quiet moments settle between the three of us. The sound of cars in the distance, driving along PCH, echoed in the worn walls of the warehouse.

"Seems like a fair reason to get sent to the Gravhune," I muttered. Drustan killed two people—political leaders. "And he wasn't supposed to leave?"

"Nobody expected him to live long enough to," Audrey replied.

I blinked at her. "What does that mean?"

"The magic of the Gravhune is cruel," Liam explained. "You enter the Gravhune, and your own mind turns on you. You see things that aren't there. You remember things incorrectly; the mental torture begins within minutes of entering the darkness."

Well, shit.

"People end up taking their own lives if they don't kill their prison mates first," Audrey murmured. "It's where they send the worst criminals. The most dangerous Hyvenmerians."

Liam nodded, "However...Drustan crawled out after completing his five-year sentence."

"And you all just like...let that happen?"

"He waited out his sentence." Audrey frowned, before lifting her hand and splaying her fingers. "The sentence to the Gravhune is five years, knowing that no one has lasted more than one. Drustan, however..."

Whoa.

"He lasted all five years."

I understood the challenge of fighting your own mind. Having your brain work against you more than most. Of your mind unexpectedly summoning trauma and memories you'd rather forget. I couldn't imagine having a constant stream of that for a day, let alone five straight years.

What inspires a person to survive the Gravhune?

"He crawled out, looking like hell," Liam murmured, and I recalled the footage of a mangled Drustan doing so. "And announced that he fulfilled his sentence. How he even kept track of time is beyond me. Time isn't linear there. It's part of the torture."

"Goddamn." I shook my head in shock. "So what did everyone do?"

"What could we do? He paid the punishment for his crime. Laws between our lands don't account for whether someone *completes* five years in the Gravhune. It only accounts for *sending* people there. We had no choice but to let him back into society. He has since been referred to as the Mad Siren Prince."

I widened my eyes. A murderer was just…walking around. Crashing nereid birthday parties. Pinning me against the wall. Trying to seduce me. Were his eyes changing to black because he wanted to kill me? Did they go back and forth because of the mental and emotional torture he endured for five straight years?

"This is crazy," I giggled the words, though I didn't actually feel humor in them. "I can't believe he—he and I—" I felt Audrey's hand on me before I glanced down to see her squeezing my shoulder.

"He didn't hurt you?" Audrey asked me quietly. She had already asked me that question several times since that evening, but my answer was still the same.

"No, he didn't," I replied. "He just looked…curious?" And horny. But maybe I was just projecting. My fear was present in that moment, that I knew for sure. But, thanks to Drustan, something purely visceral rose in me during those heated stares, too.

"I'm glad we got to you, Van," Liam spoke up, before sitting next to Audrey against the table. "Sirens are already dangerous, but he…"

"Will rip my heart out?" I tried to joke, but I couldn't lift my lips into a smile. I couldn't laugh or giggle. What was funny about a very real threat like that?

Liam nodded once. "That, but also never forget that sirens

can weaponize your emotions. Some have a weaker ability to do so than others but based on the wide pupils you had when we found you—" I lifted my eyebrows at that, because I hadn't realized. "—We need to remember that he *is* powerful. Anyone who can survive the Gravhune should be feared."

I nodded. "Got it."

"You'll be better prepared if you see him again," Audrey assured me, squeezing my shoulder. "Thankfully, Fergus took the knowledge of me officially slaying an 'ancient beast' well, and he seemed convinced that his parents would start to question the Siren King's title as the Chosen One on their own once they heard about it, too."

I nodded again. "And if we can keep the idea of a halfling like you being the Chosen One positive, then the Mellhawn Gates are more likely to stay open for everyone else."

"I reached out to Hush to let her know how our visit in Vanhirra went, but she hasn't had time to meet. I assume she's busy following a lead on the missing siren mothers and children," Liam added.

Shit. Right. There was so much going on in this other realm.

"What do you think is happening to those missing sirens?" I asked, wanting to change the subject from how dangerous Drustan's raw animal magnetism was for a human like me.

Liam and Audrey shared a look before Audrey replied, "I wish I knew. If they're alive, I want to help them. It would be easier if Hyvenmere officially deemed me as the Chosen One. If they're not alive...I want to stop whoever is hunting them down." A dark look flickered across Audrey's face, which was very unlike her. Or, maybe, this *was* like her now, and I was still getting to know the Hyvenmerian side of her.

"I want to know why they'd be hunted down in the first place," Liam added.

It was one of those rare moments when Liam and I agreed on something.

If the missing siren women and children were being targeted —which, let's face it, would be the only explanation for such a large number of missing persons—what was the motive? A hate group of some kind?

I was wrapping my mind around all of this, the significant amount of danger I was in, when Audrey stood up and clapped her hands together once.

"Alright. Let's work on some basics for today to get you warmed up." Audrey pointed toward the knife I was still fiddling with in my hands before she and Liam strode toward the exercise mats.

"What are you reading?" I asked Shane as I stretched my back out against the counter of my coffee shop. I started training with Liam and Audrey three days a week, and I was very much out of shape. I was getting better, though. I also managed to get a hit on Liam yesterday, which made my day.

I made sure not to stare at Shane as I asked him my question, because he conversed better without direct eye contact, so I focused on the parts of the espresso machine I had taken apart and was washing out before I took a stretching break.

"Sorry—I'll stop and help you." Shane rose from his seat at the table, closed his book, and tucked it into the back pocket of his jeans. He trimmed his hair recently and let his stubble grow into a thicker beard.

He looked handsome. I was curious what inspired the new look, if anything.

"I'm not asking because I'm annoyed that you're reading," I clarified. Shane shrugged, stepping behind the counter to pick up a nozzle to rinse. "I'm genuinely curious about what you're reading."

Shane hummed, "A historical."

I nodded. "What's it about?"

Shane gave me his back and lifted his shoulder as his response. I would bet his next paycheck that it was a bodice ripper, if it was small enough to fit in the back pocket of his jeans and everything.

I ducked under the counter to glance for replacement parts right when the chime over the door to the coffee shop rang. Shane turned to attach the clean nozzle and raised his voice as he asked, "What can I get you?"

He must be in a good mood today if he is speaking in fuller sentences with the customers. *Where the hell is that box?* I got on my knees and started shifting boxes around next to him.

A woman's voice answered, "A coffee."

Shane replied, and I could hear the smile in his voice as he asked, "What kind?" *What the hell? Was Shane flirting with a customer?*

"Get whatever you want," another man's voice said. Awareness tickled my spine. *Oh, he sounded attractive.*

I scrambled out from underneath the counter, which probably wasn't the sexiest thing to do, but I didn't want to miss out on this opportunity. I popped up right next to Shane, tucking stray curls behind my ears, and smiled brightly.

My handsome stranger was back. He wore sunglasses, a dress shirt rolled up to his elbows, and slacks that had no wrinkles. Next to him stood a blonde woman who also wore sunglasses.

She was gorgeous. Tall, almost my exact height. Her dark blonde hair was pulled back in a half braid, and she wore a cropped blush tank top with a flowy skirt that skimmed over her sandal-covered toes.

My smile wavered a little bit at the sight of her. *Shit, this was probably his date.* I gave her a warm smile as I ignored the funny look Shane gave me for popping up so suddenly.

"The one he ordered last time is our most popular, by far," I assured her. A pinch formed in her brow as she gave me a noticeably uncomfortable smile in return. She took a small step away from my handsome stranger to glance at our menu.

"That sounds good." She nodded, turning to look at Shane. He rang up their order on the register, but before he could ask them for payment, I waved him off, "I got this."

Shane lifted an eyebrow at me. "Yeah?"

"Yeah." It was the least I could do, after thirsting over a man who was taken and all. He probably realized how hard I was flirting with him last time and didn't want to come back until he could bring his partner. Sending a clear message that he was off limits.

I was a girls-girl first, so comping their order made me feel like I was apologizing.

"What? No." The man stepped forward, reaching into the pocket of his slacks to pull out some crisp bills. "I'm going to pay."

I suppressed a shiver from the command in his voice. It sounded *so* soothing.

I waved him off and said, "We've had a busy day, enjoy the treat."

The man frowned before glancing at the tip jar and shoving the bills inside it. Shane was already making their drinks, watching this exchange out of the corner of his eye. The woman had stepped down to the counter, curiously studying the way that Shane mixed their coffee order.

The man stood at the counter, daring me to remove his money from the tip jar. I shrugged and turned, helping Shane. The man's shoulders relaxed, and he followed his date down to the opposite side of the countertop, where their drinks would be picked up.

Shane and I worked in silence, as he preferred. Once the order was done, I took both cups and slipped the cardboard cozies onto them to help protect their hands.

"Here you go." I gave him my best shit-eating smile.

The woman smirked as she sipped her drink and led them to one of the tables by a window. Before the man could sit down, he huffed and marched back to the countertop.

"Problem?" I asked with an innocent expression.

In response, he held up the bills I had snuck out of the tip jar and tucked into the cardboard cozy of his drink.

"Look, man." I sighed and laid my palms flat on the counter. "I know it's important for your big, masculine ego to show your date that you can afford to pay for things, but I promise you it's not that deep. It's getting weird now." He quirked a dark eyebrow at me, the corner of his lips tipped up with it as he leaned on the counter, resting one large palm on the wood surface.

"She's not my date," he said. My heart started beating rapidly in my chest. From the corner of my eye, I noticed Shane turn his head to look at the woman sitting quietly at the table.

"Okay." I lifted a shoulder.

I will not drool over a man.

I will not drool over a man.

"Okay," he replied. After a moment of intense eye contact— if you could even call it that while he was wearing sunglasses— he reached across the counter. His hand was slow and confident as he slowly reached for my chest. I held perfectly still, too curious about where this was going. The man tucked one large finger into the breast pocket of my apron, pulling it open just enough for him to slide the bills into the fabric.

Heat scorched my cheeks. His smirk kicked up a notch, probably noticing the visceral reaction that move triggered in my body.

"You win," I murmured. When he leaned back, I had to dig my fingertips into the countertop to keep myself from leaning after him.

He chuckled, drumming his fingertips on his side of the

counter as he rested his other hand on his hip. "What do I win?"

I pressed my lips together as I snuck a glance over at the woman sitting at the table. She wasn't watching us; her gaze was focused on Shane, who was wiping down tables.

If he said she isn't a date…

"What do you want?" I asked.

I couldn't track his eye movement, but the subtle tip of his head and the way he inhaled let me know that he was perusing me. Studying my entire body.

I quickly sent a silent prayer up to the sky for good measure.

Please, if there is a deity out there, please let this GQ model of a man know where the clit is. If I hook up with one more man who doesn't know how to get me off, I will literally burn this shop to the ground.

During my prayer, the man's eyebrows almost hit his hairline, and I wondered what he was thinking as he pressed his lips together in thought. He was about to open them to say something right when the back door was thrown open, causing a loud bang to echo in the shop. All of us jolted at the sound, so I turned toward the back hallway just in time to see Emma storming in and throwing her bag down on the counter.

"Whoa there." I rested a hand on my hip to look at my employee. "What's with the 'tude?" Before she could sneak back into the kitchen, she turned to look at me. Her eyes were red-rimmed. Tears had already streaked down her cheeks, smudging her mascara as she glanced at me. She wiped a hand under her nose and continued into the back kitchen.

Shit.

I glanced back at my handsome stranger, whose name I didn't even have yet, and lifted my finger up at him. A silent command to wait. Then I followed Emma back into the kitchen.

"Hey, what's going on?" I asked in a softer tone. She was angrily tying her apron on, sniffling and agitated.

"Brody cheated on me."

Ugh, men.

"What an ass." I stepped up and threw my arms around her shoulders. She didn't finish tying her apron. She gave up entirely as soon as I wrapped her much smaller body into my own. Dysregulation wasn't a fun thing to experience. I hated that some tool would think to cheat on sweet Emma, but I wasn't surprised. His name was Brody. I'd be lying if I said I didn't see this coming a mile away.

"I'm so sorry," I murmured as I squeezed her tighter. She sniffled and managed to wrap one arm around my waist. Emma was only a couple of years younger than me, but I loved her. She started working at my shop fresh out of high school, and I considered us friends as well as colleagues.

Ten minutes passed with me consoling her, double-checking that she was able to work her shift today. I wouldn't have blamed her if she couldn't, but she insisted that she needed something to do, so she didn't focus on Brody. When I finally emerged from the kitchen, I visibly frowned when I saw that my mystery man and his not-date had disappeared.

"They left?" I asked Shane, who was back to reading his paperback.

He nodded, not bothering to look up from the pages. His dark brows pinched in thought as he read.

I groaned. "Dammit, I was *confident* he was going to ask for my number this time." Emma, still with excellent timing, emerged from the kitchen right as I said that. Her wide eyes and pouty lip were hurting my heart.

"I'm so sorry," she murmured.

I shook my head and pointed at her. "Don't you dare. It's fine. If he's interested, he'll be back."

She sniffled. "Are you sure? I feel so bad—" I shook my head and gave her another side hug and squeeze, before continuing on with our workday.

God, I hoped he'd be back.

CHAPTER 11

Karaoke night at the Sun Bean was a couple of nights later.

Perks of owning a coffee shop included doing whatever the hell I wanted, which meant that I could go out of my way to host community events in the space. As someone who often felt desperate to find things to do as a teenager, unsure of when the system would ship me to a new family to live with, I attempted to give back to my community. To provide relatively safe opportunities for teens and young adults that Audrey and I had learned to seek out ourselves when we were younger.

The night itself was free, which was worth it when people bought drinks. I think the live-band karaoke was what brought the crowd, though.

A college student just finished his performance of some old school rock song that, frankly, he killed at. When the drummer for the night hopped off the small stage and ran over to the counter, I already had a bottle of water waiting for him.

"How's it going, Kyle?" I asked him.

He used both of his hands to push his sweat-slicked hair back. The sweat made the blue he dyed it shinier.

"That kid has some pipes," Kyle breathed. The crowd was young enough that no one had recognized him or his husband yet. No one here knew that they were currently singing karaoke with two members of the world-famous rock band, *Carbon Cut.* "I'm so glad I made Tom get a babysitter."

I smiled. "Enjoying child-free time?"

"We always *miss* them." Kyle gave me a warm smile before snagging an extra water bottle for his husband, who was tuning his bass. "But we enjoy pretending we're still relevant, too."

"Can't waste a good babysitter."

"I noticed you and Aud haven't gotten up there yet." Kyle winked at me, and I smiled at him. Audrey and I loved karaoke, but I wasn't sure she was as musically motivated lately, considering, well, her possibly being the Chosen One to unite realms and all that. I, however, have often found myself on my composition software, desperate to flesh out the melody I only seemed to hear in Hyvenmere.

"If she shows up, we will."

"Even if she doesn't!" Kyle threw his arms out wide, each one holding a water bottle, as he walked backward toward the stage. I crossed my fingers at him before I turned back toward the counter, ready to take the next customer's order, when my breath caught in my throat.

"Hi," I breathed out.

"Did I startle you?" My handsome stranger smiled at me. His gaze left where Kyle retreated and landed on me. He wasn't wearing sunglasses this time. Instead, his dark eyes landed on me directly, and something pulsed in my veins from the direct attention. Freshly shaven. His shoulder-length dark hair was styled perfectly, and he wore a simple white t-shirt and dark-wash jeans. Not a wrinkle in sight.

After I studied his face, he quirked a dark eyebrow at my silence.

I cleared my throat, remembering to respond, "Nope. Just—"

I waved my hands around the chaos happening at the shop. "It's busy."

"It is." He glanced around the space, as if just realizing he was one wrong step away from bumping into other patrons. "I should order before you're out of supplies."

I grinned. "Your usual?"

He bit his lip in thought as his eyes flicked over the updated menu.

"Perhaps something stronger?" he asked, and even with all the noise, I could pick up on the flirtatious tone in his voice. It made my chest heat with excitement.

"*Perhaps*," I repeated. It was my turn to quirk an eyebrow at him. "So formal." He gave me a quizzical look, as if my words threw him off. I was teasing, but he seemed genuinely worried that he had slipped up somehow.

"Well, I'm not serving alcohol tonight, because of the minors present." I nodded to a group of high schoolers, singing the lyrics to the latest pop song. "But, lucky for you..." I waved Emma over to take over my spot. "...I know the owner." My handsome stranger grinned, following me around the counter as I took off my apron and hung it up, "Emma, you're in charge!" I told her.

She gave me a thumbs up and a wink, smiling brightly at the sight of me leading him back toward my office.

"This way," I called over my shoulder, strolling with my head held high down the narrow hallway. I pulled the keys out of my pocket, glancing behind me to see that he had followed me but was staying a respectable distance away. He glanced up to make eye contact with me, his smile warming up a bit more now that we were away from the noise.

He blinked, and I noticed something.

"Do you wear contacts?" I asked as I unlocked the door. I could see the faint line against the white of his eyes.

His smile fell for a second before he casually replied, "Yeah."

"Are your sunglasses prescription lenses too?" I followed up while holding the door open for him.

My handsome stranger cleared his throat and nodded. "Yes."

"Ah." I walked over to the other side of my desk, pulling out a box of some Swedish vodka I kept back here for special occasions. Or if I wanted to get fucked on my desk. Either or. I pulled out a glass bottle and two whiskey glasses.

"I don't have anything to mix it with, but I could find something out there if you'd like?"

"No, no." He shook his head and took a glass, holding it out for me to pour. "This is great."

"Great." I poured him two fingers, feeling generous with the good stuff. "I have a rule, though, before you drink." I poured myself two fingers as he held his glass in his large hand. His fingers practically wrapped around the entire thing. He waited patiently for me to elaborate.

"What is your rule?"

"You have to tell me your name." I leaned against my desk, my glass in my hands, crossing one arm over myself. "I've been referring to you as my handsome stranger in my head this whole time, and I just don't think I can moan that well enough."

His lips parted. Heat ignited in his gaze as he studied me. Something about watching a man sharply inhale, watching his chest expand as my words sank in for him, gave me a thrill.

He stepped toward me, and I clenched my thighs together in anticipation. Instead of crowding my space like I expected him to, he leaned against my desk beside me, his lips twitching with humor at my obvious disappointment. I leaned back to watch how his firm ass pressed against the wood before sitting up straight again.

I mostly dated men shorter than me, but I wasn't against dating a man taller than me, either.

"I'm waiting," I gently sang, taking a sip of my drink in a taunt.

"Why don't you guess?" He copied my pose, crossing one of his arms over his chest while holding his drink with the other.

"Hmm." I studied him. "Blake?"

He frowned, shaking his head. The way he considered it for a moment threw me, but I ignored that as I took another sip of the vodka and tried again.

"Jackson?"

"No." He chuckled.

"Jake?"

He shook his head.

"John?"

"Do all your options start with the letter J?" He countered with a warm chuckle. I caught a whiff of his cologne, and it was as if the smell was crafted just for me. I tensed, stopping myself from leaning into him and smelling it more.

"Should I start from the top of the alphabet?" I giggled. "Aiden? Alex? Andrew?"

"Yes." He jerked his head up, a devilish smile tugging at his lips as he finally took a sip of his drink. I watched his throat bob with a swallow, and suddenly, my mouth lost all its moisture.

"Which one? Andrew?"

"Yes," he confirmed as he took another sip. "Andrew."

"Huh..." I tilted my head. It didn't feel right, but I couldn't exactly place why. It wasn't as if I had a specific image of what an Andrew looked like. If he said his name was Chad, I'd ask where his blonde hair and polo shirt with the popped collar were.

"...Andrew..." I said it again, shaking my head once. "Does anyone call you Drew?" That sounded better. I still couldn't explain why. But it did.

His dark brows furrowed, emotion flickering across his face too quickly for me to clock it. "Yes."

I grinned. "Can I call you Drew?" He gave me a silent nod of consent. "So, Drew," I bit my lip. "...Do you even care to know my name?"

"Vanessa," he replied without hesitation. Which made alarm bells go off in the back of my mind.

"How do you know it already?" I questioned. He stared at me, the corner of his lips turning up a slight degree before he replied, "It's stitched onto your apron."

Oh. Oh, duh.

"Well, Van is stitched. Not Vanessa."

"What else could Van be short for?" Drew challenged.

"Van...nerism?"

He scoffed, shaking his head at my silly suggestion.

"Okay, Van would obviously be short for Vanessa. Good guess."

He lifted his glass toward me in a silent thanks before studying the rest of my office. I followed his gaze with mine, noticing how he was looking at all the little trinkets and things. All the same things Hush studied and fiddled with when she was here last time.

Something fluttered in my stomach, unease of some kind. I liked this moment; it felt human. Natural. Not that Hyvenmere was unnatural, it just...wasn't totally familiar to me, yet. I would always find comfort in the familiar. Sitting in my office, having a drink with Drew, after tiptoeing around each other for a little bit...I liked it.

"So." I scooted closer to him, fiddling with my cup in my hand. Electricity skittered up my arm from the contact I initiated when our arms brushed against each other. "What brings you back tonight?"

He didn't look at me, which gave me a moment to study his profile. The straight line of his nose, the sharp lines of his jaw and neck. He looked both familiar and not. He was a fit guy; his clothing was snug against his biceps and thighs.

Eventually, without looking at me, Drew replied with a low tone, "I guess I'm not quite sure."

I quirked my lips to the side at that. "Hmm…"

What did I say to that?

I had already made that quip about moaning his name. I couldn't possibly be more forward than that. I was the one who scooted closer to him. The one who casually brushed our arms together.

But he followed me back into my office.

"You look displeased with that answer." Drew's lips smirked before throwing me a glance out of the corner of his eye.

"I feel confused, I guess. I can't tell if you're interested in me or if I'm completely misreading these signals."

He turned to face me, saying earnestly, "I am *very* interested, Vanessa."

The sound of my name on his lips made chills erupt down my spine, and goosebumps pebble on my arms. God, what was it like having this much sex appeal without having to try?

I pulled my lips back in a grin. It wasn't a sexy grin by any means, but it was a grin that usually made men drop to their knees in front of me. The way his gaze lowered to my lips, while parting his own, made me hopeful that Drew would be there soon.

"You like *that* answer," Drew murmured to my lips as he moistened his own.

"I do. I'm glad we're on the same page." I set my glass down so I could lean back on my palms, casually showing off my body. I loved a good tank top. Most of my wardrobe was tank tops at this point. My cutoff jean shorts were a little higher than usual, showcasing my toned legs.

Thank god I decided to shave this morning. Leaning back like this also popped my chest out a bit. I wasn't wearing a bra, because fuck bras.

I *felt* it when Drew's eyes lowered to my chest in appreciation. My nipples stiffened under his attention, which made him grumble something low in his throat. He leaned closer, brushing his knuckles down my arm, sending goosebumps all over my body. Noticing my physical reaction to his gentle touch, he grinned and stood up from his seat on the edge of my desk.

I frowned at his back as he strolled across the small room, studying the pictures and clutter on my shelves. He knocked back the rest of his vodka in one sip, keeping the cup in his hands.

"So..." I stood from my desk too, folding both of my arms over my chest again.

"I don't think I wish to rush things with you, Vanessa," Drew announced with a sigh as he turned to face me from the other side of the small room. "Which is a shame." He quirked his lips at that. "Because while I would deeply enjoy our carnal—"

I snorted. "Carnal?"

He raised an eyebrow at me in a challenge. "Do you not want a carnal relationship?"

"I mean," I lifted a shoulder as I elaborated. "I enjoy sex as much as any other woman. I'm not opposed to casual relationships."

Drew nodded with a grin that practically made my clothes want to burn off my body. "Are you so desperate for my touch that you can't wait for me to learn your mind as well?"

I raised my eyebrows at him as I replied, "I—I guess I'm not used to a man being interested in anything more than physical touch."

Drew frowned at that, confused. "You are not used to men showing interest in you?"

I smirked. "I never said that. Men just aren't usually interested in anything that isn't purely...*carnal*." I used his weird word back at him.

He pressed his lips together as he glared at his glass, pondering my response.

Part of me hoped that he was upset that men only seemed to be interested in me for their pleasure, but another part of me was worried that he was upset over the idea of me being sexually experienced.

"I'm thirty years old," I reminded him. "I'm not ashamed of the fact that I have needs. If a man is interested in meeting my needs, I'm going to take him up on it."

A pinch formed between his brows as he glanced up at me. "What?"

"If you're getting uncomfortable over the fact that I have a sexual history..." I crossed my arms, not in a protective stance, but in a secure one. "You need to get over it if you want to explore anything between us." The pinch in his brow smoothed, and a smirk pulled at his lips as he raised his glass to brush his thumb against his bottom lip.

Even though my underwear was getting more damp by the second, I held my ground, waiting for him to respond before I said anything more. No matter how delicious he looked casually dragging his thumb over his lower lip in thought.

"I'm not a man who gets *jealous*, Vanessa," Drew muttered. His tone sent chills down my spine. "I'm not worried about any potential competition." He smiled again as he lowered his hand, as if the idea truly amused him.

"Okay," I replied, surprised at his confidence. "So what was your weird look about?"

He chuckled to himself before setting the empty glass on the shelf. Drew shoved his hands in his pockets as he approached, a signal that things weren't about to get sexy even though I was desperate for them to.

"You may not be used to it, but I think the idea of a man trying to *earn* your affections excites you," Drew spoke with a low clarity, and his dark eyes bounced between the two of mine.

"I'm simply wondering if I have it within me to play this game without needing to satiate my own, overwhelming, need."

I scoffed and turned away, trying to shake off the way his words made something flutter in my chest. "You don't want to just get to the fun stuff?"

"Oh, I have every intention to have *fun* with you, Vanessa." From the way his gaze trailed over my body again, focusing on my legs, I believed his sensual threat. "But I also find myself wondering what drives you. I want to learn what ignites your passion. What do you enjoy?" He tucked his lips between his teeth for a brief moment as he scanned my body head to toe, making every muscle in me melt, before he continued, "I have a feeling that once my curiosity is satisfied, it will make learning how you like to be touched, and where you are most sensitive, that much more thrilling."

I studied him, unfolding my arms and resting my hands on the edge of my desk. He let me, completely at ease under my attempted scrutiny, as he stood tall and assured. As if his words didn't just send a fire throughout every vein in my body.

"...You're right," I finally admitted, attempting to control my breathing. "I'm not used to taking things slow." I gnawed on the inside of my cheek. "Though, I'm intrigued that you want to." Drew's chest puffed as he inhaled deeply. His eyes lifted to the ceiling as he blew the air out of his lungs in thought.

"Perhaps, I'm a romantic."

I snorted. "You'd be the first man I've met that is."

Minus Fergus, if my suspicion about the nereid was correct.

He chuckled at that before removing his hands from his pockets and resting his large palms on either side of me. Hands flat on the table, letting him both tower over me and engage in direct eye contact.

"I'm honored to be the first romantic you've met." Drew's eyes softened a little as he studied me, and I found myself eyeing the almost invisible line of his contacts. "Are we in agreement?"

I pressed my lips together. The way he spoke was so *formal*, I just wasn't used to it.

"Almost." I nodded once, trying to ignore the delicious masculine scent that was enveloping me with his proximity. "I have some questions." I needed to turn the tables, to not end the conversation like some simpering woman.

Drew nodded, looking way too serious about this conversation.

"Number one." I lifted a finger between us, the tip brushed against his chest. "How flirty can I be with you?"

He grinned at that. "Flirty?"

"If we aren't getting to the fun stuff, what are we doing?" I asked, trailing my finger up his chest. The divot between his firm pecks made heat scorch my cheeks. "How much touch is too much?" The next breath Drew released was a little shakier, and I got a thrill from being able to make a man like him weak kneed.

"That's acceptable," Drew whispered.

I grinned wider, trailing my finger across his collar bones, dipping my finger under the hem of his shirt briefly. "And this?"

All he did was nod.

His eyes were getting hooded, and all I had done was rest my fingertip on him.

"...This?" I asked, feeling a little bolder. I rested both of my hands on his wide shoulders, slowly dragging my palms closer to his neck. Touching his skin was electrifying; it sent a sensation down my limbs that I wasn't used to feeling. A specific type of awareness that made the hairs on my arms rise with my pebbled skin. I wanted to rub all over him, feel every part of him on every part of me. It was significantly harder to keep my cool.

"Acceptable," Drew barely whispered the word. I bit my lip, loving when his eyes lowered to the movement and stayed there. Wrapping one hand around the back of his neck, I gently pulled him closer to me. He allowed me to, closer, closer, until my lips ghosted over the skin at the base of his throat.

A low moan escaped his mouth, and I smiled against him. I wasn't kissing him, just teasing him with my lips as I gently trailed up his neck, along the sharp line of his jaw. Right when my lips started to travel toward his, he shifted away just enough to avoid a real kiss.

"That's the boundary, then," I whispered to him.

He looked ragged. The calm, cool, collected Drew was gone. Simple, gentle touches from me made him look undone. His eyes were hooded, and his eye color was too dark for me to see if his pupils were wide in the dim light of my office, but I assumed they were.

Even though he leaned away to avoid a kiss, he lifted his hands to rest them on the tops of my thighs. Engaging in contact in a different, less intimate way.

"Are—" He stopped to clear his throat, and I threw him a wide smile as he did. "Are these terms acceptable to you?"

I nodded once. "I find these terms acceptable." He didn't seem to pick up on the fact that I was teasing his formal language, or maybe he just didn't care. Drew's hands gently squeezed my thighs.

"So…" I was reluctant to say this, but I had to. "I should probably get back to work."

Drew nodded. "I shouldn't keep you, but I want to."

"That doesn't sound horrible." I placed my hands on top of his and squeezed, enjoying the feel of his touch. "But it sounds like you have to start planning fun dates and stuff to properly *court* me." I smiled at my clever formal terminology, but he didn't react to it. He just threw me a charming smirk as he stood tall and gave me space to stand as well.

"I look forward to courting you, Vanessa."

I snorted, blushing from his words, but tried to play it cool by patting his cheek and leading him out of my office. The noise from karaoke night was loud, but instead of joining everyone, Drew ducked out of my shop and into the night as I stepped behind the counter.

"You good?" Emma asked as she glanced toward where Drew had left.

I grinned at her and replied, "Really good."

There was a presence behind me as I slept in my bed that night, but I was so deep in my slumber that I couldn't come out of it. I was vaguely aware of movement. Of warmth. I wanted to startle away, but my mind was so heavy with exhaustion that I couldn't do it. The gummy I took kept me under, just like it was supposed to. It was as if there was a weighted blanket on each one of my limbs, keeping me in place.

The presence shifted, and I sighed in surprised relief when heat coated my back, my butt, and the backs of my thighs.

The presence was safe.

I allowed my mind to drift off into a deeper sleep.

CHAPTER 12

Audrey had just kicked the shit out of me, leaving me prone on my back as I struggled to catch my breath, when her messy bun came into view.

"Are you done for today?" she asked, all seriousness, barely breaking a sweat.

I choked my reply, "I think so."

"You're getting stronger and faster, Van," Liam gave me his hand as he complimented me, pulling me off the ground as Audrey handed me a water bottle. "Your one-on-one skills are definitely improving." Most of what they were teaching me was self-defense, since I never pictured myself charging anyone in Hyvenmere.

"You're helping the human train. This is good," Hush's voice echoed in the abandoned warehouse, startling me. "She'll need to be on guard the next time she sets foot in our realm."

I exchanged a concerned look with Audrey, who didn't seem as surprised to see Hush in our secret training spot as I did.

"Why is that?" Audrey asked.

"Ilia is suddenly feeling very confident about closing the Mellhawn Gates soon," Hush replied, stepping out of the shadows. She approached our little table of weaponry, perusing everything Audrey and Liam brought for me to test out. "I guess sending his son to the nereid's birthday ended up being fruitful."

Liam stiffened. "What do you mean? All he did was harass Van." He lifted a hand toward me, and I glared at the fae for reminding me of it. Hush lifted a blonde eyebrow at Liam. Again, her face and most of her body were covered, but her eyes carried enough expression in them to let me know she was lowkey disappointed in Liam.

"Do you really think the Mad Siren Prince would bother crashing the Nereid Prince's birthday celebration—for the first time in over a decade—with no other ulterior motives?" Hush asked. When she said it like that, it felt obvious that Drustan wasn't there just to fuck around. "Where do you think Caelena was while Drustan kept all the attention on him—"

"Who the hell is Caelena?" I asked, desperate to keep up.

"His date, Drustan's cousin," Audrey answered. I locked that information away and gestured toward Hush.

"Got it, proceed."

Hush gave me an annoyed look before continuing, "After Drustan and Caelena left, rumor has it that Ilia has been in talks with the nereid and fae governments, who have all suddenly been more open to bringing the issue of the Mellhawn Gates to a vote."

Liam crossed his arms and said, "Ada hasn't mentioned any of this to me."

"Which should concern you," Hush concluded. "I doubt Fergus is aware of what his parents might have been discussing with Ilia, either. Whatever Drustan and his cousin found that night, it's starting to sway the nereids' initial support of having the gates open. Rumors throughout Ilia's guard on what to do once they have everyone's vote secure are already being spread to my unit."

"*Shit.*" Audrey scraped her hands down her neck as she began to pace. "Shit. Shit. Shit. What could Ilia possibly have on the nereids and fae to feel this confident?"

"That, I haven't been able to figure out quite yet." Hush's brows pinched together, "Though, based on the rumors I'm hearing, I'm positive that there is a text involved."

"Like a book?" I asked.

"More like a journal," Hush replied, trailing her finger along one of the swords on the table. "Is there anything of significance like that in the fae territory?" she asked Liam.

His expression pinched as he thought. "I mean, yes. There are lots of historical and precious texts in the Dahl family archives. As I'm sure the Shaws and the Ahlstroms have in their territories."

Hush hummed in thought. "We need to find out what Ilia has."

"You can't do that for us?" I asked Hush. "I mean, you're literally part of Ilia's guard."

"Yes, but to maintain my cover of complete loyalty to the old male," Hush spat with irritation. "I must continue to run his errands and serve in my unit as expected. My time is not entirely my own, regardless of my proximity."

"What if *we* go snooping?" Audrey asked, her hazel eyes on the ground. All three of us stared at her in confusion.

I pointed to myself, just to make my question clear as I asked, "We, as in, you want *us* to go to the siren territory?"

"We can't let Ilia pressure the fae and nereid governments to close the gates." Audrey was shaking her head, and I caught an undercurrent of panic in her voice. "I haven't even found my actual family, yet. We need more time. The knowledge of me defeating the solvyrn is probably just lighting a fire under Ilia to close the gates for good." Audrey stopped pacing and looked at Liam and me. "We could go, maybe cause a distraction, and hopefully one of us could look around and see if we can find whatever Ilia has on everyone else."

"Your presence in Lydhavn will be a spectacle," Hush said. "I doubt you will be able to snoop sufficiently."

"My presence will always be a spectacle," Audrey said, flitting her gaze over to me. "But *both* of us would be even more so." I immediately picked up on her train of thought.

"I'm sorry." I lifted a palm at her. "Are you about to suggest using me as bait, with you, so someone else could look around?"

"Yes." Audrey blinked at me before turning to Liam. "Perhaps you could sneak away while Van and I create a distraction."

"Just existing in the Shaw estate will be a distraction enough, I'm sure," Hush scoffed as she studied me behind her facial coverings.

"When we were teens…Caelena had an interest in me." Liam scrubbed his jaw in thought. "Perhaps I could fuel that again and use it to get her to show me around. Sneak me off, maybe even persuade her to share what she knows if I act like I'm on her side."

Hush's eyebrows jumped at his suggestion. "That's not an entirely bad idea, fae. No one takes the Shaw cousin that seriously." She waved a dismissive hand in the air. "She's a pretty face who often flies under the radar. I doubt Ilia would be worried about her pulling you into a dark corner."

Audrey's hands were balled into fists, and her mouth was in a firm line, as if she was clenching her jaw.

"When do we do this?" Audrey asked through clenched teeth. All three of us gave her confused looks, but I assumed I was the only one who picked up on how much she absolutely loathed the idea of Liam getting close and personal with another woman. Even if it was for the greater good.

"Bandthral is in a week. Very few outsiders join, but it would make sense for the halfling who wants to step into the role of the Chosen One destined to unite the realms to make an appearance, in an attempt to make peace with Ilia—not that he'd ever consider it."

"What is Bandthral?" I asked.

"Our seasonal mating ritual," Hush replied.

My brain immediately translated that to an orgy. I had way too many questions floating to the front of my brain; I didn't even know where to start. Instead of pressing for every single detail I could gain from Hush about a "mating ritual," I decided to let it pass, because I seemed to be the only one in the warehouse spiraling about those particular words.

"I may or may not be stationed during the ritual," Hush added, "However, we obviously cannot act like we know each other if we are in the same room. I will be Ilia's loyal pet, and you will have never heard of me. The next time we communicate will have to be after you visit the Shaw estate."

"Understood," Audrey confirmed. "Thank you for helping us."

Hush shook her head before walking backward toward the warehouse exit, "I'm not just doing this for you. This is for the good of all Hyvenmerians."

"Of course," Audrey replied. "Regardless, your help is appreciated."

"I know." With that, Hush disappeared into the shadows.

"He's been texting you?" Audrey asked me later that evening.

Liam was here again. He had just popped popcorn and brought us each our own bowls and plopped his massive body on the floor. Audrey and I each took an end of our couch, and Liam sat with his back against Audrey's side.

I got why he felt the need to be so present, to keep us both safe, but it also annoyed the hell out of me.

"He has," I replied, focusing back on our conversation.

Drew didn't have his phone on him when we chatted in my office, and part of me wondered if I was getting ready to be *courted* by some annoying hipster who turned his nose up at normal things, like always having a phone on your person.

However, I had given him my number on a scrap of paper before we left my office, and he said he'd call.

I hoped he *wouldn't* call. I hoped that he would send a text like a normal person. Thankfully, two days later, I got my first text from him.

> Drew: Vanessa?

> Me: You got her.

> Drew: Hmm, not quite yet, but I will.

> Me: You seem very confident about that.

> Drew: I still think about the way your entire body flushed during our conversation in your office, so yes, I am feeling very confident about that.

And that was the point that I whipped out the vibrator before replying. We'd texted only a couple of times since. Thankfully, though, our first date was going to involve dancing, and I was very excited to show him one of my favorite pastimes this weekend.

"He is very familiar with texting women," I added, after eating a bite of popcorn. "I get the feeling that he's dated a lot, because his intensity can be panty-melting." I tilted my head in thought, ignoring the sitcom we were watching. Liam, though he tried to act like he didn't, was very enthralled with the plot of

Gilmore Girls. I guess they didn't have human programs in his realm, and he was fascinated by human culture from a few decades ago.

"Intense, huh?" Audrey smiled at me, sitting cross-legged in her seat on the couch. "You haven't dated anyone like that before. That's kind of fun."

"Yeah." I smiled, then frowned. "I'm going to wear out the batteries in my vibrator, though." Audrey laughed while Liam gave me an annoyed frown. "You still don't have to be here," I reminded him. "This is our house. Don't you have some castle to count your gold coins in or something?" Liam sighed, then shoved an insane handful of popcorn into his mouth as he focused on his favorite show.

"My family isn't *that* wealthy."

"If your sister is queen, I'm sure you are."

Liam frowned but didn't fight me on it.

"Are you ready to go to Hyvenmere again?" Audrey ignored our bickering and kicked me with her foot. "We're going to Lydhavn on Sunday."

I raised an eyebrow and asked, "Where is that, again?"

"Lydhavn is the capital of Lyndoruun, where Ilia's court is," Liam explained.

"It's this Sunday, right?" It was the day after my date with Drew. I knew I wasn't going to get lucky with him yet, so it wasn't like there was a benefit to having the condo to myself the next day.

"Yes. That's when Bandthral is happening," Audrey explained, before I could ask.

I grimaced. "Speaking of Bandthral, Hush referring to it as a 'mating ritual' was very odd to hear."

"Why?" Liam asked.

I opened my mouth to explain how barbaric it sounded, but then realized that might be offensive, so instead I decided to say, "It just sounds so sexual."

"That's because it is." Audrey explained. "Sex isn't nearly as stigmatized in Hyvenmere as it is in our realm."

"It sounds *so* much better over there," I murmured. "Minus the problem with siren women and children disappearing. And that Ilia is being a huge dick." Liam snorted while Audrey shook her head at my over-simplified words. "So is this orgy strictly between mated Hyvenmerians, or is this just kind of a come one, come all, free-for-all situation?"

Liam gave me a confused look while Audrey choked on her bite of popcorn.

"That's not—oh my god." Audrey chuckled a little as she cleared her throat. "No. Bandthral is what sirens do to try to *find* their mates. Each territory has its own version of this every season."

"Oh." I blinked at her, then turned to Liam. "So you have a Bandthral, too?"

"In a way, though it's more of a formality. We've seen some success with fae finding their mates the last couple of years, though."

I tilted my head at Liam in thought. "How do Hyvenmerians find their mate? I'm getting the impression that it's a little bit more than just basic sexual attraction."

"For my people, the fae, it's a core feeling. My parents knew they were destined to be together because they could feel a connection between each other's heartbeats," Liam replied.

I widened my eyes. "How did they discover that?"

"My father felt my mother's heartbeat in the market. He was selling his leather work, and she was asking the people questions about what they needed from her." I gave Liam a funny look before Audrey chimed in.

"His mother was queen."

"Got it, proceed." I nodded.

"My father described it as an overwhelming feeling. Like a rope was wrapped around his heart, tugging him in the direction of hers, putting their heartbeats in sync. She felt it too, but she was busy conversing with her people. She didn't want to be rude, but she could feel him getting closer and closer. Finally, my father made his way through the crowd of people and found her." Liam's smile was warm, the smile of a child who grew up with loving parents, who probably shared their story with him multiple times.

Must be nice.

"Then what happened?" I pressed.

"I mean, everyone around them kind of realized what was happening. The crowd made room for her to approach my father, who was sweating after realizing that the queen herself was, well, *his*." He chuckled. "The first thing he tried to do was bow and be respectful. Even though he could feel deep in his bones that he was meant for her, my mother had a very calm poker face. He couldn't tell if she was feeling the same way. It wasn't until she studied him, up and down, that she finally addressed him. All she said was, 'Come with me.'"

"Damn." I started snapping my fingers. "I respect a woman with a no-nonsense attitude."

"I wish I could meet her." Audrey sighed.

"I wish you could, too." Liam's face fell, mourning his parents' horrible loss. "Anyway, she moved him into her residence. They spent a couple of weeks getting to know each other."

"Biblically." Audrey grinned. He grimaced, the face of a child who had no desire to picture their parents being intimate like that.

"Doing whatever they did." Liam gave Audrey a look. "And the rest is history."

"And then you and your sister were born." Audrey sighed, reaching over and pinching his cheek. He let Audrey tease him until she pulled back.

"My twin and I were miracles, considering the fertility issue being present at the time," Liam finished. "But all that to say, a mating bond is a very deep connection, and it's a tragedy when the bond is unexpectedly broken. When one mate dies an unnatural death, the other struggles to regulate and recover from the trauma. Some...never do. But assuming no tragic events occur, it's a wonderful bond to experience with someone. My parents could feel where the other was within a certain amount of space. They could always sense how the other was feeling, based on the beat of their hearts."

"That's insane," I whispered. "Imagine being able to feel someone else's heartbeat."

"We can hear someone else's heartbeat, though," Audrey replied. "As you know, Hyvenmerian's all have excellent hearing, so hearing heartbeats isn't that odd an experience. My hearing isn't as good as Liam's, but yeah, I can hear your heartbeat right now."

I widened my eyes at her. "What the hell?"

"I know." Audrey snickered. "But the difference Liam is saying is that there's hearing a heartbeat and *feeling* someone else's."

"It's almost as if your heart is irrevocably connected to another's."

I tilted my head. "Do you have someone you share that with, Liam?"

He wasn't moving, but he visibly tensed in his seat before turning to give me a dry look, "I haven't mated with someone like that yet, no."

"It's just..." I paused to shrug. "You sound like someone who has experienced it."

Liam frowned before turning back toward the TV and saying, "My parents spent a lot of time telling us about it growing up."

I nodded, not believing him at all, but not wanting to push it either.

"How do the other creatures form bonds?" I asked instead.

Audrey grinned. "Fergus's father is one of the Kings of the Nereids, and he has formed two. According to him, he and his mates touched the same body of water at the same time. The waves made from their feet felt like a direct touch between the three of them. So now there are two Kings and a Queen of the Nereids."

"Fascinating." I sat up and tucked my knees to my chest, wrapping my arms around them. "So the mermaids needed the water to know who they were compatible with?"

"A lot of it is still pheromones, though the people of Hyvenmere have a different chemical and biological makeup than humans. I assume that because part of their biology is so connected to the water, it makes sense for the water to also assist in helping them find their partners."

"How do sirens discover their mates, then?" I pressed, my curiosity taking me by storm.

Liam shrugged, and Audrey's expression became thoughtful, "We aren't quite sure. Sirens are private about those things."

I hummed, "Which would add to Ilia's overall anxiety about humans and halflings just trampling into Hyvenmere."

Audrey quirked her eyebrow and replied in a deadpan tone, "Yeah. That's what I do. I trample through the Mellhawn Gates."

I snickered at her, visualizing her doing just that.

Liam gave us a confused look before turning back to his TV show.

"Maybe we'll find out how sirens find their mates on Sunday," I added.

"Hopefully, we find out what Ilia is up to first," Liam retorted. I crossed my eyes at him even though he couldn't see, which earned me a gentle kick from Audrey from her end of the couch.

I loved the familiarity of the moment. Watching TV on the couch, shooting the shit with my best friend of fifteen years, looking forward to my date with a man who could probably get me off with nothing more than a firm hug.

And then after I soaked in the normalcy of my human dating life, I was going to travel with my best friend to a secret magical realm where we'd snoop through, what I assumed to be, another castle.

This was our life now, and as insane as it was when I let myself dwell on it too long, I was just grateful to have Audrey back.

CHAPTER 13

I wanted to bite Drew's ass, but I resisted.

Only because of our fun little boundaries and stuff.

"You made it." I pushed off the brick exterior wall I was waiting by, appreciating how his eyes were already admiring the skimpy little black dress I wore for the occasion.

I wanted him to understand *exactly* what he was missing out on by choosing to edge me instead. While I was fine with him waiting to be physical, this felt more like a game of chicken. Who could go the longest without giving in to what we both obviously wanted?

"My, my." As he approached, he leaned in to press his lips to my cheek. He was only a little taller than me, but still, I couldn't deny the thrill in my chest from the visual of him standing tall next to me. Making me tilt my gaze up *just* enough.

"Wow." I crossed my arms and took in his outfit. More slacks and a cream button-up shirt with the sleeves rolled to his elbows. "You look so good every time I see you."

He didn't respond with a thank you. Instead, he groaned and said, "How dare you look so tempting." His brown gaze briefly dipped to my cleavage, amplified by my crossed arms.

Got him.

"I'm glad you're going to suffer a little tonight." I grinned as I took his hand in mine, "Let's see how well you move."

Drew grinned at me and squeezed my hand as I pulled him into the club.

Dancing was my favorite form of exercise. It was a talent my foster mother helped me nourish during the remaining year of high school that Audrey and I shared with her. She helped me get on the dance team and determine which groups and clubs outside of school were worth my time. She helped me study choreography and gave me the support and space I needed when I wanted to practice. The garage of her home transformed into a makeshift dance studio, and I had always been grateful to her for helping me learn to dance with confidence.

This club, however, was a little different.

"You made it!" Trey smiled as I pulled Drew onto the main floor, where everyone was already gathered. The walls were lined with red velvet and gold, giving the space an old-timey feel.

"Yes, and I brought a date." I gestured toward Drew. "Drew, this is Trey, the head of the company." Drew held his hand out and gently shook Trey's hand. When Drew squeezed, Trey winced a little and pulled his hand free.

"Pleasure," Drew greeted him.

God, he was so formal all the time.

"Can I admit something?" Trey smiled up at Drew with a conspiratorial look. "I'm hoping you're a horrible dancer and that Van will take me back." Trey winked at me as Drew smiled politely at him. The blond-haired man was only five seven, a few inches shorter than me. He was also an excellent dance partner. We usually had a lot of fun on improv nights like this one. But Trey knew I was testing a guy out; seeing if he could pass a vibe check. Could Drew have fun? Was he able to keep up with me, even if dancing wasn't his strong suit?

How would he feel with the peer pressure to perform on the spot?

Would he get upset if he messed up, or would he go with the flow?

"She won't," Drew replied, and while I usually didn't love the domineering assholes, something about his confidence sent a thrill through me.

Trey grinned at me before clapping his hands and announcing the start of improv night. Drew smirked at me, and the flutter in my chest from his handsome grin made me practically bounce on the balls of my feet.

"I'll lead," I told Drew when I pulled him out onto the floor.

"If you must," he replied, tightening his hold on my hand. The music started, and it was a popular radio hit. It wasn't one specific genre, but a mix of a few; the main genre the song built on was Latin. Guiding Drew's hand to my waist and the other to my palm, I locked eyes with him.

"Ready?" I asked him. Instead of voicing a response, he tightened his hold and pulled me flush against his hard body. The move flustered me. I could feel the heat of him against my entire front, but I leaned into it. My body came alive from the contact, even with our clothes protecting us. I narrowed my eyes at him, and his eyes flared in response, as if he knew exactly how my body reacted to him.

Without another word, I led him into a dance. And the man could dance. He followed my lead but took over when he wanted to experiment with a move. He was showing off, and the two of us earned several cheers and claps from Trey and other regulars. Our dancing slowly became a competition of sorts, because when I turned around to gently roll my hips against his, he would respond by dragging his large, warm hands up and down my waist, across my pelvis, lighting me up from the inside out.

He had a hard-on for most of the night, but it stayed hidden because our bodies were practically glued together for two hours straight. Whenever I started to feel like I was getting the upper hand, listening to his breath catch and feeling his heart rapidly race in his chest, he would throw me off by pulling me close and whispering unexpected Get-To-Know-You questions in my ear.

"How do you like your coffee?" was the first question he murmured against me, making me laugh a little at how casual his questions were versus how sensual our dancing was.

"As long as it's in my mouth, I'm a happy woman," I replied just below his earlobe. He would groan, and we'd dance, and then he'd try to distract me again.

"What color brings you the most joy?" It was an odd way to ask what my favorite color was. What was even more odd was the visual my brain conjured up of golden eyes paired with dark, blood red hair.

"Y-Yellow," I stuttered out. Drew pressed me against his erection again, allowing me to roll my ass against him once, twice, before he adjusted our bodies and kept talking.

"Mine is green," he murmured against me. *Like my eyes*, I thought. "What is your favorite instrument to play?"

"Drums, I—" I turned around to lift a brow at him. "Why do you assume I know how to play more than one?" He smirked, pulling me back against his body again.

"You come alive under music, Vanessa." He trailed his finger down my jaw. "Any man with eyes can see that, and assume your skillset is vast." I tucked my lips between my teeth, fighting a full-body blush.

"I see." The conversation stalled for a little bit, the songs changing, our dancing styles adjusting, but throughout it all, Drew kept up with me. He wasn't panting from exhaustion; he was just meeting me exactly where I was. Trey gave me several eyebrow wiggles from across the room, clearly impressed with Drew's moves.

I was on cloud nine. Dancing with a handsome, fit man who

was confident and made me feel like a *woman*. Whose touch made my skin sizzle in the best way. Someone who liked the idea of making whatever was happening between us last, instead of a "fuck and release." Perhaps he was just stringing me along, and I realized in that moment that I would be okay with that. That whatever time I got to spend with Drew would be worth it, because I couldn't remember the last time that I was *this* excited about a man. When I had this much fun with a man.

I even answered his random questions.

"Favorite flower?"

"Am I boring if I say all of them?"

"Do you like spending time in nature?"

"As long as some form of plumbing is available, yes."

"Do you prefer sweet or savory desserts?"

"Both—but mostly sweet."

"Do you love that you're making me have to hide my arousal behind your perfect ass?"

"I do. I really do."

"You've been smiling and humming all morning," Audrey noted around a mouthful of cereal. I grinned at her and swung my hips side to side, happily recalling my date the night before.

"I'm crushing so hard, you have no idea," I proudly admitted. I turned around to sit at the folding table with her, my freshly brewed coffee accompanying me. I took a deep and satisfying pull of the drink before setting the mug down and grinning.

I even went as far as to cup my hands on my cheeks and give a little squeal.

"Oh my god. I've never seen you act like this over a man." Audrey placed a hand on her heart.

"I know." I flattened my hands and rested them under my chin. "But he's perfect."

"Tell me everything," Audrey ordered as she shoved another spoonful of cereal in her mouth.

"Well, first, he's an *excellent* dancer." As I spoke, I started listing things off on my fingers. "He totally matched my energy during the improv. When I went goofy, so did he. When I tried to throw him off, he seemed to anticipate it and adjusted. When I went sensual and seductive, he was right behind me." I winked at her after that, which made her cackle.

"I love when men can have fun without feeling self-conscious," Audrey added.

"That's exactly it!" I said, remembering his laugh as I pulled out the sprinkler move near the end of the night. "He and I just had so much fun. It's been so long since, I don't know, I just had *fun* with someone."

Audrey's smile faltered at that, but before I could question her about it, she recovered and asked, "And you still aren't even kissing?"

"No." I frowned, but then I couldn't help myself, and a grin spread across my cheeks again. "Not on the mouth, at least." Audrey choked on her cereal and pounded her chest with her fist.

I laughed at her until she recovered and asked, "Where did he kiss you?" Her hazel eyes glanced down, where my legs rested under the table.

"I *wish*," I groaned. "When he walked me to my building, he kissed my knuckles—" which reminded me a lot of Fergus, but I was quickly learning how into hand kisses I was, "Then, he turned my hand over and kissed the inside of my wrist." I held my wrist up, as if I could show her the evidence of his warm lips there, but I didn't have any, just the memory of it. The way my pulse spiked as soon as he brushed his lips against my skin. "Then he kissed me right here." I tapped the spot on my neck just below my ear. The spot that sent shivers down my body, making me melt into him.

How I had to hold back a whimper when he pulled away with a soft look in his eyes, as if he didn't want to go either.

"Then," I continued. "He wished me goodnight and left."

"Oh, he's *good*," Audrey wiggled her eyebrows with her words. "He left you wanting more."

"I know," I pouted. "He's playing me like a fiddle. If you hear an increase in buzzing noises coming from my bedroom, you know why." Audrey laughed before she lifted her cereal bowl to drink the remaining dregs of milk.

"Are you going to see him again?" she asked as she stood to put her bowl in the sink.

"Oh yeah, he—" I stopped talking when my phone vibrated on the tabletop. Displayed on the screen was a text from him. "Please hold." I snatched my phone off the table to open his text.

"I love this so much," Audrey giggled from the sink.

Drew: I hope you slept well, Vanessa.

"Aww." I lifted my phone to show Audrey. "He hopes I slept well."

"Stop it." Audrey groaned dramatically and plopped herself in her chair again. She rested her chin on my shoulder as I rattled off my response.

Me: I hope you didn't.

Audrey snickered when three dots kept appearing and disappearing. Finally, his message came through.

Drew: Can I ask why?

Me: I hope you slept just as badly as I did.

His three dots danced on and off again, and I held back an evil laugh at the sight as I thumbed my next message before he could come up with a response.

Me: I hope you tossed and turned all night, just like me. Aching, unsatisfied. Thinking of you. Wishing your hands were on me. Remembering the feel of your lips on my skin.

"Why are you so good at this?" Audrey murmured. "I need to remember how to flirt via text."

"I'll give you some pointers next time Liam texts you." I turned to look at her while we waited for Drew to respond. She blushed and rolled her eyes, ignoring my prying comment. Then my cell vibrated in my hands.

"Oh, what did Mr. Proper say?" Audrey tapped her fingertips together in anticipation.

Drew: I don't think you comprehend the anguish I felt leaving you last night. I had to grasp an immeasurable amount of self-control, just so that I didn't knock on your door, invite myself in, and drag you to your bed. The hunger I feel for you is all-consuming. Does that paint an adequate picture of how I slept last night, Vanessa?

"Jesus Christ," Audrey wheezed. When I looked at her, her cheeks were flushed red just like mine were. "Talk about matching energy."

"No, I think actually he won this round." I tugged at the collar of my shirt and fanned myself, trying to control my racing heart. His text got me so heated, I was worried I'd start sweating right here and now.

"What are you going to say back?" Audrey asked.

"Crap, I have to think." I rubbed the side of my neck, staring at his words on the screen, "I'm genuinely so horned up right now." I was squeezing my legs together and everything.

Audrey hummed, then looked down at her own phone with a grin.

"What? Did Liam text you?" I asked her.

"Yeah." She pocketed the phone and stood from her chair. "He's just making sure we're ready. We're not sailing into Hyvenmere this time.

"Oh shit." I stood up, too. "How are we going?"

"We're lyskifting," Audrey replied, but then stopped to give me a funny look. "You haven't done that yet, have you?" I gave her a look of disbelief.

"No. Believe it or not, I haven't teleported yet."

"I meant to ask, *we* haven't lyskifted with you yet?" Audrey chuckled to herself. "It's a lot faster than sailing. This way, if things go south at Bandthral, we can escape without having to leave your boat in Hyvenmere."

I quirked my lips to the side in thought. Made sense, though I couldn't deny that the thought of me teleporting intimidated me.

Audrey stared at me again, a new kind of hopefulness in her expression. "I know you and I haven't had a lot of *fun* together recently." Ah, that's what her previous look was for. "But I love sharing this with you. Not hiding anything. Not having any more secrets. It almost feels like we're us again."

I grinned. "That's all I want. And if that means teleporting with you to snoop through magical castles in magical realms, then I'll take it. My boat has probably got more mileage on it in the last few weeks than it has in years, anyway."

Audrey bit her bottom lip, a look of guilt passing over her expression. "Van?"

"Yeah?" I turned to grab my jacket off the back of our couch.

"You know you don't actually have a distant aunt that died and left you an inheritance, right?"

I froze. "What?"

"That was Liam." Audrey grimaced when she saw whatever expression I was making. "I told him I wanted you to be protected from all of this. How you and I didn't have much. And he, well…bought some old woman's estate. He managed to beef up the accounts, too. That way, if anything happened to me, you'd be set."

"Audrey." I gaped at her, thoroughly astonished. "You're telling me I bought the Sun Bean and own a boat because of Liam's wealth?"

Audrey tugged on the hem of her shirt as she shrank away from me. "Yeah…"

I let her sit in the silence for several moments. The discomfort from this revelation settled over her like a weighted cloak, drawing her shoulders up higher and higher the longer I let her absorb this. The thought of all my success being because Liam decided to throw his wealth at me, even when I wasn't aware of his world or true existence, made my pride take a hit. But, he was also spending half his nights here in our apartment, sleeping in Audrey's bed platonically, helping us stay safe even though Ilia's men haven't come searching for me again.

"Well." I lifted a shoulder. "Whatever."

Audrey blinked. "Whatever?"

"Yeah, whatever. I guess I'm okay with taking handouts from the one percent."

Audrey's eyes widened with amusement, and an unsure laugh erupted from her lips.

"You consider Liam the one percent?"

"He was able to dump money into our accounts and gift me a boat just like that." I emphasized my words with a snap of my fingers.

"Okay, the boat was never meant to be a significant part of

this. I'm still genuinely surprised I convinced you to keep it. But anyway, Liam's part of an entirely different socio-economic structure—"

"He's still basically a millionaire—hell, maybe even a billionaire. So, yeah…" I waved her off. "I'm not upset that Liam provided me with financial security. It's the least he could do after kidnapping you and making our friendship weird for two years, honestly."

"You know what?" Audrey furrowed her red brows and stood straight. "Hell yeah. It *was* the least he could do."

"Now we're talking." I gave her finger guns with my words, as I walked backward down the hallway. "What time does Liam want to meet?"

"An hour."

"I'll be ready!" I closed myself in my bedroom, pulling my phone out of my pocket to read Drew's text again. And again. And again. Goddamn, I was becoming completely smitten with this man. Finally, I took a moment to type a response because leaving him on read after that masterpiece of a text would be diabolical.

I shrugged out of my jacket, ripping off the t-shirt I threw on to have coffee with Audrey this morning, and jumped into my bed. I wore a thin-strap silky sleep shirt, fanned my hair out on my pillows, and lifted my phone up in the air.

The key was to leave out the bottom half of my body, which was donned in sweatpants with holes in the crotch. Instead, I cropped the photo so Drew could still get a peek at my exposed stomach and the way my breasts fell under the silk top.

I even bit my lip, like a cherry on top. Then I sent him the selfie, along with:

> Me: Next time, leave your self-control at my door.

CHAPTER 14

After emptying my breakfast into the grass, I rolled over and tried to catch my breath.

"I'm so sorry." Audrey had been holding my hair out of my face, rubbing my back as I vomited seconds after touching ground again. "I didn't realize Liam lyskifting us would make you this sick."

Liam chuckled off to the side.

My eyes were closed, I was flat on my back, but I still managed to lift a hand to flip him off again. I just knew deep in my bones that the asshole took off without proper warning on purpose. One moment, we were standing in our little condo, letting Liam grasp each of our hands. The next, the world spun, and I was thrown on the grass in Hyvenmere.

"Give me a minute," I breathed. Audrey pressed my water bottle to my lips, so I took a few sips and wiped the back of my sweaty forehead with my hand. I recovered relatively quickly, which was a relief. I'd be completely useless to Audrey and Liam, and our sneaky plan, if I were queasy and dizzy.

"Feeling better?" Audrey asked. I opened my eyes and

glanced up at the sky. The air tasted different here. Fuller. Fresher.

Each lungful helped bring me back to earth. When I sat up, we were on a hill that gave us a clearer view of the distant Fjellenheim Mountains.

"That's where we're going." Audrey stood tall and stared at the landscape. "We're standing in Lyndoruun, the sirens' territory. Your grant has already alerted Queen Ada that you're in Hyvenmere, though. If you get nervous or feel like someone is trying to take you, take comfort in that."

I rested my hands on my hips. "Are we teleporting to the orgy?"

Liam shook his head, ignoring my bait by calling these things the wrong names. "If danger arises and I need to lyskift out, I want my energy to do so. So, to get to Lydhavn, we're going to take the train. It'll be about an hour's travel. If we don't need to lyskift back, we can take the train back too, and you won't vomit all over us."

I grinned and said, "I love the train." Liam's lips twitched, but he held his smile in until he saw Audrey stand beside us, ready to depart.

"Me, too." Audrey grinned, but it felt forced. She was nervous, which made me feel anxious as well. We were walking into a court with a suspiciously dangerous king and a murderous prince. A murderous prince who could read minds. Who could reveal our plan. We chatted a lot in our apartment about the importance of not dwelling on the plan. Of changing our train of thought if Drustan was around. I then went out of my way to pull Audrey aside and let her know she can't get angry when Liam starts flirting it up with Drustan's cousin.

Audrey assured me she could keep her cool, and I believed her. Her crushes usually didn't affect her moods that dramatically. Audrey had never been a territorial person. While we rode the train, I did my best to come up with routes my train of thought could take me instead, in case Drustan was there and wanted to pry.

All I kept thinking about, though, was our moment in the drapes, and as the soft melody danced throughout the air now that I was in Hyvenmere again, getting more distinct the longer the train ride lasted, I wondered if perhaps I was too confident in my ability to handle being in his presence again.

I kept my growing concerns to myself. Once we had finalized the plan one last time before stepping off the train at Lydhavn, it was basically showtime.

However, there was something about the land of Lyndoruun that just...calmed me.

It wasn't the kind of calm that I experienced sitting on a beach or inhaling the salty sea air like in Vanhirra. No, the tropical beach scene in the nereid territory made me relax in a way like I was rushed for time. Like I needed to force myself to lie back on the beach because the moment was fleeting.

The calm I felt in the city of Lydhavn was deep in my bones. Perhaps that's the reaction I'd always have while being surrounded by the largest pine trees I'd ever seen, while breathing in the trees' scent mixed with the mountain air. It wasn't nearly as dry as the mountain air would be in California, but...crisper.

Perhaps the large lake just behind the city, separating Lydhavn from the base of the Fjellenheim Mountains, added enough humidity to the air.

The siren capital was magical, but in a reverent way. As soon as we stepped off the train into the main part of the city, which wasn't nearly as busy as Sammara, siren soldiers in their identifiable leather grey uniforms calmly approached us at the stone platform.

"What brings you to Lydhavn?" the younger-looking soldier asked. He was wearing his siren mask, but from the way his eyes crinkled, he was smiling at us.

"We're here for Bandthral," Audrey replied with a calm tone.

His eyebrows rose, and he shared a look with his companion that was difficult to decipher while they wore those facial coverings.

"I'll escort you." The soldier nodded in agreement, while his companion waited for us to step ahead so he could walk behind us.

Sirens of all shapes, sizes, and colors littered the main road. Playing music on the side of the street, having meals at a table with friends and family. Riding e-bikes with little baskets on the front and back, filled with purchases.

As a cream-colored castle came into view, surrounded by trimmed pine trees and wild grasses, an excited squeal made me turn my head to the side. A group of teenage siren girls were on their phones, talking in a language I didn't understand. I smiled at them, something the siren soldier behind me noticed as he turned to see what caught my attention.

"They seem excited," I whispered to the soldier behind me.

"They're talking about Bandthral," he replied. He sounded young, maybe early twenties.

"Oh, right," I replied. "Does everyone participate in that?" I asked.

"If they want." The soldier nodded forward, indicating that I needed to keep moving. "And as long as they are of the age of maturity."

Twenty-six.

That must be the equivalent of being a legal adult here.

"Are you going to participate?" I asked him.

His eyes widened a fraction before they scanned me from head to toe quickly. So quickly, I could have missed it.

"Are you?" he asked, instead of a response. *Easy, tiger.* I smiled. I still had no idea what Bandthral was. Audrey said it wasn't, but I was still convinced it was just a massive orgy.

"I'm not sure if humans are allowed." I replied. His brow pinched at that before he cleared his throat and stood taller. The conversation was over, because suddenly we were being led through large, wooden gates into the Siren King's estate. Another courtyard came into view, and in the center of it, a large stone statue of a woman with long hair and a formal gown, donning a crown, stood tall. She wore a bright smile, with her hand angled toward the gates, as if inviting people in.

I stepped up to Audrey and whispered in her ear, "Who's that?"

"The former Siren Queen, Astrid Shaw," she replied. "Ilia had it made immediately after her passing." Ah, Drustan's mother. At least Ilia wasn't a total piece of shit to not memorialize his dead mate.

As we approached the front doors to the castle, I inhaled a breath of confidence.

Here we go.

Sitting on a throne that wasn't nearly as elaborate or decorative as I expected it to be, was King Ilia.

He sat stiffly, with a ramrod straight back. Based on the age in his face, I would have guessed he was about sixty years old, not well over a hundred. His long fingers curled over the armrests of his seat, tapping a rhythm of impatience as we approached the center of the courtroom. His gold eyes narrowed on us; mistrust was evident in his scowl. He had a trimmed white beard, accompanying his pale blonde hair that fell just past his shoulders.

A thin gold crown with emeralds rested on his head, as well as gold medals on the breast of his shirt. He didn't wear a cape or anything else super *kingly*, but his dress clothes elevated his status above everyone else in the room, who dressed in what looked like staff uniforms. He held himself with unmistakable authority.

Next to him, casually leaning against the throne with his weight shifted on one hip, one ankle crossed over the other, was his son.

Drustan.

His arms were crossed over his chest as we approached; his shoulder-length dark red hair was down. When he lifted an arm to brush his fingers through it, away from his face, it showed off golden loops in his pointed ears.

While Ilia's body language portrayed strict dominance, Drustan's body language was lazy and sensual. Relaxed. I was immediately flooded with the reminder of how it felt for Drustan to tower over me at Fergus's party. How he smelled, how my body reacted to the barest of touches from him. How my arousal from his proximity and manhandling felt so natural and yet out of my control at the same time.

I was better prepared this time.

Drustan wore a billowy cream tunic that was completely open. Enough for me to see his pierced navel. He paired the shirt with an open grey vest, stitched with delicate golden thread, illustrating artistic images throughout the material. The vest and shirt combo accentuated the hard dips and planes of his exposed torso, the bulge of his biceps. The large thighs that pulled tight at the tan pants he wore.

I knew better than to get too distracted by him, though. I had a thorough understanding of how dangerous a siren's ability to manipulate emotions and hormones could be. Assuming he intended to get close enough to sniff my neck again. Perhaps I was being overdramatic.

Drustan's eyes locked on me, and even though we were fairly far from each other, I could see something flare in them.

I could tell he was looking at me specifically, and not us in general, based on the jump my heart made in my chest from his direct attention. Drustan's fingers tightened on his bicep, and when I forced myself to mold my face into one of nonchalance, the corner of his lips tipped up.

Handsome, lethal siren, I thought to myself, fighting every urge in me that wanted to smirk back at him.

His grin widened after my thought, proving that he was using his whismerra to its full ability. His gaze lowered to what I was wearing, which wasn't nearly as revealing as the last time we saw each other.

This time, I was wearing dark grey cargo pants that cinched at the ankles, making room for my leather boots. My leather jacket covered my heather grey tank top.

There was nothing particularly enticing about my outfit, but his perusal made heat burn throughout my body, regardless, before he lifted his eyes to meet mine again. Drustan raised his hand just enough to wiggle his fingers at me in a flirtatious greeting.

I suppressed a snort at the playful, boyish charm he was throwing out next to his stone-faced father. Audrey turned to give me a concerned look over her shoulder. I just rolled my eyes at her, an attempt to assure her that I wasn't becoming a blushing, flustered mess.

She smiled at me and faced forward.

"Welcome," Ilia's voice boomed over the court, drawing our attention back to him.

I wanted to ask, "Are we, though?" but I refrained.

A shift in posture from one of the guards to the side of the throne caught my attention. Because their face coverings were pulled down, I recognized the two sirens who attacked me on my boat.

Sergei and Leon. But who was who? I'd already forgotten.

A cold chill of fear skittered down my spine and arms, making me cross them over my chest. The blond siren narrowed his eyes at me in a sneer, and the brunet one straightened his posture. I didn't want to deal with the blond. Something in my gut churned from his attention, something I didn't want to toy with.

The brunet, however, I locked eyes on.

I lifted my fist to brush my thumb over my jaw before reaching higher to swipe at my nose once.

The brunet siren pinched his brows together, watching me, but not catching on. I smirked before gently tapping my fist against my cheek, reminding him of the solid hit I got that night on my boat. The brunet frowned at me, so I grinned even wider.

"I hear Bandthral is open to anyone outside of Lydhavn, too," Audrey explained, shoving her hands in her jeans pockets. She leaned her weight onto one hip, and I was low-key proud of her for looking so relaxed in the face of someone as dangerous as Ilia.

Ilia leaned forward, ignoring her question as he asked, "It generally is, but what brings you here tonight, of all nights?"

Audrey tipped her head and replied, "I figured it was time for me to learn more about Lyndoruun culture."

Ilia's eyes narrowed, then shifted, locking on me. *Bad*, my stomach told me, *evil, dangerous, bad.*

"And who is your friend, halfling?" Ilia asked, ignoring her question again. I raised my brows at the king's audacity. *Damn, you know her name, you pretentious prick.* Drustan grinned at me again, but I did my best to ignore him.

"This is my friend, Van." Audrey introduced me casually, as if I weren't that important. I appreciated it; her nonchalance made me seem less threatening.

"Is she a halfling as well?" Ilia pressed, scanning me from head to toe. I didn't flinch under his examination. He leered, but he wasn't studying me in a way that made me feel naked. Like his son did. No, Ilia studied me like he was looking for flaws. Cracks in my composition. Eager to point them out.

"Nope," I answered for myself, popping the p.

Ilia's brow furrowed. "What gives this human the right to be in our realm?"

I don't know, man, the fact that I'm not a total piece of shit?

Drustan pressed his lips together in a way that made me suspect that he was holding back another grin or smirk. Trying to stay composed. Perhaps he was just lingering in my head this entire time. Setting himself up with front row seats to my every thought. Was he in Audrey's head, too? Liam's? What about all the other sirens here?

Drustan's eyes lifted toward the wall on my right when a door creaked open, and a tall, stunning blonde woman strode through.

Caelena.

Ilia didn't acknowledge her presence with anything more than a fleeting glance as she smiled at her cousin and stepped up on the dais, standing next to him.

"Van is not a threat," Audrey assured the Siren King. "She holds a grant gifted to her by Queen Ada herself."

Ilia grunted a noncommittal response as someone from the back stepped up to murmur something urgent in his ear. I took the opportunity to take in our surroundings. More siren soldiers lined the wall. They were men and women in varying sizes, all with their masks and hoods down. They stood at attention, legs hip-width apart, hands behind their back, facing the king.

Varying shades of blonde, red, and brown hair were braided back and away from their faces, and part of me wondered if I was seeing Hush's face for the first time and didn't realize it.

I forced myself to glance around the rest of the room, where more siren soldiers stood at attention. Ilia must have gotten word we were headed his way when we got off the train. He clearly wanted to intimidate us, otherwise, he wouldn't have lined the walls of his court with so many of his militia.

Interesting. Was he truly that scared of Audrey?

"I find it suspicious." Ilia leaned to the side on one of his elbows, rubbing his jaw with his hand. "That you three came to visit during Bandthral."

"My sister wants to maintain our peaceful treaty." Liam stepped forward to stand next to Audrey, leaving me behind the two of them. At his approach, I noticed Caelena's gaze lock on him. "She sent me here in good faith, to ensure the halfling and human treat the siren celebration with utmost respect."

"Hmm." Ilia's lips flattened at that.

I narrowed my eyes at him. Something felt off. I couldn't name it, though.

"Does everyone from outside of Lyndoruun receive this same interrogation?" Audrey asked, clearly feeling the same thing as I. But Ilia didn't cower. Instead, he stared at her with a judgement only a disappointed father could produce.

Ilia leaned back in his chair, before addressing all the soldiers in the room with a command in his native language.

Most of the soldiers turned on their heels and marched out of the room through side exits. Liam, Audrey, and I all shared curious looks with each other.

"Come." Ilia gestured for the three of us to approach him on the dais, excitement lighting Caelena's eyes as she focused on Liam. Liam went up first, then Audrey, then me. Once I stood next to them again, I checked Audrey to ensure the heart-eyes Caelena was giving Liam wasn't affecting her. Thankfully, Audrey wore a cool mask of indifference.

"You're lucky, human." Ilia's voice sent a sharp, sick feeling in my stomach as he leaned forward to study me, but I held my ground. "No human has borne witness to Bandthral for hundreds of years."

"I'm honored." I gave Ilia a smile that I didn't try to pretend wasn't fake, as I slid my gaze over to his son, whose nostrils flared with my approach.

Audrey and Liam flanked my sides at the same time that Ilia lifted his hand to gesture to the side of the dais.

"Please be patient while my staff finds you accommodations."

CHAPTER 15

I had no idea what I was expecting when Hush originally said the words "mating ritual" back at the Sun Bean, but it wasn't this.

About thirty minutes after the court cleared out, someone produced cushioned stools for the three of us to sit on. All I could think in the moment was, *what a great place to start getting cramps*, because *of course*, I would start to cramp during this whole experience. There was no backrest, and the ottoman was just small enough for a butt to sit on. I couldn't even sit criss-cross apple sauce. Was I really expected to just sit on this for an hour? Or however long this ritual would last?

Liam originally moved to sit next to the king, but Caelena quickly cleared her throat and tapped the ottoman next to her, which would place him right between Audrey and Caelena.

Which left me sitting right next to King Ilia.

I immediately tried to fidget less on the ottoman. I didn't want him getting offended and sending his men back to kidnap me in the human realm again. I wanted to end this one-sided beef once and for all. Being cordial was the way to go.

"Do you know much about our culture, Van?" Ilia asked. Part

of me liked that he didn't use my full name. I liked the respect a full name provided, like when Drew used it, and one thing was for sure: I did not want respect from someone like Ilia.

"I know little to nothing about your culture," I replied.

"Oh?" He lifted a blond eyebrow at me, shifting in his seat to rest his fist on his cheek. "I'm sure your friends have informed you of their...perspectives." He grinned, and I blinked at him because of how similar his son had grinned at me moments earlier.

His son, who had disappeared somewhere.

I lifted an eyebrow at the king before shrugging. "I know that sirens like to keep to themselves, which is fair." His eyebrows rose at that, surprised. "And...that sirens are shapeshifters."

"True." Ilia nodded.

"And...that's pretty much it."

He chuckled. "I'm surprised you know so little."

"That's funny." I gave him an unimpressed look. "Because I'm surprised to know about this realm at all."

I locked eyes with him.

It was *his* fault I was here. If he hadn't sent his men to kidnap me that night, Audrey wouldn't have had to intervene. I would have never met Liam. I would have never discovered her magical powers. I would not be slowly dipping my feet into this otherworldly culture.

If Ilia was upset that a human was traipsing around Hyvenmere, he needed to look in the mirror, for exposing his realm to me in the first place. Ilia gave me a narrow-eyed look, clearly not liking the confrontation I was giving him.

Perhaps I needed to back off, so I adjusted my uncomfortable seat on this cushion and added, "I'm grateful to learn what I can, though." The fine lines around his eyes relaxed at that, and he settled back in his seat.

"Do you know why we like to, as you said, keep to ourselves?" Ilia asked, staring at the staff setting up the room for the ritual that may or may not be an orgy. I could feel Audrey listening intently to our conversation, and even though I didn't know much about things in this realm, I figured now was my time to get Ilia yapping. In the corner of my eye, I noticed Caelena grasp Liam's hand and pull him to a standing position, before leading him through a door near the back of the dais.

Leaving Audrey and me with King Ilia.

"I do not," I replied. Cordial. Pliant.

"Sirens are safer together." Ilia lifted an ankle to rest on his opposite knee as he spoke, the posture of an underwhelming man about to weaponize a woman's silence so he had an excuse to hear his own voice. "Our magic is more connected between our people, unlike other creatures, such as the fae, for example. Sirens rely on each other to truly thrive." He turned his head toward us, rubbing his white beard in thought. "The larger the number of sirens that are together in proximity, the stronger our magic and, therefore, our people, are."

This was interesting.

I didn't love the fact that he was offering me this information freely, because why would he feel so comfortable doing so? Unless he wasn't intending for us to leave with it.

"Strength in numbers, and all that," I added, not wanting to add my opinion one way or the other.

"Precisely." Ilia smiled at me, showing off the fine wrinkles in his cheeks and eyes. Though his smile looked more like a threat than anything, "But there is a condition, as the Goddess Tynara demands of all things."

I nodded, pretending to be fully aware of all things goddess in Hyvenmere.

"The goddess who used to live in the Fjellenheim Mountains," I added.

"The goddess of nature, balance, justice, and prosperity," Ilia continued. "This is why the siren's main settlement is the closest to the Fjellenheim Mountains. To protect Tynara's home from those who seek to bring imbalance and pain to Hyvenmere. The siren who sits on this very throne…" He tapped his knuckles on the arm of it. "…is also considered the guardian of the Fjellenheim Mountains. The last known spot she resided before she considered Hyvenmerians mature enough to look after this continent ourselves. Before she *trusted* us enough to look after the continent. However, the siren on the throne is only as strong as his people allow him to be."

I nodded in thought, absorbing his words.

As flowery as his story was, all I seemed to take from it was that as long as Ilia's people stayed close to him in the city of Lydhavn, then he would be considered strong enough to guard his people and the mountains.

Or, if he was simply a bad person like I suspected, strong enough to be a threat to other territories.

Which was probably difficult to do when the women of your territory were being hunted down.

"It sounds like an honor to be in that position," I said.

Ilia slid his gold, suspicious eyes over to me. Clearly, I hadn't quite won him over, yet.

"It is." Ilia nodded once with his agreement. "Do you understand then, why I would be hesitant to allow your kind to roam so freely in our realm?"

"I do," I agreed. Ilia hadn't been expecting that answer. He narrowed his eyes at me.

"You understand why I'm cautious of humans like *you*." Ilia's words dripped with derision as he gave me a once-over. "Coming into my realm, into my city, making yourself at home during one of our most sacred rituals of the season, whereas the number of missing females and children in my territory only seems to rise."

My face fell from his words. *Where were they? What was happening to them?*

"I understand your concern." I tried to lace as much

sympathy in my voice as I could, but Ilia—based on his own expression—wasn't buying it. "I don't want to be rude, but I can leave right now if you'd feel safer."

That, unfortunately, was the wrong thing to say.

I only realized it a moment too late.

"I do not feel *unsafe* by your presence, human." Ilia's lip curled with his words. "Do not be ridiculous." Right. Insinuating he felt unsafe probably made him feel weak. Pathetic. Because not only was I a human, but I was a human *female*, as he would refer to me.

Men like Ilia wouldn't tolerate anything suggesting he wasn't the biggest, baddest, and strongest in the realm. This was why Audrey's existence was enough of a threat to him at this point.

Off to the side, a small orchestra was set up and ready to go. Ilia lifted his sleeve to check the time on his watch, and soon the doors to the court opened. The sun was setting, filling the large marble room with oranges and pinks and warm light. Entering, I assumed, were the soldiers from before.

And a *lot* more sirens.

Everyone was dressed the same; variations of whites, tans, creams, and linens. Gold, shimmering jewelry. Dresses, floor-length skirts, pants, and capris. Some wore cropped shirts and others wore baggy long-sleeved tops. Everyone wore clothing that they were comfortable in. The only similarity was the bland, monotonous color choice. Sirens of all shapes, sizes, and colors got the same dress code.

Everyone filed in right when Ilia's staff finished setting up a table on the left side, against all the open pillars that displayed the sunset over the glistening lake, facing the mountains in the not-so-far distance. The table was covered in food and appetizers. Some vegetables and fruits looked familiar; others were unrecognizable to me.

"You good?" Audrey asked me on my right. I glanced at her and nodded, not wanting to look nervous in front of Ilia.

The band started to play, and I struggled to not tap a finger to the beat. No one said a word. There must have been at least three hundred sirens in this large room, and no one was speaking. They were snacking, standing with friends, and...just chilling.

The music shifted after a few minutes of silence; a beat started to thump heavily.

I found myself studying the faces of the blonde women more and more. The blonde women with pale skin tones, specifically.

Movement from the side caught my eye, and when I turned to see if Liam and Caelena returned, instead I locked eyes with the siren prince, and frowned.

"Nice of you to join us." Ilia sighed in annoyance as his son smirked. Drustan pulled half of his hair away from his face to tie it back as he approached us.

I knew, deep in my soul, that Drustan was doing it to show off the bare muscles in his arms and chest. Because he was wearing even less clothing now. No billowy shirt, only a small cream-colored corset, a size or two too small for his massive torso. His gold navel ring dangled with a green jewel, and because of how small his corset was, I could see another gold hoop through one of his nipples. A gold septum ring adorned his nose, as well as many gold studs and piercings in either of his pointed ears.

His linen pants were loose, but very thin.

One wrong gust of wind, and everyone in the room could see everything the man was packing. I quickly averted my gaze, not wanting to give him the attention he was seeking.

"I wouldn't miss it," Drustan purred, bowing quickly to his father as he walked past his throne. "Halfling." He nodded to my friend before stepping directly in front of me, blocking the rest of the room from my view. "Vanessa."

Good god.

I leaned to the side, pretending I was focusing on something in the crowd.

"Hey." I nodded at him as dismissively as possible.

Drustan chuckled as he stepped between his father and me, standing tall and tucking his hands behind his back. I couldn't tell if I was relieved or annoyed. Relieved, because Ilia couldn't address me as easily, but the alternative was his son. With Drustan standing so close, I could capture whiffs of his spicy scent. Was it a cologne? Was it just what sirens smelled like? Was their body odor enough to lure humans like me in?

His deep, amber eyes staring at me in the drapes of Fergus's party flashed in my memory. The thrill of being trapped against a wall by a large body like his. The heat coursing through my veins when his lips skimmed my cheek. The contrast of the cold stone on my back in comparison to his large body pressed against my front.

The *intensity* of his eyes.

Next to me, Drustan shifted on his feet.

Get out of my head, siren. I demanded in my thoughts, just like I practiced.

He simply chuckled at me. Perfect. Keep focusing on the helpless, horny human. On his other side, his father turned and made a simple hand gesture toward the musicians, and the music shifted again.

Something calmer, melodic. Soft.

I really liked it. It reminded me of the harmony I would hear in the air whenever I set foot in this realm. But I haven't focused on it since I stepped foot in Lydhavn, too intent on cautiously taking in my surroundings.

I found myself studying the string instruments the sirens were playing. They looked similar to what I was used to, but different as well. They had artistic, intricate designs and swirls carved into the wood. They were shaped differently, too. Instead of the classic figure eight, hourglass shape, they were more oval.

Part of me wondered if we could buy one in this realm, so I could take it home and play with it.

Audrey huffed a quiet laugh next to me. I glanced at her, and she nodded gently toward the musicians I was watching. "Classic Van."

Ilia cleared his throat, and we faced forward again.

In front of us, near the feet of the dais, a siren woman pulled a small golden scarf out of her pants pocket. She decided to wear a corset too, with skintight leggings that fell to her ankles. A skirt with dramatic slits cut up the sides of her legs, creating two panels of fabric in front and behind her.

With her black hair secured out of her way in a braid down her back, she tied the gold scarf around her eyes. It complemented her dark brown skin beautifully.

I tilted my head at her.

She glanced around, and I never would have been able to guess that she couldn't see with the blindfold on, because she started to navigate herself through the crowd with ease. Avoiding bumping into people by anticipating their location ahead. Resting her hand on their shoulder as she searched for…something.

"Her mate," Drustan murmured to my side.

"Hmm?" I glanced at Ilia, wondering if he was going to scold his son for talking, but then I heard a low hum throughout the crowd. The sirens were starting to speak in low, whispered conversations.

"She's looking for her mate. They all are," the siren prince elaborated. I scanned the room, seeing a handful of other men and women starting to secure golden blindfolds over their eyes as well.

"How?" Audrey asked from my other side.

Part of me was low-key happy that she was talking to Drustan without any animosity, but it was also confusing. He was the enemy, as far as I could tell. But the fact that Audrey was being amicable toward him made me confirm that my "play nice" approach was probably the best one.

"By dulling one sense." Drustan sighed, keeping his hands secured behind his lower back. "We can better search for the sounds of our mate." I raised my eyebrows at that.

Interesting.

Fae could feel their mates' heartbeats.

Nereids could feel their mates' waves in the water.

Sirens could *hear* their mate.

It was all so...poetic.

"Your bonds are discovered through sound?" I asked.

"But..." I glanced to the side to see Audrey biting her lip in hesitation before continuing with her question, "What does that mean for deaf sirens?"

Drustan gave my friend an unimpressed look. "What do you mean?"

"If sirens find their mates through sound, what happens if you can't hear?" Audrey clarified. Her eyes were wide with curiosity as she studied the crowd in front of us. Drustan rolled his eyes and faced forward, apparently done conversing with my friend.

Dick, I scolded him in my head—just in case he was lingering in there. Based on the way his hands flexed behind his back, I assumed he was.

"Sound isn't just noise," I murmured to Audrey. "Sound has waves. Vibrations." I drummed my finger on the side of my ottoman, demonstrating for her. Drustan glanced down at my hand as I theorized with her, but I ignored him. "I'm assuming that *hearing* isn't exactly all of it. Just like how Fergus's people can intimately *feel* the waves their mate makes in the water, and how the fae can *feel* their mate's heartbeat, I'm assuming sirens can also *feel* the vibrations their mate makes through their surroundings."

"Oh." Audrey nodded but looked a little bewildered at the idea. "That makes more sense."

Drustan continued to stare down at us, so I looked up at him to ask, "Does that mean the sound doesn't necessarily have to come from a siren's body or voice?" I nodded toward the musicians in the small orchestra. "Theoretically, anyone playing an instrument over there would be creating sound. That would mean that any step they take, any noise they produce." I drummed my fingertips on my ottoman again, and his golden eyes tracked the movement. "Any of that can produce vibrations sensitive enough for their mate to locate, right?"

Drustan's lips parted, and a divot formed in his brow as he studied me.

"The human is sharp, I'll give her that," Ilia spoke, leaning back in his throne as he gave me a dismissive side glance, before focusing back on the ritual. His son didn't utter another word; he pressed his lips together and faced forward again.

You're no fun, I taunted him in my thoughts.

A dark-haired siren woman dressed in a simple shirt and linen pants approached the dais, holding a tray of drinks. Behind her, the blond siren guard who attacked me on my boat held another.

I couldn't stop the frown that pulled at my lips, so I just let it happen.

I didn't need to put on a show for *this* guy. I could make my disdain for him clear. What was he going to do to me here, with his king sitting amicably nearby?

"Your majesty," the man said.

"Leon." Ilia nodded toward him. A smile slid across Leon's lips as he glanced at me and saw my frown. This meant the brunet siren who attacked me was Sergei. Leon's blond hair was almost completely white. Uncomfortably pale. The complete opposite of the siren woman who stood a couple of inches shorter than him, carrying a tray of beverages.

"Amber." Ilia nodded, accepting the glass she handed him. She silently nodded before handing Drustan a mug as well, which he accepted silently.

When she went to give me one, I lifted a brow at her as I accepted it. "What is it?" Amber glanced nervously over at the king, and that was all I needed to know.

"Wine," she replied, before meeting my eyes again, "Do you need something else?" I shook my head. It probably didn't matter what beverage she brought us, I still wasn't drinking it.

"Is tonight your lucky night, Leon? Or perhaps your sister Amber will find a match before you," Drustan spoke before sipping his drink. Meanwhile, Sergei approached the king's other side, and the two of them started conversing in hushed whispers as they studied the crowd in front of us.

"One can only hope." Leon winked at me then, standing next to Drustan. "Are the outsiders able to participate as well?"

I lifted a brow at him and said, "Explain to me, in detail, exactly what you feel when I talk to you."

"Oh my god." I could hear Audrey smack a palm across her forehead at my words, but I held my ground. Drustan grinned widely. His eyes practically sparkled as he took a sip from his mug and waited for Leon's rebuttal.

Amber frowned at me, giving the tray to someone who looked more like a servant than a ritual participant, and shared an irritated look with her brother.

"Come." Leon gave me a narrow-eyed look of disappoint-ment as he held his hand out for Amber to take. She obliged, sending Drustan a small smile as her brother escorted her down the steps of the dais and joined the party.

"You don't like him," Drustan murmured. I didn't respond, because *obviously*. "...But you like me." Drustan stood taller with his words, smug. I frowned, *wrong*.

"When was the last time a mated pair was formed during this?" Audrey asked. She sounded reluctant about it. Like she was desperate to save the mood after I essentially gave Leon the middle finger.

"A few years." Drustan sighed. "Though other matches are often still made for those interested in a...*fun* night." He sent a flirtatious wink down to me. I scoffed before facing forward. So, no mating matches for a few years. But people still go home together and "have fun," as he so delicately put it.

Frankly, good for them.

I was watching men and women restrain their vision, relying completely on sound waves for this ritual. The whole thing reminded me of one big game of Marco-Polo. I'd be lying if I said I wasn't a little disappointed that this didn't turn into an orgy. That would have been wild to see.

Drustan's head whipped toward me at the thought, his red brows raised and eyes wider than I'd seen, with his lips parted. He looked like he was about to say something, but suddenly, after finishing his conversation with Sergei, Ilia stood from his throne.

Everyone walking around stopped moving, including the sirens with blindfolds on. All heads turned to face their king as hushed conversations came to a stop.

"Proceed." Ilia waved a hand over the crowd. "My son will oversee in my absence." With that, Ilia and Sergei strode off to the side door that Liam and Caelena had left out of earlier. I caught a glimpse of the king's expression, which looked more annoyed than anything. Panic spiked in my gut, and I hoped that Liam and Caelena had just gotten caught canoodling and nothing else.

As soon as Ilia was out of sight, hushed conversations continued throughout the party.

"Freaky," Audrey whispered to me as she kept her eyes on the door.

To my left, Drustan stepped toward the throne before lazily falling into the seat. His father sat with a straight back, but

Drustan's posture was confidently relaxed. His legs were spread wide; his weight shifted to the side as he studied his people.

His abs and chest were perfectly on display thanks to the smallest, flimsiest corset I had ever seen.

I adjusted, reaching my hands behind me as I attempted to stretch my back out. The throne at least had a backrest. Whereas this glorified ottoman I was sitting on had no back support whatsoever. I found myself slouching in my seat often, which made my lower back ache worse. Thanks, cramps.

I wondered if Audrey was also struggling, or if this situation was just made worse with my looming period on its way.

"Come here." Drustan's words made me whip my head to the side to see him holding a hand toward me, over the armrest of his throne. I studied his hand, then his face.

"No thanks," I replied. I snuck a peek at Audrey, whose wide eyes were staring at me in silent concern.

"Come here, Van," Drustan ordered again. Something pulled in my chest toward him. Perhaps it was his sinndra, encouraging me to obey his words. I rubbed at the foreign feeling in my chest before I shook my head again, determined to hold my ground.

"Actually..." Audrey cleared her throat, leaning forward to get the prince's attention. "We probably have overstayed our welcome. We should—"

"I will not ask again, Vanessa." Something dark laced Drustan's tone, interrupting my friend. A warm shiver raced down my spine from his words, and that solidified it for me. Drustan was trying to use his sinndra on me. Just a little bit. But I could still shrug it off.

"I think we should go," I murmured, trying not to cause a scene, while allowing us to escape.

Audrey slowly stood; her eyes locked on Drustan over my head. As soon as I got to my feet, I immediately placed a hand on my lower back and pushed. Desperate to relieve the ache.

Drustan, still slouched in his throne, openly glowered at us.

"It would be a shame for the only full-blooded human to step foot into Hyvenmere in hundreds of years to disrespect the Prince of Lyndoruun on Bandthral, wouldn't it?" Drustan threatened.

I whirled on him, my fists clenched at my sides. Audrey whispered a low curse at his words. His lips twitched in the corners, heat flaring in his golden irises.

Fuck you, I thought with all the rage I could feel.

Is that a request? his voice whispered in my mind.

"Five minutes of your time." Drustan splayed his hand, widening all fingers. "Then you may leave with your friends without any fuss."

I glanced back at Audrey. Liam wasn't back yet. Her fingers were twitching, and behind her, a potted plant with large, green leaves the size of my face twitched in response.

Huffing a sigh of annoyance, I nodded once at Drustan, stepping closer to his throne. He widened his legs for me to step between; his lips pressed together in a tight smirk. Instead, I stood to the side. My hip rested casually against his armrest.

Audrey slowly, cautiously, sat down on her ottoman again, watching me like a hawk.

Drustan chuckled while leaning forward. He hooked a slender finger through the belt loop at my hip.

"So shy," he murmured, tugging me around to the front of the throne. As if I were an animal on a leash, he forced me to stand between his legs before gently pulling me down onto his lap. I was so stiff, every muscle in my body was locked and on alert. I snuck a glance out toward the party ahead of us, but hardly anyone was paying attention. Conversing and wandering the party themselves, looking for their mates.

As soon as my butt hit the muscle of his warm, large thigh, it took everything in me to support as much of my own weight as I could. But Drustan wasn't having it. He leaned forward, adjusting his seat so he could sit up straighter, and draped one long, bare arm around my waist.

Slowly, slowly, he pulled me in tighter. Until my back was flush against his chest, and my toes were lifted off the ground. I was dependent on his support to stay upright.

His body was producing so much heat; it was as if he were a furnace. I wondered if my back was going to start sweating.

"Better," Drustan hummed. Releasing my waist, he allowed me to lean forward a little bit. I wasn't flush to his front anymore, but before I could create even more space and put my feet on the ground, both of his large hands gripped either side of my waist.

When I froze in his hold, his thumbs slowly started to massage my lower back.

Without hesitation, I moaned from the pressure he put on my sore muscles. Horrified, I slapped a hand over my mouth. Audrey glared at Drustan as he rubbed my sore muscles with his massive hands.

"No need to be embarrassed," Drustan murmured to me, his timbre low and soothing. "My father is remarkably petty. Those seats are torturous." With his hot, large hands touching me, his muscled thigh flexing under my ass, and the soothing press of his thumbs up and down my lower spine, warmth started to burn between my legs.

Oh god, no. Absolutely not. I tried to think about other things, not sexy things. *Old, saggy, wrinkly men. The full dumpster outside Sun Bean. Socks and sandals.*

Drustan chuckled, putting more effort into his ministrations, successfully loosening my back with his massage.

"How much time is left?" I asked him through clenched teeth.

"Still desperate to leave?" he asked, and I could hear the smile in his voice. His scent was invading my senses, making the room feel like it was spinning. It took every drop of willpower I had left within me not to fall limp in his lap, mold against his warm body, and allow him to soothe me in all the ways I never knew I needed.

His use of sinndra was strong and dangerous.

I nodded to his question, because my pitiful human libido was no match for him, and I needed to get the hell out of here.

He hummed something, sending a pleasurable heat down my spine. My cheeks were flushed, both from how warm he was and how good his hands were making me feel. The familiar sound of sand started to rush in my ears from being this vulnerable and this aware of the pulse between my legs.

I couldn't remember the last time I had a massage as good as this that I didn't pay for. His hands moved lower, lower, lower. His thumbs eventually dipped underneath the waistband of my pants. My vagina clenched from awareness, and I shifted uncomfortably on his lap. Desperate to relieve a new ache building inside of me.

"Your friends can leave whenever they want, but I still have three minutes left with you," Drustan whispered near my ear, his nose teasing my hair.

My heart was hammering, practically begging to race out of my ribcage. My nervous system was completely shot from his proximity. His thumbs dipped past my waistband again, teasing the flesh of my ass cheeks with gentle but firm circles. I pressed my thighs together, only staying balanced on his thigh because of the hold his hands had on my hips.

"Two minutes," Drustan breathed against my neck.

I bit my lip, desperate not to make any more embarrassing moans or whimpers or *anything*.

To the side of me, I wondered if Audrey would be disappointed in how little effort it took for Drustan to manipulate my body to his liking. But then I remembered that Drustan was a powerful and sexy siren, and I was just a human, so she could fuck right off with any judgment she may have.

I shifted, rubbing my thighs together as he moved lower on my back again, slowly pulling the back of my pants down as his thumbs rubbed further into my glutes.

Oh god, oh god, oh god.

Behind me, Drustan's chest expanded, pressing against my back. I shifted again, silently noting the wetness in my underwear.

I hated it.

I loved it.

"One minute," Drustan hummed, his fingers flexed against my hips with his words. As if he was worried that I'd try to jump off him before our time was up. He had good instincts, at least. "Unless," Drustan continued. "You'd like more. You just have to say the words."

I pressed my lips together, and the spicy scent of him burned into my nostrils and made me lose my train of thought. My hands were balled into fists on my lap, desperate to hold my ground and not spread my legs so I could hump his leg like a dog in heat.

"Time's up," Audrey said. My head jolted to the side to see her standing and stepping in front of us.

I moved to jump off of Drustan's lap, but his fingers flexed on my hips, keeping me there. I turned to look at him over my shoulder, noting how expanded his pupils were. Blackness practically overtook his gold irises.

Silently shaking my head at him once, I grasped his hands and gently pushed them off of me.

As soon as I landed on my feet, the side door on the dais opened, and Liam was storming through without Caelena. He gave the two of us his outstretched hand, and without hesitating, we slapped our palms in his.

And then the world started spinning.

CHAPTER 16

Liam said his sleuthing with Caelena was a bust. She even went as far as to take Liam past Ilia's office in search of a more "private" area for the two of them, but when Liam walked by, he realized the space was unusually bare. No filing cabinets, no drawers, nothing. Just a plain desk. When Audrey asked if Ilia and Sergei had found them, Liam looked confused and shook his head. Which made us all wonder, why did the Siren King leave in the middle of Bandthral when the halfling he hates and a human he tried to kidnap waltzed right through his front doors?

Audrey made a snarky comment asking if Liam at least got lucky while off with Caelena, and Liam adamantly promised that no bodily fluids were exchanged between them. I ended up announcing that my period was starting and I was going to bed, during their bickering about it. I popped a gummy and crashed. The next day was Monday, so I went to work and acted like I didn't just spend the previous day in a secret magical realm and focused on getting through the shift without bleeding through my pants.

When I got home, though, I slammed the front door behind

me and slouched against it as I felt another cramp sharpen its attack. I breathed through it, used to period cramps while also cursing them.

"How *dare* I not get pregnant this month?" I groaned into our condo.

"So," Audrey's voice made me open my eyes as she slowly approached me. "I know you're in a lot of pain."

"Spot on." I nodded. I stood tall and glanced at the mug in her hands. "Is that for me?"

"Only if you want. This tea isn't from here, it's from Hyvenmere—Enharra, specifically." I reached forward and held the warm mug as she continued, "I started taking it a year or so ago for my own cramps. It's pretty strong, but safe for humans."

I grinned. "Taste?"

"Delicious." Audrey smiled. I started taking large gulps, ignoring the slight burn from the hot beverage. "Damn." Audrey giggled, before she reached for the keys in the bowl we kept by the door. "I know you're probably going to lock yourself in your room the rest of the night, but another halfling just became mated to a fae in Enharra, and Liam and Ada asked me to join them in celebrating the new bond." I grunted my confirmation that I would not be doing that with her, "But you definitely shouldn't operate any heavy machinery or go anywhere alone. I'll lock the door behind me."

I sighed. "Like cinnamon sugar," I murmured with a lick of my lips. "But you're right. I'll be in my room for the foreseeable future. I hope you have fun not telling Liam how badly you want him and pretending that your feelings for each other are entirely platonic." Audrey rolled her eyes and pinched my side before exiting the apartment.

Some indeterminate amount of time after drinking the Hyvenmerian tea, I was lying in my bed. Nothing but my salt lamp on my nightstand illuminated the space. A heating pad rested on my stomach, but I didn't need it anymore.

Because I was tripping fucking balls.

Whatever Audrey gave me, I wanted more of it immediately. It didn't have any side effects that usually came when I took a hallucinogen. No dizziness, no nausea, no anxiety. I felt light. Airy. Safe. Warm. A little giggly.

This tea was the fucking best. I kept forgetting that I was even on my period right now.

Usually, I'd be sound asleep at this point in the night after taking two gummies. I guess I *could* still fall asleep, but I was so focused on how *good* I was feeling that I didn't want to. Time was crazy, as it usually was when I was high. What I thought was thirty minutes was only two. What I thought was ten seconds was ten minutes.

Wild.

I giggled to myself when I saw the time on the clock. An hour later than when I usually fell asleep. Would I even regret staying up, staring at my ceiling in the morning? Or would the afterglow of this stuff linger too long for me to care?

Something creaked near my door.

I glanced over there, ignoring all the sparkles and rainbows that danced in the peripheries of my vision to do so. The texture swirling on my ceiling was a little distracting, but I had been staring at it long enough, I supposed. I was curious what was happening to my bedroom door.

There was someone outside of it. Which couldn't happen, unless it was Audrey, but I doubted that she'd be back so soon. There probably wasn't anyone behind it. Just another hallucination.

"Come in!" I sang to my door. I curled up on my side, tucking the blankets around me more as I stared at the shadowed figure standing in the partial opening. "How can I help you?" I blinked several times because the pictures I had on the wall near the door were starting to move, too. They were waving and smiling at me, but I ignored them. I wanted to focus on *this* hallucination more.

The door started to open wider, slowly.

It was opening *so* slowly. I almost got bored; I found myself staring at my moving picture frames before I realized it finally opened enough for a leg to step through.

"God, you're *taking forever*," I groaned, rolling my eyes. *Whoa, bad idea.* I reached up and covered my hands over my eyes, willing all the colorful shapes and designs to stay still long enough for me to be able to focus.

I could hear someone stepping on the carpet in my bedroom. The sound of the bedroom door closing behind them. Breathing.

This was *crazy*.

I parted my fingers and stared at the black linen pants of a man. Why did I know that waist belonged to a man? No idea. Wait, no. That was a slight bulge. Was this man freeballing? Regardless, I knew it was a man.

I dragged my eyes up, up, up, because this hallucination was *tall*. What surprised me, though, was *who* my big fat brain conjured up.

"This is unexpected," I murmured behind my hands.

Gold eyes and chiseled facial features, a clenched jaw, and dark red hair greeted me. Half of his hair was pulled back, away from his face. Just like at Bandthral. His linen pants were tied low at the waist, and his dark grey shirt had a deep V in the neckline, showing off the defined pecs I admired.

Nice.

Drustan stood in my bedroom, his thick arms crossed over his chest. A muscle popped in his jaw as he let me stare my fill.

"...Why *you*?" I wondered. I still thought about Drew often. He had texted me this morning, trying to nail down plans for our next date.

"...Were you expecting someone else?" Drustan asked, a deep pinch formed in his brow. His fists balled tighter under his arms, emphasizing his biceps under his long sleeves. I grinned up at him, because fucking hell, I *loved* Drustan's voice. My memory did an excellent job recreating his soothing timbre.

I steepled my fingertips together, still lying under the blanket on my side, my grin in place, "What brings you here today, good sir?" Drustan frowned, narrowing his eyes at me. His nostrils flared once, and he dragged his eyes over my lump of a body under the covers.

"You're bleeding," he muttered, unfolding his arms and reaching for the blanket. Before I could react, he pulled the covers back and reached for me.

"Wow, getting right to it, huh?" I snickered as his warm fingers prodded my body, turning me over this way and that. By the time he flopped me onto my back again, confusion marred his features.

"Ah, I forgot you're on your cycle," he said, sitting on the edge of my bed. One of his long legs tucked up against me, and his knee hit my hip.

"I forgot you're on your cycle," I repeated in the deepest voice I could make before snorting to myself. I reached for his knee, wrapping my hand around the ball of it.

God, he was just *huge*. He was huge when I saw him in person; he *felt* huge, but seeing how little my hand was on his leg was mystifying. I swore I could *feel* him. I squeezed my fingers around his kneecap before I glanced up at him again.

He looked at me with so much confusion; I ended up barking a laugh at his expression.

"Is this the part where we do it?" I've had wet dreams as an adult before, but I hardly ever remember them. I had a feeling I would remember this one, though.

Drustan's lips opened and closed as he stared at me. He shook his head once before replying.

"Do it?"

"Bone." I tucked my lips together, but he still stared at me, wanting me to elaborate. I frowned at him then. I didn't like that my hallucination wasn't playing along. This was *my* fantasy, dammit. He needed to be obsessed with me, or I needed to conjure up something else horny.

I squeezed my eyes closed and tried to picture Drew instead. It didn't work. I was too aware of my Drustan hallucination sitting next to me.

I grumbled, sitting up and getting to my knees next to him, "Do you want me or not?"

The pinch between his brows smoothed at my words. His pale pink lips parted at my question, and his golden gaze dragged over my body. *That's more like it.*

"Do you want me?" he asked. He was staring at my stomach while licking his lips. I glanced down, forgetting what I was wearing. I wore a silk spaghetti strap tank top, but I was a tall woman, so it exposed an inch or two of skin between that and the hem of my silk pajama shorts. I glanced up at him with a bite on my bottom lip, gently dragging my index finger across my exposed waist.

"I want you very badly," I admitted. Drustan was mouthwatering. I could admit it to myself in my stoned state of mind. Something about his height and muscle and voice and piercing gold eyes and dark red hair just did it for me.

Warmth was already pooling in my lower belly at the thought of him touching me. Something flickered across Drustan's expression before he leaned toward me. His hand wrapped around my hip, and right when he started pulling me closer, he stopped.

"What the—" I stammered when he stopped. He released his hold on my waist, so I grabbed his large hand with both of mine and tried to put it back on me.

"Ah, did you drink this?" Drustan asked with a mischievous look in his eye. "Is this why you're so friendly?" It took me a moment to realize he held my empty tea mug; he must have grabbed it off my nightstand with his other hand. He sniffed it once, before smirking and glancing up at me.

"Sure did," I nodded, "Anyway…" I awkwardly wabbled over him, pressing my body against his side as I looped both of my arms around his neck.

He was *so* warm.

He had a very large neck. Supported by firm shoulders that my hands squeezed of their own volition. I wanted to feel his large hands on me again. I wanted to be able to *enjoy* it this time. This tea made me very horned up.

Drustan released a whimper in his throat. His hot breath fanned against my shoulder, and I shivered from the feel of it. I slowly slid my hands up his neck, tangling my fingers into his hair.

"This color reminds me of blood," I murmured against him. I inhaled through my nose. Thank god he smelled good. Spicy. My drugged-up brain knew exactly what I needed right now.

"Don't tempt me, Vanessa." Both of his large hands gripped my waist as his fingertips pressed into my skin. "I'm not an honorable male." I shushed him before dragging the pad of my tongue up his neck like the animal inside me demanded. He tasted *good*.

I mean, he just tasted like skin.

But my tongue reacted as if I had just licked a decadent ice cream cone.

Something buzzed in me from the action.

These were quite possibly the best drugs I'd ever taken.

"*Vanessa*," Drustan groaned, tilting his head back to give me more room. "I'm not confident you won't regret this when your mind is clear."

"Shh," I whispered against his ear, before nipping at his earlobe. "This isn't real. It doesn't count." The point of his ear made me giggle, because what grown ass man had pointy elf ears like this? I traced the shape of it with my index finger. It twitched from my caress.

"Vanessa, it—it would very much count," he murmured. "I would ensure you understood just how much it counts, actual-ly." He used his grip on my waist to pull me off of him, making me sit back on my heels. The pinch in his brow illustrated an entirely new emotion.

Drustan looked hungry.

But I glanced down, taking in what had just happened. Because he had just...pushed me off of him.

"No, this isn't right." I shook my head with my words, resting my own hands against either side of my neck. Oh, wow. My own touch felt good, too. Okay. That's fine.

"Hmm." Halluci-Drustan, or maybe Dru-cinagin, sighed while tucking a strand of my dark curly hair behind my ear. "No. I guess you wouldn't think so." His eyes softened, and I blinked, struggling to clear my vision enough to find heat in his eyes. Flushed cheeks. Anything to indicate he wanted me.

I...couldn't find anything.

What the hell?

I groaned. "You're supposed to *ravish* me." I dragged one hand up into my hair, while the other slid down my front. It pulled the low neckline of my tank down, almost creating a nip slip. Drustan grumbled something incoherent to himself before he clasped my hand with his to hold it still.

"Do you even know who I am, Vanessa? Where you are?" Drustan asked me. He looked amused at my behavior. Like a man watching a show. He shook his head once, as if clearing his thoughts.

"*...Is that a request?*" I quoted the words he whispered in my mind back at Bandthral. Drustan's eyes locked on me then, and the intensity of them made me lose my breath. He was so focused on me; *maybe* I could convince him to keep touching me.

"You..." I poked the center of his firm chest, noticing a

difference in texture. I dragged my finger to the side, parting the deep V of his shirt to see what I touched. A very faint, jagged scar dragged across one of his pecks. I didn't notice this at Bandthral. I was so determined not to look at him too much, but for some reason, my mind decided to give him scars. The *details* these drugs could conjure up in my head were miraculous.

Drustan trapped my hand before I could tug it away. I leaned into him instead, remembering to finish my train of thought, "...should take your pants off."

Drustan grinned as his gaze became hooded. I stared at him, waiting.

"I enjoy you like this," he murmured. "Completely hopeless for me."

I frowned, noting how his pants stayed very much on. This fantasy was *not* going how I wanted. What the hell was the point of hallucinating a huge, sexy siren sneaking into my bedroom if he wasn't going to go down on me even a little bit?

"Okay," I grumbled, time to take care of things myself.

"Vanessa, I can't know if it's safe for us to—" I interrupted him by tugging my hands out of his grip and grabbing the bottom of my tank. In one swift movement, I pulled it off.

"*Fuck*," Drustan breathed as his gaze bounced between my face and chest. He leaned over from his seat on my bed, resting his elbows on his thighs, muttering something that sounded a lot like curses. "I don't know if what the halfling gave you is entirely safe for humans, Van. Increasing your heart rate more could..." *Blah, blah, blah, who cares?*

I stared at Drustan, hyper-focused on the large, beautiful man. My thoughts started racing faster than I could truly process them.

He...doesn't want me. Which, logically, was fine. *But he doesn't want me.*

I wanted him, for reasons that were none of my business. But I was being rejected by my own fucking *hallucination*. What was happening right now? The light and airy feelings were slowly fading from me. Creeping in around the edges of my consciousness, rejection and pain were starting to ooze into my chest. My pictures on the wall danced less. The patterns on my ceiling stilled.

My heart was racing, and my face burned with humiliation.

He doesn't want me.

He's rejecting me.

He doesn't want me.

He's rejecting me.

I couldn't escape these thoughts. They kept playing on a loop. Over and over again.

I watched Drustan lower his hand and lift his head to stare at me, horror starting to wash over his features. I gripped the roots of my hair, pulling hard. I wanted to feel anything, *anything* else beyond this ice-cold rock forming in my stomach.

These drugs fucking *sucked*.

"No, no, no." I dropped to my side, facing away from my hallucination, tucking my legs up toward my chest as I tried to fold the pain away. "No, no, no."

"Vanessa." The mattress dipped behind me, his warm words blanketed my ear, "You know that I want you." My body didn't believe him. My mind didn't believe him. I shook my head; my breath became shorter and shorter under the weight of my panic.

He's rejecting me.

"I'm not. You're *mine*, Vanessa." Right—his mind-reading and stuff.

I shook my head again. This isn't how I wanted this to go. I wanted him to *want* me, to *need* me. I wanted to *feel* wanted. When was the last time I was *truly*, passionately wanted? Why was my brain attacking me like this? I felt unstable enough with a sober mind. My world was turned upside down, and I was just barely starting to fill the large canyon that formed between my best friend and me.

My brain formed Drustan when I drank this hallucinogen. Not Drew, who also wouldn't just fuck me already. My subconscious clearly formed Drustan because I had a better chance, but I was wrong. I just needed to get Drustan out of my system. I needed to play out the fantasy of being with him. But I couldn't. Because my brain felt like it was working against me and plucking at weaknesses that I didn't even know I had.

I had never cried over a man in my adult life. So why the hell was my heart being ripped apart? Why were silent tears streaking down my face? Why did I *want* him? Why did I need him to want me *so* badly?

I smacked myself on the forehead, desperate to get a grip and escape this horrible high.

"Vanessa!" Drustan growled. He roughly grabbed my shoulders and slammed me onto my back. His body blanketed over mine, his golden glare inches from my face. He smelled too good. His weight felt like a breath of air in my lungs. His dark red hair draped over the side of us like a curtain, blocking the window from view. "Fine, fine. Just breathe, my song."

I gasped for frantic breath, desperate to cooperate, but looking at his face, the face of someone who wouldn't rip my clothes off and fuck my brains out, made something crack in my chest.

I squeezed my eyes closed. I slapped my hand over my mouth, desperate to cover the sob that wanted to escape.

Drustan growled, "Look at me." I shook my head at him. Warm, large hands cupped either side of my face. "My song, open your eyes." The weird term of endearment made me comply. My vision was a little blurry, but his features were still there. His face was so close to mine. Eventually, his forehead pressed against my own.

"Vanessa, breathe."

"I'm trying," I gasped. "I need—" His hips shifted, and suddenly something long and very hard was pressing against my thigh. A myriad of emotions coursed through me at the feel of his erection against my bare leg.

Drustan lifted a dark red eyebrow and smirked when I rolled my hips against him, searching.

"You know I want you," he announced. It wasn't a question, but I nodded; all I could focus on was the evidence of his want against my thigh.

"You want me," I murmured back to him. I leaned up to press my lips against his. I startled him by doing this, based on how his entire body stiffened. It wasn't a dirty kiss, just a simple press of my lips against his soft, warm ones.

I flopped back on my bed. I was getting dizzy. Shapes and colors were frolicking around him. My ceiling was going crazy again. His pupils were doing crazy things, expanding and contracting. He licked his lips, as if tasting me on them. Watching him do that made my body burn with need.

"When I take you," Drustan murmured. "You should beg me again, just like this."

I groaned and shook my head. "I'm not begging." I wasn't begging him…was I? Panicking, I pushed on his shoulders. He complied, shifting his massive body off me.

"No!" I gasped, grasping fistfuls of his linen shirt to pull him back on top of me. I didn't want to push him away *completely*. Just enough to let him know I was in charge.

I wrapped both of my legs around his narrow waist, searching for that brief feeling of evidence that he was just as desperate for me as I was for him. I wanted him all over me. On top of me. Inside of me. Smothering me. Whatever I could take. I wanted to crawl underneath his skin and settle in. I wanted him to break me open and undo me.

"You'll beg me," Drustan repeated, gently brushing his lips against my temple, "But you'll do so with a sound mind.

Understanding exactly *who* you're talking to, and *what* you're begging me for."

Shaking my head against his soft lips, I rolled my pelvis against him again.

"Take me," I whimpered.

Drustan chuckled, shifting us. I grumbled, but my limbs were becoming loose and weak, so I had no choice but to comply when he tucked himself behind me, wrapping me in his long arms. Tossing a leg between both of mine. The hot breath of his voice coated my neck and ear when he murmured, "Touch yourself."

I didn't even hesitate.

Reaching into my pajama bottoms, I found exactly what I needed. I had never responded this immediately to my own touch. But...I wanted *his* hand on me, not my own.

"Touch me." My eyes were closed, but colors and shapes still danced behind my lids. I patted behind me, smacking his large thigh and firm ass in search of his hand. He grasped my wandering fingers before guiding my own hand into my pajama bottoms again.

"Show me what you like, my song. I need to know." Drustan's lips moved against the shell of my ear, making me groan with need. I couldn't wait any longer. If I didn't come soon, I was going to die. I was a mess between my legs, made even worse by my arousal, but I ignored it while rubbing myself with gentle, rapid movements of my fingers circling where I was most sensitive.

"Touch me." I pleaded again. Fine, *technically*, I was begging. But he was a drug-induced hallucination, so I wouldn't beat myself up about it too much.

"Oh, I will," Drustan promised. "Show me, first." Still, he refused to touch me. Instead, he simply held me in his arms. Tucking me against his chest as I worked my fingers over my clit.

Drustan's voice was in my ear, telling me how well I was going to take him one day.

Picturing him undoing his otherworldly pants and lining himself up with me is what sent me over the edge.

Even though orgasms were always wonderful, especially whilst stoned, I knew as soon as it started cresting within me that it wasn't enough. I throbbed, I gasped, and fire exploded between my legs, warming my veins, all the way down to my fingertips and toes. And yet, when I floated back down to earth and pulled my hand out of my shorts, I felt…unsatisfied.

Exhausted, but needing more.

Sleep was slowly smothering me, pulling me under against my will. I was falling asleep while fully aware of the unconsciousness taking over.

I made a sound of protest against the phenomenon. Warmth greeted me again, calming my restless body and mind, wrapping me in its arms and tucking me against its chest.

I knew what that warmth was now, but I soon forgot what it was. All I knew was that it was safe.

When my new favorite melody started to hum in my ears, I was willing to allow sleep to finally happen. I had one last lingering thought before soothing darkness took over my mind.

…These drugs were strictly *okay*.

I hadn't had that deep of a sleep in a very long time. The next morning, I felt snuggly and warm and safe. I pried my eyes open, stretching and taking my sweet ass time getting out of bed.

Though I was pretty sure I experienced some out-of-pocket hallucinations last night, that tea Audrey gave me sure did the trick. I couldn't feel a single cramp or ache in my body. No random boob pain. No nausea. Nothing.

What a beautiful thing to exist.

Stretching again, I rolled onto my side, and my hand smacked something hard. Tapping my hand on it again, I finally registered what I was feeling next to me.

A string instrument.

The same one I saw at Bandthral. And it was beautiful.

Audrey really didn't have to do that for me, but I appreciated her little gift regardless.

I immediately sat up, grabbing the neck of it and resting it in my lap, like it was a precious infant or something. It looked like a violin, but with two necks and an oblong shape.

I loved it.

Grabbing my phone off the nightstand, I sent Audrey a quick thank-you text. Within a minute, she responded.

Audrey: You're welcome?

Short. Sweet. Simple. She always got uncomfortable whenever I fawned over her for taking care of me or doing nice things. Audrey was genuine like that. So now that the obligatory *thank you, you're welcome* exchange was out of the way, I adjusted my seat so that my back was resting against the headboard and started plucking away.

CHAPTER 17

"Are we just back to square one, then? Since Bandthral was a bust?" I asked Liam and Audrey a couple of days later. We were all in the office of my coffee shop, and Audrey was massaging my shoulders. Training that morning was rough, but the good news was that I was able to roll a massive Liam off of me with success. He tried pinning my body to the ground with his entire weight, but I stuck my arm out above my head and rolled, using it as leverage to throw him off. Audrey and Liam were excited by that move, confident in the fact that most Hyvenmerians wouldn't expect a human to accomplish such a feat, which would work in my favor, should I need it.

"I couldn't find anything useful," Liam replied as he sipped the cold brew I made for him. He was manspreading on my office loveseat as he hummed his appreciation for the lavender syrup I added to it. "Caelena was eager, but a little *too* eager." Pink stained his cheeks. "I couldn't figure out how to encourage her to take me anywhere important without actually..." Liam shook his head as he stared down at his drink.

"Why didn't you just go for it?" I asked Liam, wincing when Audrey's grip on me tightened even more.

"I'm going for a run," Audrey randomly announced, obvious irritation lacing her words. Liam and I both stared at her wide-eyed as she called over her shoulder, "I'll be right back."

I waited until Audrey's heavy footfalls led her outside the back door of my coffee shop, and when the door slammed closed, I leaned forward in my chair. I folded my arms and rested my elbows on the desktop as I gave Liam my best stern expression.

We fell into silence, and he seemed very unbothered by it. I was staring daggers at him for what felt like five solid minutes before I finally groaned and broke the silence for us.

"Can you just fuck each other already?" I asked him. Liam choked on his cold brew but managed not to make a mess of himself as he turned to stare at me wide-eyed.

"I beg your pardon?" he gasped out, pounding his chest with his fist.

"You're both clearly into each other. It's been years. Why haven't you *done* anything?" I was tired of playing around with this. Liam blushed again as he flattened his lips together.

"It's complicated," he muttered.

I lifted an eyebrow at him in disbelief. "Are you saying that you aren't interested in her? Because I'm calling bullshit—"

"You cannot fathom how very *interested* I am, Van," Liam interrupted me, "Unfortunately, it's not that simple." He frowned at his drink as one large hand rose and rubbed his chest absentmindedly.

"Why? What's holding you back?" I pressed. Liam glared at me, but I held my ground. My friend was sexually frustrated, and if Liam was "very interested," then I didn't see why he hadn't gone for it yet. What was stopping two consenting, age-appropriate adults from—

Fergus's longing expression at his birthday party floated to the forefront of my mind, and it clicked.

"You're waiting for your mate," I whispered. Liam's light

blue eyes drifting over to me were all the confirmation I needed. *Oh my god*, were all the men in Hyvenmere hopeless romantics? "That's so messed up," I scolded Liam with a point of my index finger. "You need to turn her down gently. Let Audrey move on. Give her space. Let her meet someone else if—"

"Audrey is *mine*," Liam practically growled the words, which made every muscle in my body lock up. "I knew it the moment I laid eyes on her, curled up behind her library, confused about her new powers." I sat up and leaned back in my chair, anxiety filling my chest at what he was saying.

"Audrey is your mate..." I didn't ask; it was obvious at this point. *How did I miss that?*

"Yes." Liam nodded once. "Why else would I leave my sister on her own, to deal with the politics of my territory, so often? Audrey is powerful; she can easily protect both of you on her own without my assistance." He gained a few extra points in my book by acknowledging how Audrey didn't need a big, strong man in her life. "But it physically *hurts* to stay away from Audrey too much. I was hoping that the longer she spent in Hyvenmere, the more the realm's magic would fuse with her cells, producing the same pull I feel for her every time—" He cut himself off, shaking his head. "Unfortunately, our hearts are still out of sync. I'm terrified that while she is *my* mate, I might not be—" he groaned and scraped a large hand down his face.

I didn't know what to say to that. This man had just admitted to hopelessly pining for my best friend for years, holding himself back, because he was waiting for her to feel the same magical pull that he felt.

I drummed my fingers on the wood of the desk. "Have you ever considered that because she's half human, she won't ever feel the same pull as you?" Liam hummed as he leaned back on the loveseat and stared at the ceiling.

"Yes. However, every other mated halfling that has fae blood has eventually felt the pull—but it only took them a couple of months to establish." Then Liam snapped his head up to me, "You cannot tell Audrey yet."

I scoffed and said, "I'm obviously going to tell her immediately."

"No, Van," Liam argued. "Audrey already has too much to balance right now. Taking an important title from Ilia. Ensuring the gates stay open. She's even worrying about the missing sirens. I don't want to add to her list of concerns. If she truly wants to be with me, I want her to be without the obligation of how—how *unbearable* my need for her is." Liam gave me a pleading look. "Please, promise me that you won't tell her."

I groaned in irritation at him. "We can't just keep this from her forever. She deserves to know. She deserves to have all the information available to her. I know what it's like when someone you trust keeps big secrets from you—" I gave him a pointed look, and panic rose in his features. "So, I'll make you a deal."

"Anything," Liam agreed.

"I won't tell Audrey that you think she's your mate, but only if you promise to tell her yourself." Liam stared at me, his expression marred by conflict, as unease created fine lines around his eyes. I didn't back down. I kept my expression cool but stern as I waited for his response.

"Fine," Liam muttered after several unbearable moments of silence. "Fine. Agreed."

"What are you agreeing to?" Audrey's voice echoed down the hallway, seconds before she walked through my office again. Liam and I gave each other a look before I chimed in.

"I agreed to be a little nicer to him." I grinned at my best friend. "Since we're working together to help you bring peace to the realms and whatnot."

Audrey smiled, looking between the two of us. "Really?" I nodded while Liam mouthed *thank you* to me behind her back. I raised my eyebrows at him in a silent reply, *uphold your end of the deal.*

Audrey plopped herself down next to Liam on the loveseat, rubbing her hands together.

"I had an idea while I was on my run." Audrey didn't even look sweaty, as if going on an impromptu run didn't ruin her hair or energy level at all. Must be the fae side of her. "Since we have no leads, we need to confront Ada about what the hell is going on with Ilia and the nereids."

"I've been thinking the same thing," Liam admitted before draining the last of his cold brew. He held the empty glass up at me in silent appreciation and continued, "I would be genuinely shocked if Ada felt influenced or manipulated by Ilia at all. I wonder if the rumors she's heard in her unit aren't fully biased."

"Also, I just really miss Enhavenn," Audrey sighed. "It's so beautiful there. It's my favorite city in Hyvenmere." I lifted an eyebrow at Liam, acknowledging that this must be good news for him, but he ignored me.

"Are there any fae mating rituals we could crash?"

Liam snorted. "That was last month for us." I was mostly joking, but it brought me joy that mating rituals were such a normal thing in his realm. "Additionally, we don't need a formal reason to visit my sister. I'm her brother, and she already loves Audrey like a sister." *Well, thank god for that,* I thought to myself.

"Let me check my calendar, and I can go with you, if you want." I lifted a shoulder as I pulled my phone out of my jeans.

"You're always invited to join me in Hyvenmere, Van." Audrey grinned. "God, I love that you're in on all of this."

"You're preaching to the choir, my friend." I scoffed, quirking my lips to the side in mild annoyance that my empty calendar reminded me that Drew and I hadn't been able to nail down another date quite yet. I had fun dancing with him, and I swore he had fun, too, based on those sexy texts we've exchanged since. "How about tomorrow? We have no events, which means Shane will be able to handle running this place without me."

"Works for me." Audrey nodded.

"It's settled." Liam clapped his hands together and stood from the loveseat. When he reached down to grab his empty cold brew cup off the arm, he lifted it at me with a sheepish expression. "Can I have another?"

I rolled my eyes but pushed myself away from my desk, not wanting to admit that he enjoyed my recipes. "Sure, big guy."

"Wow, you were serious about being more cordial." Audrey grinned. "Thank you."

"I wish I had more answers for you," Queen Ada said as she bent to admire a pale pink rose with a deep inhale. We were wandering through her gardens in the back of the courtyard. The sun was setting, already hidden beyond the horizon, inviting a deep blue to take the place of the pinks and oranges that danced in the clouds when we first arrived.

I made sure to take an allergy pill before we left, and after some bickering between Liam and me, we all decided to lyskift here again. I didn't puke this time, but I was still disoriented when we landed at the front gates of the Dahl family estate.

"The Kings and Queen of the Nereids haven't said or done anything suspicious?" Liam pressed his sister. We followed her as she stepped toward the next rosebush, pouring water over the rich soil. The flowers visibly perked up, even with the setting sun. Audrey trailed her fingers over the soft petals of one, and the flower leaned into her caress like a cat would with a human it didn't hate.

"None that I've heard, and I'm not sure why Ilia would feel like I'm about to endorse his position on the Mellhawn Gates activity." Ada frowned. "Though the very idea that he might be feeling that way concerns me."

"Maybe our source was just mistaken." I lifted a shoulder, fighting the urge to sneeze. This land was not for me. I much preferred Fergus's territory. Even Lyndoruun seemed more my speed. There was just way too much pollen constantly in the air here.

"And you still can't tell me who your source is?" Ada asked. Liam and Audrey shook their heads, and I felt a rush of relief over the fact that Ada didn't seem to push them for more. She trusted my friends; I trusted her.

"Hmm." Ada pressed her lips together in thought. She wasn't dressed in a formal gown this time; she wore what looked like a fancy matching pale green lounge set. Her blonde hair was thrown up in a top knot on her head, and I had a feeling that she dressed this way when she was "off the clock," so to speak. "Perhaps I can—" A distressed masculine shout halted whatever she was about to suggest, and all four of us turned toward the castle half a football field away.

There was a short but heavy silence, and then a crash through a window. Several fae guards emerged from their posts around the courtyard and started to charge the castle.

"What is happening—"

"Stay with the human, Audrey," Ada's tone hardened, her transparent wings struck out of her body in what looked like a defensive position, before she hovered in the air. "Liam, you're with me." Without another word, Liam summoned his personal sword with his fae magic again, before clapping a palm on Audrey's shoulder.

Then the two fae were gone, and Audrey and I were left alone.

"When I tell you to run..." Audrey slid her hazel eyes over to me, right when the last of the suns light became swallowed by the night sky. "You run." I nodded, not needing to be told twice.

A twig snapped nearby, and arrows ended up in the chests of the nearest fae guards who stuck around in the courtyard. Their large bodies dropped.

"They must be stunning them with a poisonous herb on the arrows," Audrey murmured, "That's the only reason they'd drop immediately." Right, I remembered how unaffected Drustan was when I stabbed him in the kidney. Made sense that a thin arrow in the chest wouldn't be that big of a deal to the average Hyvenmerian. We still didn't know who *they* were, though.

A twig snapped in the distance, and soon three figures were storming out of the Dahl family castle. Audrey braced herself before jogging after them. She didn't tell me to run, so I awkwardly followed her a moment later.

"Stop!" Audrey demanded with a grasp of her hand. The foliage of Ada's garden responded, erupting from the earth and twirling around the three figures. Two of them became suspended in the air, and I almost tripped over myself when I recognized the faces of Sergei and Leon grunting around their environmental restraints.

The third figure, though, sliced through the foliage with a blade before throwing it at Audrey. The blade struck through Audrey's shoulder, making her shout and stumble to her knees. The foliage released Sergei and Leon, and soon all three started approaching.

When Hush stepped into the moonlight, revealing that she was the one who struck Audrey with the knife, I panicked.

Hush was a double agent, I reminded myself; she was playing a role right now.

"Halfling," Leon spat, shouldering a bag with a sneer.

Audrey turned over her injured shoulder, which she grasped with her good hand, meeting my eyes.

"Run. Hide," she ordered.

She was right. I was probably mostly useless here. I turned on my heel, not loving the fact that I heard footsteps coming after me. When I glanced over my shoulder, I widened my eyes in fear when I saw Hush following me.

"Fuck me," I gasped, turning a corner and running into a wall.

Nope, not a wall, a person. A person whose spicy scent I recognized all too well.

"Only if you ask nicely," Drustan purred, clasping his hands on my biceps to keep me from stumbling away from him.

"Your highness," Hush's voice cooed behind me. I threw her the most annoyed look I could create over my shoulder, before being pulled into Drustan's body again.

"What errand has my father sent you on this time?" Drustan asked Hush. I tried to force my thoughts into another direction, locking my eyes on a flowery plant next to us. *Flowers, flowers, flowers, Audrey, flowers.*

"That I cannot say until we return to the king himself, I'm afraid," Hush replied. "Are we taking the human with us?"

"No," I replied at the same time Drustan said, "Maybe." I kicked him, getting his shin with my sneaker. Instead of reacting in pain, he tucked a hand underneath my chin and tilted my face up toward him.

"Will you come with me now, my song?" he asked with a warm, seductive tone. I frowned at the endearment and tried to shake my head out of his grasp, but he held strong. I could already feel his sinndra start to take effect. My body was struggling less and less against him. Warming up to his body heat. Molding against his dark leather militia outfit, so similar to what the other sirens wore. His scent made me instinctively inhale several lungsful of it, and I started to panic in his hold.

"Are you and your unit ready to leave?" Drustan asked Hush, keeping his eyes on me. I shouted in irritation before finally leaning up toward him. Surprise coated Drustan's expression as I latched my mouth to his.

It wasn't a kiss; it was an attack. Both of my arms were

pinned against myself. My mouth was all I had to use. I bit my teeth into the skin of his bottom lip as hard as I could, ignoring how the taste of him sent my core buzzing with want. I just needed to hurt him, not become subdued with his weaponized sinndra.

Drustan groaned, leaning into my bite, pressing me against his front.

His erection against my hip made my thighs clench, and I hated myself.

I pulled away, satisfied to see my teeth marks on his bottom lip. But instead of getting angry or upset or irritated that I broke his skin, his lips pulled back in a dangerous grin. Blood dripped out of his mouth, pooling against the bottom gums of his teeth as his eyes started to flicker between black and gold again.

"So eager to take a bite," Drustan cooed. "If you wanted a taste, just say so."

"Drop her!" Audrey's voice was a shout of anger as Leon and Sergei dragged her around the corner to where I was trapped against the Mad Siren Prince's body. Her shoulders looked wrong, like the two of them were broken. Her fingers flexed, and the foliage around us twitched, as if confused and nervous.

She couldn't use her powers if her arms weren't useful.

Shit.

"Aud," I gasped, wiggling again. Drustan grunted, and I realized that I was still very much pressed up against his arousal. He ended up dropping me enough to let my feet land on the earth again, before turning me around so that my back was to his front, his hand wrapped around my jaw as he leaned down close to my ear.

"What a tempting little thing you've introduced into our realm, halfling," Drustan spoke. Where the hell were Ada and Liam? Based on the shouts and the sound of metal clanging, I assumed they were busy inside fighting other siren intruders.

"We could have some fun with that one," Leon added with a

look that made my blood run cold, in contrast to Drustan's warmth. The siren prince's hand tightened on my jaw in reaction to his words. I couldn't tell if Leon's words excited him or challenged him.

"If I recall correctly..." Hush tilted her head at me, as if studying an animal and not a person, "The Fae Queen issued her grant. The human is technically her property." *Okay, that was* not *my understanding of how that works—*

"Pity." Drustan tsked his tongue, before trailing his other hand across my naval, teasing my exposed skin from my shirt that had ridden up. "I'm sure you would be much happier in my court."

"Don't touch her!" Audrey spat through clenched teeth.

"We have what we came for," Sergei announced. I could have sworn he was avoiding my eyes. "We should leave."

"I suppose you're right." Drustan turned his head toward the shouts of Ada and Liam, echoing from inside the castle. They sounded like they were getting closer. Drustan grumbled, turning his nose toward the crown of my head, and inhaled deeply before whispering, "Until next time, Vanessa."

Then I was falling to the ground, no longer supported by his grasp. My knees hit the earth in a rough *thunk*, my palms scratching on the stray twigs of the garden. Audrey shouted, and an unnatural cracking sound made me look up just in time for her shoulders to be popped back into place. Her Hyvenmerian genes were healing her.

But Hush, Leon, and Sergei were gone.

All of them had lyskifted out of here, seconds before Ada and Liam burst through side doors, finding Audrey and me on the ground.

"We're okay," Audrey gasped, my mind whirling from the events that took place. Drustan's scent was still lingering in my nose, and the sudden loss of his warmth made my stomach churn in a way I couldn't comprehend.

Liam growled—literally growled—when he dropped to Audrey's side, checking her for more injuries. Meanwhile, Ada gave me her hand and helped me up.

"Those bastards," Ada cursed, brushing dirt off the knees of my jeans.

"What happened out here?" Liam demanded with rage at Audrey's wince.

I was shaking; my body trembling. Ada noticed and wrapped me in her arms.

"It was Drustan," I muttered, making Ada and Liam freeze, "Drustan and Leon and Sergei and—" I shook my head, stopping myself from revealing Hush's involvement.

"What?" Liam asked, turning to Audrey for confirmation. She nodded.

"They were a distraction," Ada whispered as her pale blue eyes locked on the ground. "They sent siren adolescents to try to steal from our vaults, knowing they'd fail."

I forced my words out through my shock, "They said they got what they came for. That's—that's why we're—" *alive.* Liam growled again, wrapping Audrey up in his arms, inhaling the crown of her head. Much like Drustan just did to me.

"That means they weren't after your money," Audrey muttered, leaning into Liam's embrace without hesitation. He kept petting her hair, inhaling her, his eyes closed as he focused on nothing but Audrey.

"Check the cameras!" Ada shouted at a nearby guard who approached our group. "Search every vault, every archive." She sounded so authoritative, so powerful, and I realized she was no longer considering herself off the clock. "Search every drawer and shelf inside, find out what was just stolen from us."

The guard nodded and marched off inside, shouting orders to his unit members in the fae language. Ada followed him inside.

"Are you okay?" Audrey asked, gently nudging Liam off her. His hands balled into fists, but then she reached back and clasped her hand with his, so he pulled her closer again. She seemed surprised by his actions but accepted his embrace again.

I waved her off. "I'm fine, just console your grumpy ma—" I stopped myself, snapping my mouth closed. Audrey stiffened, her eyes widening.

"My what?" Audrey asked.

I locked eyes with Liam, who was glaring at me, but his expression was melting in real time. As if his initial reaction was anger, that was now simmering into something more resigned. He still maintained his hold on Audrey, though.

"Nothing, we should go."

"Were you about to refer to Liam as my mate?" Audrey's nostrils flared with indignation, shoving herself out of Liam's arms as she spat. "Because you should not make fun of something like that, Van. Mating bonds are sacred here, you can't just—"

"*Audrey.*" Liam pulled on her arm, drawing her attention toward him. Audrey's mouth dropped open, disbelief coloring her face. Liam's gaze was hooded, his jaw flexed as he ground his teeth together. His shoulders were hunched with stress, and he kept staring at the little space that separated the two of them.

"Liam? What are you...?" Audrey whispered.

Liam gave me one last look, as if to accept his fate, before turning to Audrey. "I'm sorry I haven't told you earlier."

Audrey's mouth snapped closed, and she ripped her hand from his. "Explain to me exactly what you're implying."

"Let me take you both home first."

"Good idea." I nodded.

Even I was able to see that accidentally announcing that Liam and Audrey were mates was a real dick move on my part. I wanted to apologize to Audrey about it, but I hadn't had the time to, yet. The two of them were currently in her room, murmuring in low voices. Eventually, her bedroom door flew open, and their voices grew louder.

I was sitting at my desk, layering a soft violin over my track, when I paused what I was doing and stood to investigate.

"Aud, please—" Liam's voice sounded desperate. I quietly opened my door and tiptoed down the hallway to see Audrey pacing back and forth in our living room.

"Why didn't you *say* anything?" Audrey grumbled. She was in her angry phase of this revelation, which I fully understood.

"What was I *supposed* to say?" Liam threw his hands up in the air. "Hi, I'm fae, and half of your lineage is from my realm—none of which you've ever heard of before—and also, you're my mate, so every facet of your life is over."

I crossed my arms and leaned against the wall, still ignored by the two of them.

Audrey grumbled before stomping toward him and jabbing a finger in his chest. "You could have said *anything* over the last *two years*, you asshole! Were you *ever* going to tell me?" He snatched her hand and wrapped an arm around her waist. I pulled away from the wall, standing tall and ready in case she needed me to intervene.

The men in Hyvenmere were entirely too comfortable putting their hands on women, as Drustan proved earlier tonight. I could still feel his fingers trailing against my lower stomach, his huge body pressed against mine.

Shaking my head once, I focused back on the drama in front of me.

"I was waiting for you to recognize it. To feel the bond *yourself*," Liam murmured in her face, holding direct eye contact. "Do you have any idea what it's been like for me, Audrey?" His voice was shifting, and I could see Audrey's cheeks blush as she held her glare on him. "I've been so close to my mate for *years*." Liam pressed his forehead to hers. "Able to touch her. Hear her voice. Smell her. Discover everything about her...why would I risk such a gift by scaring you off with the permeance of a mating bond you *just* learned about?"

Audrey didn't say anything. They just stood there. Wrapped up with each other. I thought maybe they'd kiss or something, like in the movies. But Audrey grumbled and pushed herself out of his arms.

I cleared my throat and strode through the space. They both glared at me. Flustered. Clearly horny.

"I'm just getting some tea," I murmured. "Then you two can go back to whatever the hell you're doing."

Liam cleared his throat, and Audrey crossed her arms over her chest. I whistled my new favorite tune I picked up on during our last dangerous visit to Hyvenmere while I microwaved my water and grabbed a tea bag.

After what must have been an uncomfortable amount of time for the two of them, I turned around and studied them, my mug in hand.

"Look," I sighed toward Audrey. "I'm so sorry I just blurted it out. Liam only told me about it yesterday. And regardless of my promising not to say anything, as your friend, I should have just told you. That being said...maybe you should cut Liam a *little* bit of slack."

Liam's blue eyes shot to mine, surprise evident in his expression. I rarely sided with him. But I was trying.

Audrey raised a brow at me. "What?"

"And," I continued, addressing Liam. "I think you should cut *her* some slack." I sipped my tea, desperate to cut through the mess of emotions filling the space and get on with things. "She's been popping bean to the thought of you for two years and is just now realizing how much she's been missing out on the real thing. Sexual frustration is real, my guy."

Audrey's mouth dropped as her face turned red with humiliation.

"Oh my god, Van, what the hell?" Audrey gasped. She kept glancing at Liam, though. Embarrassment and arousal flushed her face and neck.

Liam choked as he studied her flustered behavior. "That so?"

I rolled my eyes. "It's none of my business, but it's a small apartment. You're both very, um, *heightened* right now." They didn't say anything, but based on their expressions, they agreed with me. "What if you two just need to bang one out? Then you can have a rational conversation about, you know…" I waved my hand between the two of them.

Audrey's eyes were wide, and she opened her mouth to say something to me. However, her attention was diverted to Liam, because something feral and hungry coated his face as he stared at her. Whatever protest Audrey was about to give me quickly died as her gaze became hooded.

Oh god, they were really about to just go for it.

"But it's none of my business." I lifted my hand and mug up in the air as a surrender, "I'll just go to my room. Goodnight." I smiled at a conflicted Audrey before strolling past the two of them toward the hallway. "I'll wear earplugs," I called over my shoulder before I closed my bedroom door. I lingered by the wood, listening to see what would happen. There was uncomfortable silence for a while, until Liam finally broke it.

"Should…I mean…"

"Not here," Audrey snapped. "I'm not—with you—with her just down the hall—"

Her voice got cut off, and I would bet all the money in my account that he had interrupted her with a kiss. I found myself pressing my fingertips to my own lips, a pang of longing cutting through my chest at the thought.

When was the last time a man interrupted my rambling with a kiss? When was the last time a man kissed me in a way that made my toes curl? The last time a man's lips came close to mine was when I bit Drustan's lip.

Drew still hadn't even really kissed me yet.

"Not here—" Audrey panted again, confirming that her lips were otherwise occupied before. "The—the boat—" The front door creaked open before slamming shut, and silence filled the apartment. I stepped out of my room to lock the front door before returning, locking my bedroom door behind me, too.

I was used to spending nights alone in the apartment after years of Audrey ghosting me every other day.

But now, I didn't quite feel lonely. If anything, I felt a bit of relief that this all finally came to a head. Audrey and Liam both knew they were mates. The awkward tension between them might not be as unbearable. I knew Audrey would come back.

Sure, Liam would be right on her heels, but she'd come back.

We'd talk about their first kiss, their first hookup, everything we usually did whenever one of us was dating someone new. This felt more permanent, though, which I guess made sense if they were mated magically.

While I sent a silent prayer up to any higher power that Liam knew what he was doing and that their first time wouldn't be a bust, I donned my headphones and focused back on my composition.

Adding the sounds from the Hyvenmerian string instrument I had recorded earlier.

CHAPTER 18

I didn't see Audrey for several days. I texted her to check in, and all I could get back were quick responses. A thumbs up. A simple, "I'm alive." Nothing else. I jumped in my seat on the couch when she burst through the front door four days after she and Liam ran off to my boat, flushed, rushing to the kitchen to grab water.

"What happened to hello?" I turned around on the couch, digging my knees into the cushions so I could rest my arms and head on the back of the furniture, facing the kitchen.

Audrey grinned before filling a glass with water and draining it in three gulps. She sighed dramatically before leaning against the counter.

"Hello." She laughed, fanning her neck. "God, I'm so drained."

I lifted an eyebrow at her. "Why?"

She shook her head and pulled her hair back in a ponytail, before rummaging in the pantry for food. "The heat."

I frowned at her. "What?"

"The heat." She leaned out from the pantry door to tell me, before hiding behind it again. The sound of bags and boxes of snacks rustling accompanied her explanation, "The mating heat."

It took every muscle in my body to mask my facial expression to a normal one, but I couldn't stop myself from asking, "What are you, farm animals?" Audrey cackled before kicking the pantry door shut with her foot, her arms full of boxes of cookies and popcorn and other snacks she unceremoniously dumped on the folding table.

"I mean, I'd heard about how intense it was." She waved her hand in the air before she ripped into a box of cookies and started shoving some in her mouth, letting crumbs spill out of her lips as she continued, "But I had no idea it was like this."

"So, like…" I waited for her to finish another mouthful of cookies before I finished my question, "I take it the sex is good, at least?" Audrey's eyes widened as she nodded her head enthusiastically, her cheeks puffed out with cookies before she swallowed.

"I can't put into words how good it is," she breathed. "It's like everything I've been doing before doesn't even count as sex."

"Goddamn." I grinned at her. "I'm happy you and Liam are having a good time." Her cheeks flushed at the mention of his name, and she rested her hand on her chest as she took a few steady inhales of breaths.

"He had to run back to Enhavenn to tell his sister about us, and why he's been so MIA after the robbery, but he should be back soon." Audrey ripped open a bag of chips before shoving a handful in her mouth and swallowing. "The heat should subside in a couple of days, so I'll be back around then, probably. Also, we hired a cleaning service for your boat. That's all I'm going to say about that."

My jaw dropped as I asked, "Are you deadass?"

"I'm so sorry." She started fanning herself. "I—" she hesitated, lifting her gaze toward the door. I waited for her to finish her sentence, but when heavy footfalls sounded outside our door, I realized she wouldn't. Two quick knocks were all the warning we had before Liam let himself in with the key Audrey had made for him.

Somehow, he looked even bigger. He reminded me of the bodybuilder bros at the gym who took enhancements. His eyes had a similar look in them when they were hopped up, and his muscles all seemed to be flexing. Liam's cheeks were just as flushed as Audrey's, and when he saw her, he immediately strode toward her before realizing I was also in the room, and halting.

"Sorry, um—" Liam awkwardly tipped his chin toward me in acknowledgement. "Hi, Van."

"Hi Liam." I held my fist out for him to bump, and he skeptically returned it. "Also, nice." I winked at him, determined to embarrass him for the sudden surge in hormones he and Audrey were experiencing, but he took the jest in stride.

"Thanks," Liam deadpanned, before turning to look at Audrey again. When his attention was back to her, Audrey bit her bottom lip, and her eyes flickered completely black.

"What the hell was that?" I asked. I stood straighter on my knees, pointing at her face right when her eyes flickered back to their normal, light hazel color.

"Sorry." Audrey rubbed her eyes. "Did they do the thing again?"

"Yes." Liam sounded amused by it. "You have nothing to apologize for."

"Why did her eyes just do that, though?" I asked. I had only ever seen Drustan's eyes flicker to black like that. I thought that was a Drustan-specific thing, fighting against his true siren form.

"She recognizes me as her mate," Liam spoke the words reverently, before turning to show me when his eyes shifted to black, too. "It's a common mate recognition sign in Hyvenmere, especially between interracial mates."

I froze with his words.

What.

No.

What?

"Everyone's eyes do that when they, um, recognize their partner?" I started picking at stray lint on the back couch cushions.

"Not everyone's," Audrey explained. "But it's a symptom that's becoming way more common than it used to be."

I couldn't move. My hands were stuck on a stray thread on the couch. I absorbed this revelation with a racing heart and a twist in my gut. But Audrey was half-fae. Half Hyvenmerian. That's probably why she triggered it so smoothly.

Drustan's eyes always seemed to fight against the shift to black. It was a slow transition. It was different than what Audrey and Liam just did. Probably because I was human, and not really his—

"You should bring those with you." Liam stepped toward the table and scooped up Audrey's snacks with one arm, holding his other hand out for her to grab.

"Do you need anything from us, Van?" Audrey asked, wrapping both of her hands around his arm instead. I held in a scoff when I saw her hand not so subtly squeeze his large bicep.

"Absolutely not." I shook my head and frowned. "I don't expect to see you back until this…" I pointed between the two of them. "Has cooled down." Audrey laughed as Liam led her toward the front door of our condo.

"Hey, real quick," I asked right when Liam's hand landed on the doorknob. "Did your sister find out what the sirens stole?" Liam frowned as he looked down at Audrey, who preened under his gaze.

"No," Liam sighed. "She also can't press charges against

anyone except the adolescents, since we were only able to detain them when they targeted the vaults. They are claiming the crime as their own, denying Ilia or Drustan's involvement. All security systems were taken down before Drustan and his minions even set foot on our estate. We have no proof that the Mad Siren Prince or Ilia were responsible for the robbery. Yours and Audrey's word are not enough."

I gave them both a thumbs down. "That sucks." They both looked painfully uncomfortable as they stood in the entryway. "Now get out of here." I shooed them away with my hands, while Audrey mouthed a silent *thank you* to me over her shoulder before they disappeared through the front door.

I settled back on the couch, replaying Liam's words in my head.

She recognizes me as her mate. Then I thought about the first time Drustan and I met, at Fergus's ball.

Mine, he had said. I shook my head.

"Nope." I lifted the remote and switched the TV to something else. Desperate to change the environment enough to move on from that conversation. To pretend like I wasn't hypothesizing something absolutely crazy. "Nope. Nope. Nope."

Audrey and Liam didn't return to society until three days later, and while they were clearly in some type of honeymoon phase, desperate to hold hands or touch each other as much as possible, they weren't nearly as *obsessed* with each other as they were before.

However, the recent development in their relationship soon took a back burner, because Hush had reached out to Liam to meet up again. It's how we ended up in my back office a week and a half after I visited Enhavenn with them, and Drustan pinned me against himself and sniffed my hair. Only days after, I gained newfound knowledge about Hyvenmerian's eyes shifting to solid black.

But I refused to waste energy hyper-fixating on the silly hypothesis I had, so I locked in when Hush entered my office with an object in her hand, lifted in the air for everyone to see.

"This is the former Siren Queen's private journal." She let her gaze flick across all of us in the room. "Before I share more information, *you*, halfling, need to read the passages I marked." Hush dropped the worn journal on my desk without flourish, making Audrey jump. "Now."

My friend lifted an eyebrow at Hush before tentatively taking the journal in her hands, gazing at the page Hush flopped open to. The room was silent and tense as Audrey's eyes quickly began skimming the pages filled with a beautiful written language I still couldn't interpret.

"This...this is about me." Audrey's face paled with her whispered words. Liam immediately stepped to her side, protective instincts kicking in.

"What does it say?" I asked, shifting my weight from one leg to the other.

Audrey shook her head as she held the journal closer to her face. It looked like she was reading the same line again and again as she whispered, "I'm not fae."

"What are you talking about?" I asked. Liam's eyes widened before he snatched the book from her hands and read the pages more intently.

"I'm—" Audrey shook her head again, her gaze looked distant as she stared at a spot on my desk. "I'm not half-fae..."

"So then, what are you?" I asked.

Audrey's hazel eyes locked on mine, the sun setting outside shone through the window at an angle that illuminated them just right, brightening the warm undertones of the hazel in them. The gold streaks in her irises gave me the answer before she could.

My lips parted in surprise. The room's silence was thick, and when Liam read the same passage, his whole body stiffened. His gaze also kept scanning the pages, reading and rereading the language I couldn't.

"…I'm half siren…" Audrey breathed.

Oh my god.

My best friend, who was mated to a fae prince, wasn't half of *his* people like she thought. Instead, Liam's mate was half of his worst enemy. Half of Audrey's DNA was from a people who betrayed Liam in the worst possible way.

"…That's why you didn't recognize Liam for so long," I murmured, rubbing the side of my neck as I held eye contact with her. "You wouldn't feel his heartbeat when you recognized your mate. You would recognize his sound." I recalled Audrey stopping mid-sentence when she *heard* Liam approaching the condo a few days ago.

It was why Liam felt their connection in his heart immediately, but Audrey didn't. It was why Liam waited *years* to tell Audrey what he knew. How much longer would he have waited had I not accidentally revealed their bond to Audrey?

Hush dropped her head and cursed, rubbing her brow with pinched fingers.

Liam tilted his head toward Hush. "Did you suspect this?"

Hush lifted her gaze to stare at the ceiling. "Yes. This confirms my suspicions."

I gaped at her. "You suspected that Audrey was half-siren and not fae this whole time?"

Hush lifted a shoulder. "Not initially. But it makes more sense that Audrey is a siren."

"How?" I questioned.

"Not recognizing her mate the standard fae way, for one, implied that she is something else—" She turned to Liam, who stiffened. "Yes, I recognized your heart desperately trying to time itself with hers every time we were in the same room.

Siren ears are better at picking up patterns like that." Liam squeezed Audrey's shoulder, tucking her closer to his body. I was side eyeing him, knowing he had disdain toward sirens in general because of what Drustan did to his parents, but he seemed to be taking Audrey's new identity in stride, from the way he didn't hesitate to hold her through this.

Perhaps the mating bond between them put things into perspective for him. I studied Audrey's dark red hair, so similar to...

"If that's Drustan's mother's journal, are you and Drustan related?" I raised my eyebrows. Hush and Audrey nodded while Liam frowned. "Wow..." I scraped a hand on my cheek in thought. "You're siblings with Drustan?"

"Half-siblings," Liam muttered.

"Blood related all the same," Hush added before stepping forward to face Liam head-on. "It's time for *you* to learn more about your parents, fae."

Liam immediately stiffened with defensiveness. "What about my parents? What do they have to do with this?"

"The question you *should* be asking is why Ilia sent us to rob *your* parents' private journals a week ago." Hush shifted her weight to one hip as she crossed her arms to address Liam, authority and dominance straightening her spine. Liam didn't cower but instead held her gaze with his. Hush just revealed what they stole that night. Something Ada and her guard hadn't been able to figure out, yet.

"What do you mean?" Audrey asked as she rubbed Liam's chest, right over his heart. Hush reached into the inside pocket of her cloak before pulling out another worn journal. Liam's eyes widened in recognition. She tossed it to him, and he snatched it out of the air with ease.

"This was the goal of our mission," Hush explained. "While the teenagers distracted the queen and prince."

"This was my mother's?" Liam asked as he held the new

journal in his hands. Hush simply nodded. "This page?" Liam asked, finding where the bookmark was.

"Yes," Hush confirmed. She gave Liam a few moments to start reading, but when his eyes widened and color started to drain from his face, she spoke up again, "You recognize your own mother's handwriting, yes?" Liam nodded. "Do you get it now?"

I raised my hand, still sitting on my little loveseat. "Can someone explain what you're all reading for the human in the room?" Liam slumped, never turning the page. His eyes frantically kept rereading the passage over and over again. Audrey, reading over his shoulder, also looked crushed. She kept rubbing his arm and back, attempting to soothe him.

I'd never seen Liam so distressed.

Hush took it upon herself to answer my question.

"Sometimes the answers we seek don't bring the comfort we expected." Hush sighed, leaning against the wall and propping one foot against it. "Why did Drustan kill the former Fae King and Queen? Why would the Siren Prince of Lyndoruun even consider fulfilling such a heinous, morbid act of war?" Silence filled the room while Hush let her words settle over us. "It must have been something personal."

"This says—" Audrey cleared her throat, distress soaking her voice. "Liam's mother's journal is documenting when—when—"

"They killed Queen Astrid. Drustan's mother." Liam said in a flat tone of disbelief.

My jaw dropped.

"But...why?" Another question popped into my head. "Why kill the Siren Queen?"

Hush simply replied, "The unnatural death of one's mate can have a negative effect on the living partner."

"But *why* would Liam's parents kill the Siren Queen?" I asked.

"Because Ilia asked them to..." Liam whispered. I froze as

Audrey lifted her gaze to look at the former Siren Queen's leather journal now resting on my desk, whispering as it clicked for her, "…Because she had me."

I gasped.

"Oh my god." I tucked my legs underneath me. "Oh my *god*." That's how Audrey and Drustan were half-siblings.

"Ilia is a prideful male," Hush continued. "Once Queen Astrid gave birth to Audrey, he smelled the human in her immediately. Discovered his queen's disloyalty. Ilia realized that even though killing the solvyrn earned him the right to *marry* Astrid, without a formal mating bond, Queen Astrid may have a mate of her own—in the human realm. Which would be another threat to one of his titles. He bought Astrid's hand through the act of fulfilling a part of an ancient prophecy, but if word got out that Astrid had a human mate, that would negate the legitimacy of his rule beside her. According to her journal, Ilia ordered Astrid to get rid of Audrey. However." Hush lifted a shoulder. "Ilia underestimated the devotion a mother can have to her child."

Cold dread seeped into my gut. Audrey was close to death since the day she was born.

"How is Audrey alive right now?" I asked.

Audrey wrapped her arms around Liam's waist, who eventually dropped the journal and tucked her into his chest. He dropped his nose, inhaling her hair as they sought comfort in each other's embrace.

"Losing a child at birth is not uncommon, especially due to the fertility issues our realm had struggled with up until about thirty years ago," Hush said with reverence. "It was easy for the people of Lyndoruun to believe their queen experienced the same tragedy so many others have. Eventually, though, Ilia must have learned that his queen simply sent Audrey away…to the human realm."

"And that wasn't enough for him?" I asked, letting my hatred for Ilia coat my words.

"No," Hush sighed. "A pompous male like him couldn't continue living his days knowing that the evidence of his queen's affair was walking around. But he couldn't find Audrey, and Astrid wouldn't help him. The queen probably grew more distant. He couldn't trust that she wouldn't seek out her human mate again, so..." Hush nodded toward Liam.

"...Ilia asked my parents to kill Astrid," Liam finished, before shaking his head. "No. Ilia probably forced my parents' hand. My parents were *good* fae. They wouldn't just blindly do Ilia's bidding unless they were put in an impossible position—"

"Do their words read like fae who were forced against their will to take a life?" Hush countered, and when Liam stayed silent, she muttered, "Precisely."

"But—but that means that Drustan killed my parents for nothing more than petty revenge." Liam's face was turning red now. "Despicable."

Hush took a moment to let Liam mourn the image he'd held of his parents his entire life, before saying, "If a male like Ilia is willing to harm an innocent child, why wouldn't he be just as willing to harm his own queen? An alliance easily formed between Ilia and the former fae royals, because your parents thought removing one siren royal would make the other look weaker."

"...If Ilia and Astrid were mates, he *would* have grown weaker over time, but they weren't..." Audrey whispered.

"The nereids had two kings and a queen, the fae had both a king and a queen, but then there was just the Siren King. Only having one siren royal was a strategy your parents would directly benefit from," Hush sighed to a glaring Liam. "They probably assumed they could manipulate him to agree to their trade deals more easily. Based on how they describe sirens in their own private words, they didn't consider us to be held to the same air as fae and nereids."

Something didn't make sense in my head, even after the

four of us sat in silence over this revelation. "Why didn't Ilia send someone to, um, take care of Audrey?" Audrey lifted her gaze to stare at Hush, as if she were wondering the same thing.

"He did." Hush stared at the ground. "But Queen Astrid was smart. She knew he wasn't above murdering a child born out of a marital bond." Something soft flickered across her expression, but difficult for me to clock behind her mask. "However, I believe the former queen reached out to a powerful witch to cast a protection over Audrey."

Liam lifted his head, his brows furrowed in thought. "But protection spells wear off. They're not permanent. The fact that this one seemed to last three decades was already an impressive feat."

"Which is exactly why you were suddenly able to track her and the other halflings down in this realm a couple of years ago," Hush stated matter-of-factly. All our eyes widened at that. It was all starting to make sense.

"Drustan's mom didn't just protect *her* daughter." I pressed a hand to my chest, a simmering of hope burning my heart. "... She protected all the half-human children."

Hush nodded in agreement. Audrey's lips parted.

Liam frowned. "And her mate had her killed for it, because he couldn't get to Audrey." He released one of his arms around Audrey to scrape down his face. "And then my parents even documented what they considered their...*alliance*. Because even though Ilia thought he was strong enough to combat the long-term effects of losing a mate, they probably assumed what it would do to him." He released Audrey to slump against the wall, sliding down until his ass hit the ground. Folding his arms over his knees, he rested his head on them.

"Jesus," I muttered. "Drustan discovered all this, then? You think that's why he killed Liam's parents?"

Hush lifted a shoulder. "It would make the most sense."

"Does your sister know?" Audrey asked Liam, crouching down on the floor with him.

Hush shook her head. "I doubt Queen Ada is aware. I stole this from a corner of your archives that had many artifacts and keepsakes that hold no value. Masterfully hidden by the formal fae royals, where no one would think to keep something so important, but they could easily access it whenever they needed. I would be surprised if Ada ever got her hands on this specific journal of theirs."

Liam released a loud exhale as he nodded against his arms, feeling relief, but probably not enough of it.

"We should tell Drustan about Ilia's kill order," I muttered.

All three of them lifted their eyes to look at me, so I elaborated.

"We have to tell him." I nodded. "If he knew what his *father* did, that would be a game changer. No man can stomach the fact that his father killed his mother. It would get Drustan completely on our side."

Hush lifted a shoulder. "It wouldn't suck to have the Mad Siren Prince supporting us."

Liam grumbled, "Dammit. Drustan is a *murderer*."

"Apparently, so were your parents," I retorted.

"We need some time," Audrey muttered as she glared at me. "I don't think that Liam and I are in the mental space to make any major decisions right now."

Hush's blonde brows furrowed. "I'm not so sure you have the time you want."

"I don't care," Audrey snapped at her. "You just dumped a lot of information on us. Our entire view of ourselves just got thwarted. We need time to process. To regroup how we approach Ilia, the nereids, and even Ada."

Hush and I exchanged a look. It was like we were both saying, ...*really?* Not to be insensitive, but Audrey had only considered herself to be half-fae for about two years. Adjusting to learn that she's half-siren shouldn't be that crazy. But maybe that was a privileged, full-blooded human take for me to have.

"I must take these back," Hush sighed as she stood from the wall and collected the journals. "I was barely able to leave the Shaw Estate with them. I need to return them, so I don't reveal my cover." She locked her eyes on all of us. "I'll be checking in. We can plan more specifically another time. I can only give you a day or so."

Audrey and Liam didn't say anything to her, so I chimed in, "Sounds good." Hush nodded at me before studying Liam and Audrey with a look I couldn't decipher behind her mask. Within a blink, she lyskifted and she was gone.

CHAPTER 19

I weirdly became both Liam and Audrey's emotional support the rest of the day. Offering them comforting caffeinated drinks; helping them build Audrey's new, bigger bed that took up most of her bedroom—but hey, at least Liam fit in that one.

Liam was basically a third roommate at this point, and even though I still got annoyed with him, I accepted the fact that he would be wherever Audrey was. I fought the urge to escape to my boat so that the two of them could play house together at the condo, but I decided I wouldn't remove myself from my own home just to make them feel more comfortable being in it as a couple.

That evening, my phone buzzed.

Drew: Are you free tomorrow?

It was a Saturday, so I grinned with my reply.

Me: Yes, but I'm planning the date again.

"Are you punishing him?" Audrey asked with a laugh as she tossed some protein bars in her backpack.

I shrugged as I leaned against the doorway to her bedroom. "Maybe a little bit. But also, he would end up collecting trash with me regardless."

"That's true." Audrey nodded as she grabbed her hoodie and zipped it up. She and Liam were heading back to Enhavenn to formally announce Audrey as his mate, per Ada's suggestion. His sister wanted to give them space to enjoy their new mating bond in peace, but the prince of Enharra finding his mate, was newsworthy to his people. Audrey and Liam would spend the next couple of days conducting interviews, visiting families in his territory, and engaging in general royal activities.

Plus, they had to delicately handle the PR aspect of announcing Audrey's true lineage, without also announcing how they discovered this news.

Audrey already had a target on her back from Ilia as is. Liam's sister agreed that they would wait to tell Hyvenmere Audrey's real identity. Until it was a more stable time to be half siren and mated to the Fae Prince.

When I asked if they'd heard from Hush yet, Audrey shook her head.

"Maybe I'm being irresponsible," Audrey said. "But I need to not focus on Ilia or the nereids or the gates. I just want to keep focusing on the fact that Liam and I are mates for a little longer, no matter how selfish that makes me sound." I did not envy Audrey. The relationship that she had been yearning for, for years, suddenly got a thousand times more complicated.

I, however, was just grateful to be casually dating a basic human man.

Part of me wondered how Drustan would react to the knowledge of my situationship with a human, since he seemed to be hitting on me. Though, most of his flirting felt like a mockery. Like a handsome popular kid in middle school teasing the nerd with braces and acne.

Mine, one of the first words Drustan ever said to me. But then I reminded myself that it didn't matter how Drustan felt about me. Who I dated was no one's business but mine, and mine alone.

So, when Audrey and Liam waved goodbye, promising to be back the next day, just in case Drew (hopefully) decided to take our relationship to the next level, I focused on which swimsuit I wanted to wear when I took him out on the boat. Most of the ones I had in mind would show off my many tan lines—the cost of being a white woman who perked up like a flower as soon as direct sunlight touched her skin—so trying to hide those was out.

Which swimsuit successfully portrayed the message that I *wanted* Drew? I respected his boundary, but as soon as he gave the green light, he could take me right then and there on the boat.

Pulling my hair back into a braid, I checked my phone one last time.

The last message we sent was me texting him the address of where to meet up. Just outside the docks. Slipping my sandals on, I did a little happy shimmy with my shoulders as I grabbed my backpack and headed out.

Later that day, Drew and I were out on my boat, rocking with the gentle waves of the ocean on a clear, sunny day.

Our relationship was burning slowly, which wasn't something I was used to. I was a proudly sexual woman. I didn't mind jumping into bed the first night if that's what felt right for me. However, Drew putting up some clear boundaries at the beginning of all this didn't upset me either.

Taking things slowly made me feel like what we had could become special. It felt like he intended to gain a deeper understanding than men usually wanted to have with me, while still being super horny for each other.

"Ready?" I asked as I slid my cutoff jean shorts down my legs. Obviously, I did it as seductively as possible. Just because we hadn't gotten naked in bed yet didn't mean I wasn't ready to do so whenever he gave the okay.

His dark eyes tracked the movement of my shorts as he replied, "Yes."

I grabbed a mesh bag before snapping goggles over my eyes. I had oxygen tanks and masks on the boat in case of an emergency, but I had also spent time training my lungs to hold my breath for longer periods. I could do it for almost a solid minute. Plus, the ocean floor wasn't that far beneath the boat on this spot. I wouldn't have to dive as deep to pick out trash from the coral.

Following my lead, Drew pulled his shirt off, folded it, and gently set it on the bench seat next to him. I smiled and shook my head, not surprised at how much he cared for his clothes.

His sculpted chest was…magnificent. Perfectly sun-kissed, not a farmer's tan in sight. He must have shaved his chest, because there wasn't any chest hair on it. *Maybe he'd be willing to grow a little out for me.* Focusing back on our date, I walked toward the ladder before waving him over.

"Cannonball?" I asked him.

He tilted his head at me as he inspected the goggles I gave him. "What?"

"Want to do a cannonball?"

"What's that?" he asked with a smile.

I shook my head and laughed. "Shut up." I stepped up onto the edge of the boat, surprised when he dropped the goggles on the boat floor, and stepped up next to me, clasping our hands together.

"No goggles?" I asked.

"I can see just fine in the water," he assured me with a smirk. Men. Always wanting to show off. I shrugged before pulling my hand free of his and launching my body off the boat.

Seconds before I hit the water, I shouted, "Cannonball!" I couldn't see it, but I had a feeling I made a decent splash. Maybe I soaked him, too. I popped up out of the salty surface, grasping the mesh bag in my hand as I wiped loose strands of wet hair from my goggles to look up.

Drew was standing right where I left him.

He smirked before shaking his head once and saying, "I think I can cannonball better."

"Those are fighting words, Drew," I taunted. He chuckled before launching his large body off the boat and folding himself up, splashing right next to me. I was laughing and scraping salt water off the bottom half of my face where the goggles didn't protect, when he popped his dark head out of the water.

He turned to grin at me, a beautiful, happy grin—that quickly morphed into a grimace as he squeezed his eyes closed.

"Are you okay?" I asked, paddling toward him. Drew lifted his hands to his eyes, which were blinking rapidly and struggling to stay open.

"Shit," he muttered.

"Oh, no." I rested a hand on his shoulder. "You forgot to take your contacts out."

He turned away from me, his hands raised to adjust his contacts. Drew gave me his back and swam back toward the boat, swiftly pulling himself up the ladder with his strong arms.

Something small grazed my shoulder in the water, and when I reached my hand up to grab what I suspected was a small piece of trash, I was surprised to see his contact in the palm of my hand.

"Oh, I found one!" I clasped it in my hand as I made it back to the ladder, pulling myself out carefully. I didn't want to bend or warp his contact. I had no idea how expensive these were. Drew was hunched as he stood in the middle of the boat deck, still messing with his eyes.

"We have to go," he grunted.

"I found one of your contacts." I raised my palm as my feet landed on the deck. After removing my goggles, I glanced down to make sure I didn't damage it.

That's when I noticed something.

It wasn't a typical contact. It was a contact that changed the color of someone's eyes. A type of contact that actors used. His dark brown eyes were clearly not actually dark brown, because I could see the ring of color on the small disk.

"Take us back," Drew said again. His tone was off. He sounded angry and irritated.

I frowned. "Seriously? What's wrong? Let me see." I stepped forward, dropping my mesh bag from my other hand to rest it on his large shoulder. Drew shouldered me off, turning away from me again.

"Let's just go!" he demanded.

Unfortunately for him, I'd rather die than let a man tell me what to do. *Especially* while he was angry.

"Don't talk to me like that," I replied. "Did you scratch your eye? Let me see. You might need a doctor—"

"I don't need a doctor, Van—" Drew cut me off. "I need to go."

"Let me see—"

"—It's fine."

"It's *not* fine." I frowned, raising my voice. "You're being a dick and barking orders at me. If you're in that much pain, I need to see what happened to your eye!"

"Van, stop." He was struggling to compose his voice, which I appreciated, but when I rested my hand on his shoulder, he shrugged me off again. He just kept hiding his face from me.

"Drew, you're freaking me out." I grabbed his shoulder, fighting off his shrug to pull him toward me. "What the hell is going on?"

"Please, Van, please—"

"Let me see!" I yelled at him, finally getting his body to face me, but he kept one hand over the eye that didn't have a contact in it. Then he grumbled and shoved away from me, giving me his back. I hopped on him, like a koala.

"You're freaking me out, Drew!" I yelled in his ear. He grunted and tried to throw me off, so I bit down on his shoulder in irritation. Shocked that this situation brought that urge out of me, Drew yelped and dropped his hands to grab my arms. I kept my legs locked around his narrow waist, which made him slide me to the front of him.

I grinned because both of his hands were on me to support my body, wrapped around his. But then my smile immediately fell when I looked at him.

He realized what he did, then. He practically dropped me to cover his eye, but it was too late. I had already seen it.

A gold, otherworldly iris.

With a gasp, I dropped to my feet and stepped away from him. His hand released my waist, but he clenched his hands into fists after.

"Van—wait—"

"You're a siren?" I shook my head with my question, before turning on my heel and bolted into the main cabin. Drew cursed before following me, his speed too fast to be human. I reached for my backpack, where I kept the pepper spray. But large bands of muscle wrapped around my waist, pinning my arms to my side.

"Van, please—"

"Let go of me!" I yelled. I thrashed and kicked and threw my head back, but it landed on a shoulder, not his nose like I wanted. "Let go, now!"

"I can't," he yelled back, pulling me away from my backpack while struggling to still me.

I wouldn't still. I was terrified. I was filled with rage.

"Who *are* you?" I screeched at him.

Did some random siren wander over to the human realm in search of a mate? Did he view himself as a tourist?

Oh god, we were out on the ocean. Isolated.

This siren could kill me right here and now if he wanted to.

"Vanessa, please," his voice was low near my ear, and though his strong arms were still wrapped around me tight, he wasn't trying to hurt me.

Yet. I kept thrashing in his grasp. Eventually, he grunted and pinned me against the interior of my boat, up against the pantry cabinet.

"Vanessa, calm—"

"Who are you?" I interrupted, still struggling but unable to move nearly as much, pinned between him and the pantry doors like this. "What is this? What do you want with me?"

"Vanessa—"

"—Who *are* you?!" I screamed before falling limp in his hold. Exhaustion overpowered me, perhaps due to fear of how vulnerable I was. Trapped on my own boat with a siren, capable of killing me in seconds. Capable of using his sinndra on me.

Oh my god. Was I ever truly attracted to Drew? Or was it all some horrible emotional siren manipulation? Drew's breath was sawing in and out of him behind me, almost frantic. But neither of us spoke. We just stood there, his large body pinning mine. Rocking gently with the steady waves of the ocean.

My eyes started to burn, and a single tear escaped to trail down my cheek. His breath caught, and I wondered if he saw the tear.

"...I'm sorry..." he muttered. I didn't say anything. He knew the jig was up. I knew the jig was up. What did we even do from here? Would he kill me for discovering his secret?

Silent, painful moments filled the space between us. Eventually, fear twisted my chest enough to make me choke out, "…What are you going to do to me?"

His body tensed, and he dropped his hold on me immediately. Cool air brushed against my back, where the warmth of his body had been. I collapsed and slumped against the wood of the pantry cupboard, resting my forehead against it as another tear escaped my eye—a tear of anger.

"Did your king send you?" I asked in a low whisper.

I held my breath as I waited for his response.

"No." His voice changed, but I couldn't tell how until he continued in his natural accent, "…this was just for me." My eyes opened wide before I whirled around to confirm who was standing in my boat with me.

His dark, blood red hair was damp from our jump in the ocean. Pointed ears with no gold hoops poked out of the strands. No jewelry on any part of his body. He grew almost a foot from what Drew's height was, making him awkwardly hunch in the cabin to avoid knocking his head against the ceiling. His naked torso was significantly paler, no longer sporting the skin of a Californian who spent most of their time in the sun. He had taken out his second contact, unveiling a pair of those distinct, siren irises. His torso was wider, too. Perhaps he looked so big because of the smaller quarters of the cabin. Perhaps he looked so big because he genuinely was *so* big.

I gaped at the siren prince, standing there with a stone-cold facial expression, complete with a clenched jaw. His eyes locked me in place. I both wanted to freeze and run away at the same time.

Instead, I ground my teeth together and glared at Drustan Shaw.

"What the hell?" I muttered, before balling my hands into

fists. I got to my feet and started marching toward him. Drustan wasn't expecting that. His eyes widened in surprise before he quickly trapped my wrists in his large hands to keep me from hitting his chest with them. Perhaps my emotions and thoughts were racing too fast for him to keep up with.

"Fuck you," I grunted between clenched teeth as I struggled to free myself. I wanted to hit him. I wanted to punch him. Rocks were forming in my gut, and betrayal and loss filled my chest with ice.

"Vanessa." Drustan tsked at me. "You're going to hurt yourself."

I kicked him in the shin, but he didn't react to it. I did, however, feel a small crunch in one of my toes before I yelped and my knees buckled. Drustan cursed again as he released his hold on my wrists to drop to his knees. He clasped my foot in one of his hands to study it. "Dammit."

"No!" I yanked my foot out of his hold, falling backward on my ass. I tucked my foot, which for sure had a broken toe now, closer to my body as I yelled at him, "Don't do that. Don't pretend that you care."

Drustan frowned at me before he snapped, "You assume I'm pretending?"

I scoffed at him and asked, "Are you shitting me?"

Drustan grumbled as he shook his head in irritation. Then, using his hands and knees, he stalked toward me. It took no effort for him to crowd me against the pantry again, because the cabin was so small. My heart was racing; something was thawing in my chest. Excitement? Adrenaline? Because his stupid handsome siren magnetism was on full display now, and my pitiful human nervous system didn't stand a chance.

"Do you think I enjoyed the ruse?" Drustan spat as his golden eyes flared with his words. "That I enjoyed playing the part of a pitiful human male?"

"Yeah." I widened my eyes at him, curling up in a ball

against the pantry. "I think you did. You probably got off thinking about how stupid I was."

Drustan frowned. "You are not stupid. It was challenging to keep up the deception."

I widened my eyes in horror and shook my head. My mouth opened and shut as words escaped me. I pressed both of my palms to my cheeks, unable to process this.

Andrew wasn't *real*.

Drew was Drustan.

Drew…was *Drustan*.

I'm such a moron.

"W-why?" I finally settled on.

"*Why?*" Drustan asked as he shifted closer. He rested his massive body on his knees as he braced both of his palms against the pantry doors. Caging me between his arms as I struggled to press as much of my curled-up side against the pantry as possible, "Why do *you* think, Vanessa?"

"To fuck with me?"

Drustan shook his head, frowning with his words, "We've already established your competence, Vanessa. You know I wouldn't put in that much time and effort for a prank. So, tell me, why would I spend weeks masquerading as a human with you in your realm?"

I frowned at him, pissed that he dared to seem irritated with me right now.

"To taunt Audrey? Give the halfling and fae that you hate the finger?"

Drustan's nostrils flared. From the way he squeezed his eyes closed for a moment, I had a feeling he was struggling not to roll them. "Wrong again. The realms don't revolve entirely around the halfling and her mate."

"Don't they? Why else—"

Something he said tugged at my chest. Her mate.

Mate.

My expression fell, not in disappointment, but in bewilderment.

Mine.

My lips parted, and his gaze dropped to them momentarily before raising to meet my eyes again.

No.

There's no way. Did he really think…?

"Why would I do any of this, Vanessa?" Drustan asked again, leaning toward me. His nose was centimeters from mine now. His body was tense, his eyes held mine hostage. He knew where my mind had drifted; he was following my thoughts in real time.

I blinked at him, heat burning in my chest and cheeks. A little from embarrassment, but mostly confusion.

"You can't be serious," I muttered.

"Can't I?" Drustan challenged.

I shook my head at him, sucking in a sharp breath. His masculine scent filled my nostrils and throat. I swallowed around dryness.

"But—but I'm not like you," I said.

"I'm aware," Drustan replied.

"But humans don't—we don't—I can't have a m—" I cut myself off. Nerves twisted my gut too much to allow me to say the word out loud.

He narrowed his eyes at me and tilted his head to the side, something flashing in them that I couldn't identify. "If you truly believed humans couldn't, why has the halfling spent years trying to convince the people of my realm that they can—and should? Do you truly think your friend is so dim?"

I shook my head. I slid my palms into my hair. I gripped the roots of the strands, tugging against the damp braid at my back. I still didn't comprehend a lot about bonds like this, but Audrey made it clear that the connection was somewhat devastating. Forming a bond and potentially losing that bond could weaken a creature like him.

If Drustan had a mate and lost them…

But Drustan had already fought madness of some kind, hadn't he? He crawled out of the Gravhune. He's the only one on record who has completed a five-year sentence. If he were able to survive the Gravhune, it would make sense that the loss of a mate wouldn't be as concerning to him as it would be to a typical siren.

"You seriously believe—"

"I *know* what we are," Drustan abruptly cut me off. I flinched from his stern tone, and he frowned. "Contrary to what you're assuming, I do not want to hurt you."

"Why would I believe that?" I countered. "This isn't, like, a *good* thing for you, right? If what you're thinking is real, this makes *you* vulnerable, right?"

"I'd like to see anyone try to use this against me." His lips turned up in the corner, as if my train of thought was amusing to him. "…Mates are always a good—"

I shoved him away with my hands, startling him again. He didn't go far because he was still a massive man, so when he tried to reach for me again, I lifted my foot that didn't have a throbbing, painful broken toe and pressed it against his bare chest.

Right between his massive pecks. Heat flared in his eyes at the move, and I tried my best to ignore it.

"You *killed* Liam's *parents*—you ripped their hearts out—" Drustan cut me off by grabbing my ankle with one hand. His fingers folded over each other.

"—and I would do it again if given the chance," he scowled with his words. A frown pulled at his lips.

"Because you loved killing them so much?" I asked through a shiver. Cold chills had raced down my arms at the thought. I was again reminded of how *alone* we were. He could rip my heart out, too, with little thought, and no one would find me.

He could dump my body in the ocean, only for it to wash up on shore days later. "B-because—"

His grip on my ankle tightened a moment before he roughly yanked me under him, sliding me away from the pantry doors so that I was flat on my back. He braced one large arm on his elbow near my shoulder so that he could lean down toward my shocked face. His damp red hair tickled my shoulders.

"I don't lose any sleep over killing those fae, Vanessa." Drustan shook his head. "I'd do it again, and again, and again. I lull myself to sleep at night, recalling the sounds of their screams, slowly morphing into pathetic gurgling as they drowned in their own blood. I will *never* apologize for finding pleasure in that memory."

A sharp pang of understanding hit my ribcage, and I hated that I sympathized with someone like this. That I had a past that even allowed me to sympathize with someone like this. From my vulnerable position on my back, I was still willing to argue with him. "All the more reason for me to be fucking terrified of you right now."

Drustan's lips pulled back, slowly, slowly. As if my words humored him. Something flashed in his eyes. Was it heavy emotion? Was it insanity? I couldn't tell. I was too distracted by the speed of my heart rapidly beating in my ribcage.

"You're a *little* frightened of me, that I will concede," Drustan murmured. He pressed his lips together in that shit-eating grin before he continued, "…but that also excites you."

I made a *what the fuck* face at him, "No. It doesn't. I am not *excited* to be alone on a boat, in the middle of the ocean, with a killer."

Drustan smirked as he dragged his tongue across his teeth, letting his gaze travel over me again before replying, "Fortunately for you, I'm *your* killer. Whether you want to accept it or not."

"Dude!" I lifted my hands to shove him off of me, and he let me push him away with a low chuckle. I stood and marched toward the captain's deck, ignoring my throbbing toe—which probably wasn't truly broken if I could walk on it—determined to take us back to shore. I could hear his footsteps as he followed me; my body could *feel* his approach. Fine hairs rose on the back of my neck the closer he came.

Was this…was this a mate thing? No. It's a woman being pursued by a dangerous man thing.

I huffed, threw myself into the captain's chair, and started to draw up the anchor. Drustan sat in the passenger seat next to me, just like he had arrived. Except he was a huge siren now, so the chair looked significantly smaller underneath him than it did in his human disguise.

"I take it that we are going to let the fish choke on plastic today?" Drustan asked as he struggled to find a comfortable position with his larger body.

"Eat glass," I snapped at him.

"The fish probably will without our help," he replied with a quiet laugh to himself, before he frowned at the chair and murmured, "I was promised a date that involved cleaning up the reefs, but now we're leaving. It almost feels like you don't like me anym—"

"What the hell is wrong with you?" I asked as I checked the tank levels.

"Where would you like to start?" Drustan replied without looking at me. He was still frowning at the chair, and how he didn't fit in it anymore in his actual size. "Perhaps it was the pure joy I felt ripping the hearts out of the worst fae in the realm. Maybe it was five years of torture in the Gravhune. Maybe it's because my mate doesn't seem—"

"Stop it." I glared at him. "Sit still and stop talking."

Drustan laughed at that. He lifted his molten gaze to mine and smiled with his words, "I know you enjoy the sound of my voice, my song. It would be a shame to deny you it." I widened my eyes at him in disbelief, fighting the urge to scream in frustration at him. His eyes flared in response, his grin picked up a notch.

"I hate your voice." I lied.

"No, you don't." Drustan lifted his arms to hold both of his hands behind his head. He turned the chair toward me, showing off his bare, toned torso, his large arms, and that dangerously handsome face.

"I do hate it," I grumbled through clenched teeth. I was determined to stand my ground.

"You are drawn to my voice, Vanessa. As I am drawn to yours," Drustan explained.

I shook my head and replied, "My draw to you isn't real. It's just your siren *sinndra*—"

Drustan lifted an eyebrow as he replied, "You are completely immune to my sinndra, Vanessa."

I snapped my mouth closed, not expecting that response. "What?"

"Mates are equals, in every way. I cannot use my sinndra on you—and trust me, I've tried. Several times, in fact, only to prove exactly what we are to each other."

I balled my hands into fists. "We're nothing to each other."

"You're drawn to my voice, my smell, my body," Drustan continued, ignoring my protest. "As I am to you. Because I was designed by the goddess Tynara herself to specifically appeal to *you*. Because you're mine, and I'm *yours*."

"You're not—" I groaned, ignoring the fluttering in my heart, and pinched the bridge of my nose with my fingers. I squeezed my eyes closed to fight the headache that was starting to form. "We're not what you think we are. I'm just a horny woman. Just because there's sexual chemistry doesn't mean that we're—that you're..." I couldn't even finish the sentence.

I opened my eyes and dropped my hand on the steering

wheel of my boat to study him. Drustan pressed his lips together and hummed in thought.

"Do you think this is our first fight as a couple? Or—" He was interrupted when I grabbed my insulated water bottle and threw it at his head. He dodged it, laughing as he did so. It spilled somewhere, but I didn't care about that right now.

"We are not a couple, Dru—" I cut myself off and shook my head, glaring at the ceiling of the cabin as I gripped the steering wheel with one hand. The anchor was secured now, but we hadn't taken off yet. We were floating in the calm waters of the Pacific. As if Mother Nature herself was letting us hash this out before we got a move on.

"I must admit," Drustan replied, his tone a little lower. "I'm still learning the details about human courting customs, but—"

I laughed.

It wasn't a cute one; it was a hysterical one. I used both of my hands to cover my face as I laughed into my palms. My entire body shook with it. I couldn't believe this was my reality. The deadliest siren in the magical realm was sitting on my boat, talking about courting me.

It was all so insane.

"I wasn't expecting you to find this so amusing." Drustan dared to sound mildly offended.

"Nothing is *funny*," I laughed with my words. "This is just so crazy. *You're* crazy."

"I hear that's a side-effect of the Gravhune," he deadpanned.

"What is your angle?" I lowered my hands to glare at him, finally able to compose myself. "What do you gain from messing with me like this?"

His hands were still behind his back, his legs stretched as far as the space allowed him to, one ankle crossed over the other. Drustan frowned at me.

"Beyond the supposed bliss of a mating bond, you mean?"

"Why the hell would you, Drustan, give a single shit about ma—about bonds?"

I still couldn't say the word out loud.

Drustan stared at me, his lips pressed together. A muscle popped in his jaw as he let the noise of the ocean soak into the moment. I held my glare on him, determined to wait him out. To not fold under his scrutiny.

Slowly, he lowered his hands and leaned forward. Drustan was sitting, but he still managed to feel like he was taking up the entirety of the captain's quarters. When he rested both of his hands on either side of my chair to turn me toward him, my face heated.

His nose was only inches from mine as we locked eyes.

"For some reason," Drustan murmured. "The goddess blessed me with this gift." The way he spoke made me sink into my chair, but he didn't let me escape. He maintained the distance between us, scooting to the edge of his seat. It creaked under his massive frame. "Don't get me wrong, Vanessa. I may be the Mad Siren Prince, but it would be completely foolish of me to ignore what's between us."

I narrowed my eyes at him. "You're seriously..." I shook my head, struggling to get the words out when I could feel his body heat this close to me. "You're trying to claim you *want* to be m —" I hesitated, but forced myself to say it this once, "Mated to me?" I shook my head at him, "What would your daddy say about that?"

"Fuck my father," Drustan snapped.

I jumped at his tone.

Didn't expect that response.

He tensed his body over me for a moment before he closed his eyes and exhaled. The heat of his breath brushed against my neck and chest, making me shiver underneath him. Suddenly, Drustan opened his eyes and stood. He grabbed my hands and yanked me out of my seat.

"What the fu—let me go!" I pulled against him, but it was useless. He dragged me through the boat until we got to the small restroom and shoved open the pocket door. I protested, but he ignored me until he pushed my body into the small room. I had to brace both hands on the sink and catch myself. When I glanced up at the mirror, he was caging us in the bathroom. Drustan had to duck for his head to be visible in the doorway, and his large arms held either side of the frame.

"Do you see yourself?" Drustan asked me through the mirror. I had to force myself to respond; I could feel his body heat behind me. I still wore my thong bikini; my ass was exposed to him. But he held eye contact with me in the mirror.

"What?"

"I know human senses aren't as strong as ours," Drustan continued with a nod of his head toward me. "But you can see yourself clearly, yes?"

I frowned, "Yeah. What—"

"Then is it really so unbelievable," Drustan interrupted. "For a male like me to show even the *slightest* bit of interest in a woman like you?"

I froze. My cheeks heated. My heart thumped erratically, almost stopping, before picking up a steady rhythm again. Maybe it was his use of the word *woman* in lieu of *female*, but I couldn't be sure. I parted my lips in confusion at his reflection.

Drustan's lips were in a firm line, his gold irises bounced around my face in the mirror, before making eye contact again.

"Don't misunderstand," his voice was lower, that silk honey coating my nerves. "I have happily killed, and I will most likely kill again. I expect everyone to be fully aware of that truth." Shivers raced down my spine as he slowly, slowly stepped toward me. Both of his arms bracketed each of mine, his chest pressed against my back, my bare ass against the fabric of his swim trunks that hung low on his hips. His large hands gripped either side of the sink, just like mine. Caging me in.

My breath was coming to me in shorter, frantic puffs.

Drustan lowered his head as he continued to murmur, "Imagine, if you will..." He slowly shifted one of his hands to tease the top of mine with the pads of his fingers. "Growing up in that wretched estate. Watching my father throw together failed Bandthral rituals year after year, snuffing out any hope for such a rare gift...only to find you."

I had to force myself to breathe. Memories from our first meeting at Fergus's castle filled my mind. Memories that I knew he was seeing, too. My face was hot, and my chest was too tight. Sand was rushing in my ears, and as soon as I caught myself leaning into his body more, I bit my lip to stop myself.

"To discover a creature perfectly designed to seduce me, hiding in the drapes..." Drustan continued, lifting his gaze to lock on mine in the mirror.

I was hypnotized. Not by him, but by the moment. By his proximity. The heat of him caging me in against the tiny sink. The tease of his fingers on my hand, traveling up my arm, until one of his hands grazed my shoulder.

"Lulling me in with her delicious scent." Drustan turned his nose toward my hair and inhaled, expanding his chest enough to emphasize the contact between us. "Hopelessly tangled in your trance. Enchanting me with your beauty. Your eyes..." His hand on my shoulder slowly dragged over my collar bones, then flattened over my chest. His pinky finger pressed against the swell of my breast, his thumb brushed against the sensitive pulse point at the base of my neck. "Even the deadliest monster would crumble to his knees for a chance with a stunning creature like you, my song."

I exhaled a ragged breath, leaning back, exposing more of my neck for him.

Drustan took the silent invitation. His lips first teased the shell of my ear before gently nipping it. I pressed my lips together to keep my whimper at bay, but it was difficult as his palm on my chest pulled me entirely flush against him. My hips were pinned against the sink. No part of my back or ass was untouched by his massive body.

His masculine scent was making me lightheaded.

The soothing heat of his skin on mine made muscles in my body slowly relax into his hold. A low sound rumbled in his chest as he nipped at my neck. I could hear the intake of breath through his nostrils, as if he was inhaling as much of me as he could.

I pressed my ass against him, desperate to confirm this physical attraction between us.

He responded by pressing his hips into me. Letting me feel the rigid evidence of his arousal on my lower back, teasing against my cheeks.

My thighs pressed together at the size of what I was feeling.

"Oh." I moaned as his hand slowly slid down my chest, not quite grabbing my breasts, but teasing the tops of them as his golden eyes flashed to mine in the mirror. His lips traveled up my neck to pull at my earlobe, and both of our gazes dropped when we saw hard peaks on full display underneath my bikini top. His pupils widened, wider than normal.

Suddenly, his golden irises were black.

"Your eyes," I managed to gasp as I lifted my hand to cover his. I tried to pull his hand down, to palm where my chest was visibly begging him to touch, but he held his hand firm as he continued to ravish my neck and ear.

My other hand was pinned underneath his, holding onto the sink.

"I can't help it," he murmured against my skin. "You awaken the monster in me, Vanessa."

I pressed my lips together to hold in a pathetic, submissive sound.

Why did my body like the sound of that so much?

I gasped when he finally slid his hand over my bathing suit. His palm and fingers were flush against my body, but instead of staying at my chest, his hand continued down my abdomen. Toward my pelvis.

My core pulsed in awareness, and I found myself pushing my ass against him again.

Drustan groaned, and the sound practically made my mind go numb.

I shifted, and his heavy erection was firmly between my ass cheeks as I pressed against him some more. My hand pushed on his, silently pleading with him to tease me underneath my swim bottoms, but he held his hand firm on my pelvis.

"Do you want it now?" Drustan growled against my neck.

I was getting ready to say yes, when I froze.

Drustan didn't hesitate to react, stiffening as soon as he felt me tense.

"Wait..." I dropped my head, bracing both hands on the sink again. "Wait..."

I turned, and he stepped back enough to allow me room to do so in the small bathroom.

I stared at him, and something like concern filled his expression as his eyes slowly faded from black to gold again.

Was he—did he—

"Were you—"

But I didn't get to finish my question. Before I could confirm my suspicion, Drustan was gone.

He was gone.

Drustan lyskifted off my fucking boat.

I searched the entire vessel for him but found nothing.

He probably hightailed it back to Hyvenmere as soon as he saw where my train of thought was going in my head. With my swimsuit uncomfortably wet and my mind spinning with how this day turned out, I finally started the engine and sailed my way back to the harbor.

What would I tell Audrey?

What did this mean?

Was that really Drustan that night Audrey drugged me?

CHAPTER 20

I decided to conduct a little experiment as soon as I docked my *Knotty Boy*.

If my theory was correct, I needed to go to sleep tonight as if nothing was amiss. Including taking my regular nighttime cannabis gummies. The only difference between tonight and the other nights I went to sleep, was the tiny little camera I had hidden on my dresser that faced the foot of my bed. I purchased it before I went home, after my disaster of a date.

It was nestled in a pile of clothes I kept on top of the dresser. Used, but not dirty enough to warrant a wash. The pile was almost always present, and I felt like I did a good job concealing the camera in it.

I tested it on my phone and set up the settings so that the recording would automatically upload to the cloud if the connection was lost or the device turned off. After testing some recordings and seeing for myself how clear the nighttime vision on the camera was, I popped two gummies and went through my nighttime skincare routine.

I went to grab one of my oversized t-shirts to sleep in but then decided to slip on a pair of men's boxers, too.

It was a cooler night, so the extra layer wouldn't be too odd. I cracked my window an inch, tapping the screen barrier on the outside to ensure it wouldn't pop off easily, and crawled into bed.

I was hyper-aware of the gummies hitting me. My body felt both light and heavy at the same time. The bed sheets familiarly caressed my skin, and I dozed off with strange dreams and a flutter in my lower stomach that I didn't want to focus on too much.

The next morning, I stretched my arms awkwardly above my head as I awoke. The sun poked through the crack in my open window, and I lay there in the lovely comfort that only a marijuana induced sleep could provide.

Then I remembered. Part of me wondered if I should be embarrassed by how quickly I jumped out of bed to grab my hidden camera. There was no light on the front, only on the back, and it was still bright red, meaning it was still recording.

Excellent.

I brewed some coffee and grabbed a protein bar as I settled in at my desk. Powering on my laptop, I eagerly found the nine-hour-long video and expanded the image to fill the screen. The entirety of my bedroom was in view. All three walls were visible in my smaller space. My desk, my bookshelf, my nightstands, and the artwork on my walls.

The only thing the camera didn't catch was the wall the dresser and bedroom door were on, because that's the wall it was set up against.

I didn't want to miss a single thing.

I pressed play and smirked at how nervous I looked setting the camera up. The video was completely black and white because of the nighttime mode. It made my t-shirt and boxers look brighter than they were. After a few moments of watching me toss and turn to get comfy in bed, I decided to speed up the video.

It wasn't until an hour after I had fallen asleep that something flashed by the camera.

My finger paused the video immediately.

My pulse was racing.

Obviously, I thought this was a possibility, but I knew that as I rewound the clip to seconds before the flash, and resumed normal speed, that I wouldn't be able to unsee whatever I was about to see.

One deep breath for bravery later, I pressed play. Within seconds, a tall, masculine body strolled in front of the camera. Because the video was in black and white, his hair looked black instead of red, but I still knew it was him.

Anxiety filled my chest as Drustan slowly strolled across the frame, most of his face cut off from being too close to the camera. This meant that he came in through my bedroom door. Which was locked.

How the f—

Drustan had clearly been in my bedroom before while I slept. He tiptoed around with familiarity. Knowing exactly where to step so that he didn't cause a creak or a shift in the floorboards underneath the carpet.

My hands shook.

Drustan was in my bedroom last night.

Drustan was in my bedroom last night.

He wore casual wear, something that looked a lot like the outfit he wore during the trip I had from the Hyvenmerian tea. Which means that it must have truly been *him* that night. I wasn't hallucinating that night. Drustan was actually in my room. He was real. I was pretty confident I licked his neck at one point.

Do you want it now?

His chuckle on the camera made me jump in my seat, and I had to press a palm to my chest to make sure my heart wasn't about to beat out of my chest. In the video, Drustan had wandered over to my desk, pulled one of my favorite romances off the shelf, and sat in the very chair I was currently in to start casually reading. He had flipped to a specific page in the book to do so. Ignoring where my own bookmark was.

Drustan sat in my desk chair, reading a romance novel in the dark for an hour. I had to speed up the video again because I was going to lose my mind if that's all the siren prince did while he was stalking me. After an hour of casual reading, he gently slid the book back on the shelf. At the same time, I had rolled over in my sleep. A loud, unladylike snort came from me as I adjusted.

Drustan's back was mostly to me, but the camera allowed me to see him turn toward the sound of my sleepy snort. And he smiled. A lot was shocking me right now, but for some reason, watching Drustan's cheek pull back in an obvious grin as he watched me snore in my sleep made me feel…confused.

Flutters erupted in my stomach, and I couldn't finish eating my protein bar.

Drustan gently stood from my desk chair and strolled to the side of the bed. He bent his large frame down to pull open my nightstand drawer slowly.

Jesus Christ, my vibrators were in there.

He was just…snooping. When he pulled out a sleeve of condoms I had recently bought, I tugged the collar of my shirt over my mouth and nose, not knowing how to feel about what I was seeing.

In the video, I threw my arm to the side in my sleep. The sudden movement made him freeze and turn to look at me. His eyes were eerie looking in the nighttime vision. It almost looked like bright lights coming from his face. After waiting a minute to ensure I didn't wake, he lifted the sleeve of condoms to his face with what looked like a confused expression.

Did they not have condoms in the magical realm?

He held the strip to his nose and sniffed before grimacing and inspecting it again.

Then he quirked his lips to the side and slowly tiptoed back to my desk and took a seat. He clicked my laptop to life and quickly dimmed the brightness. The vision on the camera adjusted from the sudden bright light a few moments before I realized that he still held the strip of condoms in his hand.

I couldn't even hear him tap the keys; he was being so quiet. It wasn't until I saw him hold up the strip again, while glancing at the keys on the keyboard, that I realized he was looking up the brand of the condoms.

I experienced a unique kind of embarrassment watching Drustan Shaw, the Mad Siren Prince of Lyndoruun, research what condoms were on my laptop. All while I quietly snored a few feet away. When he leaned toward the monitor to read what he found, I held my breath again.

Then he suddenly leaned back, looked at the condoms again, and frowned, before clicking out of the browser and closing the laptop.

I paused the video and opened my web browser to look at my internet history. Sure enough, my favorite condom brand was the last thing searched. When the list of results pulled up, the link he had viewed was highlighted in purple text. I clicked on it.

It was a Reddit thread, with various accounts discussing favorite condom brands. The first was from a woman going into detail about how much she preferred these condoms because she could still feel—and *ohmygod Drustan read all of this.*

Clicking back to my video, I pressed play, only to see Drustan clench his hand to bundle up the strip of condoms and shove them into the pocket of his linen pants.

That son of a bitch just stole my condoms.

I paused the video.

"Girl…" I scolded myself as I scraped a hand down my face. I was already losing the plot here. A killer was in my bedroom last night, and I was getting heated over the fact that he pocketed my condoms.

I needed to stay mad over the fact that a killer was *in my room while I was sleeping.*

I played the video again, not totally surprised to see Drustan saunter back to my nightstand and grab the rest of the condoms. A comical frown marred his face as he opened the box to pocket the rest of the strips inside it.

What the hell is happening?

After he carefully put the box back in my nightstand and closed the drawer, Drustan paused to stare at my sleeping form.

My skin felt hot. I leaned onto my elbows to steeple my fingers together and rest them against my face. He was still as he studied me. Was he…contemplating something? To kill me? To steal more of my contraception?

With dropped shoulders, Drustan released a sigh loud enough for the camera to pick up and slowly sat down on the side of the bed I wasn't on. I had to force myself to breathe through my nose as I watched Drustan slowly, carefully, lie his massive body on top of the covers next to me.

He fluffed my other pillow and everything. As if he'd done this a thousand times. One ankle crossed over the other, one large hand tucked behind his head, while the other rested on his abdomen. His feet, obviously, hung off the end of my king-sized bed.

Drustan was a big man. Taller, wider, larger, everything. The visual of seeing Drustan lay next to me, even as I was bundled underneath my covers, was eye-opening. I had already understood that, as a relatively tall woman.

Lying side-by-side like this?

It was both terrifying and thrilling to witness.

He stayed there, blinking up at the ceiling. Could he see perfectly in the dark? Were his siren senses that much better than my human ones? I sped up the video, noticing that he stayed there in my bed, silent, unmoving, staring at my ceiling in thought for another hour before I shifted.

I backed it up and hit play at a normal speed. Flopping over again, I was now facing Drustan, who looked over at me as I mumbled nonsense and settled again.

The way he stared at me, watching me sleep, should have made my skin crawl. And yet, it didn't. Instead, I felt this burning awareness in my core. Drustan hadn't tried to harm me once during his entire visit. He snooped, read my book, and lay in my bed. But he never touched me.

That is, until I touched him first.

Gasping, I watched as my hand reached out toward him, still fully asleep. I rested it on him. Drustan watched the whole thing, not moving a muscle. His gaze lowered to where my hand rested on his stomach, not flinching when my hand balled the fabric of his shirt into my fist.

When I softly tugged in my sleep, he sighed again, before grasping my wrist and gently removing my hand from his shirt. I made a weird sound, but it didn't sound clear in the video. I rewound a couple of seconds to hear it again, turning up the volume.

When Drustan slowly removed my hand from his body, I... *whined*. Still fully, completely asleep. I *whined* when he pulled my hand off of him.

His mouth twisted at the sound, and a deep pinch formed in his brow. My hand wrapped around his, and I sloppily tried tugging him toward me again. Drustan gently removed his hand from my grasp, and I whined *again*. I flopped over, giving him my back, but I didn't still. I was restless, my legs kept twitching and adjusting. As if I couldn't get comfortable.

As if something was wrong.

"Shh," Drustan shushed as he leaned toward me, hovering his hand over my bare arm, before he hesitated and rested his hand on my waist, which was covered by my blanket that he was lying on.

My body stilled, and the rise in my chest indicated that I was sinking into a deep sleep again...but my hand still snuck out from the covers and grabbed the one he had resting on my waist.

Drustan dropped his head but didn't remove his hand. His shoulders rose. He looked like he was taking a deep breath as he closed his eyes and frowned at the covers between us.

Suddenly, his hand was sliding around my waist over the covers—no—wait—I rewound the video, watching our hands, to see that *I* was pulling *his* arm around me.

"Alright, alright," Drustan whispered, scooting closer to my body.

I rubbed my eyes, blinking at the computer screen to make sure I was truly seeing this. Drustan was spooning me over the covers, while I snuggled into his warmth. His *warmth*.

The warmth I've been dreaming about.

I gasped and slammed the laptop closed.

"Jesus," I wheezed, standing up from my desk quickly enough to almost tip my chair over. I paced my bedroom, rubbing my hands through my hair, gripping the roots in anxiousness as I processed what I had just watched.

How many times had Drustan done this?

Were my gummies really that strong? How did I not wake up to a killer snuggling up with me? Why did I keep *reaching* for him in my sleep? Why was he snooping through my things and soothing me in my sleep?

Why would I do any of this, Vanessa?

My knees buckled. He was serious. Drustan genuinely believed that I was...

I slapped my hand over my mouth and screeched. My nervous system was shot. I needed to release some pent-up emotion to help me think through this. I fell to the floor and curled into a ball. With both hands over my mouth, I squeezed my eyes shut and screamed.

I screamed and screamed until my body started to relax. Holding my jaw with my hands, I slumped against the foot of my bed, breathing.

Thinking.

Processing.

Spiraling.

What did I do next?

Did I have a say in any of this?

I did to some degree. Audrey could help me figure out how to lock our apartment better, probably. Liam could just officially move in, act as a guard dog, so Drustan couldn't sneak into my bedroom again.

A cold, hard feeling solidified in my chest at the thought.

"What the fuck is wrong with me?" I groaned, pressing my fists against my forehead. "He's dangerous, he's a murderer."

He's yours.

I glanced up, my vision blurry from squeezing my eyes shut. My laptop still sat closed. Shaking my head at myself, I crawled back to my desk, sat in my chair, and opened it up again. Resuming the video, I watched as Drustan settled into sleep himself. The hard lines of his face smoothed as he held me. His chest and shoulders rose and fell with steady breaths.

He never got handsy. He never tried to wake me up or take advantage of my vulnerable position. Drustan just held me until I fell back asleep, and he did, too.

This part, at least, was not that surprising to me. I knew he was dangerous. That he could kill. But watching Drustan act like an innocent lover instead of a monster solidified something in my gut.

Drustan would never force himself on me.

Cross other obvious boundaries? Sure.

Invade my privacy and steal my condoms? Of course.

Use his size and strength to hurt me? Never.

Do you want it now?

What if he was genuinely asking?

We lay like that for a few hours. It wasn't until four a.m. when Drustan stirred, yawning like a regular human man waking up from a good night's sleep, that he slowly, carefully, gently unwrapped himself from me to let me continue to slumber.

He sat up, rubbed his eyes, and blinked at the camera.

Oh no.

Drustan's brow furrowed, his head tilted, and within a blink, he was standing in front of my dresser, bending down to study the camera.

No, no, no.

Drustan's hand lifted to shift something, probably clothing, to reveal the rest of the device. His face was so close to it, I could see all his sharp, stunning features in perfect detail. His cheek twitched before the corner of his mouth pulled back in a slow, devastating smile.

His eyes fell, making direct eye contact with me through the camera.

"I told you," Drustan whispered to the camera, making my chest heat. "You are brilliant, Vanessa."

Then, he was gone.

And so were any plans I had for the rest of the day.

CHAPTER 21

"Wake up." I was being shaken in my sleep, and I grumbled in annoyance as I swatted random hands away from me. "Wake up, Van."

Audrey sounded serious, which helped me shake off my sleepy fog.

I didn't realize she was back. I spiraled all morning about what I had discovered in my bedroom the night before, wondering how the hell I was going to tell Audrey everything I found when she and Liam already had their hands full with their own drama.

She must have gotten back during my nap on the couch.

I rolled onto my back and stretched, peeking an eye open to find Audrey.

But she was fully dressed, and when I clocked movement in my peripheral vision, I saw Hush in all her leather siren militia clothes. Looking very out of place in our living room.

"What's going on?" I asked, forcing myself to sit up.

Audrey frowned at Hush as she turned toward our coat closet to pull out a hoodie for me.

"Yes, Hush." Audrey sounded very annoyed. "What *is* going on?"

"I gave you two days to enjoy your new mate," Hush replied. "But time is up. I have something to share with you two." Hush stood tall with her arms folded, mask perfectly in place, as her gold gaze bounced between the two of us. "But *only* you two."

Something in her tone got to me, so I struggled to put my hoodie on as fast as I could. By the time Audrey tossed me some sneakers, I was able to slip them on and tie them without too much sleepy fumbling.

"Where's Liam?" I asked.

"He's still in Enhavenn," Audrey replied. "I needed a break, but he was in the middle of an interview when I left."

Once dressed, Hush stepped toward us and said, "Let's go."

I stepped back. "How are we getting there?"

"I'll lyskift us." Hush reached for my hand, and I immediately snatched it back.

"No thanks, let's take the boat."

"What? No. Lyskifting is more efficient." Hush argued.

"Please—"

Hush grumbled in annoyance as she grasped Audrey's wrist and reached for mine anyway.

"Wait, wait!" But my plea fell silent, because within milliseconds, I was squinting my eyes closed and preparing for the dizziness and nausea that inevitably came with lyskifting. I hated it. I braced myself for the worst of this experience.

What surprised me, however, was the complete lack of nausea and dizziness. A powerful gust of wind hit my face, and suddenly my feet were back on solid earth again. I stayed there, waiting, wondering why the nausea and my sensitive equilibrium weren't wreaking havoc on me.

"We're here, open your eyes," Hush barked. I raised my eyebrows but slowly complied. We were...here. In Hyvenmere.

The moon was high in the night sky, right as the sun was almost done setting, illuminating the otherworldly trees.

"Whoa." I slowly took a step, then another, wondering why I felt so stable. "I don't feel sick at all."

"Glad to hear it." Hush didn't sound glad to hear it at all. "Follow me, please."

Audrey gave me a wide-eyed look, an attempt to communicate how she was also surprised I wasn't sick. With Hush, no nausea at all. Perhaps Hush was just better at lyskifting? I made a mental note to remember to roast Liam for his subpar teleporting skills later.

I had to jog to catch up to Hush's fast-paced steps, glancing around to see if I could recognize exactly where we were. The woods, based on how dense the tall trees around us were. But unfamiliar woods.

"Where are we?" Audrey asked with a whisper.

"Lyndoruun," Hush whispered, then turned to lift a finger over her mask where her lips would be, telling us to be quiet.

We walked in silence, carefully stepping over loose stones, and branches, and roots. This wasn't a regularly walked path, which made my hackles rise. Where was Hush taking us? Why did she need to rush us? Why couldn't we speak? Who was listening that felt like a threat to her? Eventually, after about thirty minutes of walking, we made it to the base of a large mountain range. Not just any mountain range.

The Fjellenheim Mountains.

It was difficult to spot it in the distance based on how dense the forest was, but it was definitely the Fjellenheim Mountains based on their size. The height of them almost hid the moon from view, casting a deep shadow right where Hush quietly led us.

I tapped Audrey on the back of her hand. She squeezed my fingers back. Reassuring, but also nervous. We were on the same page.

Hush stopped and stared at us, something flickering over her molten eyes that I couldn't catch in the darkness, before she lifted overgrown shrubbery out of the way and revealed a small, run-down cabin built right against a surface of the mountains. Vines of ivy crawled up the sides of the wood that could use a new paint job. There was a crack in one of the glass windows on the second floor. Flower boxes that hung off the front porch were overgrown with various weeds and—based on the smell in the air—herbs.

Audrey and I stared at each other, having a silent conversation.

Do we do it?

We're already here, I guess.

It could be a trap.

We're probably dead anyway if it's a trap.

…Might as well.

After that, Audrey followed Hush up the wooden steps, across the porch, and into the cabin. Before I followed, I studied my surroundings, committing whatever I could see to memory.

It was musky in the clearly abandoned home Hush quietly led us through. Dusty, worn books lined the far wall of what looked like a sitting room. There was a fireplace bracketed by two floor-to-ceiling windows, exposing a view to the dark woods along the side of the mountains. Halos of dust and dirt circled random spots on the walls, where picture frames used to be. A broken flat screen TV sat in the far corner.

But Hush didn't acknowledge any of it, taking us to the very back of the cabin, into an empty room that looked like a study. Brushing her fingers over the paneling of the far wall, she slowly pulled it back to reveal a dark tunnel and promptly disappeared through it.

Audrey shook her head before following Hush. And I followed Audrey.

Hush waited until we were through before she pushed the

paneling shut behind us, encasing us in complete darkness. I trailed my fingertips on the rough stone walls on either side of me, keeping up solely based on the sound of their steps as my eyes struggled to adjust to the dark. Audrey and Hush's footsteps were the only confirmation I had that I wasn't left behind in here. We turned a corner, I assumed. A few more quiet moments passed, and a light started to shine up ahead. It was muted, but a light at the end of the tunnel all the same.

The small tunnel that could barely fit the width of two of us finally widened, revealing a large wooden door. Ancient designs were carved into it; images I couldn't quite make sense of. Next to the door, a small sconce. The only one in here.

Hush turned to face us, giving her back the door, as we finally made it to the opening.

"Do you truly want to help Hyvenmerians? All Hyvenmerians?" Hush asked us. She still wore her mask, like always, but after maybe an hour of silence, her voice startled me. It sounded loud.

Audrey swallowed and nodded. "Yes, of course."

Hush narrowed her eyes at her. "What I'm about to show you could get all of us killed."

I raised my eyebrows at her. "...You didn't want to mention that before you dragged us here?"

Hush popped her shoulders and said, "I trust you two."

"...Does Liam know about this?" Audrey's voice was quieter. Hush studied her for a moment before shaking her head. Silence hung in the air again.

"...Why do we get to see, and not Liam?"

Hush crossed her arms and braced her stance, replying in a low voice, "Because males have failed us. Perhaps showing his mate first, however, will get him to understand why I've done everything that I have." Audrey and I let her sentence sink in, and I couldn't speak for Audrey, but something deep in my bones confirmed the truth of her words.

Were things escalating more than I realized in Hyvenmere?

What about Audrey and me made Hush feel the need to expose whatever was behind the door?

"If I show you this..." Hush tipped her head toward the wooden entrance behind her. "And if, for some reason, you two decide you are no longer with us..." I lifted an eyebrow at her, wondering what that meant. "I will lock you both out of Hyvenmere myself."

Audrey stiffened at that, I didn't. I ended up crossing my arms and studying the designs on the wood. My eyes were still adjusting, and I could make out the faded markings better. It was a root system, that much was obvious. A large tree, with branches and roots connecting what looked like thousands of different icons. Animals. Plants. Oceans. People.

Children.

I squinted, focusing on a smaller carving in particular. Branches in the shape of hands and fingers, cradling children. Something sank low in my gut, and I cut my gaze over to Hush, who was watching me closely.

"Show us," I said. "You know we'll be on your side," I spoke to Hush quietly. "That's why you felt safe bringing us here."

Hush's eyes darted between the two of us, landing on Audrey and waiting. Audrey inhaled a deep breath, nodded her consent, and said, "Show us." Giving us one last lingering look, Hush turned and banged on the door with the side of her fist.

Thump, thump, thump...thump...thump, thump...thump.

A specific pattern. A code, I realized.

Moments later, the large door groaned on its hinges as it opened, and distant noise echoed out to us.

A *lot* of people were in there.

One of Ilia's siren guards was on the other side of the door, dressed just like Hush with the siren mask over his mouth and everything. Holding it open with one arm, he allowed us to follow Hush through.

I didn't look behind me when he shut the door; I could hear it echo when it closed. Light bulbs lined the hallway we walked through, and drapes covered most of the stone of the mountain. Soon, we stepped onto what looked like floorboards. Two heavy drapes were covering what I assumed was a large room, based on the amount of chatter coming from the other side.

Hush gave us one last, lingering look before lifting her arm and pulling the drapes aside.

Revealing...children.

And mothers.

Hundreds of children with their mothers, too many for me to count. Some were at tables, writing in books. Schoolwork, maybe? Younger children were playing with each other, with toys and puzzles. Teenagers were huddled together in small groups, too, reading thicker books that could be schoolwork as well. Mothers were scattered around. In front of us, a mother lifted her chubby baby up into the air before nuzzling their cheeks. Eliciting a sharp, baby siren squeal that echoed throughout the chamber.

Nearby, someone gasped, and everyone slowly went onto alert. Eyes tore away from whatever project they were focused on, locking on Audrey and me.

Every single pair of eyes was golden.

"Wh—why are they down here?" Audrey whispered. Hush stepped to the side, following the wooden platform that elevated our entrance from the rest of the room, toward doors to other rooms on the far side of the cavern wall. It looked like it was all carved out long ago by a very skilled hand, but part of me wondered what the likelihood of the mountain caving in on top of us was. The ceilings were so high.

As Audrey and I followed Hush to the side, I noticed a small opening near the top of the cavern. Past all the wires from the lightbulbs and TV screens illuminating the space. There were no windows, no exterior doors, and almost no source of natural light.

Except for one at the top, higher than most skyscrapers I'd seen. The bright moon from the night sky shown through the opening, providing oxygen.

Wow.

I glanced around, smiling what I hoped was a warm greeting at passing siren mothers and not one of confusion. Emotions started flooding my system: *Safe. Hungry. Confused. Annoyed. Scared. Warm. Curious.*

Hush took us into what looked like an office space, and when I saw Sergei towering over documents scattered on a large wooden desk, I stiffened at the threshold. Sergei's golden eyes locked on me; a dark brow lifted in what might have been confusion.

"Come in and close the door." Her voice was firm and authoritative. Audrey tugged me through the threshold and kicked the door shut. The war of emotions within my nervous system immediately tempered.

Odd.

"What is all this?" Audrey asked, with more volume to her voice. Sergei ignored us and continued perusing the papers on the large wooden desk. Hush approached him before turning and resting her butt on the edge of it.

"This is a sanctuary," Hush explained.

"For whom?" I asked. Though part of me already suspected the answer.

"For the siren children who have developed the gift of whis-merra," Hush confirmed. "…and their mothers." Audrey cursed, plopping herself down into a cushioned chair on the far wall. She bent over, scraping her nails through her hairline.

I leaned my head back to admire the high ceiling; another skylight was cut out near the top, what felt like miles above. I rubbed my hands on either side of my neck, tugging.

"Okay." I nodded at the ceiling, "Okay. This is good."

Audrey lifted her head to stare at me. "Good?"

"Yes." I nodded. "Because now we know Ilia isn't killing the missing siren women. Or sirens with whismerra. They're alive."

Audrey shook her head before staring at Hush. "...But why do the mothers and children need to hide?" Hush and Sergei shared a look before letting silence answer for them.

"Shit," I grumbled. "Of course Ilia would."

Sergei was the one who responded, and I tried hard not to physically jump when he did. "We have received enough evidence that Ilia would uphold the ancient law."

I shook my head. "But—but no." I balled my hands into fists. "These aren't twenty-six-year-olds. These are *children*. Infants."

"Thus..." Hush gestured toward the closed door behind me.

"He's evil..." Audrey whispered, folding her arms across her chest. "Ilia is just...pure evil."

I blurted out my next question, "I thought sirens didn't develop whismerra until the age of maturity? Why can these children—how can they—" I shook my head again, struggling to wrap my head around it all.

"That, we don't know for sure," Hush answered. "Just that, for some reason, the goddess Tynara is allowing this gift to develop in those as young as infants."

It was a terrifying reality.

"I felt so emotional in there with them," I murmured. "I felt like I was spiraling."

"That's because of the infants and young children," Hush explained. "They're still learning how to stop projecting their emotions into the minds of others. My door is laced with a spell that helps temper the onslaught of their whismerra."

I raised my eyebrows. "Jesus." The secrecy made sense. I felt their emotions almost immediately upon entering that room. As if they were my own. It would be nearly impossible to keep that contained in a crowded society. All the mothers, all the missing siren women, were *here*. Hidden in the Fjellenheim Mountains.

Protecting their children.

It didn't look like a glorious experience in here. Things were a bit cramped, the air was stale, and the constant fear of the unknown was floating around in the space. Tables and chairs were squished together. There was a cot that was folded up, with a single blanket and pillow stacked on top of it. Boxes were stacked on the opposite wall, and an open one revealed what looked like cans of food.

This was a harsh place to raise children. Was there even running water in here? This deep into the mountains? What other option did everyone have?

"How do we—what do we—" I pinched the bridge of my nose, struggling to compose my thoughts.

"How—?" Audrey stopped to clear her throat before trying again. "How many are in there?"

Hush glanced up to Sergei, who released a heavy sigh as he rubbed the back of his neck before answering.

"Upwards of a thousand children reside in the Fjellenheim tunnels." He winced as he delivered the numbers, and I felt reassured that this visibly pained him in some way. "Along with roughly seven hundred mothers."

"Oh my god." Tears escaped my eyes at the thought.

The bravery those women must have had to conjure up. "... When did this start?"

"Right around the time all of this started." Hush waved vaguely in the air, but toward Audrey. Right when more mating bonds started to snap into place. When nature and the goddess Tynara deemed it time to be.

"What..." Audrey pulled a chair over so she could sit down. "What do we do?" Silence hung in the air again. A thick, daunting silence that also spoke volumes.

"Ilia has to die," I breathed. Sergei and Hush didn't react to my words. Sergei just nodded once, while Hush studied Audrey.

"No one *has* to die," Audrey retorted. "We can disarm him. Restrain him. Give a formal sentence and send him to the Gravhune properly."

I gave her a wide-eyed look of disbelief. "I'd argue that he definitely has to die. Don't you *get* it, Audrey?" I waved toward the door where the missing siren families resided in fear, "His literal soldier…" I gestured toward Sergei, who stood tall with his bulky arms crossed. "Is telling us that Ilia wouldn't hesitate to wipe out generations of his own people—the *children* of his own people."

Audrey squeezed her eyes closed and rubbed her temples with her fingertips. "But no one *has* to die. We don't just kill people to resolve conflict. That doesn't make us any better than Ilia." I threw my hands up in the air in frustration, comforted to see that Hush and Sergei also looked annoyed with my best friend.

"Spoken by someone privileged enough to never experience life-threatening danger," Hush murmured, and before Audrey could remind Hush of how she became Hyvenmere's sweetheart by killing the solvyrn, Hush added, "At the hands of others."

Audrey flinched. "That's not fair." Then she turned to look at me. "We both have experienced that." I didn't meet her gaze. I shoved my hands in my pockets and stared at the ground. We hardly talked about our past, the evil I had to commit as a teenager to save us from our foster father.

"Van," Audrey whispered. "I'm sorry. I'm not saying what you did was unnecessary—you did what you had—"

"I'd do it again." I ignored how familiar those words sounded on my lips, and I lifted my gaze to meet hers, just in time to watch her widen her eyes and part her lips in surprise. "I have to live with that horrid memory for the rest of my life." I glanced up to see Hush and Sergei studying us with cool expressions. "Knowing I'll always hear his screams." I locked back on Audrey's face. "Because I did what I did."

I had seen the bruises on Heather, our foster mother. I had gained a few bruises of my own, especially when I stepped in to protect Audrey from his wrath. I had always gone out of my way to never think of our foster father's name, because his name didn't deserve the respect of memory.

Unfortunately, when you take a life at such a young age, your brain seems to stitch every second of that moment in your cells forever. I could still smell the burnt zucchini casserole Heather had made that night, the last straw for her husband before he took the sizzling casserole dish and used it as a weapon against his wife. I could still remember the sound of Audrey and me running downstairs with heavy footfalls. Audrey with the landline to her ear as she called 911.

The operator who paused her instructions for Audrey when she heard Heather's screams.

I still remember something cold and numb settling in my chest, watching him swing the casserole dish across Heather's face and knocking her unconscious. How he didn't want to stop. He marched toward her still body, his fists tight. How I jumped on his back, determined to stop him from hurting her more. I knew, deep in my gut, at the ripe age of fifteen years old, that he was going to kill her that night.

He threw me off, making me fall into the cabinets near the stove. He made sure to kick his unconscious wife in the ribs before he stalked toward me with a drunken, maniacal look in his eye. Then Audrey tried to stop him by throwing the landline at his head.

When he turned to advance toward her, wrapping both of his large hands around Audrey's throat, something in me snapped. A darkness crawled over my skin, the adrenaline buzzing in my ears went silent except for a sharp ring resembling a high C, and I pulled open a kitchen drawer to grab Heather's chef knife.

The soft sound the blade made as it pierced his skin and entered his throat.

I was worried for a moment that I had pushed the knife too far, that I might accidentally hit Audrey, but no. Her horrified hazel eyes were just staring at the tip of the blade as it exited the front of his jugular. The sounds of him gasping, struggling to comprehend what had happened to him as he dropped his hold on Audrey to grasp his throat, brought me *relief*.

The cries and screams he made when I kept stabbing him. Over and over and over again. Determined to get him to *stop screaming*. To silence him once and for all.

Audrey and I dragged Heather out of the house, who was starting to stir but was still very disoriented.

"You killed him," Audrey kept saying, going into shock as bruises formed around her neck. "You killed him, Van." And I had no regrets. As Audrey attempted to soothe Heather, I went back into the house. I didn't bother looking at the bloody, mangled body of my old foster father. Instead, I flipped on the gas on the stove and reached inside the kitchen drawer to find a box of matches.

The house was completely engulfed in flames by the time my foster father's colleagues showed up in their police cars, and paramedics were treating Heather and Audrey.

I spent the next year homeschooled, on a special type of house arrest, complete with daily visitations from child mental health professionals. An alternative to juvenile detention that a talented lawyer fought for. Heather fought to keep us, and we begged the state to stay with Heather until we turned eighteen. She felt responsible for us, and the guilt of what her deceased spouse did to us ate at her day by day. When we graduated from high school, we told her she needed to leave. To start a new life. To go where the memories of that man wouldn't be able to haunt her every day.

She only waited a week more before leaving the country.

Then Audrey and I moved into our first dorm together at college. Thoroughly trauma bonded.

"Van." Audrey's voice snapped me back into the present. Inside the depths of the Fjellenheim Mountains. "What you did was forced upon you. You had no choice. He would have—he would have killed—"

"So, you get it, then," I interrupted her, gesturing toward the children on the other side of the door. "You get that, because we *know* what Ilia is going to do, that we have *no* other choice here."

Audrey's lip quivered. Silent tears started to pour from her eyes.

"…I hate this…" Audrey whimpered. "To take a life is so—so—"

"Necessary," Sergei said. "Ilia thinks that upholding the law and ridding Hyvenmere of any whismerric sirens is his duty as both the Chosen One and the Guardian of the Fjellenheim Mountains. He fears retribution from ancient gods and goddesses if he doesn't maintain, what he believes, is necessary to uphold peace in the realm."

I loved her. Audrey was my best friend. The closest thing to a sister I'd ever have. But I was grateful to Sergei for gently giving her a wake-up call. If what Sergei said was true, Ilia was no more than a delusional religious extremist. Unable to be reasoned with, held back by his own pride.

"I hate this," Audrey groaned, the weight of the issue settling on her shoulders.

"I promise you," I told Audrey, "Those mothers out there, clutching their children, hate it more." Hush nodded with agreement at my words, before sharing a look with Sergei that I couldn't interpret. Audrey gnawed on her bottom lip; her eyes locked on my shoes as she wrapped her head around the severity of the situation.

All three of us stared at her, waiting impatiently, based on the way Hush's fingertips drummed on her bicep.

"I don't understand," Audrey finally whispered through an exhale. "Why can't we take what we know to the fae? The nereids? Why can't we unite the realm by working together to arrest Ilia, and send him to the Gravhune properly, instead of just killing him?"

"Because Ilia has blackmail on them, now," Hush explained. "It's why we stole the journals. Ada doesn't want her people to know that her parents killed Queen Astrid. It would ruin the relationship she has with them, make people question her rule, and consider challenging her. Additionally, during the night of Fergus's party, Drustan and Caelena were able to grab ancient, illegal recipes for dark magic that would put the same distrust in the nereid kings and queens."

Audrey paled, her hazel eyes widening with each word Hush spoke.

"…That was how Ilia was going to get them to vote to close the Mellhawn Gates," Audrey realized. "Just…blackmail. It's so simple. So stupid."

Hush hummed in agreement, "However, if we can convince the fae and nereids that Ilia needs to die, by helping them see the benefit of swiftly executing him, everyone would win. Because we need the fae and nereids to be in support of us when we do this."

"How are you going to do it?" I asked her.

Hush sighed and rubbed the bridge of her nose with her finger and thumb. "I'm not quite sure."

"Wait." Audrey sat up straighter. "If Ilia is, well, out of the picture…" The question didn't need to get finished, because we all knew what she was asking.

"Prince Drustan will obviously take the throne," Sergei replied.

I let out a laugh, but it wasn't a humorous one. "He'll *love* that." The sarcasm in my voice was thick.

Hush gave me a funny look, a crinkle formed near her eyes, as if she was grinning at my retort. "You have a very accurate understanding of our prince."

Audrey gave me a questioning look before speaking up, "Van has always been excellent at reading people."

Hush lifted an eyebrow at Audrey, "And what does Van think about Prince Drustan?"

I popped my shoulders. "I think that he'll reluctantly be king for a day before clawing his own eyes out. He's not exactly looking for more responsibility." Sergei released a low chuckle and shook his head, as if we were in on a secret.

"We still need the fae and nereids to understand what needs to happen, and what will happen after," Sergei reminded us.

"I can talk to Liam and Ada." Audrey nodded. She interlaced her fingers as she rested her elbows on her legs. "And once they're on board, he'll probably come with me to talk to Fergus and his parents."

"We need to be expedient." Hush leaned a hand on the desk and shifted her weight onto her hip. "I've tried to throw Ilia and the guard off our scent for years, but they're becoming more and more curious about these mountains. I've already had to go on several patrols, finding reasons to lead my unit away from here."

Audrey nodded and pulled out her cell from this realm. "I can get in contact with Liam tonight." Then she frowned, lifting the device in the air.

"You won't have any signal for a fifteen-mile radius. The ancient magic of the mountains halts any signal from outside. Our electricity is produced from the water running through the aquifers underneath the mountains, making us completely off grid." Sergei explained.

Audrey nodded. "Makes sense."

"When do you think you'll be back?" Hush asked, leaning her hip against the desk and crossing her arms.

Audrey tilted her head side to side before saying, "A day? Maybe two, depending on how it goes with the nereids. But they've felt a companionship with sirens better than the fae have. So hopefully Fergus can help us navigate the conversation sensitively with his parents, so it doesn't go poorly."

Hush nodded. "Alright." Audrey stood, brushing her dark red hair behind her ears as we both walked toward the door. "What if Sergei goes with you?" Hush suggested.

I frowned. "No thanks."

Sergei dared to look offended and asked, "Why not?"

"I'm still mad at you," I explained.

Sergei looked confused, before it clicked for him, "Because of what happened on the boat?"

"Obviously. You and your buddy attacked me. I had nightmares about it," I replied. Sergei shook his head at me.

"Leon is a sad excuse for a male," he said. "We are not 'buddies' as you said." I gave him a suspicious look, not budging on not inviting him with us.

"What if you go?" Audrey asked Hush. "Ada knows we have someone giving us information, acting as a double agent for Ilia. If you came with, it would make our case stronger."

Hush considered, drumming her fingertips on the desktop.

"I'll consider it as I walk you both out of here. Sergei, you will stay with the women and children, with the rest of your men." Hush decided.

I laughed at him and gave him my middle finger. He smirked before murmuring, "I do apologize for terrorizing you that day. I hope you understand that I had no choice but to follow orders."

He seemed so genuine, and all I felt like I could say in response was, "Thanks."

Sergei dipped his chin at me before opening a side door

hidden behind more maroon drapes, revealing another way out than the way we came.

"We must hurry," Hush reiterated. "I don't think Ilia is going to wait much longer before closing the gates or ordering more units to investigate this mountain." The worry in her voice cut through me, and admiration for everything Hush had accomplished while also successfully being a double agent made me wish I could be her when I grew up.

We exited the Fjellenheim Mountains in silence. I wondered if Hush was giving us time to process everything that was discussed in her office. Once we all stepped outside, I inhaled a deep breath of mountain air through my nose.

"This way," Hush instructed. The two of us followed her, and after walking for twenty more minutes, Audrey finally spoke up. I looked over at her, realizing that Audrey didn't exactly look like a Chosen One destined to unite realms. She wore a hoodie, just like me. Her hands were casually tucked into the pockets of it.

"We should go to Queen Ada first—"

Hush cursed and shoved both of us behind her, reaching for the blades strapped to her thighs.

"What is hap—" I didn't need to finish asking my question, because in front of us, appearing at a speed I couldn't catch with my human eyes, were five siren guards. In front of them stood Leon, with an excited grin that made my blood run cold.

"Well," Leon chuckled to himself, rolling his wrist that carried a sword. "What do we have here?"

CHAPTER 22

Leon's smile was just as gross as the first time I saw it, back on my boat.

The three of us said nothing, not even when the siren guards fanned out and started to surround us. Weapons drawn. Masks up. Audrey's fingers started to flex, and Hush rested her hand on the hilt of one of her knives.

"How interesting," Leon continued after lowering his mask to speak. "That one of Ilia's top generals is wandering the base of the Fjellenheim Mountains with a halfling and a human." I didn't realize how high up in rank Hush was, but I couldn't say I was surprised. "The halfling specifically attempting to disrupt the peace our prophesied protector has fought so hard to maintain, no less."

That was a very inaccurate and one-sided view of events, but I didn't think it was in my best interest to try to educate him. Hush and Audrey said nothing, so I copied their tactic. I slid my gaze over to a siren guard to my right, staring at his lifted sword, as if he were worried that I would strike him first. Because my green hoodie, jeans, and sneakers gave me no ability to hide a weapon on my person, I determined this guard to be a complete dumbass. I gave him a pitiful look, and he narrowed his eyes at me.

"It's disappointing that my sister was right." Leon shook his head in mock disappointment. "I didn't think you would be stupid enough to conspire against our king," he said to Hush. The black-haired siren who sneered at me at Bandthral came to mind. "When Amber suggested that someone from our guard was working against our own people, I brushed her off. My unit here can confirm that the only reason we're even patrolling this area right now was to prove she was wrong—unfortunately," Leon sighed. "Now I must tell her she was right. Do you understand how frustrating that is for me?"

It wasn't easy to focus on what he was saying while keeping a constant eye on his unit, with their weapons ready to strike.

Leon sighed dramatically as he strolled up to us, and I internally rolled my eyes at how much this man loved the sound of his own voice. "I hate losing bets to Amber. She's insufferable about it." But then Leon looked down at Hush, who didn't back down from his approach, "However, I can't lie and say I won't enjoy dragging you to the Gravhune."

My heart sank in my gut, and right as Leon nodded toward his unit, hands were on me. I was thrust to the ground. I blinked, disoriented, and tried to stand up. But something cold and hard was pressed at my neck.

Freezing, I realized it was a blade.

"Van," Audrey gasped from nearby. She was thrust completely to the ground, hands behind her back. Three guards were on top of her, one of them holding her hands into fists, keeping her from using her gift. The shrubbery twitched around us, struggling to listen to her command and help us, but they must have learned her weakness the night of the robbery. Without the use of her hands to direct her powers, Audrey couldn't strike.

Hush was also on the ground. A guard had his knee on her

back as he gripped her hooded head upward and held a knife to her throat as well. I, however, was on my hands and knees with a knife to mine.

"You know where the missing females and children are, don't you?" Leon asked all of us this with disgust, but again, we stayed silent. "This is what happens when females are given too much authority."

"Oh my god," I spoke up, making Hush and Audrey throw me panicked looks. "Are you seriously making your inability to convince a woman to fuck you, everyone else's problem?" I realized as soon as the blade touched my skin that I was probably fucked. Audrey and Hush were strong enough to fight their way out of this, but even though I've been training, I hadn't been trained on how to get out of this specific position. I would most likely die.

If that was the case, the least I could do was buy my friends time.

Leon turned his glare on me, stepping away from Hush to drop to a crouch in front of me.

"You think I'm worried about a human's opinion?" Leon murmured, low and threatening. "Unlike many in our realm, I don't have the slightest interest in reproducing with the likes of you."

"Oh no," I deadpanned. "I'm devastated." That earned me a threatening press of the knife against my throat, an attempt to remind me of the danger I was in. I was fully aware, but I'd be damned if I let these *losers* let my last breathing moments be moments of fear.

Leon opened his mouth to say something but was interrupted.

"So easily manipulated by a human, are you?" A deep, melodic voice echoed in our clearing. The hairs on my neck rose, a bass note in the melody that constantly filled the air in Hyvenmere, thrummed.

Leon and I both turned to the side to see Drustan standing there, in the same dark leather all the other sirens in the unit wore, hood and mask down, frowning at us with a lifted red eyebrow. Audrey cursed from her prone position on the ground.

"Your highness," Leon smirked, then tipped his head in my direction. "Do you see what my unit and I have found?"

"I do." Drustan strolled through the clearing, shoving his hands in the pockets of his tactical pants, studying the three of us pinned under several guards. "How disappointing."

"Fuck you." I spat at the prince, unable to control my anger. The last time I saw him in person was on my boat, after he tried convincing me that he genuinely wanted me. The next time was me watching him snoop throughout my room and steal my condoms. Now, here he was, looking like he genuinely didn't give a shit that his supposed *mate* was being held at knifepoint.

"Unlike Leon here," Drustan smirked as he addressed me. "I'm more than willing to accept the invitation if you keep offering it." Leon's brows jumped at his prince's words, before he turned to study me more intensely. He took the knife from the guard on top of me, using the flat side of the blade to tip my chin up, as if he was inspecting me.

"I guess she *is* a pretty little thing…" Leon hummed. It was like this man had one single brain cell, and all it knew how to do was agree with whatever his authority figures said. I pressed my lips together, staying as quiet as I could. Leon's gaze traveled down most of my body, and an appreciative expression coated his features as he took in my position on my knees.

"It might be beneficial to know what it's like sharing a bed with a human."

I couldn't help it. I snorted. Leon flinched from the sound.

"Is something amusing?" He pressed the blade closer to my throat, emphasizing the threat he held over me. It wasn't the smartest thing to say, but I was a petty woman. Without much thought, I let my lips pull back in a grin.

"The idea of ever spreading my legs for you is funny, yes." Leon ground his teeth together and drew his hand back. The slap across my face knocked me to my side. A ringing echoed in my ears, and my skin stung from the sharp contact. Audrey shouted, and it quickly became muffled.

But then a low growl echoed in the clearing from above, followed by a pained, gargling sound. I forced myself to sit up, my hand to my cheek, just in time to open my eyes and see Drustan yank Leon's throat out with his bare hand. I gasped, my eyes wide as I watched Leon drop to his knees after being released from the prince's hold. His hand cupped his neck as if he could put his throat back inside of it. His eyes were wide, and blood gushed from his mouth and the hole in his neck as Drustan gripped a handful of Leon's hair and sharply twisted.

Within one swift movement, Leon's head was snapped off his body.

Hush was already pinning her soldier's body to the ground with her boot and a sword when Drustan chuckled and shook some excess blood off his fingertips. Audrey was sitting on her ass, frozen in shock at the morbid image of Leon's demise.

The other soldiers and I sat there silently. Their weapons raised.

"Well then," Drustan grinned with his words.

"You—" another soldier stuttered. "You just killed one of the king's generals."

Drustan lifted an eyebrow at him, bored, "I did."

"It's treason," another whispered. The soldier pinned underneath Hush groaned, trying to fight her off, but she held him firm.

"And?" Drustan flicked more blood off his fingertips while nudging Leon's head off to the side with his foot. Slowly, cautiously, the rest of the soldiers raised their weapons higher. I was panting, unable to control my breathing at all, as I struggled to get to my feet. The ringing in my ears was still present, and my cheek was throbbing, but I was determined to focus on getting out of this alive.

"I'd drop those if I were you," Drustan warned the soldiers.

"Our loyalty is to the king," one of them recited.

"And you still stand by that?" Drustan replied.

"Do you know where the females are?" One of the soldiers was getting heated, his voice was shaking as his brow morphed into anger. "You dare to hide our females from—"

"I'd carefully consider your next words if I were you," Drustan's voice lowered to a register that sent a flash of ice down my spine. My chest felt tight, and fear and adrenaline drenched my muscles.

"Why are you defending this human and the halfling?"

"We need to tell the king."

"This is treason!"

Drustan groaned, throwing his head back in annoyance. Face tilted back toward the sky, he turned toward me enough to see his pupils expand again. Fully. Taking over the entirety of his eyes, before throwing a smirk in my direction and saying, "Close your eyes and cover your ears, Vanessa."

"Huh?"

"Do it, Van!" Hush barked.

I gasped and did what I was told. I even went as far as to crouch, because for some reason, that felt like something to do when squeezing my eyes closed and pressing my palms over my ears.

I still heard the siren's screams, though. It couldn't have been more than a minute of time. Wails, guttural choking, cries of pain, all of it. Suddenly, but not soon enough, the sounds stopped. I kept my position. My breathing was still uneven, but at least I was breathing.

Warm hands wrapped around my wrists to expose my ears. "I'm taking you out of here," Hush assured me. I nodded but kept my eyes closed as she used her lyskift. After she settled me on a rock some distance away, so I could put my head between my knees, a poor attempt to catch my breath, Drustan was with us again.

Audrey whimpered, "…You killed them all."

"Now," Drustan's tone wasn't playful, but firm. "Tell me exactly why I just ended their lives for you three." I lifted my head to stare at him. Drustan looked…terrifying. His red hair was half pulled back in his favorite style, except for a few loose strands that framed his hard face. His hands had dark red blood all over them, which he was now wiping off with a rag he pulled out of one of his pockets in his pants. Apparently, siren military uniforms also had clean-up supplies. Drustan looked mildly inconvenienced, but his eyes were pure black again. No whites, no irises.

Audrey was standing next to him, pale, staring at me as Hush knelt by my side. Her wide hazel eyes kept flicking between the three of us. I recognized the same expression from that horrible night I burned our foster home to the ground. She might have been going into shock again.

"You need to control *that* better," Hush muttered, pointing an accusing finger at Drustan's face. "Your composure is fading more and more, Dru." I flinched at her nickname for him.

"That is not something you need to concern yourself with," Drustan grunted, blinking until his eyes shifted back to gold. "Now, tell me what you're hiding." Audrey didn't seem to hear their conversation. She seemed like she was elsewhere, struggling to blink herself back to the present. Hush stood with her fists balled up, before she inhaled a deep breath to compose herself.

My heartbeat was in my ears.

"…This could risk the lives of thousands," Hush replied. Drustan stared at her, not budging, waiting her out. She lowered her voice before saying in her clear voice, "Thousands of females and children are seeking refuge from your father's rule."

Drustan didn't react, didn't blink. Just stared at her, before shifting his eyes over to me.

"I just learned about this tonight—well, last night." I glanced off into the distance, where the sun was rising and turning the sky pink and orange.

"Where?" Drustan asked.

"I can't tell you that, yet."

I started playing my favorite tune in my head, determined to focus on every single note, not to give anything away to him accidentally. I hoped Audrey was doing something similar, and based on the frown she gave the ground, I assumed she was.

"What is your plan?" Drustan pressed as he crossed his arms over his chest.

Hush tilted her head to the side. "Do you understand why Ilia cannot find them?"

Drustan huffed an annoyed breath as he responded with, "Probably the same reason he executed a seemingly random twenty-six-year-old male during Bandthral."

I widened my eyes in horror. The Bandthral I was at? The one Drustan massaged me at? Is that where his father went off to? With Sergei. That must have been why Sergei was so confident that Ilia would kill them all. He probably watched Ilia do it with his own eyes.

"You *knew* Ilia was doing this?" Hush sounded very angry, angrier than I think common sirens were allowed to be with Drustan.

"I just learned of the execution this morning," Drustan replied. "But I only assumed why the execution happened, and you seem to be confirming it."

"Oh my god." I breathed.

"I am still failing to understand Vanessa's and the halfling's involvement in all of this." Drustan's golden eyes slid over to me.

I stood from my seat on the rock and mirrored his pose. "Because I don't need your blessing to be involved."

"No, but that won't stop me from carrying you out of this realm myself," Drustan retorted. Color was slowly coming back to Audrey's face, and her stare turned skeptical as she watched Drustan and me argue back and forth.

"I fucking dare you," I threatened. Without hesitation, Drustan stepped toward me, but Hush halted him with her hand on his chest.

"The halfling and her mate need to inform the fae and nereids of the situation, immediately," Hush interrupted, making Drustan focus his attention back on her. His expression was still stony, giving nothing away. "*That's* how close your father's guard is to discovering what desires to be hidden. What do you think would have happened had Leon and his entourage found what they were looking for?"

Drustan nodded, scraping a hand down his face.

"If you're looking for my blessing to conspire with other territories to dispose of my father," Drustan muttered as a rock formed in my throat. "You don't need one. No one will be happier with his death than me."

Well. Damn.

"If that's really how you feel," Audrey narrowed her eyes at him, suspicious. "Why haven't you just killed him yourself? You have no issue taking lives as you please, it seems."

In response, Drustan gave her a bored expression and said, "Do you think the Gravhune was a pleasant experience for me? That I'm desperate to pay it another visit?" he rolled his eyes at her and continued, "Who, exactly, would vouch for me if I took it upon myself to dispose of him? Who would plead the case that I *shouldn't* be sent back to the Gravhune for his demise? Many would be happy to see me sent back for less."

"But why are you with him?" I asked, making everyone turn to face me again. "If you wish to see him dead, why are you doing his bidding?" It didn't make sense to me quite yet and based on the nod Audrey gave me, she agreed.

"My father's power is rising at an indescribable rate," Drustan replied. "For years, since before I was sent to the Gravhune, he's spoken privately about one single goal of his. When I was released from the Gravhune, there were rumors in the guard that he was closer to meeting it," he chuckled to himself. "I wasn't about to be on my father's bad side if that were the case."

"What goal did Ilia have, exactly?" Audrey crossed her arms and popped a hip out.

"Strengthening his sinndra," Drustan replied, stepping closer to me almost mindlessly as he addressed her. "Enough to command his guard himself. Enough to manipulate the fae and nereid governments to obey his every word."

Audrey paled, but Hush didn't seem too surprised by this revelation.

"The recipes you stole for him the night of Fergus's party," I whispered. "That's—that's why he felt confident the gates would be closed now. He must have found what he needed to—to—" Drustan just nodded, confirming my hypothesis.

"Why are you telling us any of this?" Audrey glared at the Mad Siren Prince. "If you're so self-centered enough to happily steal what Ilia needs and to do his bidding, why should we trust you?"

"Because the stakes have changed since you've stepped foot into Hyvenmere, halfling," Drustan lifted a brow at her. "My father is not the prophesied one he has claimed to be, is he?" Audrey frowned at Drustan as he explained, "This means that my father is not as untouchable as the realm once believed."

"Which is why he needs to go," Hush confirmed.

"But..." Audrey stuttered. "You're okay with us just killing your father instead of sending him to the Gravhune? Like you had to experience?"

Drustan gave her a look of disbelief, "I think just killing him would save everyone time and energy. But..." he lifted a shoulder. "I am not as terrified to take a life as you seem to be."

"Because I'm not a soulless monster," Audrey grumbled. I flinched at her words, which she clocked immediately. Instead of apologizing as she did before, though, Audrey just held my gaze.

"Will you be willing to do what needs to be done once Ilia is gone?" Hush asked.

Drustan rolled his eyes and scoffed. "I am not meant to rule."

"You do not have a choice." Hush stepped forward, her hands out to emphasize her words. "Whether he dies at the hands of rebels, or dies a natural death, you are still the next in line. Our lands will be uneasy, and the revolution will create extremists who will make Ilia a martyr. We need you to guide our people into peaceful living, regardless of who can touch whose mind."

"Why would you ask the Mad Siren Prince to become another Mad Siren King?" Drustan asked.

"Because you have to," I chimed in. Audrey glared at me before turning her anger to the side. I knew she was displeased by the conversation, by the reality we all had to face, but Hush was right. We were even shorter on time than we thought, if Amber and Leon were onto us.

Hush and Drustan turned to look at me, but his expression was particularly annoyed at my comment. I stepped toward them, determined not to shout or yell in case any more of Ilia's spies were lurking around. If Amber sent another unit to follow her brother's.

"You have to step up, Dru." I hesitated. I hadn't called him that since I thought he was a human. His eyes softened at the nickname, but I was determined to ignore his feelings and get my point across. "*Your* people *need* you. You're in a privileged position here. You can inspire *real* change. Just imagine all the good you can—what are you doing?"

Drustan had taken a few steps toward me, his eyes hooded and focused on my face. "Staring."

I blinked and stepped back once. "Staring? At—at my mouth?" I ignored Audrey's judgmental gaze on me as I snapped my fingers in front of Drustan's face. "You need to focus."

Drustan shrugged. "It's just such a pretty mouth."

"Oh gods." Hush pinched the bridge of her nose and grabbed Drustan's bicep to keep him from stepping toward me further. "It's challenging to believe males like you have more than a pebble bouncing around in your skull."

Drustan smirked at Hush, igniting my growing curiosity about their relationship.

I held a finger up at Drustan. "*Focus.* You need to be ready to step in."

"Okay." Drustan pressed his lips together in irritation before blowing out an inconvenienced breath. "I'll be the political figure our people need to feed the illusion of safety in this realm." Audrey's shoulders even seem to drop a smidge at that, even though her expression voiced the concerns she still had.

I nodded, "Good, then—"

"For a price," Drustan said before his lips pulled back to smile at me. Hush groaned at the same time I blinked at him.

He can't be serious.

"I'm not fucking you to convince you to be a decent person," I informed him.

"Absolutely *not*." Audrey snapped, stepping up and putting herself between the siren prince and me. Drustan barked a laugh, as if he truly thought I was funny.

I just stared at him.

"I won't go anywhere near your cunt—" Why did that word from him make me blush *so* hard? "All I ask is for a kiss."

I parted my lips in surprise and asked, "A kiss? That's it?"

"Yes," Drustan confirmed as his eyes danced all over my face. "One that doesn't end with an injury this time." Audrey scoffed, shaking her head at him.

"From me?" I stepped around her to face him, pointing to my chest, just for good measure.

"Only you." Drustan jutted his chin toward me once. Audrey was still shaking her head. I gaped and glanced at Hush, who looked *very* annoyed at her prince.

I turned back to him. "A single kiss? From me? And you'll help us stop your father and take his place?"

"Would you like this deal in writing?" Drustan asked with a chuckle.

"Kind of, yeah."

"We don't have time for that," Hush groaned, before jutting a thumb over her shoulder. "Audrey, you must speak to Queen Ada immediately." Hush pointed at me. "If you deny such a simple ask and Drustan refuses to take the throne, I swear on all that is balanced in this godforsaken realm—"

I lifted my hands to cut her off. "I got it."

"No." Audrey shook her head, clasping her fingers with mine. "I'm taking Van with me, and we're going to Queen Ada. Drustan can find anyone else to toy with, in the meantime."

Drustan lifted a shoulder, grinning at Audrey. "Then find someone else to lead the sirens into a peaceful living after my father's death." Audrey grumbled, stomping her foot. Drustan smiled down at me, fully pleased with himself.

"I hope you realize that this isn't a win for you," I told him. "Exploiting me for a kiss isn't nearly as impressive as actually convincing me to kiss you of my own free will."

"I'm willing to admit defeat," Drustan sighed.

Something flickered in his eyes with his words.

"Are you sure it's safe for Van to travel with you?" Hush asked Audrey. "You can protect yourself, as long as your hands are free," she explained, making Audrey drop her hold on my hand. "But Van can't." Audrey bit her lip, acknowledging the truth of Hush's words.

"I could stay with Hush," I suggested. Drustan's lips pulled down in the corners, disliking that idea. "You can go to Queen Ada and the Kings and Queens of the nereids faster without lugging me around, I'm sure."

"I'll protect her," Hush promised Audrey.

"What about him?" Audrey glared at Drustan, who pointed to himself in jest.

"I'll protect her," Hush repeated, stepping between Drustan and me, just as Audrey was. "But you need to hurry, Audrey. Please." Hush's tone turned pleading, and that's when Audrey's empathy cracked through her harsh exterior. "We need to return to hiding, before more of Ilia's guard finds us, and more lives are carelessly lost." This lit a match under Audrey, who pulled me in for a firm hug. I landed against her with an *oof* before wrapping my arms around her.

"I'll be safe, but she's right," I murmured against Audrey's shoulder. "You need to go."

When Audrey pulled back, her look made my stomach churn. She looked miserable and angry with me. Not enough to make me think she hated me, but enough for me to know that something needed to be addressed between us. She studied me with her gaze like she couldn't trust me, before saying, "I'll be back. Please be safe."

"I will," I promised her.

With a grumble and without acknowledging Drustan's presence, Audrey sprinted toward the trees. A whoosh sounded, and her body was gone. Lyskifted away.

Then I turned to look up at Drustan. There was vulnerability in his gaze before he threw his unaffected mask back into place. It caught me off guard, because I had never seen—or even considered—Drustan to be someone capable of feeling vulnerability at all.

"If I kiss you, that does not mean that I want to be your mate," I whispered to him.

Drustan's gaze poured into mine, his arms across his torso dropped as he expanded his chest on an inhale. "I am painfully aware of that fact." Warmth burned in my chest, a confirmation I didn't want to accept, yet. He was being genuine. Not the obnoxiously confident man he usually was. Hush grumbled something and stomped off into the woods, giving Drustan and me privacy. It was the first time I had been alone with him since our date. Since he broke into my bedroom.

"I'll agree to your terms," I murmured. Drustan blinked and grinned, though clearly startled at how quickly I agreed. I had to force myself not to stare at the beauty of his smile for too long.

I stepped toward him. His breath caught on my approach. I was convinced at this point that Drustan really did view me as some sort of magical soul mate. So much so that he was affected by my mere presence. Men could fake attraction just as well as women, but watching his face and body language as I stepped closer and closer, I knew deep in my gut that Drustan was both excited and nervous about something as simple as a *kiss*.

Why else would he rip out the throat of a man who slapped me?

Drustan's hands reached out for me, and I allowed him to rest his large palms on my waist as I pressed mine on his chest. Slowly, slowly, I slid my hands up his body, teasing the firm muscles of his chest and shoulders, anchoring myself around his neck. His delicious scent enveloped me, and I inhaled a deep lungful of it with no regrets.

Drustan's eyes were hooded as his lips parted. His pupils were overly blown out again, daring to conceal all of his gold irises.

"Are you ready?" I whispered, stretching on my toes.

Drustan's hold on my waist tightened, helping me reach his face. He leaned down toward me. We were close enough now that loose strands of his red hair kissed my shoulders.

"Always," he replied with a shallow exhale.

I nodded, licked my lips, and cautiously stretched higher. I wanted to taste him so badly. Something deep in my DNA loved being wrapped up in his embrace like this. A primal part of my brain kept chanting *yes, yes, yes, finally*. I was grateful Audrey was gone, so I could enjoy it. But then the pang of guilt stabbed through my core. I waited until our noses bumped, and right before our lips were about to touch, I smiled and said with regret that I couldn't mask in my voice, "Then you better pull through for us."

Drustan's fingers flexed on my waist, and his eyes softened at me in response. A flash of disappointment had flickered across his face as he heard the shift in me, changing my mind at the last possible moment.

"Clever woman," he muttered. I patted his cheek twice, the second time rough enough to make a gentle slap, before I dropped to my heels. Drustan held me a moment longer before finally releasing his hold on my waist. When I looked up at him, I wasn't too surprised to see his pupils fighting to dilate again.

"Help us take down your shitty father." I kept my voice low and intimate, a moment just for us. "And I'll willingly and happily kiss you. Mouth to mouth. For as long as you want." Because I would be lying to myself if I said I didn't *desperately* want to kiss him in return. That if I was going to do this, I wanted there to be a decent reason for it, so I could enjoy our first *real* kiss.

Drustan heavily exhaled at that, and goddammit, even his breath smelled good to me.

"That's a dangerous thing to say." Drustan lifted a finger to tuck a strand of hair behind my ear, and heat scorched my cheeks. "I don't know if I'll be able to stop once I do."

"We'll cross that bridge once we get there." I grinned at him, because I could. I enjoyed the idea of Drustan wanting me. I closed my lips and gave him a casual shrug. His eyes darkened, his pupils slowly covering the entirety of his eyes again, before Hush suddenly returned.

"Alright," she clapped her hands, making Drustan blink his eyes back to their natural gold. "We need to get back."

"Great." Drustan nodded. "I'll return Van to her realm."

I raised a finger at him as soon as he stepped toward me. "I want to stay, like I told Audrey, and you need to deal with it."

Drustan frowned and retorted, "And if I refuse?"

"I'll protect her," Hush argued.

"Yeah." I jerked a thumb toward her. "Hush will protect me."

"I can't," he grumbled and pressed his fingertips to his temples as he squeezed his eyes closed. "I can't just live with that."

"Figure out how to," I argued. "Because I'm leaving with Hush."

He grimaced, scraping a hand down his face, as he glared at Hush and uttered, "I'll escort you two back, then."

"Fine," Hush sighed. I didn't say anything. I just followed her. Drustan strode next to Hush, and I let them have whatever silent conversation that ensued between them while I focused on not tripping over rocks and stray twigs and other random forest debris. Based on the annoyed looks they kept giving each other, I assumed the mental conversation they were having was a heated one.

After a few more moments of heavy silence, I decided to break it.

"I can't believe you stole my condoms," I grumbled to Drustan's back. Hush turned to look back at me with a pinch of confusion in her brows.

Drustan didn't say anything; he just kept walking.

"Really?" I asked him, "You're not even going to try to deny it?"

"Why would I deny it?" Drustan retorted, glancing around the woods.

"I guess I just want to understand *why*." I continued, "Does the idea of me being at risk thrill you?" Drustan stopped, and I had to catch myself before I walked right into his massive back. He turned, revealing his own furrowed brow.

"Why would the idea of my mate being at risk thrill me?"

I raised my eyebrows at him and crossed my arms. "Without condoms, I'm at-risk during sex."

Hush asked, "What are condoms?" It was my turn to be shocked. *Was my assumption that night correct? Did they not have those here?*

"Don't worry about it," Drustan muttered.

"Condoms are like..." This was crazy, I couldn't believe I was explaining what a *condom* was to another grown adult. "These thin latex sleeves a man puts over his..." I waved vaguely toward my crotch, making Drustan's lips twitch with amusement. "So that he doesn't spread any infection to his partner or get them pregnant."

Hush's eyes went wider and wider as I finished that sentence. "He wears a *what*?"

"Humans." Drustan rolled his eyes as he mirrored my pose, crossing his massive arms over his chest.

I lifted my hands at the two of them. "Are you seriously telling me you *don't* have condoms anywhere in Hyvenmere?"

"Why would a male wear one of those?" Hush gestured toward her own groin. "When he could just take the injections?"

"What?" I asked.

"The injections," Hush repeated, then continued to explain. "It's a medicinal cocktail designed to make a male infertile for up to a year. Injected into the shoulder. There's a second injection designed to protect males and females from infections transmitted during intercourse."

"Well, yeah, okay. In my realm, women have options like that for birth control."

Hush's eyes widened even more. "The *females* take it? Why? Males are the ones who fertilize every time they reach their pleasure." I scraped a hand down my face, trying to ignore the jealous rage over how the men in Hyvenmere seemed to handle the birth-control side of sex without question, even though misogynistic men like Leon still very much existed.

The standard for men in my realm truly was in hell.

"The point is…" I widened my eyes as I addressed Drustan. "You *stole* my protection."

Drustan opened his mouth, but Hush cut him off, "Why would human females continue to have sexual relations with human males if *they* were the ones responsible for not getting pregnant? Why not only sleep with females and avoid the risk altogether?" She shook her head and muttered, "This must be why humans have bred enough to reach their absurd population."

I opened my mouth to reply before hesitating. Hush, as always, had a damn good point.

"I don't know." I waved my hands in the air. "But the point is, you," I pointed my finger toward her prince, "Broke into my bedroom and stole my condoms. You took away my protection."

"Have you taken a male to your bed since I took them?" Drustan raised a dark red eyebrow at me.

I blinked in surprise at his question. "What? No. Because I don't have—*ohmygod*—you *fucking* dick." I balled my hands into fists. This *fucking* siren and his *fucking* audacity.

Drustan responded by pulling his pink lips back into a feral, unrepentant grin. "My motive is sound, then." Hush was still blinking in bewilderment from the newfound knowledge she had of condoms and human sexuality.

"We should keep going." She shook her head and marched on. Drustan winked at me before turning on his heel to follow. I grumbled, not too loudly, as I stomped after them.

"I'll just buy more," I muttered to his back.

Drustan turned his head just enough to tell me over his shoulder, "I will take that as a personal invitation to return and rid you of them." My blood was burning with feminine rage.

"You don't get to dictate my sex life. What I do with my body is my choice. If you think I'm above going out of my way to sleep with someone else out of pure spite, you're wrong," I informed him.

Drustan whirled on me then, making Hush groan and roll her eyes as she turned to look at the two of us. The siren prince's hand cupped my face. His fingers laced in the hair at the back of my head, while his thumb tipped my head back by resting underneath my jaw. A muscle popped in his cheek as he ground his teeth together. His brows had a deep pinch between them, and his lips were pressed in a hard line.

He held my gaze for just a moment before he said in a low voice, "If you insist on creating a death wish for humans in your realm, then by all means, bed as many as you want."

I glared up at him, determined to ignore how warm his hand felt on my face. "You can't be serious."

"You know that I am deadly serious, my song," Drustan's words practically rumbled out of his chest. "You have said how dangerous I am. Just imagine my wrath when another pitiful human mistakenly puts their hands on you."

"What do you think is going to happen here?" I stepped closer to him, poking his abdomen with my finger. "Do you think that if you threaten human lives and steal my protection, that I'll happily jump into bed with *you* instead?"

"Of course not," Drustan muttered. His shimmering eyes bounced between both of mine, "I don't care if you never join me in my bed." I widened my eyes at that, my cheeks heating as

I quicky glanced over at Hush, who just stood there with folded arms, looking bored. "Celibacy is a reality I'll happily embrace if that's what you desire." I widened my eyes at that, because I'd never heard a man utter words like that. "But the only way I can close my eyes and gain an ounce of sleep at night is if I know that you aren't being touched by some weak human. Unsatisfied."

"Just because you're practically a giant, doesn't mean that all humans are weak," I retorted. My mind was still whirling over his words.

"She's right," Hush muttered to herself, glancing over her shoulder in the direction we needed to continue walking.

"Compared to your mate, they are," Drustan replied. He didn't even sound cocky as he said it. In his mind, it was probably a simple fact. The equivalent of saying, "the grass is green" or "the sky is blue."

I grumbled and pushed on Drustan's chest, making him release his hold on my face. He frowned as he stared down at me, his hands balled into fists.

"You're overstepping here big time," I informed him. "I'm not some simpering, controllable woman, you manipulative ass."

"Oh, I'm *very* aware," Drustan replied, holding his ground.

"I can't—oh my god," I grumbled and gripped the roots of my hair, something I often seemed to do in his presence. "If there was *ever* a chance of you getting into my pants before, there sure as hell isn't one now." I was so heated, I wanted to punch him, "I'll kiss you after you take your throne, but then that's *it*. One kiss, and you'll *never* be able to put your hands on me again. Your celibacy will be officially activated."

Drustan lifted a shoulder and said, "As you wish."

I hated this. He truly seemed unbothered. *Asshole.*

"If you two are done," Hush muttered, "This is where we leave you, your highness."

I recognized the area immediately, and to keep my thoughts to myself, I started thinking about my composition, containing my favorite melody that has been haunting me for months.

Drustan gave me a look I couldn't decipher before he nodded and scanned the surrounding area with his eyes. "I'm going to linger, ensure no more of my father's guard are present."

"Thank you," Hush muttered, "But you need to leave us before we continue." The siren prince rolled his eyes and silently muttered her words back to her, as if he were mocking a sibling, and not a double agent. He turned to stalk off, but before he did, his hands clenched at his sides. Drustan took one more step forward before shaking his head turning around to march back toward me.

Alerted, I started backing away from him. "What are you—" But my air was cut off. Drustan had wrapped his hands under my arms, around my waist, and lifted me in the air so he could bury his face in my neck. For stability, my arms wrapped around his large shoulders while the toes of my sneakers dangled in the air, not touching the ground. I couldn't remember the last time I had been lifted in the air for a hug. Perhaps I was a child. But this, this didn't make me feel like a child.

The way Drustan's breath inhaled against my skin, rubbing his face against my neck, as if absorbing as much of me as he could, I felt...*cherished*. He didn't say anything. Just...breathed me in. His chest pressed against mine with his inhale, tightening his hug around me.

I took a moment to indulge myself. I dipped my nose toward his neck, tightening my hold around his shoulders, and breathed in his spicy, delectable scent. Forcing away the guilt that burned from my indulgence. Audrey wasn't here to judge me. Hush didn't seem to give a shit if I sniffed her prince. My nervous system liked it. I became grounded as Drustan wrapped his entire body around me like this, but I couldn't explain why.

It was just a hug. But I could feel his heartbeat against my chest. I soaked in the warmth of his large body, seeping into my own. His soft hair brushed against my arms, and my eyes fell shut for a moment as I calmly breathed him in.

Just like he was doing with me.

After a few tense moments, Drustan sighed and lowered me to the ground. His hands lingered on me, though. His large palms cupped either side of my jaw as he rested his forehead against mine. He had to bend quite a bit to make it happen, since my feet were flat on the ground again. But he just held me, pressing his lips together, squeezing his eyes shut, as he held my face.

Then, without a word, he disappeared.

"Let's go." Hush didn't give me time to adjust to what the hell Drustan and I just experienced. Instead, she grabbed my hand and led me deep inside the Fjellenheim tunnels.

CHAPTER 23

Audrey returned later that day, right when the sun was setting on the horizon. Not that I could keep track of time that well in the tunnels.

I was sitting with a group of teenagers in a little alcove where some instruments lingered for entertainment. Hush assured us that we were deep enough in the mountains not to be heard by anyone potentially stalking the surrounding area, so we had a quiet little jam session.

This was where Audrey found me.

"No, no." A teenage boy, I would guess he was about seventeen, put his hand on mine when I played a note incorrectly again. "Like this." He took the instrument from my hands, one that reminded me of a bass guitar, and strummed it with precision.

"Sorry." I giggled to myself, amused at how strict these kids were with music.

Throughout the day I spent here, I learned that playing music was similar to a religious experience for sirens. Something all siren children dabbled in at a young age. The type of instrument didn't matter: string, wooden, wind, or even their own voice. Music, of all genres, was a heavy part of siren culture. Though I was amused at how strict and serious a teenage boy was acting, I tried my hardest to show the craft the respect it demanded.

"You're really talented," I said when he was done demonstrating.

"I keep telling him that!" A teenage girl in the group piped up who had been busy giving him big, dreamy eyes as he played. He let his dark shaggy hair fall over his face more, his gold eyes quickly glanced up at her before he focused back on the bass in his hands. "I'm no more talented than anyone else."

The teenage girl made a scoffing sound. Teenage crushes and angst were a thing no matter what realm you were born in, apparently. I gave her a smile of camaraderie, because I, too, was a simp for emo boys with shaggy hair at her age. She grinned up at me, but her focus kept flicking back to the boy as she spoke.

"I miss my band," she sighed. My heart twisted for her. She couldn't live like she used to, because she randomly woke up with the gift of whismerra at sixteen years old, unable to control it. Her mother had scooped her up and kept her hidden until, somehow, Hush found them in the woods days later.

This was only a month ago.

Why doesn't he notice me? Her thoughts echoed in my head.

The boy stiffened, making me suspect that he heard her, too. From the way her eyes widened and her cheeks turned dark pink, I became desperate to save the situation. I remembered the horror of accidentally exposing a crush at that age, and if these kids couldn't live normal teenage lives with the rest of their peers, I was determined to try to ease things as much as I could.

"Show me how this one works." I picked up an instrument that reminded me a lot of a harmonica, and the boy happily took the distraction. He set the bass down and clasped the wooden box with both hands before blowing into it.

I grinned, pleased that my guess was correct.

It didn't sound like a screeching harmonica, though. The sound was crisper. A clean whistle, but gentle enough not to make listeners tense from the sound.

"Van." My head jerked toward the sound of Audrey's voice, and all the other kids around me followed suit. "Oh, thank god you're alright."

"I'm okay." I pointed to the harmonica-like instrument in the boy's hand. "I want one of these next."

Audrey smirked, even though a visible sadness lingered in her eyes. "Next? Is there a list?"

"Yup." I nodded, standing from my cross-legged position to leave the teenagers to their soul-crushing angst. "How did it go?" Audrey and I waved goodbye to the teens as we walked throughout the cavern, keeping our voices low in a space that echoed, filled with thousands of ears that could hear better than I'll ever be able to.

"Okay," Audrey replied with a shrug. "Ada feels horrible about all of this." I pressed a hand to my chest in relief. "Liam is at Fergus's now, asking the Nereid Kings and Queen for assistance." She bit her lip as her gaze flicked back to me. "I didn't want to leave you alone here for much longer."

"Thank you." I elbowed her arm as we walked. "And I'm glad to hear Ada understands the problem and wants to help," I replied.

"Well." Audrey kept her gaze down as she spoke. "The problem is, we kind of are on our own."

I frowned at her, "What do you mean? I thought that things went well. They don't want to help us take down Ilia?"

Audrey shook her head. "Ada is sympathetic and agrees that Ilia is a huge threat. But it's a bit more complicated than that. Now that he has her parents' journals, *and* she knows what's in them." Audrey looked defeated as she explained, "Ada is hesitant to directly attack or oppose him. It's very complicated knowing what Ilia has on her—and when I relayed the information Drustan shared about Ilia's amplified sinndra, she just looked...terrified."

I widened my eyes. "Agreed. So how is any of this too complicated for her to join us?" I gestured to the huge cavern of women and children at risk of being executed.

Audrey sighed, rubbing her forehead. "Ada can't just invade. It'll break several treaties and laws, laws older than anyone alive in this realm at the moment."

I shook my head at her, "So?"

"So," Audrey continued, "She can't just invade Lyndoruun and take Ilia out. However, she suggested the possibility of taking in Lyndoruun refugees if we managed to sneak anyone out under Ilia's nose. She also suggested waiting to see how talks go with Liam and the nereids. If they're willing to stand up to Ilia, Ada would feel more comfortable doing so as well."

I blinked at her. "Okay, that's not terrible. But what happens when Ilia discovers the refugees first? Or learns that we're trying to turn the other territories against him?"

Audrey blew out a breath through her lips. "I don't know. That's something that Ada mentioned, and it made her a little more concerned for her own people's safety and trust in her rule." We made it to Hush's quarters in an emptier area of the cavern. Audrey knocked on the door, which was immediately opened by Sergei, who gestured to us to enter. Hush, always donned with her face mask and military leather, was pacing the room with a distressed look on her brow. The two of them were staring at two large monitors on the far wall, displaying security footage.

"We're monitoring a unit that is currently patrolling near the tunnel's entrance. They haven't found the cabin yet," Hush explained. I panicked, but Hush and Sergei's level-headedness made me think they were prepared for something like this. Or perhaps they were used to patrols getting close to their secret.

"It might be worth trying to get the sirens out, without alerting Ilia to their departure and risking an attack on the fae and nereid territories," I summarized.

"Correct." Sergei nodded.

"Yeah." Audrey plopped down in a nearby chair. She had dark circles under her eyes, and I felt bad for my friend and the weight she was carrying now. "According to a call I had with Liam, Fergus at least seemed very willing to help relocate the families to Vanhirra, which would make more sense logistically than Enharra. Fergus was hopeful that his parents would, too."

"Okay." I nodded. "Good, good."

"We also need to find a way to remove Ilia, assuming we get little to no support from the fae or nereids," Sergei muttered, rubbing his hand on his jaw. "Ideally with minimal civilian casualties and public backlash."

"We need to ensure that the sirens of Lyndoruun, and the rest of Hyvenmere, understand *why* rebels are doing this," Hush added. "We need to take control of the narrative before Ilia can."

I grimaced. Hush and Sergei gave me funny looks.

"What?" Hush asked.

"I'm sorry." I waved my hand to shoo my weird feelings away. "It's just odd discussing the PR aspect of removing a dictator from office."

Audrey snorted, but it wasn't humorous.

"This is all such a mess," Audrey said. I watched her as she rubbed her temples with her fingertips, her eyes closed as she struggled to gather her strength.

"The good news is, Ilia still doesn't know where the females and children are," Sergei muttered. "But he probably knows that Leon and his unit are disposed of at this point, since they failed to check back in. We don't have a lot of time to come up with a realistic plan to relocate over a thousand sirens."

"Okay, so, what do we do right now?" I asked.

Hush pulled a vibrating phone out of her pocket before

furrowing her blonde brows at the screen. Sergei pulled out his own phone that was vibrating as well, and the two of them shared a very, very concerned look.

"Amber must have realized her brother won't be returning," Sergei grumbled. "There is another unit of guards several clicks from the cabin, searching."

"It also looks like we were just given a new assignment." Hush pinched the bridge of her nose with her fingers as she murmured angry words I couldn't pick up on.

"What's your assignment?" Audrey pressed.

Silently, Hush strolled up to us to show her the screen of her phone, and on it, was a picture of me. It was from my first and only visit to Lydhavn, unaware that my picture was being taken as I sat on my ottoman at Bandthral between Audrey and Drustan. The language written underneath my picture was in the runes I couldn't read, but a cold twist in my chest helped me guess what exactly was being ordered.

"They want you to kill Van..." Audrey barely spoke the words loud enough for me to hear. "...If Leon's sister suspects that I killed her brother, then her revenge would be killing Van." Audrey scrubbed both of her hands down her face in exasperation.

"This is also clearly a test," Hush murmured. "This was sent to the generals of Ilia's guard. If what Leon said was true, and that Amber is suspicious of me conspiring with the halfling and human, then I need to be the one to prove my loyalty to Ilia." Hush pocketed her phone and slapped her hand down on the desktop in frustration.

"It's almost as if impulsively killing people isn't always the correct answer," Audrey spoke, her voice dripping with derision as she crossed her arms.

Hush snapped at Audrey, "Would you rather we sent Leon and his unit back to Ilia? Let them report exactly where the thousands of missing females and children are? After they already killed Van for spite, of course."

Audrey flinched and crossed her arms. Not willing to argue with her.

"Leon was a repulsive male," Sergei chimed in. "Hyvenmere is a better realm without him, regardless of how or why he was disposed of." I silently agreed with Sergei. Leon always made my skin crawl, and I liked the idea of never having to face him again. "His sister is spiteful and petty in her own way. Even if Leon and his unit made it back to her without finding you three, I would assume that she would have continued investigating the mountains anyway. Once she has a theory in her mind, she won't let it go until she has answers." Sergei spoke his theory while opening a laptop on the desk, tapping away on the keys. He grinned at it. "Thankfully, it seems as if the talks with Prince Fergus have gone well." He pointed to the computer screens, and all of us watched as Liam and Fergus stalked behind the unit that was spread throughout the trees.

Fergus and Liam were undetected, and Fergus threw a wink at Liam before raising his hands and lifting his gaze toward the sky.

Thunder erupted, and within seconds, heavy rainfall descended on the siren guards.

The unit was annoyed, completely soaked. Within minutes, the unit regrouped and retreated.

"I'll fetch them," Hush murmured, throwing her hood up as she strode across the office. We all watched as Hush appeared on the security footage, startling the men. They followed her, Liam looking much more skeptical than Fergus. Later, the two princes strode through Hush's office door.

"We are running out of time to get all the females and children out," Liam announced as he entered Hush's office. Following behind him was the nereid prince, who greeted Audrey and me with a wide smile.

"Ah, if it isn't my favorite halfling and human," Fergus grinned. "Though I wish we were meeting again under better circumstances."

Sergei flattened his palms on either side of the map he was studying.

"I just feel the need to say it out loud..." I lifted a finger to get the attention of everyone in the room. "Regardless of what our plan is, I'd like to stay alive. No matter what." Audrey continued to frown at that, not appreciating my attempt to lighten the mood at all.

Hush gave me a funny look. "Are you always so desperate to be unserious?"

"It's *my* death that's being discussed," I argued. "I'm the one who gets to decide how seriously to take it. But I'm deadass when I ask, from the bottom of my heart, please don't kill me to prove your loyalty to Ilia."

"Killing you would be idiotic for us to do." Sergei finally looked up from his map, his dark hair fell over his forehead, his smirk visible because his mask was down. "It would be a death sentence for us." Audrey pinched her eyebrows but didn't voice the question that inspired her confused expression.

"What are we doing instead?" I asked, trying to move the conversation along.

"I need to prove our loyalty to Ilia, to buy us more time to figure out if we can relocate everyone, before Ilia feels the need to send more of his army here to investigate." Hush nodded toward Fergus, who was leaning against the back wall.

"My parents have been unable to make a firm decision either way," Fergus announced with annoyance. "Unfortunately, the dark recipes Drustan and his cousin stole from them the night of my birthday not only made them fear Ilia *more*, they also lost some trust in *me* for allowing it to happen." Fergus lifted a dark eyebrow as he smirked conspiratorially. "However, I am still the beloved Prince of Vanyara. Several Vanyaran guards are working on preparations to host refugees as we speak, without the official order from my parents," Fergus added, before turning to Audrey and me to inform us. "I can have two trusted spies explore the back end of these tunnels. But based on what that map shows..." Fergus pointed a finger adorned in gold rings to the old parchment laid out on Hush's desk. "There is a specific route leading to the ocean. That might be the best way for us to transport the refugees out."

Sergei pointed to the map Fergus referenced as he added, "There is a sizeable gulf between Lyndoruun and Vanyara." His finger dragged across the map where the ocean was illustrated. "Prince Fergus is right, that might be our best shot of getting everyone out safely. The handful of Fergus's guards operating the mission will have strength from the ocean, and siren adults with stronger shapeshifting abilities will be capable of swimming themselves to the shores of Vanhirra, if something happens to the ships."

If Ilia targets the ships and they all capsized, he meant.

I nodded. "Okay, how much time do we need?"

"A few days at least," Fergus replied. "It's not easy for members of the guard to find time to go directly against my parents' orders."

"What happens when your parents realize what's happened?" I asked. "Will your parents ship all the refugees back to Lyndoruun?"

"No." Fergus shook his head. "If the refugees happen to find their own way into our lands, my parents will welcome them. My people have always felt a companionship with the sirens, so it would be very foolish for my parents to go against public opinion and send the refugees back Lyndoruun."

"That's great," Hush started to pace the room with her words. "Ilia told us to confirm Van's death by tonight," Hush added, rubbing her forehead in thought.

"Damn," I muttered. "Ilia has no chill."

"None of this is fucking *funny*, Van," Audrey snapped. I jumped, surprised at her heated tone. I glared at her and snapped back.

"If I don't get to laugh about any of this, I'll start screaming," I explained. She ground her jaw and looked away from me, silently fuming.

Hush rolled her eyes before leveling everyone in the room with a stern look, "Any suggestions on how to buy time for Fergus's spies to set up an escape plan, while proving my loyalty to Ilia by tonight, would be helpful."

Everyone thought in silence. Brainstorming.

"...What if we just killed Van?" Fergus suggested, the first to break the silence.

"Dude." I glared at him.

"Not *literally*," Fergus smirked at my offense as he explained. "But we need to confirm your death, right? What better way than to make Ilia believe they actually killed you?"

"How?" Audrey questioned.

Fergus stood from the wall, his dark blue eyes sparked with confidence as he continued his train of thought, "We have this herb in Vanyara." He pointed to me. "It's strong enough to knock out a nereid. Slow their heart rate. It's medically used to combat extreme levels of stress and anxiety. To slow the body down." He glanced over at me. "I'm sure it could do more to a human."

I frowned. "This just sounds a lot like killing me, but gently."

"It can slow our heart rate down to less than five beats per minute." He pointed to his chest.

"For context," Audrey spoke up for my benefit. "The average resting heart rate for a Hyvenmerian is around two hundred beats per minute."

"Goddamn," I replied as I lifted a skeptical eyebrow at

Fergus. "So if mine is half that rate, and I take one of your herbs..."

"It will get dangerously close to stopping your heart entirely..." Fergus tilted his head with his words, "Though, not completely."

"But what if this herb actually does just stop Van's heart?" Audrey argued.

"It shouldn't," Fergus replied. "It's designed to slow the heart down, not to stop a heart completely. Though, if it does, you could just heal Van."

"I can only heal what's alive. I can't bring someone back from the dead." Audrey bit her lip in worry. "Have you even tested this on a human?"

Fergus shook his head. "Not officially." Though the way he said it made my suspicion rise.

"What does—" I frowned, thinking of the human inclusive bond Fergus and I saw at his birthday. "...You've seen this work on a halfling, though."

Fergus smiled in confirmation. "The halfling's mate was very distressed, as going several minutes without hearing their mate's heartbeat would make anyone feel, I'm sure."

"Ilia isn't patient," Hush spoke, squinting her eyes in thought at Fergus. "He wouldn't need more than a minute to confirm that Van was disposed of."

"We could fool him with a dangerously slow heart rate," I said, considering. "But I don't think the herb itself would be enough..." My brain was going through several scenarios. My unconscious body being within the same city as Ilia made me sick to my stomach, but if we were going to risk me being in the same room as him, we needed to *sell* it. Make my death as believable as possible, so that he would find comfort in Hush's loyalty again.

The room was looking at me, waiting. "...We need to make my death look gruesome."

Audrey's eyes widened in alarm before she breathed, "Excuse me?"

"I wouldn't go down without a fight," I explained. "We need to make it look believable enough to fool Ilia. Slowing my heart rate so Ilia can give me a once-over is great, but not *enough*. I need to be beaten and…wounded."

Audrey paled, and she was shaking her head at the same time Liam spoke up, "That isn't a bad idea."

I lifted a finger at him. "Watch it, you."

Liam gave me a forlorn look as he explained, "I am not eager to see you wounded, Van."

I gave him a skeptical look and replied, "If you say so."

Liam gave me a small smile. "Whoever is important to my mate…" With his words, he laced his fingers together with Audrey's, tugging her closer to his body. "Is important to me. However we choose to see a plan through, your safety will be a priority."

I believed him, returning his smile in thanks before facing the two sirens and nereid in the room. "I think this could work. But I need to look like I put up a *good* fight. My clothes should probably be torn. Go as far as to trash my bedroom. Like you jumped me when I wasn't expecting it—just in case Ilia feels the need to send scouts to confirm your story."

Hush and Sergei shared a look, before Hush addressed Fergus, "When can you get us that herb?"

"Give me two hours to lyskift there and back," Fergus replied with a wink thrown at me, before disappearing out the door.

"Okay." I ran my fingers through my hair, nodding, hyping myself up for the plan I helped put together. "Okay. So, you knock me unconscious and then beat me up and drain me of some blood to sell it." I glanced up at Hush as I rested my hands on the back of my neck. "Then what?"

"I'll heal you." Audrey waved a hand as if this was obvious. "If your wounds are as bad as I'm assuming, it'll take me some time." She gave me a soft expression, reminding me of how far back our friendship went. "But, I'll do everything I can to make it feel like you never experienced the physical trauma in the first place.

"Good," Hush said, focusing back on the topic. "That should be enough time to let Fergus's spies get their affairs in order, before Ilia discovers the missing sirens."

"Ilia still doesn't know where the missing sirens are?" Liam questioned.

"No." Hush shook her head. "He suspects Amber might be onto something, but he doesn't have confirmation."

"But how do you know that?" Liam pressed. "How can you be so confident assuming what Ilia actually knows?"

"I just am." Hush sounded tired as she stood next to Sergei, her golden gaze flitting over the map.

Liam pressed, "I just don't feel as confident as you are. If Ilia sent his militia here once, he must be confident about his suspicions. I consider us lucky that Fergus's storm managed to fend them off."

"Ilia has suspected that Audrey and Van are behind the missing sirens for a while," Hush lifted her gaze to Liam with her reply. "He currently suspects that *I* might be assisting you both with the missing females and children. But he doesn't *know*. He has doubts."

"How do you know he has doubts?" Liam asked.

"I know," Hush snapped.

Sergei gave Hush a nervous look as Liam argued again, "*How*, though?"

"Because no one knows Ilia's mind as *I* do!" Hush yelled, slamming her palms down on her desk.

An uncomfortable, weighted silence pressed on all of us. It clicked for me then, and I inhaled a shocked breath. Everyone turned toward my gasp, studying me with various levels of confusion and suspicion.

So I said it out loud, "You have whismerra." Audrey and Liam stilled, before staring at Hush with wide eyes. Sergei didn't look surprised. He just kept his gaze locked on me. Waiting.

"You have whismerra, too?" Audrey whispered.

Hush rolled her eyes before exhaling an annoyed breath. She stepped around the front of the desk, a deep pinch formed in her brow before she yanked her mask down. A perfectly symmetrical and familiar feminine face was revealed—soft pink lips, a button nose. Hush almost looked unreal. Digitally drawn. Her beauty was otherworldly, even when she was dressed in her siren militia leather uniform.

"If we go through with this ruse, I need everyone to stop questioning me and *trust* me," Hush spoke, curling her top lip back at Liam in annoyance—so different from the starry-eyed expression she gave him at Bandthral. "So stay quiet, and let me share some context with you as a form of mutual trust." She closed her eyes and inhaled a deep breath, preparing herself, looking as strong and confident as I expected her to be, before she opened them and announced, "My name is Caelena Shaw."

CHAPTER 24

Hush was Caelena Shaw. Drustan's cousin. Ilia's niece. The one who stole the dark recipes from the nereids. The one who snuck Liam out into the hall at Bandthral.

"You—" Liam gave her a wide-eyed, bewildered look. "*You* tried seducing me at Bandthral."

Hush—Caelena—rolled her eyes at him. "I played my role as the pretty face perfectly. I *tried* encouraging *you* to take charge and search my uncle's room and office properly, but you were too flustered and worried about your mate's feelings to focus on the mission." I snickered at her version of events, but my laugh was ignored by everyone in the room.

"Wait..." Liam's face paled. "You were there the night Drustan killed—" he snapped his mouth shut, unable to say the words.

"I was," Caelena nodded. "And as much as you've been holding onto this anger and resentment toward Drustan, you need to understand what happened."

Liam frowned. "What, exactly, happened? Beyond the murder of my parents, that is."

Caelena gave Liam a stern look. "Drustan only killed your parents because of *me*."

Liam cursed, baring his teeth at Caelena, making Audrey have to hold him back.

Sergei snarled, clearing the desk and positioning himself in front of Caelena, lifting a sword to Liam as he growled, "Think very carefully about your next move, fae."

Liam was struggling to control himself. "Why? Why would Drustan do that for *you*?"

"Because." Caelena's temperament was calm, not defensive but determined. "Your parents were going to kill me first."

Liam froze, his eyes widening with horror. Why would Liam's parents care about Caelena? She herself said that no one in Hyvenmere considered her to be more than a pretty face. Something Ilia was able to weaponize to steal from other territories. What would make the former Fae King and Queen want to end Caelena's life?

Then it hit me.

"Because of your whismerra..." I whispered my assumption.

Everyone in the room stilled.

"Yes," Caelena confirmed. "I wasn't raised like all of you. I didn't grow up in society. My parents protected me. Kept me safe from the ancient law that demanded I be executed. That cabin that guards the entrance to these tunnels is my childhood home." I pictured my first impression of the cabin, how it looked lived in once upon a time. I could practically feel the warmth that was soaked into the structure over the years and years.

Caelena's family home.

"My parents first discovered my whismerra when I was an infant. I couldn't project clear thoughts, obviously. Just feelings." Caelena paced the room before deciding to lean against the wall where Fergus once was. "They took me away. To the base of the Fjellenheim Mountains. My mother was a witch—

the one Queen Astrid worked with to develop the protection spell over Audrey and the other halflings in the human realm. My father and Ilia were brothers, and my mother was from one of the small towns scattered between here and Lydhavn. It wasn't a suspicious move my parents made, and Ilia granted them his blessing to leave the city, because my father was farther away from the throne. In Ilia's eyes, his brother picking up his mate and newborn, and leaving the city, was the equivalent of giving Ilia his blessing to rule with Queen Astrid. So, I was raised here." She gestured toward the cavern. "My mother taught me *everything* she knew. Educating me on the goddess Tynara and the power she stored here." Caelena marched over to the far wall where the many maroon drapes hung and pulled one back.

This revealed a series of carvings. Old enough to be marked long ago but preserved.

"What does that say?" I asked.

There was a reverent, heavy silence in the room until Audrey started to speak, translating:

When contention shrouds the continents, an Idol shall rise.
Their hand shall heal, their roots sunk deep in timeless soil.
Guided by the holy elements, they shall cast down the ancient beast
and bind the realm in long-lost unity.

"The prophecy," Liam breathed in awe. "This must have been one of the earliest documentations of it."

"My mother believed the Goddess Tynara carved these words herself, before she left us," Caelena added. "My studies were held in this very room my entire childhood."

Audrey stared wide-eyed, releasing her hold on Liam to step forward and gently trail a finger just outside the carvings. "... Was it you?" she asked, turning to look at Caelena. "Was it you who started the rumors that it wasn't Ilia who was prophesied to unite the realm...but me?" Caelena simply nodded, making Audrey press a hand to her chest in shock.

"Yes. I studied our history here," Caelena explained. "As well as many other subjects. My father pushed me to become skilled enough to destroy any enemies should anyone discover my whismerra and demand my death."

Audrey spoke in a reverent tone, with her eyes glued to her prophecy, "But by doing that, wouldn't your parents put their own lives at risk? Breaking the law by hiding you?"

Caelena nodded solemnly, "Raising me, protecting their only child, eventually cost them their lives."

Grief that I had no right to feel, filled my chest, and I couldn't stop myself from placing a hand between my breasts to ease the ache. "I'm so sorry."

Caelena ignored me and continued, "When I was older, barely fifteen years old, my parents deemed me ready to enter Lydhavn. They introduced me to the king, my cousin, and started to educate me on proper siren society. I had passed all my parents' lessons with perfect marks, and they were confident I could keep my own secret. Drustan, however, is cleverer than anyone gives him credit for." Caelena sighed. "We returned to Lydhavn just after the Siren Queen's mysterious death." She threw a look in Liam's direction, who furrowed his brows from being reminded of his parent's crime. "I was being taught siren politics, which is why, after a few weeks in Lydhavn, I was invited to attend Queen Ada's birthday celebration that night."

Liam looked more and more uncomfortable as Caelena told her story. Perhaps that was why Sergei had slowly lowered his weapon, an untrusting eye locked on him as Caelena continued.

"I thought I was ready." Caelena leaned her head back against the wall. "I thought I was strong enough. But I wasn't." She bit her lip and closed her eyes through the next part of her story, "When I first arrived in Lydhavn, Drustan suspected my whismerra almost immediately. He and I spent the most time together, and he tricked me. Thinking something loud and clear, exactly how he would vocalize it, while his back was turned to me. I responded, assuming I had heard his voice. But no." She shook her head. "He tricked me with his mind."

Audrey exhaled a nervous gasp. "But, Drustan has whismerra, too. So, he couldn't turn you in."

Caelena gave a mischievous smirk at the ceiling before locking her gaze on Audrey. "Drustan has no whismerra at all."

I frowned. *What?* That couldn't be right.

"He's been in my mind," I argued. "How could Drustan have known my thoughts if he doesn't have whismerra?"

"There is only one other way a siren can enter the mind of another," Caelena explained. "A way that is not only allowed but sought after."

My stomach sank as Liam cursed, "Are you implying that Drustan and Vanessa are mates?"

Audrey paled and asked, "Mated sirens can enter the minds of others?"

"No." Caelena shook her head. "Mated sirens can enter the minds of their mate. That's it. No one else."

"That's why he killed Leon for slapping you..." Audrey murmured to the ground. "I suspected, obviously. I thought I saw his eyes flicker to black." She gave me an accusing look; one I didn't bother responding to. "He must have known you were his mate since Fergus's birthday." Audrey looked very confused, so when she opened her mouth to ask more questions, I tried to get the conversation back on track.

"So Drustan killed Liam's parents because they discovered your whismerra?"

Coward, Caelena taunted in my mind.

Fuck off, I thought as loudly as I could.

"Yes." Caelena looked remorseful, and part of me felt bad for diverting the subject back to such a sensitive one. "I had tried to whisper something to Drustan during dinner. He was the only one who knew my secret besides my parents...he and I hadn't known each other for more than a few weeks, but Drustan was the only friend I had." Caelena's gaze grew distant, and part of me wondered if she was reliving the memory as she told us about it. "Unfortunately, Drustan didn't hear me...your parents did."

Liam clutched Audrey closer to him, seeking her comfort while his eyes were glued to Caelena. His full attention focused on her story. I couldn't imagine being haunted by this memory. Holding a grudge against your parents' murderer for over a decade, only to discover the horrible things your parents did. To hear the perspective of someone else involved in the crime.

"I was terrified. I screamed into Drustan's mind what I had done. I was convinced I had committed my own death sentence. The entire dinner, I kept waiting for the Fae King and Queen to reveal what I did. But they didn't. I kept stealing glances in their heads, determined to figure out what their angle was." Caelena's lips pressed together, and the divot between her brows deepened. "Their minds were not a place I wanted to linger. They were cold. They were calculating—very unlike the demeanor they performed for everyone else. I almost couldn't believe it." Caelena shook her head. "I was horrified. I combed through their minds while they continued a pleasant conversation with Ilia and the Nereid Kings and Queen. That's when I found a horrid recent memory of theirs. The death of Drustan's mother."

Liam cursed, pulling Audrey in front of him so he could wrap his arms around her and rest his face in her hair. She stared wide-eyed at Hush, stroking his arms and providing comfort the best she could. Sergei continued to stand as a guard in front of Caelena, and I contemplated the clusterfuck of this situation.

"Were your parents there?" I asked Caelena with a soft, yet prying, tone.

Caelena nodded. "I didn't tell my parents what I had done. I was terrified that if I made it out of Enharra alive, they would send me back to my lonely life in the mountains. I was a stupid adolescent." Caelena's eyes started to get red with unshed tears. She desperately fought them back. "This is why, when the Fae King and Queen requested to join my parents in their chambers that night, assuming I'd be with them, my parents invited them in without question. Unaware that within seconds, the fae royals will have poisoned them..." My heart shattered for her. "I awoke to my parents screaming their last thoughts to me. Telling me to run. To get out. They were gone before I even sat up in bed." Caelena closed her eyes, allowing one single tear to trail down her cheek.

She wiped it away before continuing.

"I was staying in Drustan's chamber, who awoke from my distress. Told him my mistake, shared the memory I stole of his mother's death." Caelena locked eyes with Liam again. "Drustan attended that dinner already fully aware of who murdered his mother, and who asked them to do it. But once he saw in real time your parents planning to execute me as well...Drustan decided enough was enough. He took things into his own hands."

The room felt cold, as if the unveiling that Caelena was bestowing on us came with a haunted wind. A reverent confirmation that each of us experienced with her words. I folded my arms, rubbing my palms on the outside sleeves of my leather jacket.

"...Then Drustan was sent to the Gravhune, and Ilia—who has *never* learned about my whismerra—ordered me to train with his guard, as his last surviving heir," Caelena concluded her story; squaring her shoulders.

"Your parents' last thoughts were focused on saving you," Audrey murmured. "Every choice they ever made was to save *you*."

"Similarly to your mother," Caelena agreed with a sad, empathetic expression. Audrey sniffled, wiping from her eyes, the tears that refused to stay put.

"To think that two women, who were willing to protect their children no matter the cost..." I murmured, heavy with emotion over the concept. "Started such an important chain of events."

"Our mothers went against a law that had been upheld for thousands of years, disobeying ancient precedent, to protect their daughters," Caelena confirmed, giving all of us an intense stare.

"It's just crazy to think that if your mother hadn't hidden you from society..." I gestured to Caelena. "You wouldn't have been able to save thousands of sirens—" I stopped, a thought striking my mind. Everyone waited for me to finish my sentence, while a hypothesis suddenly started forming, but I wasn't sure if it had any merit. I spoke again in a lower voice, "...and if Audrey's mother hadn't saved her...there would be no Chosen One to fulfill this prophecy. Ilia would have just killed you."

"Thank the gods that your mothers were willing to make those choices," Liam murmured, nuzzling Audrey's hair again.

I stared at Audrey and Caelena. Audrey kept her eyes on the prophecy, but Caelena kept her eyes on me. I had a sense that she was attempting to follow my scattered train of thought, based on the way her brows pinched.

"How much older are you than Audrey?" I asked Caelena. She lifted a pale eyebrow at my seemingly random question before she replied.

"Almost a year."

"Meaning Audrey and Drustan's mother—Astrid—became pregnant soon after your parents decided to protect you and leave, correct?" I pressed. Caelena confirmed my statement with a dip of her chin.

"You said that fertility started to rise again about thirty years ago," I pointed to Liam. He also looked at me with confusion before he confirmed with, "Er, yes."

"Right around the time their mothers made these dangerous decisions, going against ancient precedent, as she said." I tipped my head toward Caelena as I stared at the prophecy. "I wouldn't be surprised if fertility rose exactly after their mother's prioritized the protection of their children—regardless of what the laws of the land demanded."

Caelena's pinch in her brow started to smooth, and I used that to continue hypothesizing, "When did fertility start to decrease significantly? You said it had been dropping gradually for thousands of years, correct?" I asked Liam again, who simply nodded his head at me, but based on his expression, he was confused by my line of questioning.

Caelena, however, wasn't.

"Gods," Caelena breathed, before rushing to her drawer and pulling out dusty old books. They looked like they were about to fall apart, but she handled them with delicacy while urgently flipping through the pages. "Fertility decreased right around the same time as..." Caelena released a shocked laugh, turning to another text, flipping it open, and dragging her finger across the page, "...the execution of whismerric sirens was put into effect." She shook her head in disbelief. "The correlation is *so* obvious."

"What correlation?" Audrey asked.

"It was a curse," Liam said, catching on. "Hyvenmere was *cursed* with infertility, because why—" He shook his head, running a hand through his blond curls as he put it together. "Why would Tynara reward Hyvenmere with more children when we were willing to execute them as soon as they reached the age of maturity?"

"But Caelena's parents changed the precedent." I pointed to her, pacing the room as I rambled, "Which would make your goddess eager to bless Queen Astrid. Opening the Mellhawn Gates after thousands of years, allowing Queen Astrid to wander through in secret, and get pregnant with a child who would be powerful enough to fulfill her prophecy—should she continue to make the correct decision and protect her daughter from death —even if it included protecting her daughter from her own king."

"Which she did." Audrey's hazel eyes were scanning the prophecy on the wall. "...But while there are other halflings like me, the spell our mothers cast to protect us probably affected fertility, which would explain—"

"—why a surge of mating bonds started snapping into place after the spell wore off and the halflings could safely travel to and from Hyvenmere," Liam finished.

"This might also explain why there was a surge in whismerric sirens the last couple of years," Sergei added, folding his arms as he studied the prophecy on the wall. "Audrey was back, her powers are intended to bring balance back to nature—a balance that our governments had been disrupting for thousands of years by executing whismeric sirens. But Caelena and Audrey were proof that the realm is ready to change."

"To unite," I murmured, studying my friend in a new light. "...Roots in soil..." I couldn't remember the prophecy exactly, but I got the gist of it. I studied Audrey's healing hands as the prophecy explained, watching as she fidgeted with her fingers. The same fingers that were sunk in eternal soil, when it hit me. "...What if the ancient beast wasn't what we thought?"

Everyone turned to look at me, but Caelena, following my train of thought, gasped.

"It was never the solvyrn...it was Ilia..." Caelena furrowed her brows. "Sirens have been going missing since before Audrey returned to Hyvenmere, but at a much slower rate—because Ilia was finding whismerric sirens and executing them." Acid churned in my stomach from her words. "But then I learned what he was doing when I joined his guard, and when Audrey returned to Hyvenmere and significantly more sirens started to develop whismerra, I started to find the sirens before Ilia, upsetting him."

"Ilia truly, deeply believes *he's* the one the prophecy is discussing," I added. "After speaking to him at Bandthral, it's clear that his titles are his entire personality. He is convinced that he needs to maintain peace and balance in this realm."

"I bet that Ilia fails to see another way to maintain peace beyond upholding the ancient laws. Maintaining the precedent that his bride and brother's mate disrupted. His queen having an affair with a human and sending her child out of his clutches not only wounded his pride, it also fed into his delusions," Audrey hypothesized. "I'd bet that he genuinely views the execution of his own queen as his duty as the Chosen One, if Astrid was willing to illegally travel to the human realm and conceive a child."

"The ancient beast wasn't either of the solvyrns..." Sergei muttered. "...It was the ancient law..."

"...That's why he needs to go..." I concluded. Audrey's hazel eyes lifted to me, and while there were layers of emotion in them, I picked up on the most important one she was experiencing. Resolution.

"If I'm the one this prophecy is discussing," Audrey whispered. "It's my responsibility to ensure Ilia is stopped."

"And if he's delusional enough to murder his own queen to keep his titles..." I let the sentence hang.

"Ilia Shaw *must* die," Sergei concluded. "Whether by the Gravhune, or the hands of the child whom Queen Astrid died protecting."

"Gods be damned," Liam choked. "It's *all* connected. Caelena. Audrey. The siren children. Even our mating bond..." Liam stared at Audrey with awe in his eyes.

*Drustan claiming he and I have a bond of our own...*I shook the thought away, too overwhelmed with this context to focus on it.

"Perhaps this is why Drustan was powerful enough to crawl

out of the Gravhune," Caelena added. "The first in documented history to be able to do so."

"He enforced the new precedent by protecting you again," I added. "When Liam's parents tried to kill you. Surviving the Gravhune could have been another blessing in response."

"Who else could inspire a siren to survive the Gravhune, if not an ancient goddess?" Audrey asked rhetorically, "I doubt Drustan's pure spite alone helped him survive five years of deadly mental and emotional torture. It *had* to be Tynara, goddess of nature and balance, granting another test of good faith, helping Drustan through it, as a reward for saving Hush—er—Caelena."

"Thank the goddess that Drustan *did* make it out," Sergei interjected. "We need someone with a decent level of spite and strength to take down his father."

"And to lead our people into the new era," Caelena added.

"I still don't know how I feel about Drustan becoming King of Lyndoruun," Liam murmured.

"But we know what it's like with Ilia as king, so," I shrugged with my reply to him. "This is what needs to be done."

"Agreed," Sergei said.

I had my own hesitations about Drustan becoming Siren King, like me kissing him as some sort of reward for doing the bare minimum, but I also knew deep in my bones that Drustan would be a much better ruler than Ilia. My intuition hadn't completely failed me yet, so I was counting on it not to lead me astray this time.

"Now we understand the *gravity* of what we're fighting for." Caelena pushed herself off the wall. "If any of this is going to work, I need you all to *trust* me, and those I also deem trustworthy." Caelena tapped the side of her head for emphasis. "I just shared vulnerable information that could get thousands of Hyvenmerians killed. Prove to me that it wasn't in vain."

"Your secret is safe with us." Audrey nodded, then she

glanced up at Liam, who silently checked in with his mate before muttering his agreement.

"Thank you," I said to Caelena. She seemed caught off guard by my words, her eyes nervously glanced around the room before she asked me, "For what?"

"For everything *you've* sacrificed," I explained. I stepped forward, slowly, carefully, not wanting to scare her away or cause alarm. Sergei stiffened but remained where he stood as I lifted my arms and wrapped Caelena in a hug. "You've sacrificed *so* much," I explained into her shoulder. Her entire body was stiff and still under my hug. "You saved all these women and children. You're helping a society that just as easily would have killed you had they been given the chance. You've been saving lives for years."

Caelena's muscles slowly, barely, relaxed under me. I squeezed her again for good measure, before unwrapping my arms and stepping away. The look on her face caught me by surprise. Her eyes were wide, her expression nervous as she pressed her lips together. The unprepared expression on her face dissolved with a few rapid blinks and a clearing of her throat.

"You're welcome," Caelena's voice sounded dry, uncomfortable with my hug and gratitude. "But you're the one about to make a big sacrifice."

I groaned and tilted my head back toward the ceiling. "Ugh, I forgot that I needed to die today."

"God dammit, Van," Audrey muttered, releasing herself from Liam's arms to run after me and wrap her in a hug of my own. "I hate this plan."

"I mean, I don't love it," I replied, catching Caelena's eye over Audrey's shoulder. "But I consent to it. I understand that this is the best option to buy us, and everyone else, time."

Caelena didn't say anything. Instead, she tentatively rested a hand on my shoulder, giving me a friendly squeeze of gratitude.

She didn't need to thank me out loud; her face said it all. As did Sergei's, who dipped his chin at me once in acknowledgement.

"Also," I said when Audrey pulled away. "Thanks for at least entertaining the fake-kill me option. You know, instead of just killing me for simplicity's sake."

Audrey snorted while Liam pinched the bridge of his nose with his fingertips, still in distress over the weight our recent conversation brought to everyone.

"Well..." Caelena squared her shoulders, lifting her mask onto her face again. "Sergei and I have done our best to be as transparent as possible with the mothers thus far." She nodded her head toward the door that led to the main cavern of refugees. "I think it's only fair they know the details of our current plan."

CHAPTER 25

I got to play with the kids and some teenagers before Fergus returned with the herbs.

Part of me got way too excited to see the two angsty teens from before holding hands, blushing, shy, not saying a word to each other. Just holding hands while she drew, and he watched her draw. Hidden in a corner, their own little reprieve where crushes could exist without the weight of the world on their shoulders.

Mothers everywhere were packing, gathering their things in case a quick getaway was needed. If our plan went as expected, they would still have several days to get ready to leave.

I hoped, I *hoped*, that what I was about to do would buy everyone enough time to properly prepare to get out.

I was sitting in a circle with some younger kids, holding a sleeping infant on my shoulder, getting random moments of his dreams pushed into my mind. The feeling of his mother's voice in his ear. How safe he felt when she fed him. Random notes from instruments he'd heard already. The baby couldn't have been more than six months old, but he was big. I had to sit to hold him because of how dense he was.

Nearby, his mother helped his older siblings wash clothes in a portable bin.

"Van," that was Audrey's voice. I slowly turned my head, determined not to wake the baby.

"Yeah?" I asked her.

Audrey bit her lip, wringing her hands together, "Fergus is back."

The kids who were chattering around me quieted their conversations. The nearby mothers paused their chores to look at me, varying looks of pity, gratitude, and pain painted their expressions. I hated seeing them. I didn't want their pity or gratitude. Part of me wished Caelena had never told the mothers what I was about to do to help buy them time.

"Alright." I slowly made my way to sit up, before the baby's mother came running over to gently lift her son off my shoulder, helping him stay asleep. I stood, straightening my clothes, which felt silly considering how abused they were going to be soon.

At least I wouldn't be conscious for any of it. A warm hand rested on my shoulder, halting my retreat.

"Thank you," the siren mother whispered. "All of us will know your name, Vanessa." I didn't know what to say to that, so I patted her hand with mine and squeezed her fingers before following Audrey back to where our friends were waiting.

"...So..." Audrey tried to sound nonchalant but failed miserably. "You and Drustan are mates." I grunted a noncommittal response, then she said, "Did you already know? Or suspect?"

"It doesn't matter, because there is no 'me and Drustan,'" I assured her, watching her shoulders relax with my words. "Just because he feels some magical pull toward me, doesn't mean I have to engage in any sort of relationship with him."

Audrey quirked her lips to the side in thought, "I don't know if it's that simple, Van."

"Well." I released a frustrated breath. "I can't just wrap my head around the fact that your half-brother—who is also the man who killed your boyfriend's parents—for reasons that feel *all too familiar* to me right now—" Audrey's head snapped in my direction in disbelief. "—seems to have some magical claim on me. For some reason, my non-existent love life feels very insignificant at the moment."

She bit her lip as her brow furrowed. "But you have Drew." I stopped walking, making her stop, too. I stared at her, waiting. I waited until her eyes widened in realization and she said, "Drew was Drustan—oh my god." She slapped a palm on her forehead. "It seems so obvious now."

"Imagine how *I* felt." I sighed. "There's more we need to catch up on." Like how he had been breaking into our condo. "But we will have to save that for after..." I tipped my head toward Caelena's office.

We walked in silence the rest of the way. Yes, Drustan was a killer. However, if we were being blunt, so was I. Even though I'd only taken one life, and he'd taken more than that, I still stood by my decision I made as a teen. I *saved* Audrey and me. That man would have killed us that night otherwise.

The idea of some fuckass human man, unknowingly murdering the Chosen One destined to fulfill a prophecy in a secret magical realm, struck me. Was killing our foster father in self-defense maintaining some sort of magical balance that the goddess of this realm demanded, too? Is that why a mate bond snapped into place between Drustan and me when we first met? Did the goddess bless me for saving us as teens, in the only way Hyvenmerians seemed to care about?

"Are you ready?" Audrey asked me as she pushed the door open to the room I hadn't been in before.

I scoffed, "Nope."

She hesitated, "Did you change your—"

"No." I strode through the threshold, where a medical-looking table sat in the center, and some monitors that reminded me of medical equipment were stationed in the corner. Everyone was there except for Sergei, who had to return to Lydhavn for his usual check-in to keep up loyal appearances: Caelena, Fergus, Liam, and Audrey.

Does Drustan know about this? I asked Caelena.

She didn't react to my words. She kept doing exactly what she was doing when we walked in, checking the monitors. She didn't flinch, didn't address me with eye contact or her body, nothing.

She was an excellent liar, having to be after experiencing firsthand what the consequences of slipping up did. *Once he arrives at the Shaw estate, Sergei is going to try to find time to speak to Drustan in private, since I'm sure the prince won't be pleased about the state his mate is about to be in.*

Well, if I do end up dying anyway, I argued, *at least Drustan won't have a powerless human mate hanging over his head.* I didn't know if I believed my own words; I just wanted to distract myself from what I was about to do.

Don't be a moron, was Caelena's immediate reply as she turned to murmur something to Sergei. Well, that was probably all the stalling I could manage.

"Okay." I plopped myself on the table, staring at the jar in Fergus's large, bronze hands. I held a palm out toward it. "How do we do this?"

"Sergei should be arriving at the Shaw Estate any minute now," Caelena explained while she walked to a countertop and started mixing a tea. "While he's updating Ilia this evening on the *nothing* he and his men have found, I will call in on our comm that I have you." Caelena walked over to me with the tea, unscrewing the jar in my hand and pinching some of the herb.

"A little less than that," Fergus said, nodding when Caelena followed his instruction. "Perfect. The halfling in my territory took no more than a teaspoon, so it would make sense for Van to consume even less since she doesn't have our strong

Hyvenmerian blood in her veins." He nudged his knee against my leg that hung off the side of the bed, and I appreciated his ribbing. It helped make this moment less terrifying.

Caelena stirred the herb into my tea, before sniffing it, and hanging it over. Fergus took the jar out of my hands so I could cup the warm mug, inhaling the smells that reminded me of citrus and lavender.

"How soon will I feel its effects?" I asked Fergus.

"Minutes, maybe less," was his reply.

"You can still say no, Van," Audrey chimed in, stepping between Caelena and Fergus to address me. "You don't have to do this. We can find another way—"

"—as long as that way allows me to prove my allegiance to Ilia in less than a handful of hours, sure." Caelena retorted. Audrey glared at her before giving me a pained expression. I waved my best friend off.

"I'm okay. I can do this," I laughed humorlessly. "If you could make sure that I'm completely under before you start beating me up, I'd appreciate it."

Caelena, all seriousness, nodded her head. "The story I'll give Ilia is that I found you and Audrey at a location far from here. Audrey and I engaged in a fight, and you were injured. During our fight, I ended up pushing you down a canyon, and your weak human body failed you."

"Wow," I deadpanned. "I was hoping my death would be less embarrassing."

"Audrey became too distressed with your death to fight back, so she ran—feeding into Ilia's assumption that you're her weakness," Caelena continued. "And I brought your body back for him to see for himself."

"And hopefully Leon's sister will get off your dicks," I finished. "Sounds good. Let's do this."

I looked everyone in the eye, trying to memorize all their faces. Their eyes. Their expressions. Their features. Caelena's military uniform, Fergus's gold rings on his fingers and dread-locks, Audrey's hoodie, and Liam's hand squeezing her shoulder in comfort.

"Well…" I lifted my mug of tea in the air. "Bottoms up." Then I tossed the entire drink back in one go. It had a sweetness that made chugging the entire thing easy. I let the last drop rush past my lips before I lowered the mug and grinned at my audience.

And then the heaviness in my body started to settle in.

I remembered uttering the words, "I think it's working." Then my vision became hazy and a darkness tunneled my vision.

The sleep I succumbed to was warm. Not as warm as I was used to, though. I felt alone in this sleep. There were no dreams for me to recall. One moment, I was holding hands with Audrey while waiting for the herbs I had consumed to kick in, the next everything was dark. All I heard was beeping. I tried to roll over and hide from it, but warm hands were gently stirring me back to the surface.

"Van!" Audrey's voice was raspy, as if she had been sobbing recently.

"Her vitals are good," Caelen's voice draped over me. "She's made a full recovery."

"Gods, that was brutal." Liam's voice sounded next.

"It had to be." Sergei was back, apparently. "It needed to be convincing."

"Hello?" I finally asked. My mouth was dry, and I tried to smack my lips to moisten it.

"Van!" Audrey's body was draped over me, making me gasp from the sudden weight, "You did it. You're safe. It's done. Ilia thinks you're dead."

"Cool, cool," I croaked. "Get off me."

"Oh!" Audrey immediately removed herself, and I was finally able to open my eyes. Everyone was standing around me, curiously studying me. I felt like a science experiment.

"You will be back to normal within a few hours," Caelena explained, staring at the nearby monitors. She walked over and tapped a sticker on my hand. "Keep this one for the rest of the day, and these." She tapped another sticker on my chest, and another on the back of my head, at the base of my hairline. "These are your vitals. They're good."

"Thanks," I yawned. "I feel exhausted."

"Your body went through a lot." Caelena squeezed my arm. "But it worked. Ilia didn't spend more than thirty seconds glancing over you before telling us to dispose of you. When we snuck you back here, Audrey healed you. It took her about half a day or so, but she did it. You'll be okay."

I gagged because the thought of my unconscious body being anywhere near that man made me want to throw up. I only took comfort in the knowledge that Caelena was there, too. Protecting me during my vulnerable state.

"Awesome." I rubbed my neck, careful of my vitals sticker. "Did you do anything fun with me while I was out? Puppeteer me around? Pose me like *Weekend at Bernie's?*"

Caelena and Sergei gave me horrified expressions before Sergei bit out, "Absolutely not. I don't know what the last thing is, but we did not *play* with your unconscious body, Vanessa."

"Sorry, sorry." I waved him off. "I was just making a stupid joke. Bad timing. My bad. I'm glad it went well."

Everyone was quiet, letting me adjust, but I took the silence as an opportunity to stretch my muscles out. I wasn't in my own clothes. Caelena must have gotten me similar clothes to mine that were made in Hyvenmere. The fabric was higher quality and breathable. Linen pants and a long-sleeved t-shirt.

"How long was I out?" I asked.

"Two days," Caelena responded.

That made a spike of adrenaline course down my spine as I asked, "Any update on if Fergus's men can get the sirens out?"

Fergus stepped forward. "My mother is suspicious of what I'm up to," he explained. "Which caused a little delay; however, she is choosing not to interfere." The nereid royals knew how to ride a fence like nobody's business, it seemed. At least Fergus seemed to be willing to stand up for what was right, which meant he would be a great ruler when his time came.

"My unit and I have helped Fergus's men route the tunnel system we'll use to lead everyone to the ships," Sergei said. "The females have been slowly packing and preparing their children for about half a day's worth of travel through the tunnels, should the time come."

"Thank you, Van." Caelena squeezed my arm, sincerity in her tone. "Your sacrifice gave everyone time. It won't go unnoticed."

"Yeah," Audrey gnawed on her lip. "Everyone was able to see Caelena present your body to Ilia from the security footage Sergei was able to steal. You probably don't want to see what you looked like for a while, but all the adults in here saw Ilia deem you dead."

"You're right." I nodded at Audrey and swiped my hands across my chest. "I don't want to see what I looked like, yet. As of right now, what happened to me during the last two days is none of my business."

Eventually, everyone gave me time to fully come to. I ate a lot of food, because I hadn't eaten anything in two whole days. We game-planned what to do next. For now, everyone was still stuck here. Another patrol was sent to the mountains after Caelena returned my body and Audrey started healing me. The patrol didn't linger, though. They simply spread out, found nothing, and returned home. This gave Caelena and Sergei hope that Ilia and Amber were becoming less confident that there was anything to find in the mountains.

But half a day later, while we were double-checking my vitals in Caelena's office again, Sergei strode in with a laptop in his hands and a sharp frown on his face.

"We have a problem," Sergei muttered. His grimace was dramatic on his face as he pulled open a laptop and showed us all the screen.

I gasped at the same time Audrey tensed, and Liam groaned out a "Shit."

On the screen was a video of Drustan.

Shackled, chained to a wall that reminded me a lot of a dungeon. It wasn't dark. The dungeon-looking space was made from a light stone, making the image's clear details easy to point out.

"What the hell?" Audrey whispered.

Drustan was thrashing against his restraints, yelling and growling as he pulled and pulled. His muscles flexed, his teeth clenched in frustration, but eventually, his body would go slack as he fell to his knees. He'd take a moment to rest before battling the restraints again.

"What the fuck is happening?" I asked. "Why is no one helping him?" I ignored how frantic my anger felt in the moment. But my chest twisted painfully watching the video. It was *wrong*. I kept clenching and unclenching my fists, unable to process the immediate rage I felt watching Drustan, chained and helpless.

Help him, help him, help him.

Caelena was scraping a hand down her face as she watched her cousin struggle. "Ilia shackled him in the dungeon."

"Gods." Liam shook his head, rubbing his jaw in thought.

Sergei cleared his throat and said, "This footage was recorded twenty-four hours after we presented Vanessa's body to Ilia. When we were back here, healing her."

On the footage, Ilia entered the cell, flanked by three of his guards. Drustan started thrashing more, and even though there was no sound, it was obvious he was shouting and cursing at his father.

Ilia stayed eerily calm, lifting a hand toward his son as his lips moved.

Drustan stilled, frozen.

"No." Caelena gasped.

Ilia spoke something else to his son, and without hesitation, Drustan dropped to his knees with his hands behind his back.

"He did it..." Audrey breathed, horror lacing her tone. "How did Ilia figure out how to—" She cut herself off by slapping a hand over her mouth in fear.

"We have to help him," I insisted with a frantic voice. "We need to get Drustan out of there."

"We will," Caelena promised. "But we need to be smart about it."

On the screen, Ilia stepped forward and produced a knife for Drustan to take, who did so stiffly. Like an emotionless robot. With another simple command from Ilia's lips, Drustan held the knife to his chest.

"No!" I gasped, stepping forward, shoving Audrey out of my way. "No, no, no." I clutched my hair in my hands, pulling at the roots, "He can't—he can't—" But right when Drustan pressed the blade to his chest, drawing blood, Ilia commanded him to stop with a shake of his head.

Drustan obeyed, dropping the knife, and gasping as if he had been holding his breath.

Relief filled my lungs; tears pricked my eyes as I watched Ilia laugh and leave his son chained in a cell.

"Audrey," I spoke with a familiar numbness coating my voice.

"Yes?" She asked, placing a hand on my shoulder.

"If you don't kill Ilia..." I turned, giving her a good look at my face so she could see exactly how serious I was. "Then I will."

Something shuttered over her eyes as she pressed her lips together. She blinked at me, squeezed my shoulder, and released her hold. Only then, when there was distance between us, did she dip her chin once in acknowledgement.

"This is bad," Liam murmured, pulling Audrey back toward him.

"Your observation skills continue to impress, Li." Fergus chuckled to himself.

"I'm afraid there is more," Sergei spoke low, turning his laptop around to tap some more. "This was just aired moments ago, before I re-entered the tunnels."

Ilia was standing at a podium. Reporters and cameras circled him as three microphones hovered over his face. He wore his crown and his medals, standing tall. His lips were tipped up in the smallest, most condescending smirk I had ever seen him wear. To his right stood Amber, wearing her guard attire with the mask and hood down.

"For too long our land has been divided," Ilia spoke, looking like every slimy politician I had ever had to watch give a press release in the human realm. "The ongoing debate on whether the Mellhawn Gates must stay open or closed has caused contention in our beloved continent. Tynara, surely, must be disappointed in the divisive behavior of my fellow Hyvenmerians."

Burning rage made my hands ball into fists. He was masterfully weaponizing a belief system to confirm his own problematic interpretations of events. "The halflings who have invaded our borders and taken up valuable space from honorable Hyvenmerians must accept the responsibility their reckless and selfish decisions have caused." Ilia stared down his audience, and the determination in his gaze made me want to claw the smug look off of his face with my own bare hands. "After discussing the issue at length with the Dahl and Ahlstrom royals, we have concluded that it will be best for all of

Hyvenmere, if the Mellhawn Gates are destroyed, once and for all."

Cold seeped into my gut. A burst of noise from the reporters holding cameras and recording devices closer to Ilia made him pause his speech for a moment to nod condescendingly at his audience.

"The halflings from the human realm have overstayed their welcome," Ilia continued. "They will have twenty-four hours to leave of their own accord, before my guard will be forced to escort them out. Once balance is restored to our sacred lands..." Ilia couldn't stop himself from smirking as he finished with, "The Mellhawn Gates will be destroyed, keeping humans out of our realm once and for all."

The reporters, thankfully, were not satisfied with that conclusion. Even as Ilia waved politely and started to wander away from his podium, a flurry of questions followed him.

"What about the halfling-inclusive mating bonds?"

"How do you plan to destroy the ancient gates?"

"What exactly made Queen Ada change her mind on this issue?"

But Ilia didn't give a shit; he just left. He didn't need to defend this decision or question the support of the fae and nereids. In his mind, it was done. That gave us less than twenty-four hours to kill Ilia, free Drustan, and release the whismerric sirens into the safety of Lyndoruun.

What none of us were expecting, though, was the grunt that came from Caelena's office door. All of us turned around to see who had entered, not realizing that Sergei had left the door open when he barged in with his laptop.

"Ilia must be stopped," one of the siren mothers said. "He cannot do this."

"We're working on that," Caelena assured her. "We need more Hyvenmerians to help overwhelm Ilia enough for us to take him down. But the fae and nereids aren't willing to help other than being a landing pad for refugees. In the meantime, Ilia's men get closer to us every passing day, so our main priority has been finding a safer place for you all to go—"

"Let us go and fight, then," one taller siren mother responded, producing a knife from a sheath on her hip and pointing it at us. "You all cannot fight every battle of ours for us." She smirked with her words, flicking her wrist to twist her knife this way and that. "I have years of pent-up rage inside of me, ready to ignite. Let us end this nonsense, once and for all."

I widened my eyes and cautiously backed away from her. "For sure."

"Ilia is done terrorizing our children," a third siren mother spoke, hands balled into fists. "He must be stopped. With the prophesied on our side..." She gestured toward Audrey, who stood tall with her acknowledgement. "Surely, Tynara will grant us her favor."

"Ilia won't stop," Caelena muttered.

"He won't," I agreed.

All of us stood in heavy, unbearable silence. The reality of what needed to be done weighed on us all like the mountains we hid under.

"It has to be now," Audrey announced reverently. "Everyone else is on the move with Fergus. We have to take him out now. Though I need to make this clear..." Audrey lifted a finger to everyone in the room, "If there is an opportunity to take down Ilia without killing him in cold blood, I'm going to take it. I am not eager to take a life, like *others*..." her words were cutting, and even though she wasn't looking at me, I still received the acknowledgement she intended, "But a message must be sent. Ilia is not the ruler of all of Hyvenmere. It doesn't matter who guards the Fjellenheim Mountains, who the prophecy is about— not one single Hyvenmerian has the authority to do what Ilia is about to do. If we don't act now, and the fae and nereids allow Ilia to see this plan through, it will set a very dangerous precedent that might be impossible for Hyvenmere to come back from. Ilia can't be so wasteful with siren lives if they happen to be whismerric, and he cannot destroy the Mellhawn Gates. Hyvenmere already knows what it's like to experience such an imbalance, and keeping the gates open and encouraging relations with humans has only proven to even the scales. Just as the goddess herself desires."

"The sooner Ilia is defeated," Liam whispered.

"The sooner innocent children no longer have to live in fear." Audrey finished.

Those seemed to be the words that made everyone come to a resolution. We all agreed we had to go do what needed to be done. I felt my own call to go to the city of Lydhavn, one I had no desire to speak aloud because, in the grand scheme of things, it didn't matter as much.

But Drustan was held captive. Mentally tortured by his own father, after surviving years of lethal torture in the Gravhune. He was in pain, and he was in danger. I didn't like that. I couldn't continue with the knowledge of Drustan in that state. The reasons why, I didn't like and weren't significant enough to voice, but I knew that if we stormed Ilia's estate, I would go out of my way to find Drustan and free him.

Caelena caught my gaze across the cavern with a knowing look in her eye.

It's natural for you to feel drawn to him, Caelena spoke in my mind.

I know, I admitted, *I don't know what to do about it. But I am. I can't find it in me to fight it right now.*

Caelena dipped her chin and replied, *Then don't.*

It took only a couple of hours to gather all the women who were willing to fight, which was more than I expected. They coordinated with each other, determining which children would be in the care of which mother, should the worst come to pass. I helped everyone load up on knives and weapons and helped other siren women pack away first aid supplies.

A woman was zipping up the pockets of her tactical pants when a handful of items fell out, so I knelt down next to her to pick them up.

"Here." I handed her the gauze and tape, and a handful of tiny matchboxes.

"These won't all fit." She pocketed everything but three matchboxes, then looked at me and the jeans I wore. "You can take these."

I wasn't wearing tactical gear. Just jeans and boots, and a long-sleeved shirt. Audrey wanted to lyskift me back to our realm, and I told her to fuck off and let me join. She grumbled but accepted that I wouldn't let her do what she was about to do alone.

"Thanks." I pocketed the matchboxes. "What's your name?"

"Martha." She shook my hand after we both stood up. "And you are Vanessa."

I grinned at her. "Yes, ma'am."

"I'm honored to know you, Vanessa." Martha gave me an appreciative smile before her eyes hardened. "I'll do my best to protect you."

I laughed at that, "I'll be okay, don't worry about me."

CHAPTER 26

"I love how after everything we've been through…" I spoke as we strolled through the city of Lydhavn, "We plan to, quite literally, just walk up to the Shaw Estate."

"We have the element of surprise on our side, and we need this to be as visible as possible," Audrey replied with a grimace. "The Lyndoruun press needs to report it to the rest of Hyvenmere."

"I know, and yet, it's still just us walking up to Ilia's castle, banging on his door, and demanding he stop being a dictator."

"He won't," Caelena grimly replied from her place a step behind us.

She was right, and even though the reality of what we were about to do made nauseating nerves churn in my stomach, I also felt peace with our decision. Ilia wouldn't just…stop. And while I admired Audrey's determination to subdue him as ethically as possible, I was wholly prepared for the reality that he needed to cease breathing.

No man who had his mate murdered because she didn't properly murder a child, like he told her to, was going to be reasonable. Like Audrey said, strolling through the streets like this alerted everyone to what we were up to, just like we wanted. After an hour of walking, sirens with cameras and boom-looking mics and badges that looked a lot like press identification, started to follow our march.

There were hundreds of siren women trained in hand-to-hand combat by Sergei and his men. I just hoped it would be enough.

The rest of the siren women and all the children stayed behind in the Fjellenheim Mountains, where Fergus and a handful of his men guarded them. We convinced Fergus to stay, so that the sirens involved can be the ones who dethrone their king. Liam, the only other non-siren besides myself, obviously would go wherever Audrey went.

We didn't all march in one group. Instead, we entered the city of Lydhavn from various entry points. We needed the attention of *everyone* if our rebellion was to generate the support needed to not only take down Ilia but also maintain a peaceful transition afterward.

"Keep your children indoors," Caelena would occasionally call to pedestrians who stared wide-eyed at our group. They listened to her instructions without hesitation. Our rebellion started to get larger, our separate clusters merging into one as we made it to the main road that would lead us directly to Ilia Shaw.

A handful of Sergei's soldiers accompanied us, less than two dozen, but the rest of our army were women. All dressed in various interpretations of siren militia. Everyone with a mask over their mouth, sending a clear message.

Ilia could try silencing these mothers, but the mothers were stronger. They had experienced more pain and suffering and paralyzing fear than Audrey and I had in a very long time.

My muscles were sore, but it was easy to ignore the pain.

If we failed, and Ilia and his men ended up killing us all, I took comfort in the fact that Fergus was already forming a plan with his men to get the rest of the refugees out of the mountains through the back tunnels, where a handful of ships were currently sailing from Vanyara to meet them. He assured us that his parents would remain unaware that they were missing a couple of ships from their fleet of thousands. The refugees were getting prepared for that reality as we walked, briefing their children on the logistics of traveling inside the mountains.

Now, as the main road we marched on widened, Ilia's estate came into view.

Caelena stepped forward on Audrey's other side, at the same time Liam stepped back, scanning and taking one last note of everyone here. Sergei stepped forward to walk on Caelena's opposite side.

The four of us led the charge, followed by Liam and the women. Sergei's soldiers marched on the outer perimeter of our army.

If I died, Audrey would be here to mourn me, at least. But a certain detained siren also came to mind. Would Drustan actually mourn me? Or would he feel relief with my loss? Would this animalistic urge inside of him dim with my death? Or would that just tip the Mad Siren Prince over the edge?

To distract myself from possibly dying today, I started whistling.

It was my favorite tune, the tune that had been stuck in my head for months. Haunting me in my sleep. The one I had been working on producing on my laptop, on the drums at the Sun Bean. The tune that always danced in the air whenever I stepped foot in this realm.

To my surprise, after a few moments of me whistling, Caelena joined in.

I grinned at her but was surprised when she started whistling the next verse.

"How do you—?" I tried not to sound too offended that she

knew my song. The song I had been desperate to write down and properly compose. I thought I had dreamt of it.

"I was going to ask you the same question," Caelena raised a brow as she replied. "Though, I have my suspicions for why you know the former Siren Queen's famous lullaby."

My lips parted.

"I hear this song every time I come to Hyvenmere," I explained "Sometimes it's faint, sometimes it's louder—"

"Does it get louder the closer you are to your mate?" Caelena asked with a raised eyebrow. Audrey stared at me after Caelena's question, her face numb with what we were about to do. I opened my mouth, ready to reply, then shut it. Realizing I had no idea how to respond.

Because the closer we marched to the Shaw estate, the clearer the tune played in my mind. Caelena hummed, clearly accepting the answer my silence provided her.

Sergei started to hum after that, and then, in a low baritone, he started to sing words in an ancient siren language.

It was reverent and haunting. A song designed to bring comfort while fully aware of the gruesome reality we faced. I couldn't understand the words, but as Caelena and other siren women behind us joined Sergei with their powerful voices, I was overwhelmed by the strength brewing in our rebellion.

Audrey and I hummed along, not needing to know the lyrics. Just honored to be part of the act of defiance.

We approached the gates to the Shaw estate, where a dozen siren soldiers stood outside of it, weapons out and defense positions taken. Eventually, the song ended on a haunting note, and Caelena lifted a hand to get everyone to halt.

Hundreds of women faced a dozen soldiers.

There was one who stepped forward, lowering his sword just a touch, as his eyes studied our group. Recognition flared.

"Is Carmen with you?" the soldier asked.

My face fell, watching his eyes continuously scan our mob

over and over again. His body was braced for battle, but his mind was elsewhere.

Caelena and Audrey stayed silent.

"What about my son?" he asked, cautiously stepping forward once more. "Is he with her? Are they safe?"

Caelena stared at him hard, and I wondered how exactly she was sifting through his mind. Weighing the pros and cons of being honest with him, while also understanding that as long as Ilia lives, secrets must be kept.

"We are here to speak to the king," Caelena answered instead.

The soldier's brows furrowed as he focused in on Sergei, "… Are you a traitor?" he asked.

Sergei didn't need a moment to think about his response.

"I am loyal to the people of Lyndoruun. Ilia is not."

Another soldier guarding the gate, standing near the back of the defense, cursed and raised his sword higher.

"You've stolen our females," he spat.

"We are not possessions to be taken," a familiar woman's voice—Martha, her name was—called out from behind me. "Or livestock to be rid of."

I smirked at her words.

All of the soldiers stiffened, glaring behind their masks, looking more alert as they studied the group in front of them. All except the one who asked about his partner. His child. He started to lower his sword just as his companions started to tighten their grip.

"Let us through." Audrey nodded toward the guards. "Or we will go through you."

"We are loyal to the king!" a different soldier near the front yelled. "Take another step, and you will be charged with treason!"

Without a word, the soldier who inquired about his family swung his sword, swiftly removing the arm of his neighbor.

"Shit," Audrey muttered.

Everything happened so fast after that.

Roots and vines erupted from the earth, startling the soldiers, who began to charge us. Audrey's red hair lifted with static as her eyes and fingertips illuminated that magical glow. The soldier who inquired about his mate shoved his companions into the snarling roots, allowing Audrey to detain all of them immediately. They cursed and shouted and gargled, gasping at the foliage that bound their bodies and necks, elevating them off the ground so their boots couldn't find stability. Some were cursing at us; others were just desperate to save their own breath.

The only soldier not bound by Audrey's command was the first soldier.

Audrey clenched her hand and instructed the roots to move the guards out of our way, making enough room for Caelena to step forward.

The first soldier turned and pulled on the handles of the gate.

"Shit," he muttered. "It's locked down." He pounded his fist against the door and yelled.

"One sec," Audrey grunted, stepping forward. Her hold on the detained soldiers was still intact. She was grinding her teeth together, and part of me wondered what kind of brain power Audrey was experiencing to control eleven different roots to hold off eleven different, powerful sirens. It wasn't until I followed her forward that I realized the roots also covered their mouths, keeping them from the ability to use their sinndra on Liam and me.

Audrey grunted and stomped her foot forward, digging the heel of her boot in the ground. At the same moment, I watched with awe as roots erupted from the earth again. This time, wrapping around the large steel door.

The roots wrapped and wrapped the majority of the gate, and

the groan of hinges being bent and damaged, played a chorus of surrender as she stomped her foot again, and the door was pushed in.

"You're amazing," Liam murmured to her as he stepped up to her side. He even went as far as to plant a kiss on the crown of her head. Behind me, siren women started yelling. Screeching. Shouting. A myriad of voices, powered by years of fear and dread finally being released on the people responsible.

Caelena and Sergei led everyone through the gates, followed by me and the hundreds of women. The eleven guards? They were now pinned against the exterior wall, completely immobile and unable to free themselves. I unsheathed my knife, allowing the adrenaline to course through my body. To activate my fight or flight, to help as many women as I could.

As expected, there were dozens and dozens of siren soldiers waiting for us in the courtyard.

Martha had pinned a soldier about to attack me, against the wall of the courtyard, her sword tucked under his chin, when recognition flared, and he halted his struggle to address her by name.

She hesitated but kept the blade under his neck. The tense moment between them was heavy, and her blade had nicked his skin enough to cause a small trickle of blood to leak down his neck.

But he didn't acknowledge it. His eyes stayed locked on her. Awestruck.

"Martha...my song?" he asked in a whisper.

Martha broke then, lowering her weapon. They couldn't embrace, because someone else tried to fight her while her back was turned.

Martha's mate didn't need any other knowledge or reason. He just started fighting on our side, as did several others.

Many guards didn't hesitate to attack us. To defend the

estate. To defend their king. There was nothing else for the rebels to do, besides fight like hell.

Weaponizing hundreds of siren women to distract all of Ilia's militia for me, I started running around the perimeter of the courtyard.

I needed to get inside. To find Drustan.

But I knew I couldn't just walk in through the main door; it was too guarded. I'd be cut down immediately by Ilia's men. I snuck around hedges and statues, making it to the side of the estate.

Windows were locked. A side door was bolted shut. The farther I got from the battle, the more split in two I became.

I needed to find Drustan, but I couldn't abandon Audrey and Caelena, either. Audrey released a loud screech, and fear raced down my spine as I jogged back toward the main fight, brainstorming ways to help while not getting in the way.

A blond siren soldier, with his mask down, appeared as soon as I re-entered the courtyard. His gold gaze was terrifying, and his grimace as he swung his sword reminded me just how useless I was in this setting.

"Shit!" I cried, barely dodging his blade as I ran away. He chased me and grabbed my hair, before throwing me on the ground. The air was knocked out of my lungs, and right when he lifted his sword to spear me, Caelena was suddenly there, hitting the back of his head with the handle of her own blade.

His eyes closed, and his body dropped to the ground in a dramatic *thump*.

A woman and another soldier approached, fighting each other with their own knives. Blocking blows, striking others.

While still on my back, I tightened my grip on my knife.

Call to Drustan! Caelena shouted in my mind before vocalizing, "Now!"

"He won't hear me!" I shouted back, slashing the back of the knees of the soldier the woman was fighting. He yelped, fell to his knees, and allowed her to take a knife to his shoulder. She twisted, before ripping the knife out and slashing him across the throat.

Blood splattered on me from the move, and I did my best to move on from it as quickly as possible. Perhaps that was all I could do. Avoid engaging in one-on-one battles myself but assist whoever I stumbled upon.

Caelena laughed darkly, shouting, "The prince will hear you just fine!"

I shook my head, "How? He's not—whoa!" I dodged the blade of a sword as a woman sliced toward a siren soldier obviously doing his best not to cause *real* harm to her.

The soldier looked very conflicted. This was good.

I finally got to my feet, losing track of where Caelena was, when she shouted at me again.

"Call to him, Van! He needs your voice!" Caelena was suddenly pinned against the wall by a soldier, who reached for a blade on his hip. I started sprinting toward her, but she was quick.

She had already grasped the blade he reached for and sliced his neck with it. He screeched, gargling, grasping his throat. Lifting her legs, she kicked him off of her and left him on the ground to heal.

"*I've* been mentally calling to Drustan the entire time." Caelena was covered in blood, dirt, and bruises. She looked ragged. Her blonde braid was coming apart. "And for some reason, all I'm hearing back from him is *your* name."

The sound of footsteps approached me from behind, and Caelena glared at whoever was charging me. I ducked right as she lifted her arm to swing. The sound of a man groaning and collapsing behind me made me turn to see a soldier grasping for his bloodied throat.

"You have a very specific style," I muttered to her. She clasped my arm and pulled me up, dragging me behind the stone statue of Queen Astrid to take a breather while the fight continued.

"Our voices are sensitive," she pointed to her neck as she spoke to me. "If a siren attacks you, slicing their throat is the best way to both stun and retreat. It takes a bit longer to heal than other injuries."

I nodded frantically, "Go for the jugular. Got it."

"Call for Drustan—mentally, if you can." Caelena looked fierce, like a true warrior. "Do it."

Drustan! I tried to mentally shout. How the hell did you raise the noise level of a thought? The concept seemed so foreign to me.

"Louder!" Caelena pushed us down as a soldier was flung over our heads. His body hit the walls of the estate with a crunching *thunk*, before he fell into the perfectly trimmed rose bushes. He didn't move, so Caelena turned back to me to say something else, before her gaze caught something over my shoulder and widened.

I turned to see what grabbed her attention, and cursed when I saw Ilia himself, perfectly groomed beard and hair, marching toward Audrey, Liam, and Sergei in the center of the courtyard. The three of them were fighting Leon's sister, Amber.

"Fuck." I turned back to Caelena. "You have to help them."

"I will." She stood and pointed an accusing finger at me. "But we *need* Drustan. His mating instincts to protect you are invaluable to us right now. Call him."

"Okay!" I nodded as she sprinted off, snagging daggers and knives off the bloodied bodies of sirens. I couldn't tell who had died and who was just healing. I couldn't feel my own heartbeat, just an ache in my chest where I was unable to process the adrenaline of this moment.

Drustan, I called in my head. *We need you. Come help us.*

I tried to focus on him but wasn't sure I even knew how to do that.

I just pictured him in that video, thrashing against his restraints. Looking the most feral I had ever seen him. Staying hidden behind the statue, I peered to the side to see how my friends were doing.

All four of them were fighting Ilia.

The other soldiers and women were busy fighting themselves, but I grinned at the sight of the four-to-one battle happening with the man who needed to die the most, whereas Amber was now up against several siren women. Fury coated her expression as she slashed and slashed and quickly became cornered.

"You got this," I muttered to everyone.

Audrey was shouting, her hair a mess, her clothing torn, as she orchestrated her hands enough to conduct the power of nature to her will. Roots and thorns and branches danced around everyone, targeting the Siren King.

But Ilia was fast and strong.

As soon as a branch as thick as my leg lifted to strike him, he would turn and grasp the branch with his bare hand, crushing the wood with his single grip.

Drustan, Drustan, Drustan, I started chanting in my head.

"I should have killed you years ago," Ilia spat at Caelena, who shouted at him with a swing of her knife. It landed true, right in his shoulder, but Ilia shook her off with no more than a wince.

Holy shit.

Ilia was too powerful.

"You!" Ilia pointed an accusing finger at Sergei, who halted his charge with a pained expression.

Sergei was frozen, wide-eyed, and trembling.

No!

"Take care of the fae!" Ilia ordered. I stared in horror as Sergei immediately turned and raised his sword toward Liam.

"No!" Audrey screamed, frantically pulling more roots and vines to the frontlines. Liam yelled as he blocked a lethal blow from Sergei. The two of them were pushed out of Ilia's space in their own fight.

"Kill the fae!" Ilia instructed Sergei. Sergei shook his head, wincing, screaming, but his body remained dutiful to the king. Striking Liam again and again, almost frantically.

Liam, wide-eyed with horror, kept up his defense.

Ilia just used his sinndra on Sergei. Ilia just used his sinndra on Sergei.

"Drustan, we need you," I spoke, wondering if my voice would be better than mentally shouting for him. "I—I need you." Watching, terrified for my friends, I immediately started clawing at the dirt at my feet. Desperate.

"You're right. You should have killed me," Caelena growled back at Ilia, focusing his attention on her. "Now, you'll be the one to die first." She raised her sword at the same time Audrey's roots circled Ilia's neck.

But he fought them.

Stepping toward Caelena regardless of the bounds Audrey created, he grabbed Caelena's blade with his bare hand. Ignoring the blood oozing from his grip, he used his other hand to grab her hood and tug it down, angling his lips toward her ears as he muttered to her.

"Kill the halfling."

Caelena stilled.

"No," I whispered, clawing at the dirt more and more, loosening it up. I started to spit in the pile I made, but my mouth was so dry, it wasn't enough. I eventually lifted a pile of dirt in my palms and shoved it in my mouth, desperate to moisten it enough.

Audrey's eyes were frantic, desperate to keep an eye on Liam as he fought off Sergei the best he could, while also watching as Caelena stiffened and fought against Ilia's sinndra with all her might.

It's up to you, Van! Caelena's voice echoed in my head. *Don't you get it? You're the only one who can release Drustan!*

I shook my head. *I'm trying!*

Try harder! Caelena shouted, making my ears ring.

Spitting out the dirt, I started to shove the moistened clay into my ears. As much as I could fit, praying that it would be enough to protect me from Ilia's lethal voice.

Suddenly, everyone started to slow. Grunts and shouts were stalling in the air. Everyone around me was falling motionless in unnatural positions, as if someone hit pause on a movie.

Then the world started to change.

CHAPTER 27

Bodies were unnaturally still. A high C rang in my skull, making me dizzy. I tried to blink it away, but my vision got fuzzier and fuzzier as I did. Because reality was fading. Dissipating like fog as new images took over my vision.

I vaguely recognized PCH, old cars and bicycles zoomed by, and the feeling of awe and wonder filled my gut with every person that passed.

Completely unaware of my, and my mother's, presence.

Wait.

I turned to look into a shop, briefly adjusting my dark red hair under my hat that so many humans wore here. A beanie. I double-checked that my ears stayed rounded, just like the humans, and trotted after my mother. I recognized the face in the reflection, but it wasn't my own.

It was Drustan's

This was Drustan's memory.

He looked younger. Much younger than how I knew him. He couldn't have been more than a late teen. Maybe twenty years old at most.

"This way," a woman with long red hair braided back,

wearing faded jeans and a tank top with beads dangling at the end of the hem, called to him.

Drustan's mother. Queen Astrid.

I could feel Drustan's excitement about visiting the human realm. The realm he only learned about in school, through history classes and textbooks. The realm his father would *never* allow him to visit. But his mother was always more fun. More encouraging. More curious.

Ilia never valued curiosity. Only obedience.

Entering a quieter neighborhood, Drustan and his mother turned a corner and approached a stucco house—a house I immediately recognized even though Drustan didn't.

Heather's house.

It was early in the morning, and Drustan's mother raised a finger to her lips and instructed Drustan to stay hidden. Obscured by the neighbor's RV and overgrown shrubbery. The front door to Heather's house opened, and Audrey, no more than fifteen years old, stepped out of it.

She held both straps of her backpack in her hands, yawning dramatically as she made it halfway down the lawn before frowning and turning to look behind her.

"Who is that?" Drustan asked with a whisper. His mother reached behind herself, grasping his hand in hers, and squeezed reassuringly.

"This is your sister," she replied in a soft voice. Drustan's surprise washed over his entire body, while also noting a hint of recognition. Audrey's hair. The specks of gold freckling her eyes. His vision was so clear. He could see the finest details on Audrey yards away.

"...My sister? I thought she passed?" Drustan questioned. But he believed his mother just the same as he realized something and asked, "Does father know?"

His mother squeezed his hand as she replied, "He can never know." Drustan frowned, feeling uneasy about keeping another secret from his father, but instinctively more loyal to his mother.

Audrey groaned, loud and annoyed, before calling toward the house, "Van! We're going to be late!"

"Wait for me!" a feminine voice yelled from inside. *My voice.*

Chills of awareness ran down Drustan's spine. Hairs on the back of his neck stood still. Muscles in his fingers loosened, and his shoulders dropped. Every cell in his body was focused on who was about to emerge from the house.

What was happening to him?

Stepping out of the house, was me. My wavy brown hair bounced as I trotted after Audrey. He noticed the freckles across my nose and cheeks, my paler skin that was still a shade darker than Audrey's from being in the sun more often. My baggy grunge clothes. I wore earbuds of some kind that rested over my head, connecting to a device on my hip that, based on the sounds Drustan picked up from this distance, he assumed was human music.

"Sorry," I murmured, pausing to adjust my Walkman. I pressed a few buttons, and it wasn't until the music played again that Drustan realized I restarted the song I was listening to back to the beginning.

I raised my gaze as I shouldered my backpack, and my green eyes took his breath away. Something in Drustan's gut tugged toward me. Longing to be near me.

Could she be...? He thought. *No. No, she couldn't.* He and I were too young. Drustan wasn't twenty-six yet. He couldn't develop a mating bond yet. I was even younger than him, so his sudden focus and infatuation had to be a mistake.

But wait. "My sister is human?" Drustan asked his mother. She nodded, and suddenly the image went blurry.

Fading. Shifting to something else entirely.

Darkness, fear, suffering, and distant screams consumed my being. Pain stabbing my skull. Drustan's cry of agony.

Kill me, Drustan begged. *End me already. Be done with it.*

Wait for me! My voice from years prior rang in his mind, causing the shadows and demons of the Gravhune to lessen their attack.

Wait for me! The memory of my voice was getting clearer the more he focused on it. Years had passed, but Drustan could still remember my face. My freckles. My green eyes. My hair. The holes in the knees of my jeans. The way I bit my bottom lip as I adjusted my Walkman to restart my music.

Wait for me! He focused on the memory of my voice as pain threatened to tear him apart. As demons and misery clawed at his mind, taunting him to end it all. The agony of the torture still registered in his body, but he disassociated from it. Focusing on me.

He'd never get to know if that human was his mate or not. Revisiting the human realm to search for me would put his sister at risk, and after that one single visit to the human realm, he'd made a promise to his mother to keep his half-sister safe. But it wasn't as if Drustan was ever going to see the light of day again anyway.

What was I doing in the human realm? Was I happy there? Did I have a family of my own now? Children? A human mate?

Wait for me!

My face solidified in his memory, moments before another prison mate growled and charged Drustan, ready to attack. Fully consumed by the madness of the Gravhune.

Wait for me! With my voice clear in his mind, grounding him, Drustan ripped apart the deranged prison mate with his bare claws.

The image shifted again. The torture of the Gravhune still haunted Drustan on occasion. Drinking helped numb him to it. Keeping the public at arm's length helped more.

What didn't help? His sister was being pulled into Hyvenmere by a lustful fae, too selfish to be near, what Drustan assumed was, his mate, to truly care about her safety. All the effort Drustan's mother put into protecting Audrey from this realm was officially wasted. Because of Liam's naïve narrative, Caelena and Drustan were ordered by Ilia to visit the human realm. To learn Audrey's weaknesses. Find a way to take her down.

"I found something earlier today that you might be interested in," Caelena told Drustan after scouting the human realm on her own that morning. She didn't share with Drustan *what* she found, ensuring that he would follow her back to the human realm that evening.

While disguised as humans, Caelena and Drustan entered a small but noisy dwelling with the words *Sun Bean* on the front. My coffee shop.

Following the scent of Audrey, they decided to take a break from their spying, sit down, and enjoy the music. Caelena was always excited to experience new things, as sheltered as she was. She hummed along with the music, smiling at all the energy and joy filling the space.

That's when Drustan heard my voice. It had been fifteen years since he heard it, but he recognized my voice as if a single day hadn't passed. The voice that Caelena could surely recognize after flitting around in Drustan's mind for years.

Drustan's body tightened on high alert. The noise of all the other humans and musicians faded into nothing. My voice, singing backup for the performer that night as I played the drums, made his chest tighten, and his ears relax. Every cell in his body wanted to jump out of his chair and run toward me.

It's her. He thought. Focusing on the stage, after humans moved out of his way, he saw me. Ripping the drums with a soft smile as I leaned over into the microphone to accompany the singer.

Everything he suspected as an adolescent was true. He and

the human female he stumbled upon years ago were bonded in a sacred way.

In a blink, the image changed again.

"Bring her to me." Drustan was drinking heavily again. *This is dangerous*, he thought. He couldn't have a mate. A *human* mate. Not in this political climate. His father would surely kill me if he found out.

But Audrey would put me in danger anyway.

"Is—is that the best option?" Caelena asked with crossed arms, frowning at the empty whiskey bottle Drustan set on the table. *If I knew you were going to act this recklessly, I would not have led you to your long-lost human mate*, Caelena scolded him in his mind.

"I can't—" Drustan couldn't stop picturing my face. All grown up. More beautiful than he remembered. My *voice*. He felt so spoiled, having practically an hour of new words I'd sung to commit to his memory. Memory he could call upon to help him whenever he felt the lingering darkness of the Gravhune start to creep into his consciousness. "I can't focus on anything else." He pinched his brow as he pointed to where Sergei stood at attention near the doors of his chamber. "Just—bring her to me —unharmed. I'll frighten her right now if I go myself."

"Dru, she won't be safe here," Caelena tried to argue. Red colored Drustan's vision. Caelena was trying to keep his mate from him. Instincts he had only read about flooded the surface of his skin. Making the monster in him desperate to claw out. He put all his energy into ensuring his claws stayed retracted. Caelena wasn't the enemy here, but this primal impulse didn't care.

Logic was threadbare at this point.

"Go." Drustan waved to Sergei. "Bring her to me. Unharmed."

That was the night that Sergei and Leon attacked me on my boat.

Ilia *never* wanted me. It was Drustan. It was *always* Drustan.

Suddenly, Drustan was stalking the corridors of Fergus's family estate, following the sound of my hum as I studied the vases and drapes of the hallway. Practically hypnotized. He had no qualms about ditching his cousin while she obtained the recipes his father asked them for.

Because here I was. Dressed as if I belonged in Hyvenmere, with him. When he startled me, and I gasped, impaling him with my cake knife, he couldn't find it in himself to focus too much on the pain. Instead, all he kept thinking was, *my mate is stunning*.

My voice echoed in his head; *I just stabbed someone. I just stabbed someone.* But as far as first meetings went, he figured things could have gone worse. What was I doing there? In the realm? He thought Audrey had fought Sergei and Leon well enough and would go out of her way to keep me *far* from Hyvenmere. Why on earth would Audrey dare to bring me here? So close to him?

Did Audrey *want* Drustan to find me?

I was terrified, but bubbling under the surface, he could smell other emotions coming from me. Curiosity. Recognition. Attraction. His mate was *so close* to realizing it.

Got it, should we go? Caelena's voice entered his mind.

Not yet, Drustan responded to Caelena as he inhaled my scent. *She is breathtaking.*

Then we were back in the human realm.

Drustan was watching me flirt with my handsome stranger for the first time, in a random human disguise as I fluttered my lashes and gave him teasing touches. *No. Wrong. Mine.* Drustan's mind kept repeating. The flirtations were cut short, and as Drustan watched me run outside the coffee shop, searching for something, he noticed how the man looked more uninterested in me than before.

Then, an idea formed in Drustan's mind. He turned a corner, needing privacy as he found a window to an empty shop to observe himself in. Staring at his reflection, Drustan shifted. Presenting himself exactly as the human male I was flirting with.

Perfect.

Then we were at Bandthral, and Drustan's hackles rose when he saw that his deranged father had made me sit next to him. It took every muscle in his body to casually place himself between his father and me.

Then we were in my room.

Drustan was determined to visit me while I was awake this time. To perhaps attempt explaining why he put his hands on me so thoroughly at Bandthral. That he couldn't sit with the knowledge that my back was in so much pain. He simply couldn't focus on anything else.

But a complicated discussion couldn't be had, because I was hallucinating in my bed. The faint smell of blood mixed with the smell of the tea Audrey gave me made Drustan's heart twist as he stared down at me.

I was smiling up at him. I hadn't done that before. Not when he looked like himself, that is. Of course, I wouldn't be of sound mind the first time I did that. When he tried to ward off my advances, and I started thrashing and crying, he gave in and ordered me to touch myself. The smell of my arousal perfumed around both of us, drugging him with need.

"You know I want you," Drustan cooed at me.

Then we were in the courtyard in Enhavenn. The night Caelena stole the former Fae Queen's journal. *Gods, she's mouth-watering like this*, Drustan thought as he stalked me in the shadows. He bit back a groan of arousal as he stepped in front of me, letting me crash into him, and pinned my body against his.

How could the simple act of holding me against his body feel *this* good? *This* right? As if our bodies should never be separated again.

Who knew that mating bonds could be so cruel? Surely, Tynara was punishing him for all the lives he'd taken.

Another change.

Drustan was chained in the cell, his father standing in front of him. His father's voice commanded every muscle in his body.

"Stop," Ilia's sharp command ghosted over Drustan's entire body, forcing him to halt his movements, but leaving the agony that filled his mind. "You will never disobey me again, son."

Then reality started to blur again.

CHAPTER 28

Caelena's command was still echoing in my head, and when reality started to fade back to me, I was only vaguely aware of what Caelena had used her whismerra for. Memories Drustan had shared with her were shoved into my brain, becoming my own. The information dump was instant, meaning time didn't actually slow down at all.

I just blinked and suddenly had new information.

Bodies that were frozen started to slowly, slowly, move again.

Caelena was grimacing, targeting Audrey, who now had to focus her strength on fighting off our ally.

But the memories felt like they were too much. I couldn't process all this new information. I desperately wanted to sit down and analyze every moment I saw. Every memory of Drustan's I gained access to.

But I couldn't. Because time was speeding up, and I was running out of it.

I shoved one last, disgusting, moist clod of dirt in my ears, silently praying to the goddesses of this realm that it would be enough to protect me from Ilia's command.

"This is ridiculous," Ilia spat, watching his sinndra control both Caelena and Sergei. How could Ilia's sinndra possibly be capable of this? Sirens couldn't manipulate other sirens, so why could Ilia? A theory hit me.

Sirens are connected. The king got his power from his people.

Strength in numbers, now used to weaponize that strength against those very numbers. Sergei fought aggressively, years and years of combat training showing through as he focused all his strength to take down Liam. Quickly, after flipping the fae over his large body, Sergei turned and raised his sword.

No!

He struck Liam directly in the chest, twisting.

"NO," Audrey screamed, drowning out Liam's own. Her scream echoed an omen across the courtyard. I was positive that if the dirt in my ears weren't protecting my ear drums, that they would start bleeding from her otherworldly pitch. Siren men and women momentarily halted their battles to register the sound of her torment, watching Sergei pull his sword from Liam's heart.

Sergei looked tortured as he studied the fae prince at his feet.

Audrey's wrath grew with the power of her agony, and light overpowered the entirety of her eyes.

"Drustan!" I yelled, hoping the sound of Audrey's continued cries of agony hid my own enough from Ilia, "Drustan!" I shouted. Audrey struck Caelena down, pinning her by the throat with thorned roots. She turned her attention to Ilia, who just smirked at her. The smirk of a man who would rather die than consider taking a woman like Audrey seriously.

The smirk of a man who should no longer exist in any realm. A fact Audrey had seemed to accept, based on the cold and lethal look in her eyes as she glared at him.

"Stop." Ilia didn't bother to project the word. He didn't need to, because Audrey obeyed. Tears streamed from her cheeks, her teeth clenched in a grimace as every muscle in her body halted from the command of Ilia's sinndra.

Drustan! I started chanting in my mind, struggling to amplify my mental cry. *Drustan! Drustan!*

"Call back your gift," Ilia ordered next. Roots, branches, and other greenery started to shrivel. A sob erupted from Audrey's throat as muscles in her neck tensed, desperate not to listen to the king. I was reduced to only mentally calling Drustan's name, because the eerie quiet of the courtyard as Ilia commanded his own people against their will, absorbed everyone's attention.

Soon, the courtyard that was once overrun with fresh, thriving growth was nothing more than shriveled, dry, dead debris.

Caelena and Sergei stayed frozen, still under Ilia's command.

"A siren's sinndra cannot be used on one of our own," a siren soldier muttered a few feet ahead of me. "It is unnatural."

Ilia turned his head toward the sound of his soldier's acknowledgement, before flicking his gaze to a nearby companion and muttering, "Kill him." I gasped, fighting the urge to cover my eyes, as a nearby soldier charged him.

"No, wait," Ilia chuckled to himself. "Let him live." The soldier had his sword raised but froze. "None of you are good to me dead. Listen to me." Ilia's voice boomed over the courtyard, making all sirens in the vicinity freeze. They held their weapons and turned their full attention toward their king. Even I could feel the power of his impulse wrap around my body, searching for my compliance.

It seemed as if the dirt in my ears was enough to protect me from his sinndra after all. I needed to call Drustan, but shouting mentally wasn't working. Perhaps I didn't even know *how* to properly shout at someone mentally. How the *hell* did one project thoughts? But Drustan and I were now the only ones not under Ilia's control. But I couldn't communicate to him, because if I called for him, Ilia would hear me.

Kill me, and then his son.

I needed a distraction. A sound barrier of some kind. I started frantically patting my pockets, desperate.

"I am tired of this foolery," Ilia spat to his people. "I am done with it. If you cannot be trusted to behave..." He shook his head, like a parent reprimanding a child. "Then you are a threat to the peace in this realm." Dread weighed in my gut as I shoved my hands in the pockets of my pants, the pockets against my calves.

My fingers folded over a small box.

A matchbox.

I stared at it in my palm before focusing on all the dried, dead foliage littering the entirety of the space. I toed a small branch curling nearby, and it shattered immediately.

I needed something to distract Ilia, so I could call for Drustan.

Do it, Caelena's voice, weakly, called into my thoughts. I whipped my head to look at her, but she hadn't moved. Her body was still under Ilia's control, but her mind was completely hers as her golden eyes slid over to where I stayed hidden, and her voice rang louder, *do it, Van. Before it's too late.*

I struck the match and dropped it on the nearby branch before running and hiding behind another retaining wall. Flames engulfed the space I previously stood, in a *whoosh.*

"Put that out," Ilia spat. Soldiers marched forward and started to pound at the flames with the soles of their boots, but it was all too dry. Too dead. The flames spread rapidly.

I lit another match and dropped it, running.

"Stop—stop this!" Ilia spluttered. I couldn't see him from my new hiding spot, but that didn't stop me from lighting another match and booking it. The flames crackling and consuming the courtyard grew to a threatening roar. Ilia started shouting and other soldiers briefly broke away from the call of his sinndra to avoid the growing fire. I made it near the front doors of the estate, knowing that Drustan was still trapped in the dungeon.

Get out! Get out! Get out! If the flames continued to grow unchecked, with all the fuel littered in this massive courtyard, the entire Shaw estate could be ashes within minutes.

I needed to light a fire under Drustan's ass to break out of the cell, while lighting a fire to his childhood home. Then it hit me.

"Wait for me!" I called to Drustan over the roar of the flames. "We're not done yet, Dru!" I dropped several more matches, breathing a sigh of relief when my friends started to gain back control of their muscles. Ilia was dodging the flames with wide eyes, but every time he tried to escape, new flames as tall as trees started to sprout. I didn't realize it until I paused my arson to take a breath, while air was still breathable, that Audrey was now crouching on the ground, her hands glowing as she fed the flames with more and more foliage. Green leaves burned in seconds, creating a thick smoke in the air.

Flame and smoke and ash created the perfect camouflage.

I ran and tripped, landing face-first on the ground. I spat dirt out of my mouth to turn and see that I had tripped over Liam.

He was gasping, blood pooled around his body, as he held a hand on his chest where Sergei had stabbed him.

"You're alive," I breathed, reaching out to put more pressure on his wound. Liam couldn't muster a response. Then Sergei was next to me, replacing my hands with his, applying more pressure to slow the bleeding.

"You can still heal Liam!" I called to Audrey, not knowing where she was, but hopefully close enough to hear me. I could hear her coughing in the distance, healing another siren woman, but she still managed to respond.

"I'm coming!"

"Listen to me, fae," I pointed an accusing finger at Liam. "Audrey needs you. You can't die yet, so hold on." In response,

Liam narrowed his eyes at me as he coughed more blood out of his mouth. With that, I left Sergei to tend to Liam and ran off.

I dropped another lit match. Another. The sound of destruction coated the entire courtyard. Hopefully, this immobilized Ilia's weaponization of his sinndra against other sirens. The roar of the fire created a shield from the sound of his voice.

A large shadow approached me through the flames.

Shit.

I ran but landed in a corner. The exterior wall of the courtyard. I frantically brushed my hands over the stone, looking for some kind of escape. But the sound of Ilia's chuckle behind me made me panic. I hoped that Audrey would at least make it out of here alive. That I was able to buy her time.

"You?"

I almost laughed at the sound of confusion coming from Ilia's voice. I rested my head against the stone, taking a moment to accept my fate, before I turned around and unsheathed my knife from my belt that I stole off someone else.

His white hair was coated with ash. His beard was disheveled. His eyes were deranged as he smiled at me.

"I thought you died?" He hummed to himself as he studied me. Cornered.

"Come and get me!" I yelled to Drustan. The Siren King cocked his head to the side, his pale brow pinched with my words.

"Why the rush?" Ilia asked. The moron thought I was talking to him.

"You've waited long enough!" I shouted, desperate for the sound to escape over the flames. "Come and get me!" It was doubtful, since the entire point of the fire was to mask my own voice from Ilia. An impossible feat with him standing in front of me now.

Ilia's brows smoothed with understanding, and a dark

chuckle accompanied his words as he spoke, "My son can't get to you, human."

"Come and get me, Dru!" I screamed again. The sound of water rushing and smoke flooding our surroundings, drew our attention. Flames as tall as a building started to die down, hissing with their extinction. I coughed against the flood of smoke, barely registering the sight of sirens standing on the exterior wall of the courtyard with hoses, shouting at each other to put the flames out.

"Are you proud of yourself?" Ilia asked me with a raised brow as he unsheathed a knife of his own. "All this destruction, and for what?"

"Come get me!" I screamed, fisting the handle of my blade so tightly I was losing feeling in my fingers, "I'm yours, aren't I? So come and get me!" My throat was raw from screaming. Inhaling ash and smoke. Lacking moisture. Ilia just laughed, determination coating his expression as he took a step toward me and wrapped a hand around my throat.

"I'm yours!" I shouted one last time before my air was cut off. Ilia shook his head in pity before throwing me against the stone wall. My head hit the stone with a crack, and I crumpled to the ground. My weapon fell from my hands, and disorientation clouded my senses. Squinting my eyes open, a blurred and dizzy vision of Ilia stepping toward me, resting his boot on my arm, made me cuss at him.

"Pathetic bastard," I wheezed. I couldn't see his face, but as he slowly applied pressure with his foot, I both heard and felt the snap of my forearm. I clenched my teeth together, groaning through a scream I didn't want to give him.

"Humans are so fragile," Ilia muttered, dropping to his haunches to tower over me. "It would be pathetic to let you live."

Thank you, I still wasn't positive Drustan could hear me, but my mind was all I had left, *...for waiting for me. After all this time.*

Abruptly, a deep, enraged roar pierced our ears. A hand with black claws the length of fingers, as if they were dipped into black ink, wrapped around Ilia's throat from behind. As soon as those claws ripped out Ilia's throat, silencing him once and for all, Ilia reached toward me as he fell to the ground. Behind him, watching his father crumble to his knees, clutching his throat in his claws, was Drustan.

Shackles dangled on his wrists and bare feet. Red rashes coated his joints. His eyes were black as night. His inky claws were bloody. Black, ominous veins haloed Drustan's eye sockets. His canine teeth were exposed, displayed with a deadly growl as he reached for his father again and sank his claws in his shoulders.

In one swift move that couldn't have been more than a second, Drustan tossed his father's body right over his shoulder, away from me. Ilia dropped to the ground right at Audrey's feet, who looked more deadly than I had ever seen her. Ilia panicked and started flailing. Unable to gasp due to the lack of a throat.

All I could do was stare at the sight.

Numb to it.

I watched as Drustan's head turned toward me, and his black eyes widened in panic.

That was the moment I registered the sharp burn in my stomach. My breath caught in my throat from the sudden pain.

Drustan screamed. A loud, outraged, painful scream. I was pretty sure my ears started bleeding based on the wetness dripping out of one.

Instinctively, my good hand dropped to where the pain was, only to come in contact with the handle of Ilia's blade. It stuck out of the center of my abdomen. The bastard must have thrown it at me before he fell to the ground. I gasped in pain; the movement made blood ooze from my body, down my clothing. A loud, throbbing clang echoed.

Surrounded by flames, shattered, broken shackles littered the ground in front of me where Drustan used to be.

Where did he go?

Audrey screamed next, but her voice was starting to sound faded. Farther away. The air was too thick with smoke from the doused fires, but I could see the silhouette of her figure ripping Ilia's arm off his body—her hand now donned with its own set of siren claws.

I could barely inhale a breath.

"Vanessa," Drustan's warm, soothing voice was in my ear. The heat of his body enveloped me, and one of his hands curled over my good one. Near the blade that his father threw into my core.

Another scream filled the space. I couldn't track who it was, but I hoped deep in my soul that it was Ilia. Even though his voice was ripped from him. The scream was feminine, and it sounded horrible. Like pain and fear and defeat.

Please, stop Ilia, I prayed to anyone who would listen. The pain from having a knife thrown at my stomach was more than enough to distract me from what I hoped was happening to him.

My vision was starting to tunnel, and blackness crept in from the edges of my sight. The tips of my fingers started to feel colder, loose, but lacking feeling. Eventually, something numb started to drape over me in a thick blanket.

"Vanessa!" Drustan shouted next to me. I should have jumped from the proximity of the sound, but I didn't. I *couldn't.* Drustan's sharp face filled my vision, void of black veins, gold irises wide and frantic. His blood red hair fell around his chiseled features, reminding me of the new taste on my tongue. Liquid that tasted metallic and salty filled my mouth before dripping out of the corner of my lip.

"You got me," I muttered to Drustan, meaning every word. Something cracked in his gold eyes, flashing black at me. A distressed shout ripped from his chest. I somehow noticed the feeling of his torso against my side.

I didn't recall being laid back, draped over his lap, but I was.

"Audrey!" Drustan shouted.

"Keep pressure on her!" his cousin called back from somewhere far away. His hand flexed on my stomach, and I whimpered at the new wave of pain and nausea filling my body. The darkness tunneling my vision was taking over now, and part of me was grateful that Drustan's handsome face was the last image I would see before I succumbed to it.

Wild eyes shifting from black and gold. His clenched jaw, inches from mine. A warm embrace, cradling me into the next plane of existence.

"I have you. Stay with me, Vanessa," he ordered.

"...I will..." I could only whisper the reply before sound was lost and darkness enveloped my vision.

Death wasn't as terrifying as some described.

Death was quiet.

Death was peace.

The last thing I remembered was exhaling one final breath, knowing I didn't have the energy to inhale another.

CHAPTER 29
DRUSTAN

Vanessa's eyes were glassy.

I worried that she was losing focus as she weakly whispered, "I will." I'd been longing to hear a form of consent from her for months, and yet, when I finally did, her body immediately fell limp in my arms.

No, no, no, no.

"Audrey!" I roared. Vanessa didn't move. Didn't even flinch. The sensation of black tar burning throughout my core continued to spread to every one of my limbs. Rage and agony were battling for their spotlight within me. Finally, my cousin was there, dropping to her knees as she swatted my hand away from the wound. I didn't remove my father's knife, terrified that it would cause Vanessa to bleed out even more. Expediting her demise.

The squelching of my father's body behind me ignited conflicting emotions. Peace and relief, because the halfling was currently ending him once and for all. Anger and rage, because *I* wasn't the one to end the sorry excuse of a male for myself.

"She's still there," Caelena muttered, her eyes looking distant as she reached for Vanessa's consciousness.

Then my sister was there, dropping to her knees next to us, silently slapping her bloody hands onto Vanessa's body. I could feel the heat from the halfling's healing touch coursing throughout my mate's mangled body.

The ash that surrounded all of us landed on her cheeks, and I used my thumb to brush it off. Revealing my mate's flawless freckles.

The city's fire control bureau had arrived and was currently putting out all the flames. Drones, capturing all the footage of the battle, flew overhead. Undoubtedly reporting the story to news stations all over Hyvenmere.

But none of those details mattered. Vanessa groaned, and the three of us watched as Vanessa's core twitched. Blood still drained from her stomach.

"He hit an artery," Audrey muttered, inhaling a deep breath before channeling more healing into her touch.

"You're taking too long," I scolded, holding Vanessa tighter to my chest. "You need to heal her faster." I leaned down, resting my nose in the dark curls falling around her head. Her floral scent filled my senses, bringing a brief hint of ease into my muscles.

I was struggling not to shake as I held her unconscious body in my arms.

"I'm drained," Audrey groaned. "It's going to work—just be patient," I growled in annoyance at her. She clenched her teeth and growled back at me, while continuing to heal Vanessa.

Finally, Caelena wrapped her fingers around my father's blade and yanked it out, making Vanessa release a soft cry from the pain of the open wound. However, Vanessa's bleeding started to slow.

"Shh," I cooed into her hair. Tears streamed down my cheeks. That was too close. My father almost killed my mate. Part of me wished that the halfling could heal him after she was finished with my mate, just so I could kill him again myself.

I could picture the feeling of my hands ripping his limbs from his body after sinking my claws deep into his throat. Unable to sound one single cry as I plucked him apart. Slowly. Torturously. His fearful and angry expression would be enough to soothe me into a peaceful slumber every night for the rest of my days.

"You're holding her too tight, Dru," Caelena scolded.

Dru. What Vanessa called me. The nickname she gave to my human identity. The nickname that I pretended was for my real name every time I stepped foot in her realm. The real me. I loosened my grip just enough to allow the halfling to keep working.

Against my stomach, Vanessa's ribs expanded on a deep inhale. Healing. My half-sibling was right, it was working. It was just taking far too long.

"Aud!" The fae prince's shrill voice made me frown as he dropped to his knees, landing on the other side of my mate's body, next to the halfling, "Get your hands off—"

I snarled at the fae. A feral sound of pure threat. Hanging onto what was left of my sanity was difficult enough without the fae wailing and trying to take my mate from me.

He halted his sentence and stared at all of us with wide eyes.

I frowned at the halfling and her mate, as I realized how good they looked.

"Did you heal him first?" I snapped at my sibling.

She leaned back on her haunches, wiping the sweat from her brow. I refrained from yelling at her to get back to work simply because Vanessa was breathing more steadily in my hold.

"Just enough." The halfling waved behind me. "I'm drained because I needed to save my strength to finish off Ilia." A quick glance over my shoulder showed what was left of my father. Perhaps the halfling and I truly were related, because the sight of my father's dismembered state, even down to the loose fingers scattered on the stone, staining the ground with his blood, made me want to grin with joy.

I glanced back at the halfling, "You should remove his head, too. His corpse doesn't deserve it." I also couldn't put it past the monster to find a way to recover from being dismembered, since he was able to figure out how to weaponize his sinndra on his own people.

Her red brows, so similar to my own, rose, "What?"

A whoosh and a *thunk* made us all flinch, before we looked back at where my father's remains were. Dozens of siren females—*women*, I corrected myself. Vanessa would want me to refer to them as women—were continuing to tear my father's body apart in rage. The *thunk* that caught our attention was the sound of a small siren woman, a frail-looking thing, swinging his own sword through his neck.

Separating his head from what was left of his body.

Surrounding the scene, my father's soldiers slowly lowered their masks as they stared wide-eyed at the sight of their people dismembering their king's corpse before them.

Ash continued to fall from the air, and nothing but char scorched the courtyard. Flames were quietly dying down, and some soldiers who were caught in the flames were helping each other put out their clothing.

In the distance, I noticed Leon's shitty sibling observing the chaos from a hill on the other side of the courtyard wall. How she and her unit escaped the battle with little to no injuries was beyond me, but when we made eye contact, I bared my teeth at her in a clear and undeniable threat.

Unsurprisingly, my father's loyal crones turned on their heels and fled.

A problem to be dealt with later, then.

Vanessa gasped, and I whipped my head around to study her face. Her eyes still weren't open. The halfling slumped, falling to her side on a pile of ash.

My mate was so *brave*. So brilliant. Willing to risk her life to burn my father's empire to rubble. Cursing him with her last breaths.

I still needed to scold her for risking her life, but I figured I could wait to do that until she was fully recovered.

"She needs more." The halfling breathed. "But...she'll live." An irritated sob tore from my throat at her words, and with Vanessa's mostly healed body still draped in my arms, I buried my head in her neck. Grounding myself in my mate's scent. The sound of her heart beating more steadily. The heat of her blood pumping in her veins, trying to pick up where her friend left off.

Soaking in the euphoria of simply *holding* my mate like this.

"...We—" the halfling cleared her throat. The sound made my eyes flash open to stare at her. She jumped at my gaze, recognizing the danger in it. *Good.*

"We should take her," she muttered, reaching her hands out toward my mate.

"I will kill you," I muttered against my mate's neck.

"Let them," Caelena argued. "She's fragile. She needs to properly rest and recover, Dru." I glared at all of them, ignoring the flakes of ash falling on us.

"No," I replied.

"We have work to do, you stubborn male," Caelena grumbled. Another soldier ran to her side, waiting for orders. But she continued to scold me, "Our people need you. Us." She glanced behind me again.

Keeping my mate safe in my hold, I followed her gaze. The flames had all died out. Sirens littering the courtyard spoke in quiet, reverent voices. Hundreds of gold eyes locked on us, as if they were waiting for something.

Everyone calmly rested in the aftermath. The sound of our breathing filled the air, accompanying the soft melody from the gentle touch of ash flakes falling from the sky like snow. Landing on us. The ground. The stone. A hymn of ashes cascading around all of our people. Penned by my mate's determined hands.

A song conducted by nature herself, consecrated by Tynara's desires being fulfilled. Hope bloomed in my chest that it wasn't too late to turn things around.

For my people. For me. For my Vanessa.

"Let us take her," The halfling's tone was quieter, reserved. "...Please." Her hands were still out, waiting for my compliance. Beside her, her mate glared at me. I refrained from rolling my eyes at him.

"Drustan," Caelena regained my attention with her determined tone, "They know she's yours." She nodded toward the halfling and her mate, who both dipped their chins in understanding, albeit reluctantly. "Let them take her. Let her rest. One step at a time."

I pressed my lips together. I loathed this. The thought of letting Vanessa go, of her friends taking her back to the human realm without me, felt wrong. So deeply, horribly wrong.

Staying in Hyvenmere to help rebuild my people's trust was the logical solution, but one I only accepted with resentment. Slowly, reluctantly, I shifted my mate's body into the arms of her most trusted person.

"If you hurt her," I muttered, "I *will* kill you." The fae curled his lips back, unhappy with the blatant threat I just gave his mate.

"The same goes for you, *brother*," my sibling replied. We stared at each other for a brief moment before she accepted Vanessa's body with a gentle hold of her own.

Perhaps the halfling—my sister—wouldn't be so annoying after all.

"We'll stay in touch," Caelena addressed them. The fae prince and his mate both nodded, and the halfling sent me a glance as her mate draped her and Vanessa in his arms.

"She'll be safe," Audrey reassured me. "She's just not like us. She needs more time to heal. Somewhere safe."

"I'm aware," I spat. I flinched at myself, remembering that my mate was now going to be in the care of this person. "Just —" I pinched the bridge of my nose, my lap and arms felt terribly cold with the loss of her warmth, "Help her get better."

"We will." My sibling bit her lip as she gave her mate a look I couldn't identify. A look that felt like a secret conversation between the two. "...Whatever Vanessa wants."

The fae pressed his lips together, nodding once, before they disappeared. Lyskifted back to the human realm. I frantically reached out toward the space they once occupied, even though it was useless. They were gone.

"She healed him too much," I growled at my cousin. "If he was able to lyskift that easily."

"She needed to stop Ilia." Caelena flipped me off with her words. I knew, logically, that she was right. But the thought of my mate getting the last remaining dregs of my sibling's gift irritated me beyond control. "...One step at a time." Caelena wrapped her fingers around mine.

One step at a time. Clean up this mess. Rebuild with the people I wasn't sure I could claim as my own. Invite those who had to flee back, without the threat of execution hanging over their heads, should they choose.

Get back to Vanessa.

She *said* she'd stay with me. I wasn't above holding her last spoken words to me over her head.

I will. Her voice sounded wrong. Weak. Too close to death. Rage flooded my veins as my gaze landed on the...mush that was once my father. And to think some males in my realm thought that *they* were the superior sex. Winning back trust with my people needed to start with the fem—the women.

"You're right," Caelena spoke, locked into my thoughts.

"First our people. Then we'll figure out how to help you get your mate back. I promise."

I nodded, squeezing her hand in acceptance.

I couldn't force my expression into one of understanding. Starving me for several days in a cell while being forced to injure myself seemed to do a number on me. The fact that I thought I heard Vanessa's voice above the cells my father kept me in was enough for me to call to that base instinct inside of me. To tear out of my cell, to throw guards out of my way, destroying my home until I made it outside, where my heart *knew* she was waiting.

I wasn't fast enough.

"I promise," Caelena repeated. I nodded once; my eyes stuck on my father's remains. Of course, my cousin had her own reasons to return to the human realm as well. That was all the assurance I needed to listen to her. I straightened my shoulders and dropped my cousin's hand to fold my arms across my chest.

I lingered back as my cousin started barking orders to set up a medical tent, while I focused on the remaining scent of Vanessa in my nose.

Clinging to it. Savoring it, already *desperate* to be close enough for her scent to fill my head again. But I couldn't. She would want me to help my cousin, I realized. That was all I needed to get myself to follow Caelena's lead.

And then, no matter what else happened, I was getting back to my mate.

Even if I had to beg her.

Get me back, I silently prayed to the old goddesses of my realm. *No matter what happens, get me back to Vanessa.*

CHAPTER 30

AUDREY

It had been two days since I killed Ilia Shaw.

"By unanimous vote, it is determined that the Mellhawn Gates will remain open indefinitely to halflings and humans who discover Hyvenmere, and wish to enter our realm peacefully," Queen Ada gently slapped her palms on the surface of the table to punctuate her decree, making the two Kings and Queen of the Nereids repeat the gesture in support. I followed suit, officially the human realm's representative as the halfling who fulfilled an ancient prophecy. However, everyone at the tribunal noticed a missing set of hands slapping their agreement, and we each turned to face the newest leader of the sirens.

Drustan Shaw.

My half-brother. He was seated beside his cousin, Caelena Shaw, who frowned and kicked him under the table in a not-so-discreet fashion. Drustan snapped out of whatever distant thought he was in as he carelessly slapped his palms on the surface.

"Yes, obviously the gates should remain open," Drustan muttered, before slouching back in his chair and resting an elbow on the arm. He was struggling to stay focused today, gazing off into a distance that wasn't visible in this room. He rested his fist against his mouth as his cousin threw him a reprimanding look, which he ignored.

"Excellent." King Einar, Fergus's biological father, nodded as he combed his fingers through his long, black beard. The move displayed his gold-painted nails, matching the many rings and bracelets decorating his umber hand. "The goddess has looked fondly on us since the elimination of Ilia and his…unpopular ways. This proves that Hyvenmere will gain much by encouraging various cultures from both realms to connect."

He wasn't wrong. Ada and Fergus's mother, Hilda, confirmed a handful of new mating bonds snapping into place between their people—some within hours of Ilia's head being removed from his body. Hilda's ivory hair was braided back from her face, in a crown that showed off her dazzling features and blue eyes that contrasted beautifully with her copper complexion.

Her expression became hopeful as her gaze turned to her son, Fergus, who stood behind all three of his parents with his arms folded. Fergus matched her expression and even gave his mother a playful wink before focusing back on the conversation at the table.

"Have the sirens seen bonds, as well?" King Algot, Fergus's other father, asked Drustan and Caelena. Drustan's gold eyes slid to acknowledge Algot, his mouth still hidden behind his fist as he shook his head once in the negative.

"We have had our hands full the last few days," Caelena answered on Drustan's behalf. "We are preparing a small settlement a couple of miles outside of Lydhavn, where the women and children Ilia had been hunting will be able to start anew. Many of our guards and carpenters are working on building homes for them as we speak."

"Do you truly think this is better than simply inviting them back to their homes in the city?" Queen Ada questioned with an empathetic expression. "I'm sure those females and children must miss their lifestyles."

"They do," Caelena confirmed. "But the children are still learning how to control their whismerra. These children and their mothers need to be prepared to face backlash from Hyvenmerians, whose knee-jerk reaction will be to fear them. Creating a space for whismerric sirens to live in peace, while learning how to use and control their gift appropriately, prepares them for navigating the rest of the realm as everyone else does." Caelena had disclosed her own whismerric gifts to the fae and nereid governments soon after Ilia's public execution. While I was nervous about her being so open about it, she must have seen enough of their minds to know that they would take her honesty as an act of good faith. To allow them to trust her, and she them.

"While my father has finally met the demise he deserved," Drustan muttered behind his hand, before sitting up in his seat and resting his elbows on the tabletop. "Amber, his second in command after Leon's death, is still alive and well. I doubt she will stay in hiding for long."

"Perhaps we can invite her back and discuss how Hyvenmere is going to run things going forward," Hilda offered. "Help her unlearn all the brainwashing your father—"

"Or we can just kill her and her unit, and be done with it," Drustan casually suggested.

All the royals at the table gave him disappointed looks.

"Do not be mistaken, young male," King Einar spoke in a low, dominant voice. "Though you are intended to be crowned king of Lyndoruun soon, you are still beholden to Hyvenmere's laws. Do not repeat the same mistakes that cost your father his life."

"My father made no *mistakes*," Drustan retorted, challenging. "My father made a series of very intentional decisions that determined his fate. Including, but not limited to, stealing very dark and very illegal magical recipes from our alliances."

The nereid royals stiffened as Hilda said, "Those were locked away, securely out of the public's reach, protected by my magic—"

"And yet Ilia still managed to tell us how to get in and steal it," Caelena interrupted, then raised her hand to halt Hilda's argument. "I'm not saying that you hiding those recipes with dark magic from your people was your mistake, but we need to figure out *who* Ilia was working with in your guard that made it so easy for us to follow Ilia's instructions."

"Concerning swaying public opinion about the integration of whismerric sirens into modern society," Queen Ada chimed in, removing her crown and rubbing the bridge of her nose, "That will, in fact, take time. However, if all of us stand united on how undoubtedly blessed our people are by saving them, I assume any conflicting murmuring throughout our lands will be diminished within a year."

"How will the sirens of Lyndoruun see the benefit of integrating with whismerric sirens, if their people have not had a significant increase in mating bonds?" King Algot questioned, folding his pale arms across his chest.

I slid my gaze over to Drustan, who felt my stare and returned his own.

"What is on your mind, halfling?" he asked me.

"My name is *Audrey*," I replied. "And you know that, considering you had no problem shouting at me to heal Vanessa in your courtyard." Drustan's face hardened with my words.

"Siblings," Fergus shook his head with a *tsk*. "I know the familial agitation all too well." I ignored Fergus's attempt to lighten the mood and answered Drustan's question.

"You and Vanessa are mates." Drustan didn't reply, so I kept speaking. "Your people already suspect that, even though it hasn't been formally announced." Footage that reporters captured that day, showing Drustan cradling Vanessa, bleeding out, angry tears streaming down his face, went viral. Drustan has stayed out of the public eye, while Caelena took the responsibility to clean up and rebuild trust with her people after leading an army to execute the Guardian of the Fjellenheim Mountains. Opinion on the theory of Drustan and Vanessa's matehood varied. Some considered it abysmal that a royal would be bonded to someone wholly human. Other opinions were more hopeful and excited at the idea.

"What is your point, *Audrey*?" Drustan asked with a bored tone. Liam grumbled next to me, annoyed with Drustan's disrespect. I attempted to calm him with a squeeze of his knee under the table.

"My point is," I continued. "If you confirmed your matehood with your people, that would help make several transitions into a more peaceful Hyvenmere run smoother." Drustan's lips pulled back in a wicked grin. Then he leaned forward, resting his forearms on the table as he clasped his fingers together.

"And how do you think our dear Vanessa will like that idea?"

I glared at him. Vanessa still hadn't awoken from her recovery. I'd healed her as much as I could, and Ada had her own healer look after Vanessa to try to assist, but Vanessa still slept in my old room in the Dahl estate. Caelena theorized that Vanessa continued to sleep because of all the trauma her body had taken within such a short amount of time. After being abused to fool Ilia about her death, only to almost die again. As if Vanessa's body was demanding a time-out from the physical trauma.

"I'm not saying you need to *act* on your bond," I clarified, "I'm saying it might be beneficial to confirm that the bond itself *exists* between you two."

"I disagree," Caelena spoke up, with her gold eyes on the table. "If Vanessa rejects the bond with Drustan, that will not win any favors with our people. In fact, it could turn even more sirens against the idea of leaving the gates open and allowing halflings and humans to explore our realm." Caelena scrubbed her jaw with her hand. "The most helpful thing would be for Drustan and Vanessa to cement their bond. It's the best way to bring unity between our people."

I paled, shaking my head at her, "If Vanessa wants to crawl into bed with him—" I crossed my arms and tipped my head at Drustan. "It should be of her own volition—not because she needs to bear the responsibility of getting all of the sirens to hold hands and sing kumbaya."

Based on everyone's confused expressions, I lost the group with that very human reference, but the gist of my words seemed to get through to them.

"Audrey has a point," Fergus strolled around the room as he spoke. "It's not fair to shoulder Vanessa with such a burden, especially after she's sacrificed so much of herself already, for a realm that she has no ties to."

"No ties—except for her mate," Caelena added.

"And what would be the point of her sacrifice," Einar argued. "If the sirens of Lyndoruun were still conflicted? The solution seems simple to me." Einar faced Drustan. "Officially bonding with your human mate will most likely be the key that unlocks your people's ability to secure their own bonds. The nereids and fae have accepted their bonds without fuss and look at the success our people are having because of it." He leaned forward, folding his hands on top of each other as he locked eyes with the siren prince. "Bonding with the one whom the goddess chose for your mate, could be what she's waiting for, to determine if the rest of your people are ready for such a gift."

Drustan drummed his fingers on the wood of the table as he asked, "And how does the council suggest I earn the acceptance of my mate, because for those of you unfamiliar with Vanessa, she is not exactly *eager* to jump into my arms...or bed."

I smirked at that. It brought me a spark of hope, at least, that

Vanessa wasn't desperate to get into Drustan's pants. I'd spend a lot of time by her bedside the last couple of days, waiting for her to wake up, thinking about her situation. At first, I was angry, because why would the goddess punish Vanessa with such a horrible man as her Hyvenmerian mate? Vanessa was too good for him, by miles. Drustan was…unbearable. The manner in which he carelessly took lives was nothing less than evil.

Just because I understood the context of *why* Drustan murdered my mate's parents didn't mean he was forgiven for it. I hated that he was bonded to my best friend in such a way. But then Vanessa's words floated in my memory, "…for reasons that feel all too familiar right now…" and a hard, cold rock filled my stomach. Did Vanessa seriously consider her and Drustan to be similar in that regard? To have the same morals and ethics? Vanessa was just a kid, and we never talked about her murdering our foster father that often because, well, I didn't think we needed to. I just assumed it was a dark, horrible memory to have, and that she wouldn't want to dwell on it. But what if that wasn't the case? What if Vanessa truly did dwell on what she did more than I thought? It would explain why she was so eager to plan to kill Ilia.

Perhaps, similarly to how I've kept part of myself from Vanessa to protect her from this life, Vanessa had been keeping dark parts of herself from me.

Just the thought made dread fill my veins.

"I think the first thing we need to focus on is ensuring Vanessa wakes," Queen Ada argued. "I'm not wasting precious time trying to help the Mad Siren Prince of Lyndoruun pick out the perfect flowers to court his mate with." I loved Liam's sister so much. "And if Vanessa has no desire to finalize the bond between them, then we will have to come up with a more creative way to unify the sirens of Lyndoruun."

Everyone murmured some form of agreement, even Drustan, who seemed more resigned than I expected him to be.

After discussing more details about the whismerric siren haven Caelena was designing, the dates on which Drustan would announce his intention to claim the throne as Guardian of the Fjellenheim Mountains, and maintaining the Mellhawn Gates, we all rose and left the chambers.

While Liam clasped his large, warm hand in mine, we watched as Fergus tapped Caelena on her shoulder before she could leave.

"Could you do me a favor and let me know what my mother would like for her birthday?" Fergus asked. Caelena released a huff of laughter.

"For you to find your mate," she replied. Fergus groaned.

"She and I both," Fergus huffed. "But genuinely, what else?"

"She's your mother, Ferg," Caelena scolded him. "I have more important things to do than help you be as lazy as possible with your mother's birthday."

Sufficiently scolded, Fergus bid us farewell and followed his parents.

When Liam and I turned a corner with Caelena, Drustan was leaning against a wall in the hallway, waiting for us.

"I'm getting tired of seeing your ugly face every other day," Liam muttered at my side. I squeezed his hand in reassurance as I fought a smile. Drustan tipped his head to the side, genuine confusion marring his features before his eyes narrowed at my mate.

"Are you still upset with me for killing your parents? Because *your* mate killed my father just days ago, and I'm already over it." I genuinely believed him. Drustan did not look or sound like someone who gave a single shit that the people he was speaking to had killed his father.

"What is it, Drustan?" I asked, standing my ground. His eerie siren gaze locked on me, and I genuinely couldn't believe that he and I shared the same mother.

"When can I see her?" Drustan asked.

"When she wants to see you," I replied. Drustan ground his jaw together, and a muscle popped in his cheek.

"You must understand how difficult that answer is for me to accept," he replied.

"She's recovering in my home," Liam explained. "And you are needed in Lyndoruun. I suggest helping your cousin lift the load, so your people have a chance at seeing you as the leader you intend to be."

Drustan glared at him, staring, letting his irritation coat over everyone in this moment.

"So that's how it's going to be, then." He determined.

I lifted a shoulder, "I'm not just going to make Van accessible to you. When she recovers, and she says she wants to see you, I won't stop her." Drustan shook his head once before pushing off the wall he was leaning on and storming off. Caelena turned to address us before following after him.

"I'll keep in touch." She held herself with such authority, such maturity, I couldn't believe she and Drustan seemed to get along as well as they did.

"Us as well," I replied. Once Caelena was gone, following after Drustan, I released a heavy breath that seemed to lift a weight off my body.

"C'mon," Liam pulled me under his arm, comforting me in the heat of his body, his orange scent that made my brain relax. "Let's go home."

I smiled at that. This was all I ever wanted. I wanted to find out who my parents were, and I discovered who my mother was, at least, which gave me a cousin and brother whom I probably wouldn't have picked out for myself. But I had Liam. And his sister Ada. My chosen family, in this realm that felt more and more like home every day that passed, as the magic continued to infuse with my cells.

As Liam pressed his lips against my head and got ready to

lyskift us back to Vanessa, I let one last selfish thought fill my mind.

I'd rather close the Mellhawn Gates myself than see Vanessa bound to someone like Drustan Shaw.

THIS CONCLUDES PART ONE.
PART TWO OF VANESSA AND DRUSTAN'S STORY IS
COMING SOON.

ACKNOWLEDGMENTS

As always, thank you, dear readers, for taking a chance on this story. My first fantasy romance, at that. That being said, I would like you all to know that if it weren't for my editor, Yara, this book would not exist.

I approached her years ago with this idea of a villain falling in love with a sidekick. While I appreciate all the readers who also showed excitement for Vanessa and Drustan's story (because you all made me want to pull this manuscript out of the hidden depths of my laptop), Yara was the one who held my hand and helped me dissect and build this story well enough even to consider publishing it. She pointed out what worked and what didn't. She's read multiple variations of this story and might understand these characters better than I do at this point.

Thank you, Yara, for working your magic on this one. I cannot wait to work with you again on the rest of this series.

Thank you to all my readers who are still with me as I tiptoe into a new genre, thank you so much. I would not have a career without you all.

Thank you to my friends and family who support my career by reading my stories, or yapping to others about them, or listening to me ramble about the fictional romances always playing in my brain, thank you.

Thank you.

ALSO BY ANDREA ANDERSEN

The SUN STEER TECH interconnected standalone series:

WRITTEN BY A WOMAN

MELTED BY A MAN

The WHAT IT MEANS interconnected standalone series:

WHAT IT MEANS TO BE WHOLE

WHAT IT MEANS TO BE BRAVE

WHAT IT MEANS TO BE FOUND

WHAT IT MEANS & SUN STEER TECH interconnected novella:

TAILORED FOR THEM

ABOUT THE AUTHOR

Andrea is originally from Oregon but now resides in southern California with her little family. When she isn't curled up on the couch writing love stories, she can be found rewatching her favorite TV shows or taking too many naps.

www.andreaandersen.com